THE

RACHEL RAWLINGS

THE MORRIGNA
A Maurin Kincaide Novel

Cover by Incredibook Design
Formatting by Max Effct
www.formaxeffect.com

DEDICATION

For my husband, who not only said I could, but that I
should. I never would have finished this book without your
support, encouragement, and belief in my writing. Thank
you for finding the typos, lending your insight
and for all of the R&D. But most importantly,
thank you for loving me.

You have all my love as always.

Books By
RACHEL RAWLINGS

The Maurin Kincaide Series
The Morrigna
Witch Hunt
Wolfsbane
Ill Fated
Mistletoe Meltdown
Payable On Death, a Jax Rhoades novel

Coming Soon
A Haunted Life
It's All Death To Me

I

ONE

I'd been leaning up against this wall as if I was the only thing holding it up for twenty minutes. Not even at work an hour and my feet were already screaming about my choice of knee-high, black leather stiletto boots. They look better with my skirt than the sensible heels I usually wear, I tried rationalizing to my feet. What the hell is taking Masarelli so long in there anyway?

A few minutes ago I'd rapped on the door to remind him I was still out here and not going anywhere no matter how much he wanted to do this interrogation by himself. I fought the urge to step back when I heard him stomping toward the door.

"Five minutes," he all but growled at me before slamming the door shut in my face.

So again, I was stuck in the hall waiting for him to open the door so I could finally have access to the interrogation room and the man in for questioning. Not to mention a damned chair. If I stand here much longer, these torturous boots are coming off. I'm not exactly sure what these boots were made for, but they obviously weren't the ones Nancy Sinatra sang about, and standing sure as hell wasn't their manufacturer's intention either.

A quick glance at my watch revealed six minutes had passed. Times up. Patience may be a virtue for some, but I sure as hell don't have any. I could hear Masarelli's temper rising through the door. Surely that was more from his lack of progress than my lack of patience. We'd always managed to work well together before, even if I wasn't his favorite person in the world.

"That better be your friggin' attorney because if it's not I've got some pretty creative ways of making you talk!" Masarelli practically spat the last few words in my face as he opened the door.

Lucky for him, I wasn't an attorney or he might be facing some charges. Any other day I might have backed down from his lack of control over his temper, but not today. If he wanted, he could slip on my stiletto boots and stand out in this hallway for almost half an hour, then we would see how many times he knocked on the door.

At five foot eight his height was average, but he knew how to fill a doorway. Smoothing the front of my charcoal-gray skirt, I did my best to ignore his glare. At my five two it wasn't that hard to do. I stared at the stains on his tie, avoiding eye contact, and pushed my way past him. He might not want me to question this suspect, but it was my job and come hell or high water, I was going to do it. He'd just have to swallow his pride along with his shortcomings as an interrogator and let me do my work.

After three years of working with Masarelli on Salem's Preternatural Task Force (SPTF) as the psychometric interrogator, I still couldn't figure him out. Why would a Norm who's obviously as uncomfortable around the Others as he is choose to work here? He seemed more like an FBI suit to me, not someone who'd be working with psychics, witches, vamps, and weres. Yet here he was, getting in my way.

Two feet into the room and the hairs on the back of my neck were standing up. Something was definitely different about this suspect, besides his unusual size. His enormity did give me a second's pause, however, as I noticed he had the height of a basketball player coupled with the width of a linebacker. But it was something else that had my other senses on high alert—a palpable power rippling through the room, more intense than just my psychic energy. What the hell was this guy, anyway? I figured there was no other way to find out than to touch him. Cautiously, that is.

I hated to touch anyone with my shields down, especially a six foot seven, two hundred and seventy-five pound stranger who was radiating a power I couldn't quite register. But I didn't have a choice. Without an empty cup, pack of cigarettes, or pen on the table, there wasn't one thing he had touched that I could use. If I wanted to follow the memory link we all leave behind in our fingerprints, I was going to have to shake his hand.

"Well it's not your attorney, asshole, but you lucked out, anyway. This is Detective Kincaide. Kincaide, this is Seamus O'Neill, summoner and general practitioner of the dark arts."

I ignored the last part of Masarelli's introduction, not wanting his opinion or thoughts to taint my reading. He mumbled something about not being able to hit O'Neill now that I was in the room, so I shot him my best 'what the hell's the matter with you' look. Something had his panties in a bunch today. Maybe he was just tired of me coming in halfway through his interrogations and getting the information from the detainees that he never could. No matter what he did, no matter how many times he asked the right questions, the suspect could still refuse to answer. That was a luxury they didn't have with me. Once I opened the mental link, I could find all the information and evidence we would ever need. Masarelli and his jealousy was something for me to worry about another day. I had my hands full with the giant sitting across the room.

I crossed the room to where O'Neill was sitting with my hand extended for a proper introduction. I was aiming for the role of the good cop to counter Masarelli's obvious role as bad cop earlier today.

"Mr. O'Neill, as Detective Masarelli explained, my name is Detective Kincaide, and I'll be taking over the questioning from here." My voice was calm and neutral, not giving away my uncertainty as to his identity.

The large man raised one eyebrow as he pierced me with his ice-blue eyes and grasped my hand. If I were lucky, he would see what everyone else saw when they looked at me. I was short with a petite frame and curves where a woman was supposed to have them. In other words, I appeared attractive and harmless. Most people who sat where O'Neill was sitting now never knew what I was and if they managed to figure it out, it was too late anyway. I'd have already penetrated his or her mind, found the information I needed, and slipped out again. From the power that zinged across my skin at his touch, I doubted very much that this case would be that easy.

It took almost a year working with SPTF before we figured out the types of beings my abilities would work on. Your bread-and-butter human, or Norm, as the Others call them, are obviously the easiest. Unless a practitioner of black magic has made them a familiar—then it's damned near impossible. Their heads are too filled with dark energy. While the practice is strictly forbidden, I've encountered it twice so far.

Witches, who were the closest relation to Norms, came in a close second. Weres are harder, but with a lot of mental effort I could usually work my way through the animal-versus-man thought process that seemed to rage in all weres' minds. Or maybe it was the nerves and adrenaline from being hauled in for questioning that caused that type of brain activity in a were.

Vamps were a complete blank, although my ability worked quite well on the vamp tramps we managed to get our hands on. I just wish it worked both ways, so there was a group I didn't have to shield against. As it was, my mind was on lockdown twenty-four-seven. Otherwise, I couldn't touch a doorknob without going completely apeshit.

Strangely, Seamus the behemoth didn't feel like any of those to me. Holding his hand was no longer necessary to continue the mental link. The initial touch was enough to get me inside his mind. I tried to slip my way inside his memories as I slipped my hand out of his grip, only to find shields as strong as my own in place. Did he know who or what I was, or did he always shield his mind with such strength?

So much for the silent approach. I'd be here all damned

day if I tried to find a chink in his mental armor. I pushed hard against his shields again and felt them bend slightly before snapping right back into place. A smug smile crept across his face. Shit, he does know about me.

It took longer than I thought for word to get around about me. Still, I shouldn't have been surprised to discover he knew who I was. When I took this job, I knew I wouldn't be winning any popularity contests, but it definitely beat working at a carnival or side-show. My gifts didn't involve telling the future. There were no readings, palm, rune, or otherwise, I could give that people would pay for. Seeing the past was not the most lucrative psychic gift I could have been given. When the SPTF came looking for me, I jumped at the chance for a legitimate and decent paying job. Now that people knew about my abilities, it just meant the work would be harder and maybe a little bit more dangerous as time passed. Maybe I could ask for hazard pay as part of my benefits package.

Suddenly the shields were down—his and mine. Neat trick. I'd never had someone take down my shields so easily. Now that I think about it, no one has ever taken down my shields before. Seamus O'Neill was a very powerful psychic, but was his only talent breaking down barriers? If so, with no partner here to finish off the job of making me helpless and hurt, all he had succeeded in doing was allowing me access to his mind.

When he spoke in my head, I realized what he had done was level the playing field and end a mental stalemate. If I wanted to see inside his mind, then he would have an equal opportunity to see inside mine. Lucky for me, there wasn't a whole lot for him to see.

I didn't summon the demon. This is a trumped-up charge to haul me in for the demon running loose in Salem. His abrupt words scratched inside my head.

Mmm, I silently replied, surprised at how easy it was to communicate with him this way.

Seamus was the first telepath I'd had in for questioning before, and I highly doubted the charges were trumped up at all. The demon was there in his house. I'd say that's evidence enough. Demons don't just roam around unaccounted for. Someone summons them. And from my perspective, it looks at lot like Mr. O'Neill here.

May I point out that if you are going to think to yourself, particularly about me, I will be able to pick up on it while this line of communication is open.

Shit, point taken, I thought, feeling slightly embarrassed, not because I cared if he knew what I thought about him, but because I'd been caught in my thoughts. I really wasn't used to having someone poke around inside my head, and I can't say I enjoyed the role swap in this case.

All they have is the fact that a demon was in my house. Did it ever occur to anyone on this so-called Preternatural Task Force that the demon could have been sent to my house? Was there a circle, chalk, scrying mirror, anything that could be used to summon demons found in my house? Suddenly he was questioning me.

Let me ask you this: If you were going to raise a demon and set it loose, would you leave evidence of your summoning laying around? For all I know, you summoned it somewhere else and bound it to you until you got home.

Do I feel like a witch or practitioner of the Dark Arts to you? Surely someone with your psychic gifts would have felt me out by now.

It's not my job to determine what you are or are not. I'm not a profiler. I ask questions. That's what I do.

No, you are a petty thief," he snarled. A stealer of thoughts and images. Well, there is nothing for you to pilfer here. It happened exactly as I explained to the other detective. The demon was already in my house, unbound, when I got home. I was looking for a banishing spell when your co-workers conveniently arrived.

So you're sticking with that story then? Can't say I'm all that convinced. Why do you think their arrival was convenient? Without the attitude. I added. There was only room for one snarky person in this conversation.

Because it is too convenient. I didn't call them. Why would I if I summoned it? So, the real question is who did, and how did they know there was an unbound demon in my kitchen unless they saw it or sent it? Why is the truth always so hard to believe?" He sounded tired. Tired of repeating himself, tired from sitting in this room so long.

I'd prefer fact over your version of the truth. We both know you're hiding something. If it really happened like you say, that you came home from a long day at work, or wherever you were, only to find a demon running loose in your house, then why don't you drop the rest of your shields and let me have a look at what it is you're keeping secret back there?

I'm not the only one keeping things locked away. There's something blocked inside your mind as well. Funny thing is, I'd swear you know it's there, but don't know what it is. His brow furrowed trying to figure it out.

He hit too close to home on that one. There was

something stirring in my psyche, and I didn't know what it was. My psychic abilities had been growing, but they were becoming unpredictable, and they didn't always work when I wanted them to. Last month, the tricky little witch who'd managed to keep her charms concealed and her secrets all to herself was proof of that. But when everything was working like it should, I was able to really see everything. Even my shields were getting stronger.

At least I thought they were. I didn't want him seeing anything about me that I didn't know. Was he that much stronger than me mentally that he could figure it out?

I'm not stronger than you. Not even close. Just better trained. Seamus acted like there were people lined up outside clamoring to help me hone my skills.

Before I could answer him, there was a knock at the door. I knew it wasn't Masarelli just from the sound of it. He usually pounded on the door. This was a very polite 'sorry to interrupt you' knock. Unfortunately for me, the person who walked through the door after that knock was someone who wouldn't feel bad at all for interrupting. Holloway. I'd seen her at work in the courtroom on more than one occasion, and she had been ruthless every time. She'd brought more than one tough-as-nails cop to tears on the stand. She might as well carry a man-card shredder around with her.

"Well, I have to say I really have enjoyed this little chat of ours, Maurin. We'll have to do this again real soon," Seamus quipped.

He perked up as soon as Holloway waltzed through the door. Can't say as I blamed him. She was good. It did make me feel a little bit better knowing he would probably be refinancing his home to pay her retainer fee.

"It's Detective Kincaide, and we'll definitely be doing this again. Sooner than you'd like, I'd wager."

Holloway set her briefcase down on the table and at the same time, I slammed my shields back into place. The connection was dead, and he was back to that smug smile. I stood, turning to walk away, not wanting to dignify that look with a response, only to smack right into Masarelli. Boiling mad, he grabbed me by the arm and dragged me out into the hallway, holding on tight enough to bruise.

"What the hell's the matter with you?" I snarled, as he closed the door behind us. "I'm gonna have your greasy fingerprints on my arm for a week."

He didn't let go, despite my desperate attempts to wrench my arm free.

"Perhaps you were too busy doing the mind meld with that guy to notice the actual facts in the file, but right now all we have is circumstantial. I've got a stack of complaints and offenses linked to this demon with no end in sight, unless we find out who summoned him. I get my first real lead, the demon in O'Neill's house, and you're going to blow it by letting him mind fuck you?" He spat the last few words out like they left a bad taste in his mouth.

Hearing them left a bad taste in mine. But I, trying to take his feelings into consideration and be the better person, calmly said, "Go. Fuck. Yourself."

He let go of my arm and then sharply spun on his heel and headed for the Captain's office. This would not end well.

TWO

I stood there blankly for a moment, unsure what to do.
Forcing out some crocodile tears to earn the sympathy vote
came to mind, but I quickly vetoed that idea. The captain
would know I was full of shit. Crying had never really been
my thing. I'd be more likely to storm into his office with my
finger pointed and my temper flaring. That sounded like a
solid plan to me. Yes, today I was going with the usual.
Now I just had to beat Masarelli to the captain's office.

He was already halfway down the corridor. I quickened
my pace, despite my boots and the screaming in my ankles,
and caught up to him just as he was opening the captain's
door. Shoving right past him into the office, I grabbed
the vacant seat across from the captain's desk.

Captain Matthison was a minimalist when it came to
personal mementos. A family photo sat on his desk. Not
because he wanted us to see what his family looked like,
but because his wife forced him to have it there. The
solitary ivy plant his wife gave him was in desperate need

of water. This was a fact I pointed out every time I was in his office, which seemed to be a lot lately. I was beginning to feel like a truant teenager in the principal's office yet again.

The battered desk was littered with case files, and the walls were plastered with photos and notes on unsolved cases. He claimed these motivated him. "Those people are the reason I do this kind of work," he once told me during one of his many lectures. I looked around the walls at all of the lost faces and felt overwhelmed more than motivated. But then I wasn't a "real" detective. A fact Masarelli continued to point out. I was just an Other as far as he was concerned, a specialist they gave a badge to in order to make me seem more official.

I sat there across from Captain Matthison, watching those steel-gray eyes peer over the rim of his glasses at me. Masarelli was standing behind me. He took in a long breath and began his rant about how I had screwed up the questioning and now O'Neill's attorney was here. Captain Matthison held up his hand to interrupt.

"What you had on him was pretty thin, Masarelli. We discussed this before you brought him in for questioning. Even without his attorney, you couldn't hold him overnight. Still, I want you to coordinate visual surveillance on him."

I couldn't help feeling a little vindicated as the Captain told Masarelli his theory was pretty much paper thin, but he hadn't even started on me yet. Matthison dismissed Masarelli with a wave of his hand, but the detective held his ground, waiting to hear me get chewed out.

"Now, Masarelli." The tone in Matthison's voice had me

sitting up straight. "Shut the door behind you."

Captain Matthison waited until Masarelli closed the door behind him and was out of earshot before he continued. Definitely not a good sign.

"You're not going to like what I have to say, Kincaide, but I'm going to say it, and you're going to listen. I'm putting you on paid administrative leave. Effective immediately." He was his usual calm self as he handed out my punishment.

"For how long? Wait a minute, what the hell did I do? I came in here, tried to do my job, and now you're punishing me because I didn't get the desired results? You never said that there would be repercussions if I didn't produce every time when you offered me this job!" He might be calm, but I was fuming.

He lowered his head and ran a hand through his short brown hair. "I realize every case can't be easy, that there will be times when you simply can't get the answers we need. That's not what this is about, and you know it."

"No, I don't actually, so why don't you enlighten me." It probably wasn't smart to get flippant with the captain, but I couldn't have cared less in the heat of the moment.

"There's something going on with you. I've noticed things over the last couple of weeks, ever since we've been dealing with this demon case. Even before that, if we're being perfectly honest. There's no way that witch should have walked out of here like she did." He was mussing up his hair again, like he didn't want to finish, so I didn't give him the chance.

"If the arresting officer had caught that witch's charms, we wouldn't even be talking about her right now! And you can't seriously think I had anything to do with any of this? That my not feeling well is in any way related to the demon running loose? So why put me on leave?" I didn't even try to hide my disgust at the thought.

"Would you shut up and let me finish. We both know it's more than you not feeling well. Not feeling well implies that you're coming down with a cold or something. That is not what is happening with you. And of course I don't think you had anything to do with the demon. As for being related? Who knows? From what Masarelli says, our best, though admitted-ly thin, lead had you in some kind of trance. You were catatonic in our interrogation room for Christ's sake! That's never happened before. Not once in the three years you've been here. You have been getting stronger. I've seen it. You spend less and less time with the suspects and walk away with more and more information. But the witch? Charms have never stopped you before. And then you face O'Neil, and it's like you've got nothing, no abilities at all. He should have been a cakewalk for you. He didn't even register on any of our psychic scans. It's like with more power comes less control. I don't know what's going on with you, and you don't either. So until you figure it out, you're on leave. I just can't risk you being injured or blowing a case, both of which are very real possi-bilities, and you know it. I don't want you near the station or anywhere near this case. That's an order." He didn't have the same tone in his voice as he had with Masarelli, but it didn't make it any easier to hear what he had just said.

"Do you want my badge too?" Okay, it was slightly juvenile, but I couldn't help myself.

"Are you offering it to me? Because as much as it would

disappoint me, I'll take it if you are," he said.

I didn't say another word. I stormed out of his office, shutting the door firmly behind me. What I really wanted to do was give him the finger and slam the door, but that would have been incredibly stupid, and I probably would have gotten unpaid admini-strative leave instead. Suddenly I realized he never said how long I was on leave. Indefinitely? Until I figured out what the hell was going on with me? How was I supposed to do that? It's not like there was a doctor I could go to for some prescription or a class I could take to get better control over my power. I'm sure that there are Others who are doctors or teachers who know about these things, but given how I've been making my living the last three years...Well, I doubt they'd be lining up to help me.

Less than ten steps into storming out of the station I noticed O'Neill's attorney headed for the captain's office. I could almost hear him sigh when she knocked on his door and announced her arrival. In the minute or so that passed as I was watching them, I realized I didn't have my purse or my keys. Storming out was only effective if you didn't have to storm right back in because you forgot something. Somehow that last part diminishes the effort.

Backtracking to my desk, I grabbed my things, which put me within eavesdropping range of the captain's office. When he told her where she could stick her complaint and to get the hell out of his office, I smiled. Not the most mature reaction, but what can I say? The fact someone else had the captain as pissed off as me was pretty satisfying.

I guess the lawyer felt the same way. As the door opened, she wore a very similar smile of satisfaction.

O'Neill would be processed and released, and she had irritated the hell out of Captain Matthison. Her work here was done. She was actually humming as she passed my desk.

Captain Matthison hollered for my new favorite person, Masarelli. I grabbed my things and strolled out of the station. No need to storm out now. Oh, I was still pissed beyond belief, but O'Neill's attorney sort of took the edge off of my outrage. All I wanted to do now was get a cup of coffee and a croissant. I could con-template my new quest for self-control and personal growth better with a steaming cup of caffeine and a flaky French pastry.

The street was crowded, but I decided to walk the four blocks to my comfort food, boots be damned. It was a beautiful fall afternoon, and the cool, crisp air felt refreshing on my face, helping to cool the heat of anger that still flushed my cheeks. I took a deep breath and could actually feel the tension leave my body as I exhaled. Fall was my favorite time of year, and despite my poor choice of shoes, I enjoyed the brisk walk to the coffee shop. There wouldn't be too many more days like this, and I was glad I had decided to walk. Soon the air would be too cold to enjoy the trek. *Besides,* a bitter little voice said inside my head, *it's not like you're in a big hurry. You have nothing better to do today now, do you?* I tried to squash down the little voice as the flush returned to my cheeks.

Turning on to Essex Street toward the old Pedestrian Mall, I pulled out the pin holding my hair in a loose twist. My long, dark-brown hair fell free and cascaded down my back. It felt good to have it down, easing the tension headache I could already feel forming behind my eyes. I caught a glimpse of my reflection in a storefront window and instantly regretted it. I looked like crap on toast.

Sleep had evaded me over the last few weeks, and it was starting to show. Dark circles under my eyes were pretty much color coordinated with the nearly black shade of my eyes. Maybe if I'd plastered on some make-up, the captain wouldn't have put me on leave. The matching set of luggage under my eyes didn't really scream confidence. I needed to get a handle on the dreams I'd been having, and fast. Over the counter sleeping pills didn't work, and the only shrink I knew worked for the department. An appointment with him would have just gotten me sent home sooner. Well, it's not like I had to get up and get dressed for work for a couple of weeks. Hell, I didn't have to even get out of bed. Damn that little voice.

I walked the four blocks in record time, wallowing in self-pity about my shitty day and deteriorating appearance the whole way. The tension headache was crashing through my head like a runaway Mack truck by the time I walked through the door of the Daily Grind. Maybe someone would have mercy on me and give me some Advil.

As soon as I crossed the threshold and the smell of the heavenly brew hit my nose, I started feeling better. My head still felt like Gallagher had confused it with one of his famous watermelons, but I could already feel the knots unwinding in my neck and shoulders. I loved this place.

The old, wooden floors creaked in protest when you walked across them, and the brick walls were warm, making the place feel smaller than it actually was. Where the franchise coffee joints tried to be beatnik and eclectic, the Daily Grind actually was. It was a coffee drinker's coffee house, not your half-caff, skinny soy, hold the foam, artificial sweetener kind of coffee house. Mismatched couches and chairs were situated around worn wooden coffee tables, which were covered with newspapers and used books. There were old, beat-up candy machines by the front door, filled with chocolate-covered espresso beans, rather than gumballs or Mike-n-Ikes. But the best part was the coffee was truly fantastic, and the croissants were always fresh. This place knew me like Cheers knew Norm. I'd come here even if it only had metal chairs and card tables.

I made my way around the tables and couches over to the counter. Amalie must have seen me walk in, because she already had my order waiting. I'd like to say it was because she was a witch, but in actuality it was because I came here that often. The coffee, with its milk and two sugars, sat next to a warm croissant. Heaven. I dug in my purse for a ten and handed it to her.

"Okay there, Maurin? Not looking so good today," she asked, as she rang me up and got my change.

Why do people always point out that you look like shit? I might have been a little offended had there not been genuine concern written all over her face when she asked.

"I'm fine, great, never better. Thanks for asking," I growled, half-kidding. She handed me the change, and I dropped it into the tip cup before making my way over to my favorite spot.

My coffee and croissant resting on the little table, I slid into the worn, brown leather chair which looked like a castoff from some rich guy's study. The seat cushion was a little flat and the tanning had almost completely worn away on the arms. I'd sat here more times than I could count trying to come up with a way to get them to sell it to me. Amalie promised to call me if they ever decided to get rid of it. Sinking into the seat cushion, I half wished it would just swallow me whole. Maybe if I closed my eyes and sat here in the quiet, I could just pretend today never happened, even if just for a little while. The morning's events were still swirling around in my head when Amalie tapped me on the arm and handed over three Advil liqui-gels. Now, that probably was because she was a witch, since I never mentioned I had a headache.

"Thought you could use these. I look like you do after I've been cramming all week for an exam," Amalie said.

She pulled a chair over and sat down. Her auburn hair was swept back, leaving a clear view of her bright, green eyes that were fixated on the circles under mine. "So, I'm done here for the day. Wanna tell me what's up your ass? I don't think I've ever seen you drag in here like that before."

I don't ever see Amalie outside of the Grind, but I have seen her here almost every day for the last couple of years. As far as friends go, she'd be the closest thing I had to one these days. She could probably make more money at one of the charm or potion shops, but her uncle owned the place so she worked here part-time while she went to school for Practical Arts. Practical, that is, if you needed to know how to use wolfs bane in a transforming spell or bleeding hearts, the plant, not a real heart, which would be gross and not her kind of magic, for a love potion. I can't say I've ever confided in her before. Our conversations were usually just small talk. Today was different. I felt the need to unload. Sometimes you just need to verbalize things in order to work them out.

"Thanks," I said and hurriedly washed the Advil down with my coffee. "I've had a horrid day so far, and it's only half over. I got sent home today for an undetermined amount of time because I need to get myself together. I'm exhausted, but don't feel like going home to sleep because the sun is still out. I've never been a big napper, and I don't feel like dreaming." I could feel my body decompress as each word left my mouth.

"Dreams huh? Is that why they sent you home? Insomnia?" She knew there was more. Her quizzical brow gave her away, but she was waiting for me to spill it.

"No. I didn't even tell the captain about my sleep deprivation for this very reason. I've, uh, been having some control issues at work," I told her.

"I imagine that you would be having control issues if you aren't getting any sleep. But I think the bags gave you away." She smiled apologetically.

"Nah, it's more than that. Sometimes it's like I'm hardwired into a person's brain. I'm in and out in seconds, and the images are clearer, more plentiful. Then other times nothing. I actually let someone get charms past me a couple of weeks ago and then got steamrolled today. Or as Masarelli so tactfully put it, 'mind fucked'," I said.

I didn't mention anything about Seamus O'Neill or the demon. I suspected she already knew about the demon given the literal circle she ran with, but I couldn't risk letting any details of the case slip.

"He's a jerk. Doesn't tip for shit either. I wouldn't worry about him. I hear the other guys when they come in here, and they seem pretty damned glad to have you around," she said.

"Yeah, well that's great and all, but warm fuzzies aren't getting me out of this extended vacation anytime soon. I've got to figure out what's going on with me and get some damned sleep. If I can get rid of these bags under my eyes, I might be able to convince the captain to let me come back sooner."

"Not likely. Look, I've got to head down to the Witch's Closet to pick up a few things for my next lab assignment. You wanna join me? There might be a couple of books about dreams you could pick up. Or, you could just stay here drowning in caffeine and self-pity." She was already standing, waiting for my reply with a compassionate smirk on her face.

"Man, I thought *I* was bad at this confiding thing. Aren't you supposed to let me wallow for a few minutes and then tell me everything's going to work itself out soon? Just look for the silver lining, that kind of stuff?" I was trying to hold back the grin I could feel forming on my face.

She snorted. "You know, I could have given you some fortune cookie Confucius bullshit or maybe a spiritually uplifting Hallmark speech, but what's the point? You'd know I was full of it and keep wallowing like a pig in mud anyway. At least my way you have shopping to take your mind off the current situation, and if you find a good dream book it might help solve one of your problems. Not to mention, that I won't feel like I'm going to puke afterward. You coming or not?"

"Yeah, I'm coming. Not like there's a whole lot on my agenda today, anyway, besides wallowing followed by Häagen-Dazs, trash TV, and more wallowing." I was grinning, almost laughing now.

I stood up a little too fast for my headache, felt the room spin a little, and grabbed my coffee and croissant.

Amalie made a beeline for the door, and I was right behind her. We left the Daily Grind and headed uptown to the Witch's Closet. It was a little over two blocks away, which we thankfully walked in silence as I busied myself with polishing off my croissant. Its light buttery perfection improved my mood slightly. The coffee was only lukewarm now, but still tasted rich as it washed down the croissant.

From the outside, the Witch's Closet looked like any other boutique that carried specialty clothing and fragrances. Beautiful dresses hung in the shop windows and when you passed through the door, there were more of the same on several round racks. There were shoes perched on shelves that neatly lined the walls. Stars, planets, and the moon hung from the ceiling. Cozy and old-fashioned, the little shop even had an old bell hanging on the door, rather than an electrical doorbell sound when someone entered. Most of the shops around here are like that, actually. They are mainly historic buildings converted into shops on the first floor and apartments on the second and third floors. I tried to get one of the apartments down here a while back, but the rent is sky high.

An elegant, older woman behind the counter waved to us as we walked by her. "Just got a shipment in. Everything you need for your lab is in the back. How's your uncle?"

"Thanks, Arcana. Uncle Garrett's good. He said to say hi. This is Maurin." Amalie kept walking as she talked to Arcana, and I followed, waving one last time as we made our way to the back of the store. The old wooden floor started to slope the farther back we got, and I wasn't prepared for it. I've never been in here before, since I'm not a witch or someone who likes to pretend she is. I stumbled forward and almost knocked Amalie down.

"Sorry," I mumbled, a little embarrassed at my clumsiness. *There's five years of ballet school paying off.*

Another room in the back of the store housed old, built-in bookshelves which lined the top half of the walls. The shelves were filled with a mix of dusty, old books bound in linen or leather and brand-new books in their glossy jackets. Built-in drawers were under the shelves, and I assumed these were stocked with all sorts of items you would need to stir a spell. Amalie confirmed my suspicions as she walked over to a drawer labeled 'levitation charms'. Inside the drawer lay beautiful malachite stones in deep shades of green with mint and ivory colored veins running through them. Not what I expected. I imagined something horribly ugly, like maybe jars filled with eye of newt and bat wings or something. I'm psychometric, not a witch expert, after all.

The look on my face must have said so because Amalie just smiled and said, "I'm not that kind of witch, and this isn't that kind of store. There are two sides to every coin. White witches just as there are dark. Lucky for you, I'm not a dark witch." She gave me a little wink and turned back to the drawers.

"I know at least that much," I muttered while I looked at the books on the shelves for anything related to dreams and their meanings.

"Hmm, three pieces ought to do it. Oh, you won't find anything but spell books back here. We'll ask Arcana. She'll know which book to get and right where it is."

With that, we made our way back to the front of the store only to find that Arcana had disappeared, and a very large man was now standing in front of the window. The sun was shining behind him making it hard to make out his face, but by the size of him I knew exactly who it was. I grabbed Amalie's arm and jerked her back toward me.

"Ouch! What's the matter with you? You're gonna pull my friggin' arm out of socket!" she snapped.

"Shh! It's him. The guy from this morning. What the hell's he doing here?" I whispered in thinly veiled panic. It would have been too much of a coincidence if he was just out for a little afternoon shopping spree as well.

"Who, the mind-meld guy? What's he want?" Amalie didn't seem quite as unnerved as me but then again, I hadn't exactly told her he was suspected of summoning demons and using dark magic.

"Maybe he wants to finish the conversation we had this morning, starting with a full confession," I said, all too aware of the fact he could squash me like a bug without even breaking a sweat.

But he wouldn't hurt me in a public place, right? If he was going to kill me or something, he'd wait until I was at home alone and send his little demon friend to slice me up, right?

"No way to find out but to talk to him," I said, as I dug deep to find my courage. I didn't even make it two steps before Amalie was yanking on my arm.

"Look, I don't claim to have precognition or anything, but I've got a bad feeling about this. I've covered for Arcana before, there's an emergency exit off the supply room. We can just slip out," she hissed.

"Why couldn't I sense him or his power like I did this morning?" The room felt dead. There was no buzzing like there had been earlier. "Hang on a sec…Captain Matthison said something about this guy not registering during screening. He said that he should have been a cakewalk. *Shit!* He's not just any old telepath. He's a void, a deadener. Ha! I'm not losing it. They didn't even know he's psychic. If he can waltz right past screening, then why should I be any different? I'll be back to work tomorrow!"

"Yeah, um thanks for the detailed summary, but can we focus a little more on why he's here and how we're going to get rid of him? I don't even know what a deadener is, and I certainly don't want to find out the hard way that he can squelch my magic like he can your psychic power," Amalie whispered.

"They're really rare. I've only read about them. I've never met one, but as far as I know he can't stop your magic. On the other hand, I might be at a slight dis-advantage. If I only had some other super psychic gift— besides hindsight. I never really have an advantage actually, except against Masarelli, that is. That's it! Masarelli was supposed to set up surveillance on Seamus. I'll call him and let him know he's here. Or that I'm in here, more importantly," I clarified.

I started digging through my purse for my phone. Why is it that even with a tiny bag I can't ever find anything?

"What are they going to charge him with, Maurin? There's no reason for him not to be in here." She didn't sound scared, but she definitely didn't want to be there.

"He'll come up with something. He was pissed as hell

that Seamus got out earlier. He'd like nothing more than to get him back in for more questioning." I tried to sound reassuring.

I was just about to dump out the entire contents of my purse when I finally found my phone. I hit the speed dial for the station and asked for Masarelli.

"Masarelli here." He even sounded like a jerk on the phone.

"It's Kincaide, I'm at the—"

"I'm pretty sure the captain sent you home, but not before telling you I'd handle the case." The line went dead.

I closed the phone and tossed it back into my purse. "Asshole. Looks like we're on our own here," I told Amalie.

Before Amalie could say another word, I made my way up to the front of the store and the behemoth that was waiting for me.

THREE

"**I think this conversation is taking place sooner than** *you'd* like, Maurin, rather than the other way around, as you wagered earlier today. What's my prize for winning the bet?" O'Neill smirked sarcastically, obviously trying to piss me off, and enjoying every minute of it.

His confidence that the odds were neatly stacked in his favor was starting to tick me off. He cocked his head to one side, sizing me up.

"Come on now, Maurin, don't you want to know what's going on? Don't you want answers to all those questions swimming around inside your head? Why is the demon here? Who sent it? Why can't I keep control of my powers?" He mocked me with his accurate list of my internal questions.

Whoa, so he *had* managed to catch a glimpse of what I was hiding before he shut down the link this morning. No wonder he thought he had the upper hand. He'd gained a little bit of information from our mind-meld this morning, whereas I knew nothing more than I did before our meeting.

"If you know something, why didn't you just tell Masarelli? Why wait 'til now? You could have cleared your name and helped us catch the person responsible for letting a demon loose on the city!" I was fighting to keep my anger out of my voice and losing pathetically.

Amalie slipped up behind me, presenting a unified front. I don't think she trusted O'Neill's presence here anymore than I did.

"Honestly, Maurin, your faith in the humans is inspiring, even if a bit blind. Do you think that little spook squad of yours is going to stop an unbound demon? Who's your little friend here? How fortunate of you to align yourself with a witch so quickly. Do you trust her?" Seamus asked.

I didn't know what to say. Did I think the SPTF could stop an unbound demon alone? Probably not. The team consisted mostly of Norms. We had one rogue wolf but no witches, and that would become a problem when it came time to dispel the demon.

Did I trust Amalie? I trusted her as much as I trusted anyone, which wasn't much. She hadn't done anything to lose my trust—she just hadn't done anything to really earn it, either. Though it looked like that might change in the next few minutes if the twitch in her hand told me anything.

"I wouldn't let that lightning loose, witch, if I were you. It'd be a shame to burn down the nice lady's shop unnecessarily. Let me introduce myself properly, since our mutual friend here is greatly lacking in manners. Seamus O'Neill. Maurin and I have some unfinished business. You're welcome to stay. Something tells me you have a part to play in all this." He stared at Amalie intently.

Amalie didn't even blink. She just stared right back at him, waiting to hear what he thought her part was.

"What, are you a clairvoyant now, too?" I asked. "The only business we have is back at the station. How about I call and get us a ride in one of those shiny cars with the bright lights that are always cruising around town?"

"Very considerate of you, but I've actually got my own car. Why don't we continue this conversation on the way to meet my employer?" Seamus grinned, and I shuddered in spite of myself.

"I don't think so. I was actually paying attention the day they told us not to get into cars with strangers when I was a kid. Who exactly do you work for, anyway?" I asked, pretending to be casual.

I could see Amalie out of the corner of my eye. Her hand was still, and she was listening, but her body posture said she didn't trust him any more than I did.

"Baylen Knightley. I'm sure you've heard of him." Seamus said that with such confidence, as if the fact he worked for Knightley would give him some credibility. That was hardly the case, as far as I was concerned.

Most people saw Baylen as the businessman he pretends to be. He makes headlines and heads turn, buying and selling businesses and properties, that sort of thing. That would be fine, since we do live in a capitalist society after all. Who am I to begrudge him his millions? Unfortunately, the staff he uses to acquire these things is unethical, if not outright unlawful.

I didn't know Baylen Knightley personally, but I knew enough of him to think he was just like every other CEO out in the world. Peons who worked for them be damned. They would get rich breaking the backs of their underlings, and the consequences did not apply to them. I watched and read enough news to know that most guys with exceptionally fat paychecks like his usually get them at the expense of the people who work for them. Sometimes it's pay cuts. Sometimes it's layoffs. Sometimes it's 'oops, no more pension, I used it all up for my golden parachute', but Knightley took it to a whole new level. He has acquired quite the staff of special skills workers as well.

Imagine how easy it would be to succeed in the stock market if you had an oracle on your payroll. It was illegal for special skills workers to be employed in a field their skills could directly affect. So, if you were gifted with foresight, for example, you could not work for any financial institution. It kept the world markets neutral. Casinos and bookies, however, reaped the benefits of having a special staff. They had people readers to combat card counters and knew just how to run the numbers on their bets. Hedging had gotten a lot more interesting since the shift.

But Knightley? He liked to break the rules, and that just chapped my ass. It really bothered me that he felt the rules didn't apply to him. It bothered me even more that the powers that be seemed to agree with him, so long as they got their cut of the revenue. I was just about to tell Seamus a thing or two about his boss when he started talking again. Or maybe he had been talking all along and I was so caught up in my mental tirade I didn't notice.

"He has information about the demon and a need for someone with your unique gifts. Perhaps a deal can be made?" he asked, raising one eyebrow.

"What, no one with the gift of hindsight on his staff? I find that hard to believe. And here I thought he was a collector. Oh, and I don't make deals. I leave that to the D.A.," I said.

"I don't have all day, Maurin. Let's stop with the games, all right?" Seamus took two steps forward, closing the distance between us.

"You're the one playing *Let's Make a Deal*. Tell me what you know, or I'll haul Knightley in for questioning. Something tells me he'd be more susceptible to my charms than you." I held my ground. Backing up like my instincts told me to would only weaken my threat.

"Fat chance of you hauling Knightley in for anything. Aren't you suspended? And even if his attorneys did slip and let you drag him in, you wouldn't be able to crack him. Do you honestly think that someone who works with the people he does is unskilled or without shields? Don't be a simpleton. We have a book. We need you to read it," he stated.

"Paid leave, thank you! Why can't you read the book? I'll buy you *Hooked On Phonics*," I growled.

How the hell did he know I was on leave? Damn Masarelli for hanging up on me.

"Not that kind of read, and you damn well know it. Knightley thinks the book will lead us to the demon. If we know where he's been and what he's planning next, we can use it to track him. Like a beacon," Seamus said.

"Yeah, that is *not* going to happen. I am not going to play demon GPS for you. I don't track demons. Hell, I don't chase down criminals. I'm not even a real cop. Just ask the other detective you met today. I'm sure he'd be happy to clear that up for you. You may not have noticed, but I have a human life-span, and I'm not bullet or demon proof. Just thought I'd point that out, in case you had me confused with someone who came equipped with a cape."

The distinct sound of crackling electricity was coming from Amalie. She was about to let loose the lightning, and if I was in O'Neill's shoes I wouldn't want to be anywhere near here. Interestingly, he didn't seem even mildly concerned.

"Look, we really need your help, but I've never been good at groveling. So, we can do this one of two ways, ladies. We can all get in the car together and go for a nice little ride to Mr. Knightley's, or I can make you get in the car for a not-so-nice ride instead." His voice was calm and cool, despite the menacing threat of his words.

"Was that a threat? Are you threatening me? On leave or not, I'll haul your ass in for that."

I was feeling emboldened by the fact that he had threatened me. Now I had a legitimate reason to haul him in, not to mention rub it right in Masarelli's face.

"Why are you doing this the hard way? I don't want to force you to come with me, Maurin, so don't make me." His voice was more seductive now, and he was already moving toward me.

"Nobody's making me do a damned thing," I warned him.

Famous last words. Hindsight's a real bitch. No good until it's too late. Why couldn't I just tell the future?

IV
FOUR

Seamus turned to leave the store with Amalie and I falling in line behind him. I didn't want to go anywhere with him, and yet couldn't seem to get my body to understand that. My movements were sluggish, and I felt like a zombie, trying to tell myself to stop. But no matter how much force I put in the thought, I just kept on following Seamus. Right into the back of his car.

He opened the car door for us, playing the gentleman card in the most ironic way possible. Amalie and I slid into the seat of the black limo waiting out front. I could only assume this was one of Knightley's cars. Seamus practically fell onto the seat across from us. Maybe keeping two people under his control was too much for him. Or he could wear himself out and give us the opportunity to jump out of the car or something. Highly unlikely. My luck's never been that good, but one could still have hope, I guess.

Salem isn't a huge town. We'd been riding in silence for about twenty minutes so I could only assume Knightley lived outside city limits. I watched familiar faces and places roll by, not looking at either of my traveling companions as we made our way to see the great Baylen Knightley.

Seamus broke the silence but unfortunately not his control over my body. "Perhaps I should bring you up to speed before you talk to Baylen," he suggested.

"That would be nice." My tone was anything but nice. "On a first name basis with the boss man, are we?"

"I've known Baylen since high school, but that's not important. A war has been raging for some time. There are forces greater than we are, trying to regain power in this realm. We've kept it from the humans so far, but if we keep losing ground it will spill over the edge of our world, which is your world too in case you've forgotten, and into people's lives. Mass panic and hysteria will ensue and he, the demon, will feed off of it. We need you. And your friend. Hell, we need all the help we can get right now." He suddenly seemed tired, and I felt my anger reluctantly seeping away.

"A war? That's a bit dramatic don't you think?" My anger flared again. "It's a good thing you waited until we got in the car to drop this bullshit on me because mind control or not, I think you would have had a hard time getting me out of the store if you said that before."

"You chose to do the work that you do. No one forced you into this field, and by choosing this path you have isolated yourself from the world in which you truly belong. You have no one to blame for that but yourself," Seamus muttered.

"Yeah, because the Others were just lining up to be friends with me before. Look, I still don't understand how my skills will be useful to you. Amalie I get. At least she's a witch. But what good is knowing where this demon has been?" I asked.

I could feel Amalie glaring a hole in my head. She didn't like being dragged into this mess any more than I did.

"I think I'll let Baylen explain that part." And that was it. We rode the rest of the way in silence.

So many things were running through my mind, but none of them made sense. Surely a prophet or a sister from the Order of Delphi would be better suited for this. There were too many unknowns. This was the most time I had spent with Amalie in all the years I'd known her. Part of me couldn't help but wonder if that wasn't a coincidence. The other part squashed down that thought. No use separating myself from the one ally I had. What I knew of Seamus and what I knew from him were far too contradictory for my tastes. And despite his public life, there was far too much unknown about Baylen Knightley. If he's just a business-man, then what exactly is his tie to all of this? He obviously wasn't the human he portrayed himself to be. So what was he?

More importantly, why couldn't they just rally the Others and conjure up some immortal army? They were all less likely to die than I was, and they all had a lot more experience in this kind of stuff than I did too.

Damn it. I had really liked my life when I got up this morning. Things had been going just friggin' fine until Seamus O'Neill showed up. Well, maybe not fine because I was definitely having some issues, but I could have handled it. Seamus being hauled in to the station today and the call for me to take over his questioning was not a coincidence. Everything happens for a reason. That much I do believe. And when I got to wherever Knightley hung his hat, I was going to ask him just what those reasons were. I was betting on him actually having some answers and hoped like hell I wasn't wrong.

FIVE

The limo slowed as we approached a break in an old stone wall and turned down the driveway. Tall maple trees, neatly planted a lifetime ago, leaned their heavy heads toward one another to create a beautiful canopy of changing leaves over our heads. At the end of the drive sat an old Victorian house with a stone foundation, freshly painted white wooden siding, and black shutters. It was fascinating to me that this is where Knightley lived. Not exactly what I had pictured for his house. Something ultra-modern and cold, like a condo or penthouse apartment in a hotel, seemed more his style. This house had life. It was warm and inviting. The opposite of what I thought of when I heard the name Baylen Knightley.

The car came to a stop, and Seamus finally let go of his hold on us. I guess he figured we wouldn't try to run now. Even if I wanted to, I couldn't. My muscles and joints felt achy and stiff. I hadn't realized how much my body had been fighting his control. Amalie and I followed him out of the car. We both stretched slowly, like cats awakening from a nap as we made our way up the stone steps to the house.

The grandeur I had expected when we first pulled up wasn't what greeted us when we stepped inside. In its prime, the house must have been breathtaking. Strip away the layers of paint and plaster, and I could run my hands along that first coat to catch a glimpse of the people for whom it had been built. Unfortunately, the original structure, down to the moldings, had been touched by a heavy-handed interior decorator, whose taste left much to be desired. It was masculine and sparse. Now this was precisely what I expected of Baylen Knightley, minus the concrete tower.

We made our way through the foyer and into a room, probably a sitting room originally, on the left. It was crammed with the entire Best Buy catalog. I was starting to think this wasn't actually where Knightley lived, but more like one of his many offices. Why was it all of the beautiful Victorians were turned into funeral homes or offices? I tried to imagine the room as it would have been, velvet settee and all, but couldn't focus on the image with the chatter coming from four different flat-screen TVs.

Each TV was tuned to a different news station. I wasn't sure why the weather or Fall Festival this weekend was more important than anything on CNN, MSNBC, or Fox until I heard the reporter talking about an ongoing investigation which had escalated to four dead vampires with zero suspects. The news story might not have seemed immediately relevant to why I was here, unless you took into consideration how hard it was to make the undead permanently dead. It's not like vampires just let you walk up and stake them. I could almost see the light bulb turn on over my own head.

Knightley knew more than he was likely to admit about the demon. He was also putting every story in the news, local and national, under the microscope. He wanted to know who was doing what and why. Another light came on suddenly, this time with an audible click.

A little fluorescent lamp turned on at the large mahogany desk behind me. Lost in my train of thought, I made a rookie mistake and was paying too little attention to my surroundings and inadvertently let someone sneak up on me. I spun around so quickly to see whom it was that I almost lost my balance. In a lame attempt to regain my composure, I started smoothing out the front of my skirt. As if anyone would think 'whew for a second there I thought she was going to fall, but no she's just fixing her skirt'.

I focused on the man now standing behind the desk. Knightley. He was more handsome in person than on TV. In my earlier disgust I may have overlooked the fact that he was attractive, but standing across from him now I couldn't deny it. He was tall with an athletic build, and he obviously had a personal trainer. His hair was a medium-brown but not boring in the least. There was a depth to the shade of his hair that would catch the sun and shine like someone had brushed honey through it. His eyes were stunning, even in the dim light. I've never seen someone with eyes like his. They were so light brown they were almost yellow, almost amber. I was having a hard time taking my gaze off him. That is, until a tall drink of water sashayed up beside him.

Cool as a cucumber in temperature and temperament,

she could be only one thing. Vampire. She stood next to him with one hip cocked to the side and her hand resting gently on it, more to draw attention to her slender waist than for actual comfort. All legs and at least six feet tall she towered over me. Admittedly my judgment with height is slightly skewed by the fact I'm so short. Everyone looks really tall when you're only five two. Dressed in jeans that hit her just below the hip and one of those red cowboy-style handkerchiefs tied around her for a top, she oozed sex and knew how to use it against you. Dark black hair with eyes to match and flawless and naturally tan skin made her look like she was spun out of caramel and dipped in dark chocolate. Her velvety-smooth voice caught me off guard when she spoke before Knightley did.

"Well, Maurin, we finally figured out a way to get you to come over for dinner. Baylen had thought to ask you many times, but felt certain the invitation would be declined. And now, here you are. And with such strong shields. Why are you so guarded tonight? I won't bite. Unless you ask me to. Please ask me soon," the vampire all but purred.

The light Spanish accent combined with her over-whelming sex appeal, almost distracted me from the hint of fangs peeking through her sly smile. Almost.

She was trying to bait me and may have succeeded, if I didn't think it would end with me on the floor and her fangs in my neck. Before I could utter a reply, however, Baylen jumped in.

"Medea, play nice with the guests. There will be plenty of time for you to get better acquainted with our new friends later. For now, let's get down to business."

I wasn't sure if that was a threat or just a false promise to placate the vampire. Either way, I let him continue.

"This must be Amalie Beaumont, quite the gifted witch from what I hear. Arcana speaks highly of you, and she doesn't give praise often. My informants failed to mention that you socialized with Miss Kincaide outside of the Daily Grind. I'll have to speak to them about that oversight. You're only as good as the information you get, after all. Wouldn't you agree, Miss Kincaide?" His amber gaze rested heavily upon me, but he didn't wait for my reply. "Where are my manners? Please, sit. Make yourselves at home. Can I offer you something to drink?" Baylen asked.

No one said anything for a moment, and then Medea chimed in. "I'll have one, thanks."

Baylen shot her a look that would stop any warm-blooded human in her tracks. "Medea." He managed to growl her name behind his clenched teeth.

I was tired, and the day was so obviously far from over. If I was going to have any chance of not losing my shit, we were going to have to pick up the pace. With all the tact I could muster, and believe me, it wasn't much, I attempted to move things along.

"Could we just skip the niceties here? This has been a real bitch of a day so far. No thanks to your crony over there." I jabbed a thumb in Seamus's direction. "It's showing no signs of improving either, so why don't we just get to the part where you unfold your master plan?"

I felt Amalie stick an elbow into my ribs and inhaled sharply. Clearly unhappy with the direction I was going, especially since we didn't even come here of our own free will, she wasn't the only one irritated with the fact I had apparently checked my manners at the door.

"Rude. You have spent far too much time among the Norms. Your host offers you refreshment, and you would refuse his offer? You have much to learn about the meetings and ways of your own community." Medea looked like she was ready to toss me out the door.

"You know, Medea, I'm sure men find you sexy and desirable, but right now you're just getting on my fucking nerves. I did not drop by to socialize. O'Neill gets his ass hauled into my interrogation room, something I doubt is a coincidence, then shows up at the store I'm shopping at with some story about how you need my help and are willing to trade information for it. Then to top it all off I end up in the back of his car on my way here against my will. I don't think I'm the one who needs a lesson in civility. So can we please just get to the reason I'm here?"

Sometime during my rant Medea moved several steps closer to me. Her power washed over me like warm water.

"I had so hoped we would have more time to play, Maurin. You are very amusing when you're angry. Alas, Baylen is also eager to move things along, so who am I to stand in the way?" She was so close to me now I could practically feel her breath on my skin.

I was beginning to feel lightheaded from the rush of her power, and I knew better than to provoke a vampire. But I really was having a crappy day. Not to mention I didn't like Baylen and had no desire to be here. Who could blame me for being in a bad mood? Medea sure seemed to, and her power pushing against me said she was going to show me too. She moved closer. With the way my day was going, it was certainly for the kill. With one hand around my neck and the other behind my back she lowered me to the floor.

The strength a vampire possessed never ceased to amaze me. Only a fool would make the mistake of thinking her weak simply because of her appearance. Able to bench press a car without breaking a sweat if she wanted to, I didn't even want to think about what she could do to me.

I was quickly moving past lightheaded and into nausea as she tried to break down my shields. They were so much a part of who I was that normally I didn't have to worry about anyone taking them down, but the stress and emotional exhaustion of today, combined with her intense power, was taking a toll. If she kept pushing I had no doubt they would come crashing down soon.

She pushed further, and I could feel the walls I had so carefully constructed inside my mind crumbling away. A vampire could roll you, and it could be the most pleasurable experience of your life, but Medea wouldn't bother to make it sweet. I asked to get on with it, and she was getting on with it all right. Note to self: be careful what you ask for when the person you are dealing with has been undead longer than you have been alive. Wording was everything when dealing with a vampire. After working with SPTF I knew better and still opened my big mouth managing to end up on the floor with a vampire inches from my virgin neck.

Why was no one pulling her off me? I'm lying here on the floor with one of the unnatural world's greatest killing machines cradling me like a freaking infant, and this doesn't warrant an interruption? Didn't they want my help? Didn't she say something about wanting to have me over for dinner? Something told me she meant as the main course. It was time to make some hard decisions about the people I associate with.

She was in my head. Her laughter rubbed against my skull like crushed velvet, sending chills down my spine. Certain I was going to drown in her power before she ever sank her teeth into my neck, it wasn't the prick of fangs against skin that I felt. Instead she pressed a torn leather book into my right hand.

The moment the book hit my hand, I could feel myself being pulled away. My physical body was still held down by Medea, but that other part of me, the part that draws on psychic energy, was quickly being dragged through the floor to the bowels of the earth beneath Baylen's house.

"What do you see, Maurin? What do you feel?" Medea's voice was closer than it should have been. She was there inside my head. Was it because she was still holding me down? I've never had someone touch me while I did a reading. Would she be pulled all the way into the vision with me?

I didn't bother to answer her. If she wanted to know what I saw, I would show her. She was obviously along for the ride. The trick would be getting us both out intact. Well, at least me, anyway, since I wasn't all that attached to her.

It got very dark, very quickly. What little light there was had a reddish glow that hurt my eyes as they strained to adjust. The images were strong, maybe the strongest I've had yet, and there was a physical weight to them. There was a lucidity to the world I saw in this vision that I have never experienced before in a reading. I couldn't see Medea, but her energy was there like a cat rubbing along the inside of my skull. I had to try to ignore her and focus

on what I saw. This place gave me the creeps, and I didn't
want to be stuck in this vision any longer than necessary.

The room, if you could call it that, had solid rock walls.
How much dirt and rock was actually above this place? It
was hard to make out anything else. My eyes adjusted, but
there just wasn't enough light to make out any real details
about the room I was in. I caught a glimpse of something
moving, almost pacing, in front of me. If I wanted to see
who it was, I was going to have to get closer.

It shouldn't have mattered if I was quiet or not, but this
place seemed so real I couldn't help but tiptoe. Moving a few
steps forward as quietly as possible, I could barely make
out the silhouette of a man walking back and forth across
the rock floor. Who lives in a place like this? What was I
seeing? Where the hell was I?

And then it occurred to me. Not 'where the hell am I', but
'holy shit, this is Hell!' Seamus said they had something of
the demon's for me to read. Ironic that it was actually a
book. How did they even acquire it in the first place? Bad
things should happen to people who have books like this.
Letters were forming in my mind, pushing away the
thoughts of why they had this book and forcing me to focus
on its original owner.

The letters left my mouth as they appeared inside my
mind. "*O. U. Z. E.*" Before I could say the last letter and
finish the name, Medea's hand clamped down over my lips.
The pull of this place was so strong that for a moment I had
forgotten I was still lying in her lap and she was still inside
my head. She brought me back a little with her touch,
which I was suddenly grateful for. I may not have liked the
lusty bloodsucker, but I didn't want to be stuck in the pits of

hell either.

I could hear Baylen talking to me, but his voice sounded far away since I was half in and half out of my vision. "Don't call him. We can't defend ourselves here if you call him."

It was too late. The last letter was there in my mind. *L. Ouzel.* The name came together like a tumbler falling into place inside a lock. As soon as I put the name together I could feel the pull on my spiritual self again.

His name literally meant arrogance, outwit, over act. All of those things seemed appropriate where he was concerned. He was there in his special little place in hell, plotting our demise. Part of me wanted to run, run as far away from this vision as I could possibly get. The other part said I was already here and if I just got the information Baylen wanted, then I could get as far away as I could from him and this whole mess.

Ouzel was still quietly ranting and pacing like something out of a Shakespearean play. He had been patient, and for a *disii*, that was saying something. But he had grown tired of waiting for us to do it ourselves. The rewards would have been sweeter, the gloating that much more fun, had we been the final means to our own end. And yet we remained, even after so much time had passed. Hell was filled with the damned after centuries of the rot in our souls contaminated our kind. We would surely do ourselves in, according to him. There was proof enough just outside the walls of his room, but it just wouldn't be fast enough for his liking.

He had decided to abandon the rules of his master. He was *disii*, after all, and what were rules to a demon? What were rules in this place? Rules were for humans to create the illusion of safety and civility. Ouzel was neither safe nor civilized, so obviously they did not apply to him. Besides, new alliances had been made.

I wanted to run, to get out of this vision and back to my reality, but Medea wouldn't let me. The weight of her body on mine, and her power in my head, kept me stuck in this vision of hell and the *disii* who inhabited it. It suddenly became apparent that while I had never taken anyone into a vision with me, she'd definitely tagged along with someone before. She wasn't letting me go anywhere until we had more information. Medea whispered for me to be still and to avoid drawing attention to myself. How could anything I do draw attention to me? This was the past. It had already happened. He was already off doing whatever it was he was planning.

His monologue was already winding down. Ouzel found the psychic, finally. He had upheld his end of the bargain, despite the setbacks in the man's house. I wondered if he meant Seamus. It wasn't like I could ask the *disii* for clarification, so I just let the vision roll on. The Triad was gathering their forces. They would be ready very soon.

It was over. The vision weakened, and I tried to pull away but couldn't break the connection. Medea slipped out of my mind and back to reality, leaving me alone in the vision.

He stopped pacing and turned to face me. Or something in the direction of where I was standing. It couldn't have been me he was boring a hole into with that terrifying gaze, since this had already happened. I looked over my shoulder to see who he was looking at.

"Peek-a-boo, I see you, Maurin Kincaide," it said.

I thought I might actually shit in my pants. He saw me! There was no way! I wasn't really there, right? This was supposed to be an imprint just like any other. It wasn't supposed to open some sort of mental gateway. If he could see me, could he follow me? He just kept staring at me, and I had my answer. Baylen hadn't thought this through. If this was his big plan, we were all fucked!

Freaking out, I scratched, kicked, and clawed, anything to get Medea off of me. Anything to bring myself back to the physical world I had somehow slipped out of. Flat on my back with her straddling me just at the waist, I managed to pull myself out.

Medea looked genuinely surprised when I bucked us both up off the floor, but I wanted up. She pulled herself out before he saw me and had no idea what was coming. I did, and I wanted to get the hell out of here before he arrived. She was holding both my arms down because I had managed to cut her up pretty good with my nails. The scratches would be gone in a minute, but undead or not, if someone is scratching the shit out of you, your first instinct is to make them stop. Caught off guard by how much trouble I was giving her she used both hands to hold me down. Without tapping into an eighth of her vampiric strength, Medea could have pinned both my arms above my head with one hand, but I wasn't about to remind her of that. With both hands occupied, she left my mouth uncovered and gave me the opportunity to scream at the top of my lungs.

Amalie's shouts to Baylen were barely audible over my screams. Static rode the air, enough to raise the hair on my head, and I knew she was pissed. Between screaming at Medea to get her cold, dead ass off me and trying to tell them he was coming, I wasn't making much sense. Everything was coming out jumbled up.

Amalie must have managed to get something out of my now raspy screams because she yelled at Baylen to get the car.

I started to feel something hot running down from my nose across my lips, and the glassy look in Medea's eyes told me it was blood. *Great.* On top of everything else, I had a nose-bleed from connecting with the demon or *disii* as he referred to himself. That hasn't happened since I was a kid and meant I had used way more energy than I thought, physically and mentally.

Medea abruptly let go of my wrists and jumped off of me before I could sling one more profane word her way.

I tried to get up off the floor, but only managed to get to my knees.

Seamus grabbed me around the waist and hauled me up to my feet. Oh sure, look who's a fucking knight in shining armor now. If he wanted to help, he could have intervened when I was screaming and fighting like a crazy person to get Medea off me.

I stepped away and instantly regretted it when my knees started to give, but Seamus scooped me up before I hit the floor. It was in my best interest to let him hold me up at this point since I was suddenly having a hard time focusing on anyone, or anything they said. The room expanded and contracted in time to the throbbing in my head, so I closed my eyes to stop the movement, afraid I'd toss my cookies right there in front of everyone. I think I blacked out for a second.

Tires screeched and brought me back long enough to see everyone piled in the back of a limo peeling away from Baylen's house. I managed to get a glimpse out the back window in time to see a black cloud rolling in behind the house. It was moving way too fast to be a storm cloud.

I finally got a complete sentence together and couldn't have given a shit about the fact that my voice sounded panicked and a little too high pitched when I asked, "What the hell is that?"

Nobody answered me. The tires let out another painful screech as we peeled away and a black cloud swirled high above the house before it seemed to swallow it whole. Only the chimney peeked out of the horrible blackness.

It was at that moment my mind decided I'd had enough. As the blackness consumed Baylen's house, a safer blackness crept in over my vision. I welcomed it this time. Anything, even unconsciousness, was better than what had just happened. It was here. The big bad ugly. The real monster under the stairs was here.

VI
SIX

It was still dark when I woke up. My mind felt fuzzy, like I'd had too much to drink, and the pain had returned behind my eyes. I don't think I dreamt the whole time I was out, which should have been a relief. Instead it left me feeling vaguely uneasy. Why hadn't the wailing woman who had haunted my dreams for the past month visited me last night? She had become such a part of my normal routine that not seeing her seemed wrong somehow. Had I been given some chemical concoction to knock me out?

I had no clue where I was or how I got there. Trying to remember was making my head feel like one of Gallagher's watermelons again. Then everything that happened yesterday all came crashing down on me. Was it yesterday, actually, or was it today? What time was it, and where the hell was my watch? I checked my wrist, despite not feeling the weight of the watch. My hand slid down smooth silk. Not the starched cotton I remembered having on before I blacked out. A new question much more urgent than the status of my watch flashed across my mind. Where the hell were my clothes? Despite still feeling a little out of it, I knew damned good and well I didn't go to Baylen Knightley's house in pajamas. Especially silk pajamas. I don't even own silk pajamas, since I am a boxers and tank top kind of girl.

Baylen. Anger flared to life inside me at the thought of him. If that son of a bitch had undressed me, I was going to kill him. Feeling slightly violated at the thought of someone undressing and dressing me like a doll, I tucked my knees into my chest and rested my chin on top. I was trying to go back over everything that had happened to see if I could remember where I was or even how I got into bed, when I noticed I was rocking. I realized two things as I ran my fingertips along the tip of my thumb, counting down the day's events. One, I must look like a crazy person, and two, I wasn't alone in the room.

He cleared his throat softly, and I pinpointed the sound to the far right corner of the room. I'm not sure how long he had been sitting there in that chair. It was so damned dark I couldn't see him until he made a sound for me to hone in on. I can only assume it was my insane-looking behavior that prompted him to speak.

"You are quite safe, Miss Kincaide, I can assure you. Miss Beaumont helped change you into more comfortable clothes, and we left you here to rest," he said.

"Back to formalities? Just call me Maurin. We moved way past Miss Kincaide the minute your vamp dropped me in your office, Knightley. Two questions. Where are we, how long have we been here, and where's Amalie?" I asked.

"That's three questions," he replied smugly. Something

like a growl made its way up my throat, prompting Baylen to answer a little more quickly.

"Right to the point as always, Maurin. It's still Thursday, but not for much longer. It's close to eleven thirty. You are in another of my homes, Medea's room to be precise, and Miss Beaumont is quite safe upstairs. You've been out for a few hours now. She wanted to wake you, but I'm afraid I insisted on your resting," he informed me.

"Well aren't you Mr. Thoughtful? I mean, it's pretty clear I wouldn't have blacked out or needed to rest if you hadn't put that damned book in my hands in the first place," I snarled.

"Yes, that was an unfortunate oversight on my part. I—" he stopped suddenly, seemingly at a loss for words.

"Oversight? That's putting it mildly. Huge, colossal mistake seems more appropriate."

"Are you going to let me apologize, Maurin?"

"Is that what you're doing?" I heard him sigh heavily and decided it was probably in my best interest to let him continue. At least if I wanted out of this room and back in my own clothes. "Fine, fine. Go ahead."

"I couldn't have predicted that would happen. If I had known your reaction would be so strong, I never would have put you in that kind of danger. You must believe me, if I had any inclination that the *disii* would be able to tap into your energy, or that you would have a physical connection to the vision, I never...well, I wouldn't have done that. At least not without your permission."

"Whatever, apology accepted. Wait. Back the truck up for a sec. Did you say the *disii* tapped my energy? As in it was draining me of my energy?" I asked.

"Yes. But as I said, if I had known that would happen, well, I certainly wouldn't have put you in that position knowingly," he replied.

Right. I'm sure he was sorry. Sorry he put himself in danger by being in the same room when Medea gave me that book. Sorry he messed up with people around to witness it. Sorry he didn't get what he wanted. But sorry that I had been outed to a freakin' *disii* as the psychic who could tap into his powers and vice versa? Somehow I doubted that very much.

"Maurin? I don't suppose you're up to telling me everything you saw while you were connected to the *disii*? You were rambling, practically in a full-blown fit when you came out of the vision. We couldn't comprehend most of it," Baylen admitted sheepishly.

"Why didn't you just ask Medea? She saw most of it, didn't she?" I wasn't feeling particularly helpful at the moment.

"She didn't see anything of value, you must know that. He let something slip, didn't he? Please, anything, any little detail may be the break we need to catch up to him," he pleaded.

"I don't have the coordinates of his next attack, if that's what you're hoping for. Look, can we do this with everybody all together? I really don't feel like reliving this more than once. And maybe we could get something to eat too?" I mumbled the last part, not wanting to admit I needed something from him.

"Of course, please excuse my manners. You must be starved. It's been a long day, and you need to recharge with food as well as rest. Let's join the others upstairs, shall we?"

Baylen sounded pleased I was cooperating.

He stood from his chair in one graceful motion, reaching out a hand to help me off the bed. I didn't need or want his help. Ignoring his offer of assistance, I pushed down on the soft mattress with both hands and scooted to the edge of the bed. His hand dropped down to his side, and he turned slowly toward the door. Putting both feet on the floor, I stood up. The stone floor was cold under my feet, and I longed for my comfy slippers back in my apartment. God, if I'd only stayed home today. Why didn't I ever call in sick? Stupid work ethic.

He didn't seem to have any trouble seeing in the dark room. I followed him out into the hallway and up the stairs. There was a faint light coming from a room at the back of the main level, and I could hear hushed voices. I could only assume it was the kitchen.

As we got closer, I could hear Amalie and Seamus talking excitedly about everything that had happened. Somewhere in all the chaos they had managed to forge a connection. Where was Medea? Not that I missed the bitch or anything. Baylen walked through the swinging door first so they couldn't see me behind him. Amalie asked for me.

"Is she awake yet? Did you talk to her?" she asked excitedly.

"See for yourself," Baylen said.

I stepped out from behind Baylen, and Amalie jumped from her stool at the island in the center of the kitchen. She came rushing over, practically knocking me down as she swooped in for a hug.

"Oh Maurin, I'm so glad you're ok. They said you'd be fine and not to worry, but I just thought...well, I mean you have seen some pretty scary stuff on your job, but nothing like him, and I was kind of worried you know that, well...oh, but you seem fine! Are you hungry? Baylen's put out quite a spread for us. Plus, coffee and croissants just for you." She finally took a breath as she half let me out of the hug to wave a hand at the food on the countertop.

"Amalie, I'm glad to see you too, but could you let go of me now? You're still squeezing me pretty tight," I said.

"Oh right, sorry. I, uh...Come and sit down. You must be starving. I'll fix you a plate while you tell us what you saw to freak you out like that," she said.

Amalie was way too chipper for me right now, even after a nap. Nap? Blackout? Whatever it was, I bet she's like this first thing in the morning too. All bright-eyed and bushy-tailed. Maybe it's a side effect from working around all that coffee at the Daily Grind. She had already busied herself piling fruit, cheese, and a croissant onto a plate.

Baylen had another think coming if he thought I could be bribed with caffeine and pastries. I grabbed a mug off the counter and fixed a cup of coffee before heading over to the table where Baylen and Seamus were sitting. To my surprise, I noticed my least favorite undead person was missing from the room.

"Where's Medea? Do you want to wait for her?" I asked Baylen.

"I sent her to your apartment to get some of your things. She should be here any second. Drink your coffee. We can wait a few more minutes." He leaned back in his seat, all too confident once again.

"Back up a second. You sent Medea to my apartment? How'd you get my keys? Let me guess, you took the liberty of going through my purse as well as my house. Nice." It would be nice to have some of my own clothes, but the thought of Medea rooting around in my stuff grated on my nerves.

As if cued by my irritation, she strolled into the kitchen with an armful of my things. "You know, when this is over, someone is going to have to take you shopping. You would be a perfect candidate for one of those makeover shows."

"I'm sorry I don't have anything more appropriate for fighting a demon," I replied dryly.

"Oh what you have is fine for fighting the *disii*. It's for everything else that your wardrobe is a problem. Even your work clothes are atrocious. If you could call them work clothes," she said.

She threw my favorite pair of Levi's, black motorcycle boots, and a long-sleeve, black V-neck tee on the table. I reached out for my clothes, pulling them close to my chest for comfort. The pajamas may have been comfortable, but they didn't do much to soothe my nerves. I really missed my boxers and tank tops right then and seriously thought about asking if I could change my clothes before we began. It would be hard enough trying to explain everything I saw without having to do it in light-pink pajamas with black polka dots.

Medea slid into a seat at the table next to Baylen with her gaze fixed on me. I am not sure why she was so intrigued with me. If it was simply to annoy me she succeeded. I had no idea what Baylen saw in her, but she must have some seriously valuable skills or he wouldn't keep someone with her personality around for long.

Amalie slid a plate in front of me and sat down in the

chair on my left. All eyes turned to me, waiting for me to begin.

"Maurin, if you would please," Baylen prodded, gesturing with his hand for me to start.

"Of course, thanks for giving me some time to rest first. I genuinely appreciate it," I said.

His eyebrows rose a little when I said it. I don't know why he seemed surprised that I had actual manners. Just because I hadn't used them yet didn't mean I didn't have any at all.

"Um, let's see. Where to begin?" I looked to Medea. "Did she start to explain anything? I mean, she rode through most of the vision with me."

It was Seamus who answered me, his Irish accent more noticeable now. "She told us some of it, but she broke the connection before the really exciting bit, apparently. Why don't you just start from the beginning as if we never heard any of it," he suggested.

"Well, I think it's pretty obvious that we all know who he is. Well, I don't really know who he is, but we do know what he calls himself. Whatever. You know what I mean. I don't know where he was, though. I know where I think he was, but that would be impossible right? It wasn't really some cavern in the pits of hell, right?" I asked, directing my question at everyone, but not really expecting an answer. I should have known better.

"I find it hard to believe that at this point you'd find anything impossible. And to answer your question, no, it wasn't hell itself, but another worldly plane very similar to the Christian Hell. Please continue, Maurin," Baylen said.

"Six impossible things before breakfast. I'm starting to

feel a little like Alice tumbling down the rabbit hole. Where was I? Oh, ok so we were in this cavern-like room, and he was ranting about something like a final battle. He said they would be pleased with his progress. That he had found the psychic, despite setbacks in the man's house." I looked toward Seamus as I said the last part.

I finished telling them everything I saw and heard during the vision, right up to the *disii* actually seeing me. We all turned to Baylen for answers. Me most of all. I wanted to know how the connection had been made. How did the *disii* see me? How did he know my name or that I was there, and why wasn't I viewing the past like I always had before? I've never been able to see the present when I made a connection.

"Won't they be pleased? He said, 'Won't they be pleased?' You're sure that's what he said, Maurin?" Baylen asked.

There was a hint of panic in his voice. I'm not sure if anyone else caught it, or maybe I did because I had grown so accustomed to hearing it after I'd told a suspect I knew all the grimy little details of the crime they'd committed. I've done enough interviews; I say interviews because what I do isn't really an interrogation. I don't have to force or coerce a confession out of anyone to know when a person's pitch or demeanor changes and what it usually means. Baylen spoke a little faster, and his voice was a hint higher than normal when he asked if I was sure.

Medea stirred in her seat. Had she noticed? Of course she had, she was a vampire. She didn't need to listen for any changes in his voice. She could simply tell from the change in his heart rate. She could practically smell fear emanating from a person.

"Well I don't know if that was what he said verbatim, but he definitely said 'they'. Why are you so surprised? You didn't think he'd be working alone did you?"

"Ouzel would be bad enough all by himself, and you know it isn't other people who are helping him." Baylen seemed to have regained some of his composure.

"Why did you just say his name? You said not to say his name. I heard you. Are you insane? He'll be coming here!" I screeched.

I could hear the panic in my voice now, and it made me uncomfortable. I was tired of feeling like I was out of control and didn't know anything about the world around me. I started to push away from the table. No way was I waiting around to see how long it took Ouzel to get here.

"Maurin, wait. It's okay." Seamus spoke with such confidence that I almost believed him. "Baylen and I performed some controlled experiments while you were sleeping. We've come to the conclusion that in order for him to come you have to want or need him to do so. He is still a *disii*, and there must be some form of raising. He shouldn't be able to come on his will alone."

"Okay, there are two problems with that. First you said shouldn't. He *shouldn't* be able to come. Not really comforting. And second, how do you explain what happened earlier? I certainly didn't want him to follow me out of the vision. Nor did I want him to see me at all!" I exclaimed.

"Maurin, we didn't expect that to happen." There was a hint of sadness in Seamus's voice now. "We're certain the reason he was able to do that was because he was drawing on your power. Once he discovered you, he was able to tap into your energy and gain strength from it. I think that explains why you blacked out. He was literally draining you. As for why he could see you and why your vision was in the present rather than the past, well, I simply don't have an answer for that. I think that has more to do with you than anything we put into motion. Let Baylen explain the rest. You need to know everything," Seamus said.

Part of me didn't want to know everything. So far everything they had told me sucked. Part of me didn't want to hear more because I knew it would only get worse.

Baylen asked Amalie to get him a book from the desk in his study before he picked up right where Seamus left off. "He almost took this city once, centuries ago. A group of foolish girls accidentally conjured him up. It would have been all too easy for him to turn saints to sinners and create mass hysteria. If not for the strong faith of some, all would have died. He is bad enough on his own. So yes, despite my suspicions, I had hoped he was working alone. But make no mistake, the entities he refers to are not working for him. He is working for them," Baylen explained.

Amalie returned with yet another very old book with a spine so brittle I thought it would fall to pieces before my eyes. The old, leather cover was cracked and torn. Amalie handed the book to Baylen but didn't move. She looked like a kid who wanted the best spot at story time.

"I don't know what you're planning to do with that book, Baylen, but it didn't go so well the last time. So, just tell me who they are, okay?" I demanded.

He cracked a smile at my comment about the book. "I wouldn't have you read this one, Maurin. It wasn't hell you saw or at least the Christian version you're used to, but it was an underworld of a sort. These are old gods, old Pagan Gods. They ruled the earth long before man found his savior and Christianity swept over the world with crosses and steeples. There was more than one god who was angry that man had found himself a new place at the feet of one true God. If they all worshiped Him, where would that leave the old gods? And while only one could truly rule the underworld, alliances were formed. There are politics even in religion. Treaties were made, and bargains were struck. The old gods could keep the souls they won for themselves, and the outcast could have those who strayed aimlessly from the flock. He would have Hell and they would have Hell on Earth," he said.

"Damn it, Baylen, who are they?" I tried to keep the impatience out of my voice. "I don't need a scary story, just tell me who or what we're dealing with."

"I'm getting to that. First and most important is Morrigan, the supreme goddess of war. She is a shape shifter, not just a were. She can take all animal forms, though she is most commonly seen as a raven. She is the goddess of lust, dark magic, prophecy, and revenge. And if she wasn't bad enough, her sisters round out the Triad. Badb commonly known as Fury, and Nemain also known as Battle. Perhaps now you see the problem?" Despite the bad news, Baylen seemed remarkably calm.

"Oh, is that all? Whew, for a second there, I thought you were going to tell me something really bad. Why didn't you just say we're screwed and save your breath?" I get a little sarcastic when I'm nervous. One of my charming defense mechanisms.

"Don't forget that she has brought desire into her fold.

She is the seven deadly sins all rolled into one," Medea said, smiling at me.

"Yes, thank you for bringing that to my attention, Medea." I really wanted to slap her. If I thought it would have done any good, I think that I would have.

Medea smiled at me again. A very cool smile, the way I imagined she smiled at her prey. It was a little unnerving. When she opened her mouth to speak again, I let out the breath I was holding. At least now I could concentrate on what she was saying, instead of worrying I was her favorite blood type.

"We aren't totally screwed yet, Maurin. If she is living sin, then we fight her with everything she is not," Medea stated.

Now I was more than irritated. This was some plan. "Great, Medea. So, what, we just think good thoughts, hold hands, and sing *Kumbaya*? I hope you have more in the arsenal than that."

She laughed at me then, a real laugh, deep and rolling. It gave me goose bumps, but not in the way she had before when she had emitted that cold, icy laugh that seemed to say, 'I want to eat you'. No, this laugh was real and made her seem more human to me for a minute, which just incensed me even more as I realized she thought I was being funny. I wasn't in the mood to be amusing to anyone.

"Perhaps Maurin should go change before the Council meeting, Baylen. As delectable as she is in her pajamas, it isn't really appropriate attire for when our guests arrive," Medea said, as she looked at me through half-lidded eyes.

"I didn't know you swung both ways Medea."

"When blood sings with power like yours, Maurin, I am

easily persuaded."

Baylen cleared his throat. "Yes, of course. Maurin, you should find everything you need to freshen up in the bathroom upstairs. Third door on your left."

I scooped up my clothes and headed for the stairs. What the hell had I gotten myself into? At least they'd called a Council meeting. Surely the oldest and strongest of the Others could come up with a plan. Representatives from all dominant groups of Others would be here tonight. I couldn't help but feel a little excitement at the thought of them all being in the same room.

I've never met most of them. Sure I'd heard of them, but none of them were ever tied closely enough to a crime for us to be formally introduced. The closest I ever got was the lackey who did the dirty work, and even then their secret was safe. There was more old-world justice than Amalie cared to admit back at the Witch's Closet.

So many thoughts were racing through my head that I was standing in front of the bathroom door before I knew it. I went inside and threw my clothes on the long, marble counter.

I quickly changed from the pajamas to more familiar clothes. I instantly felt better as I slid my jeans up my legs and fastened the button. I pulled on the black tee and caught a glimpse of myself in the huge mirror that ran the length of the bathroom wall. I started rummaging in the drawers for a brush and something to tie my hair back with. In the second drawer I found a brush and two beautiful black hair sticks with mother of pearl embedded into the wood. They were a lot fancier than the elastic bands I usually used to tie my hair back, but I wasn't complaining.

Baylen said I'd find everything I needed, and he was right.

I started twisting my hair with my left hand, grabbing the sticks with my right and caught the faintest image. Everything had been purchased especially for me. The pajamas, though what had made him pick silk polka dots I'll never know, the hair sticks, the spread in the kitchen, everything. I felt a smile creep across my lips as my thoughts slipped from the sleek hair sticks to the image of Baylen's face and his striking eyes. I felt my face warming as I finished putting up my hair.

Whoa, where did that come from? I didn't even like him and was seriously coming unglued if I was starting to be attracted to Baylen. Get it together, Maurin. He has clairvoyants working for him. They probably told him to be prepared for my extended stay. I chuckled to myself at the thought of these things meaning anything more to Baylen than being prepared.

I closed the lid on the toilet seat and snatched up my boots and socks, barely getting my left covered when I heard a car approach. Looked like the party was about to start.

VII
SEVEN

When the Others first 'came out of the coffin' as we like to say, because the vamps were the first to do it, there were some pretty bad turf wars. The Council was formed to maintain order between the vamps, weres, and witches. There were other races amongst us, but these three were the most dominant and had acquired the most wealth and power over the centuries.

I couldn't help thinking about how old the Council was when compared to the task force I worked for and how foolish and arrogant they likely thought we were. If I was honest with myself, we still needed the Council to regulate the masses. Our justice system simply couldn't handle a massive outbreak of renegade vamps or rogue weres. If I was *brutally* honest with myself, I'd have to admit the department I worked for was just a straw man to make the Norms feel better, and I worked there simply for a place to fit in. Pushing those thoughts away, I refused to let my insecurities get the best of me.

Another car pulled up. Dammit. Why didn't I get three-holed Docs instead of eight? I yanked on my other boot, not bothering to tie it, and headed down-stairs, not wanting to make a grand entrance.

Introductions were already being made by the time I reached the last step. First to arrive were the weres. Four wolves walked through the door, with Grayson in front. I'd seen him at the station giving statements, though I'd never actually spoken to him. Well over six feet and easily 260 pounds, he was all muscle, but not in that ridiculous 'I can't put my arms down' kind of way. No, Grayson was just right. Hell, if the inter-species dated, I might have asked him to take me out. His head was shaved, and he had a tribal tattoo around his neck. I'm sure more of him was tattooed—wouldn't I like to find out. He looked over to me on the stairs his light-brown eyes softening said he remembered me too.

I gave him a half smile back, trying to hide the fact I was checking him out as he came in.

Behind him was the pack leader, Roul. The regal air that swirled about him contrasted with his rugged good looks. Dark-blue eyes stood out against his salt-and-pepper black hair. I've heard, well seen, from the few wolves I've questioned that he is a fair but firm leader. Perhaps he was trying to live up to his namesake. According to local legend, a witch told Roul's mother to name him after an ancient wolf because he was destined to lead.

She didn't name him after just any wolf. She chose Roul, the most respected and first pack leader in the States. Many full moons ago, too many to even count, a lone wolf left the Scottish Highlands and ended up here. There were no established packs when he arrived, so he had to fight his way through the rogues to earn the right to stay. Stronger and smarter than most, he quickly established himself as the first pack leader, creating pack law and the hierarchy that's still in place today. Since his death, only one wolf has borne his name. That wolf was now standing in Baylen's foyer.

Beside him was his wife Olwyn. With her dark-red hair and beautiful, green eyes, I bet she made a stunning wolf. Bringing up the rear was a wolf I didn't recognize. I only caught the end of the pack introductions, but managed to catch his name. Tybalt looked younger than me. He was similar in size and shape to Grayson, but seemed more light-hearted. Maybe it was the age difference or maybe it was just his lack of experience.

I stood there on the last step, unsure if I should introduce myself or wait to be acknowledged. Olwyn must have sensed my uncertainty.

She strode over to me. "Obviously you've met Grayson, given your line of work. This is Tybalt. Tybalt, this is Maurin Kincaide," she said, making introductions.

I nodded to Tybalt, and he gave me a deviant smile in return. Yup, this one was trouble. Not trouble like he'd turn red coat on us, but trouble like boy-meets-girl trouble, with a capital *T*. My instincts are pretty good. They've gotten me this far. We'll see if I'm right about Tybalt.

I held my hand out to Olwyn. "Hello, it's nice to meet you. I just wish it were under better circumstances."

Her hand was soft and warm. The warmth didn't surprise me, since weres run hotter than the rest of us. Their normal body temperature would be a deadly fever for us.

"You're a healer!" I blurted out, before I could stop myself.

"Very good, Maurin. I didn't realize you would be able to tell such things just from shaking hands." She sounded intrigued by this little development.

I certainly was. Not by how little she knew about what I could do, but at how clearly I could read her. I didn't even realize I was doing it, and her mind was crystal clear. No interference from the wolf at all. Highly unusual. I tried to hide the fact I wasn't sure if it was another flare up in my power or if her mind was stronger than the other wolves I've questioned.

It was obvious I was nervous, hopefully her soft, pleasant laugh meant she mistook it for being around the Council.

With her hand on my back, she moved us both toward the couch in the living room. "Come along, dear. We have a few minutes before all of the Council has arrived. Sit with me," she whispered.

Olwyn sat down on a cream-colored couch that made her striking features that much more noticeable. Her black suit and emerald-green, silk shirt did wonders for her eyes. I could feel my self-esteem dropping by the second just being near her. She gently patted the cushion next to her, and I came to sit beside her with Tybalt once again bringing up the rear. He knew his place which, like any good bodyguard, was against the wall neither in front of, nor behind Olwyn, hovering without being noticeable.

"So, Maurin, Baylen has already told us that you saw the *disii* and that he could see you. Is that true?" Olwyn asked.

"Yes. It was definitely a first. Even excluding the fact

that it was a demon, I mean. I'm not used to seeing in the here and now. That's not really my forte," I confessed.

I wasn't sure how much to say to her. Was I supposed to wait for the rest of the Council? No one told me not to talk. Although, I doubt it would have mattered if they did. She could make me tell her if she wanted to which wouldn't be fun, so I was talking of my own free will.

She was still mulling that little tidbit over when there was a knock at the door. I never even heard a car pull up.

Seamus answered the door since Baylen was still fervently talking to Roul. They occasionally glanced at me, but went right back to whatever it was they were discussing.

Arcana walked through the door, calling for Amalie. She gave Baylen a gentle pat on the shoulder as she squeezed past him and Roul and kept walking back toward the kitchen. Positively radiant, younger even in her flowing charcoal-gray dress which brushed along the floor as she walked, making it look like she floated across the room.

Amalie flew out of the kitchen and rushed to give Arcana a hug, with the events of the last several hours pouring from her lips. I think Arcana already knew what had happened, as Olwyn did, but she didn't bother to stop Amalie. She just waited with a patient smile on her face. Once Amalie finally stopped to breathe, Arcana took her hand and led her over to the couch where Olwyn and I were sitting.

"Maurin." Arcana gave me a reassuring smile as she and Amalie sat down on the loveseat across from us.

I'm usually better at appearing confident, even when I don't feel it, especially when I'm at work, but my nerves were getting the better of me. And, as far as I was concerned, this was still work. Unfortunately, my body didn't agree, since it had no problem giving me away. I was so far out of my comfort zone, sitting there with Olwyn like we were long lost friends catching up. Even if this wasn't Olwyn's way of feeling me out, even if the entire Council was about to convene, and I was the first outsider to witness such a meeting, I would still be uncomfortable because I don't really have friends. Christ, Amalie was the closest thing I had to one, and I'd never seen her outside of the Daily Grind before this. So yeah, it was a little uncomfortable, this little couch time Olwyn wanted to have.

Arcana thankfully came to my rescue, drawing Olwyn's attention away from me. "Have you met my niece, Amalie?" she asked, as she gestured toward Amalie as if there was any question about which of the four of us she was.

A small sigh escaped Olwyn, accepting her defeat. The moment was lost. Anything she hoped to learn, any advantage she hoped to gain, was gone. "Lovely to see you again, Arcana. Amalie—your niece? Mmm. So this is the witch Seamus spoke of. I assume the rest of the coven will be along shortly?"

The question hidden in her comments, 'the witch Seamus spoke of' caught my attention. No doubt Arcana caught it as well. I wondered what Seamus had said to spark Olwyn's interest in Amalie. After spending so much time around the highest coven members at Council meetings, what could be so fascinating about Amalie? Maybe she was a stronger witch than I had imagined.

Amalie sighed, showing her anxiousness to meet the rest of the Council. Once again, without the sound of a car to precede it, there was a knock on the door. Before any of us could answer it, the door swung open. A wiry witch, with eyes grayer than any fog I've seen roll off the Atlantic, walked in with four other witches. Or maybe it was two witches and two wizards? Whatever the politically correct term was, there were four of them behind her. While the Council members addressed each other and Baylen, Amalie gave me the rundown on who these coven members were.

The first and oldest among them was Mahalia, High Priestess of the coven who knew every witch by name and had a heavy hand in their futures. Amalie had been brought before the High Priestess by her father before she could walk. It was Mahalia who decided what course of magic Amalie would study by reading the magic in her blood. She could feel what type of powers each witch would wield: offensive, defensive, elemental or blood magic. She could see it all in the very makeup of each witch in her coven.

Behind her was Phallon. She was a tall, lean witch with fiery-red hair and bright-green eyes. She looked like a handful. The coven's version of Tybalt? I was willing to bet she'd give him a run for his money. Amalie confirmed my suspicions by telling me she was as lethal as she was beautiful. Trained in the offensive elements, Phallon was one of the strongest witches in the coven.

Phallon's sister Juno was right beside her. Her hair was a darker red, and her eyes a deeper green, but the power radiating off of her was equal to Phallon's. The ying to her sister's yang, Juno was trained in defensive magic. The two were never far from one another in a fight. Neither held a seat on the Council, but the sisters were inseparable and invaluable to the coven leader. Mahalia was taking precautions.

Cicero may have been average in height, but he certainly made up for it in build. I couldn't help but wonder if he really spent all his spare time on his physique or if it was actually a glamour charm. He was the most well-balanced member of the coven—needing no offset to his magic, he had mastered both offensive and defensive skill sets.

Oberon rounded out the representatives of the coven. Ruggedly handsome with black hair, sad blue eyes, and a strong jaw, he was at least a foot taller than me, and I couldn't help feeling drawn to him. My hand itched to trace the tattoos peeking out from underneath his shirt. He was quickly replacing Grayson as date material. Oberon specialized in old Druid magic long forgotten by most covens and rarely practiced nowadays. Some didn't even think the old spells worked. Mahalia wasn't telling and neither was Oberon. I guess we'd find out soon enough.

The room was suddenly very noisy, with everyone talking over one another. I found myself wishing the vamps would just hurry the hell up and get here so the meeting could officially begin. At least then there would be some order and maybe some semblance of a plan could begin to form. Right now, it was just loud pointless chatter. It was too hard to process all of the little conversations that had broken off in the comfort of Baylen's living room.

And then, as if by my command, the front door swung open. Only this time there was no knock to precede it. The vamps had finally arrived. When will I ever learn to be careful what I wish for?

VIII
EIGHT

The conversations quieted down until there was nothing but the sound of our breathing. Everyone began to rise except for me because I didn't know I was supposed to.

Olwyn took me by the elbow and gently pulled me to my feet. It was still amazing how in control this were was of her strength. She could crush my skull if she wanted to, but Olwyn simply helped me off the couch like I was made of glass. The alpha's wife knew I wasn't familiar with the Council formalities and did not want to give the vampire queen and Council chair an excuse to lay claim due to my poor manners, whether they were intentional or not.

Olwyn found it insulting that the vamps held the highest seats on the Council and were given authority over all the Others. After all, was it not the wolves that descended from Remus and Romulous themselves? Or shifters as a species that could be traced back to St. Patrick who, along with his congregation, shifted to become deer to avoid religious persecution? It was one of the earliest documented shifts. If it was good enough for a revered saint and the Norms' most dominant religion, then it was certainly good enough to hold high seats on this damned Council.

While I found all of this fascinating, especially since I never knew of shifting in the early stories of Christianity— it's amazing what they leave out in bible school—I was more interested in the fact that once again I had been able to read by touching *someone* and not just *something*. The change in my ability from reading inanimate to reading animate objects was unnerving. This time it was a fully coherent thought too, not just a quick flash like I'd experienced earlier. How was this happening? Had I gained something from Ouzel as he was gaining strength from me? My skin crawled at the thought. Should I tell someone? Mahalia, or maybe Baylen? But when? I sure as hell wasn't going to just raise my hand and say 'Hi, I'm Maurin, and I have no idea what the limit or capability of my power actually is'. They would probably see it as a weakness, especially the vampires. There wasn't a person alive since the shift that didn't know the vamps, and none of the ones present were known for their forgiving nature. I was not in a room with a group of people I wanted viewing me as weak.

Agrona is ancient in modern terms. No one, even Agrona, knew how old she truly was. Really old vampires could lose their human memories over time, and she had almost no memory of her human life left. The vampire queen couldn't even remember the name her human parents had given her. She had come to be known as Agrona, which means carnage or slaughter, centuries ago

in England for the many corpses she left in her wake.
Seems the Brits thought it a fitting name for her.
Apparently so did she, since she never bothered to change
it. Her auburn hair and hazel eyes were sort of an odd
contrast to her Elmer's glue complexion. Agrona didn't
have the porcelain skin with just the slightest hint of pink
common to most red heads, though it could have changed
over time since she had been undead for so long. Her body
was stiff and cold like she had been carved from marble.
The formal dark-green ball gown she wore only added to
the hardness of her appearance. She looked like a
bridesmaid in the undead wedding of the year instead of
the high seat on the Council. The dark-green velvet of her
hem brushed the floor as she walked in with the grace of
royalty. Scary 'Off with her head' Queen of Hearts kind of
royalty, that is.

Agrona used to believe humans were merely cattle and
should be hunted at will. And while there was a part of her
that still looked down upon humans, lower on the food
chain as they were, she has come to accept the delicate
balance between vampires and humans. Obviously
stronger and harder to kill, vampires could hunt themselves
right into extinction if left unchecked. As Council chair she
worked hard to keep the vampires reigned in to maintain
the balance of their life's blood. Of course, when they speak
publicly, it's not a story of survival you'll hear, but rather
one of vampires and humans living in domesticated bliss.

Keeping her fellow vampires in check had become
much easier for Agrona since the romanticizing of
vampirism. Thanks to Anne Rice and her beloved Lestat,
there were flocks of people who wanted to be loved by a

vampire. None of us who had yet to be bitten, or rather the ones who had no intention of being bitten, were complaining. Though you might be shocked at just who was hiding bite marks under sharp business suits.

King to Agrona's Queen was Kedehern, the battle lord, in a suit tailored to both fit him and match Agrona perfectly. While the dark green made Agrona paler, it actually brought a little warmth to Kedehern's face. I was hoping it was the suit warming his complexion and not the fact that he had a snack on the way here, anyway. His single-button suit jacket did little to hide the muscular physique beneath it. He had obviously been athletic while he was still alive. Though, when he was alive most people had been farmers and weren't typically fat, regardless.

While they were not turned by the same master vamp, Kedehern and Agrona found each other in England. He went there after being chased out of Gaul. The fact he stills calls it Gaul when the rest of the world calls it France is a sign of just how old he really is, despite his youthful appearance. Whoever turned him, turned him young. He didn't look a century over twenty-one.

Like Agrona, he was renamed Kedehern. If he does remember his human name, he has never shared it. Apparently he rather likes being called "battle lord". Despite losing most of his humanity he kept his love for Agrona. He loved her the moment he laid eyes on her feeding after sunset in a dark alleyway, one cold winter night many centuries ago. Her face flushed with the rush of blood, she had taken his proverbial breath away, and he's been enraptured ever since. Kedehern still adhered to the old ways and laws of the vampires and served as their judge, and often executioner. Most vampires today had grown fat and lazy by his standards, living far too decadently and drawing far too much attention.

Compared to the two of them wrapped in velvet, the rest of us looked like crap. Well not Olwyn, Arcana, or Mahalia. At least they were in dresses and a suit. Even Baylen and Roul, who were both in business casual, looked overdressed when compared to the rest of us in jeans and T-shirts. I definitely looked unfit for a visit from the royal couple.

They were the only two vampires who came, despite having a dozen or more that belonged to them directly. Not to mention the throngs beneath those. All the other leaders had brought their own backup. All Carnage and her Battle Lord needed were each other.

Seamus had brought in the dining room chairs for those who arrived after the couches were full. Tybalt brought two more chairs for Agrona and Kedehern, closing the circle everyone formed in the room.

The air was excruciatingly tense as all eyes fell on Agrona. Everyone waited for her to begin the meeting. I don't know why I expected her to get right down to business. She didn't, choosing instead to sit there for what seemed like hours. This was her Council, and she would begin when she damned well pleased, regardless of the circumstances.

I felt Olwyn stir next to me and knew she was getting more irritated with each passing second. Olwyn could take a lesser vamp with no problem. She knew how to handle herself in a battle and was exceptionally strong, even by were standards. She had to be, or she would never have been Roul's mate. Against Agrona she wouldn't survive the challenge, so she had to endure this ridiculous behavior.

I was really trying not to freak out at how easy it was to read Olwyn. She barely brushed against me as she crossed her legs. Either she was projecting her feelings like a freight train coming at me head on, or I was getting better at this by the second. I really needed to talk to Baylen or Mahalia, alone.

Ten minutes ago, I had just wanted the meeting to start, to finally get the others planning and moving. Now, I couldn't wait for it to be over. Even more aggravating was the fact it was most likely Baylen whom I would have to ask for advice. Just the thought of it made me queasy. I didn't know Mahalia, so I couldn't be sure she wouldn't just out me as a hack to the Council. Baylen, on the other hand, is the one who dragged me into this mess. He might look bad in front of the Council if the psychic he brought was somehow misfiring and not quite in control of her powers.

Agrona's voice was cool and smooth. The tension immediately left the room when she decided to finally bless us with the sound of it. Power seeped across the room, acting as a sedative. I was sure this same power that so easily calmed us could just as easily choke the life out of us.

"Baylen has already informed us all of today's events. Therefore, there is no need to recount them now. We must focus our attention on finding the Triad, the Morrigna. It has been more centuries than I can count since all three have been united as the Morrigna. The fact that they have joined again is grave news." Agrona turned her icy gaze toward me. "I am not sure, Maurin, why you are at the center of this, but you seem to be the key. So, we must once again put your talents to use."

What? This wasn't exactly what I had been hoping for. I would have preferred to discreetly tell Baylen my powers were short-circuiting which made me stronger but less predictable, and that could backfire. I'd rather hoped to not expose myself to the entire Council and looked to Baylen and Seamus for direction, unsure of what I should do.

Agrona's voice rocked my attention back to her. "Do not look to Baylen! I hold the high seat here, and I will decide. You were the first to see anything beyond sign or suspicion, and you will repeat that performance now before the Council!"

She focused more of her energy on me, and I could feel the crushing weight of it, feel her trying to crush me into submission. With a snap of her fingers, and a vamp that I had not even seen come into the house, let alone the room, came before her like a lady in waiting. I guess that was what the lesser vamp was.

"Thank you, Cerise." At Agrona's dismissal, the vamp disappeared as silently as she had appeared.

I couldn't see what Cerise had handed to Agrona, but I had a terrible feeling that Agrona was about to hand it to me. I was wrong about the formalities, however. Agrona fashioned herself as a real queen and was, therefore, above touching her subjects. She called for someone to do it for her. Never tired of giving orders, she picked someone new to boss around.

"Medea, you helped Maurin earlier today and so, you shall help her now. Take this, and be sure that Maurin holds on to it. This item should bring greater results. We shall see if they are as Baylen suspects. Mahalia, you and your coven will raise shields to protect this house and its occupants," Agrona ordered.

Mahalia and her coven rose from their seats. The High Priestess didn't seem at all bothered by Agrona ordering her around, which surprised me. She obviously knew her place in the universe and was comfortable there. Me, I would have told her where she could stick her shields. But nothing Agrona said or did would change Mahalia's path. Knowing the course you're on and knowing your place in the world was a good feeling. I'd felt like that this morning before I got to work, before Seamus had showed up at the station. Right now, I seriously doubted I would ever feel that way again.

IX
NINE

The earth beneath the house seemed to come alive, as though it had a heartbeat and pulsed in time with the coven. They stood there in the living room, drawing on the power of the earth. A cool, damp, mossy smell drifted into the room. I kept my eyes focused on Mahalia. Drenched in power, she took on a vibrancy I hadn't seen before. Her hair blew in a breeze caused by a shift in the air molecules surrounding the coven.

They began to invoke their charm in two groups of three. Mahalia, Arcana, and Phallon were joined, as were Juno, Cicero, and Oberon. They would have needed two more for Amalie to take part, and two sets of three were more than enough to shield the house.

The number three had held great power for Druids, and that power continued today. Each line was recited three times by each group. Mahalia chose an old charm to protect the house, hoping any dark witch or warlock that had aligned with the Morrigna wouldn't recognize it. Three more times they would recite this, with each group of three in succession. It reminded me of when my class used to sing *Row, Row, Row Your Boat* in rounds when I was a kid.

The air in the house grew warm, and there was a soft buzzing that hung in my ear signaling the charm was in place, and the house was now impenetrable. At least, we hoped so. If something could come through that door, it would be too strong for us to stop. If it was that strong though, I doubted it would use the front door.

Now that the witches had completed their task, Medea's attention was back to me. She moved toward me with that same sway in her hips, always in seduction mode. Her left hand was curled into a fist. With her right she reached for me, pulling me closer to her. I didn't see the point in struggling. Medea was definitely stronger than I was physically—she could crush all the bones in my arm if she wasn't concen-trating on being gentle. Besides, Agrona was still projecting most of her power in my direction. I could never split my attention between the two of them and walk away alive. Still, I wasn't just going to walk over to her like a mindless fang banger. So I let her pull me to her.

Medea was toe to toe with me now, and I held out my right hand, ready to take whatever Agrona had given her. Her hand, still clenched in a fist, hung over mine. She had a fierce look in her eye, warning me not to touch her. I can't imagine why she wouldn't want to hold onto me this time. There wasn't a single scratch left on her beautiful tan skin, but I knew she wouldn't risk a mere mortal drawing blood from her in front of the entire Council.

With a light thump, a small, smooth, gray stone dropped into my hand. I expected it to feel cool against my skin, but it was warm. A small hum of power radiated from the center. I closed my hand around it, gently gave it a shake, and let the warm stone roll around the inside of my fist. The warmth quickly grew from comforting to hot— almost too hot to hold. I was about to drop the scalding stone, but instead it dropped me to my knees.

Almost immediately, my head was filled with images. This was the Stone of Fal. In the old days, all who would assume sovereignty were required to hold the stone. It would flare to life with power, giving off a heavenly glow if they were truly to be crowned king. So why was it coming to life now and causing a vision?

"To bring me to you," said a deep male voice that was familiar to me, even though I was sure I'd never heard it before.

He walked toward me. His black hair had a soft, natural wave and covered the collar of his ankle-length leather coat, which billowed around him as he moved. Matching, knee-high boots defined his strong legs. The word gorgeous came to mind. I wanted him to wrap me up in that coat with him. The blood in my veins felt warmer, and my face felt flushed. I was drawn to him, needed to touch him—this man who was certainly no longer alive.

He was getting closer, and my heart was beating faster. I could barely think since the sound of my heart was pounding in my ears. This was crazy. Not once in my entire life have I been drawn to someone this way. This wasn't real. It was a damned vision, and I needed to pull myself out of it before whatever power was driving it trapped me here in a place that couldn't still exist, and with a man who hadn't been alive for centuries.

And yet, I couldn't tear my gaze away from his beautiful

blue eyes. There was something so familiar about them. The stone grew hotter, finally drawing my attention away from the stranger who was quickly approaching. I looked up from the forgotten fiery stone in my hand to find him standing right in front of me. His blue eyes were burning a hole in my heart with the sadness that lay in them.

I wanted to cup his face in my hands and kiss his exquisitely full lips until all the sadness was gone. He was close enough to me now to actually do it. All I had to do was raise my hand but I stood there, unable to move, totally awestruck.

"I know you, Scota, my Goddess, my love." His voice poured over my skin like satin, and I felt goose bumps run up and down my arms.

"Rory." His name left my lips in a whisper. I felt like I had loved him once too, this man I had never met and would never have the chance to meet outside of this vision, which was beginning to feel more like a personal delusion.

He reached for me and still, I stood there. His hand brushed mine and with that one touch, a memory flared to life that was not my own and yet was still somehow about me. He did know me, in every way, but that had been a long time ago. Another life. His arms were outstretched, and I let him wrap them around me, surrendering to his embrace.

I can't remember the last time someone had held me this way. Intimacy eluded someone with my abilities. I've had relationships before, but they always ended badly. With my shields down I'd see things I shouldn't see. It's hard to get back from that. I tried not to let them see me weirded out about the things I knew, but I couldn't help it.

They then leave when they realize what I've done, intentional or not. No one, despite what they say, ever seems to really want someone to know them inside and out. So I've gotten used to being alone.

And now look at me, my faced pressed against the smooth silk shirt of a man long since dead, breathing in the herbal smell of him mixed with the leather of his coat. I was in a vision and feeling what? Peaceful? Happy? I was starting to think the recent power increase had completely fried my brain.

Heat from the stone and cool droplets of rain brought me back from my thoughts, washing away the minty leather scent I had become so comfortable with. The vision was changing. I tried to open my eyes and look up at him, but the water poured down harder, forcing me to bury my face in the protection of his chest. Until suddenly there was nothing but the water. The warmth of him, the strength and comfort of his body pressed to mine, was replaced with the cold, hard press of water against my skin.

I felt surprisingly lonely after being pulled from Rory's embrace. In just the brief moment he had held me, I felt far away from the terrible things that were going to happen when we finally faced the Morrigna. The need to be there with him felt right. It felt more real than anything that had happened in my life so far. Still, if I listened closely enough, I could hear those familiar little voices trying to tell me it wasn't my life he had been a part of. It wasn't Maurin he knew or loved.

But it didn't matter. He was gone, replaced by the cold, dark water. I was sinking fast, like someone had tied a boulder to my feet and thrown me in. My body felt denser than the water, which was getting colder and darker by the second, and there seemed to be no possible chance of floating back up. Rory was just a small glimmer of light at the surface. The water seemed to be alive, pushing me down.

I couldn't move my arms enough to swim. The water felt tight against my skin. It was still pushing me down when I realized this wasn't just water. It was power. Something or someone was in this water with me. My head should have hurt. My lungs should have hurt. I've never stayed this long underwater, and I think my untrained lungs would be screaming in pain right now. They weren't, and I kept on sinking.

I felt remarkably at peace for someone who was obviously drowning. On the brink of death, trapped in this vision, and instead of panic all I felt was a strange serenity.

I fought to swim one last time because the sane part of my brain said I should. I tried to kick my way back to the surface, back to consciousness, and back to Baylen's living room. But it was no use. The harder I struggled to get to the surface, the further away it became. My arms and legs were burning from the effort to get out of the water, and I finally gave up.

X
TEN

A hand sliced up from the bottom of the water that had become my prison and grabbed ahold of my ankle. It began pulling me down, deeper and deeper, toward the bottom of the body of water. It was so dark I couldn't see who or what was dragging me into the abyss. The hand felt small, barely able to wrap around my ankle. Was it a woman?

The pressure this far down was starting to hurt my eyes, my ears, and even my chest. My body felt like it was in a car crusher. It hurt everywhere. We had almost reached the ocean floor when I was finally close enough, despite the blackness, to determine that it was a woman pulling me to my death. I might not have known it at all, if not for her long hair floating back toward me, or the hem of her dress moving across my leg as we finally hit the bottom.

She looked like an angel, but she walked on a bed of sand instead of one made of clouds. With no other options, I followed her. As if the fact that I was walking this far down in what had to be the ocean wasn't insane enough, the blackness began to fade with each passing step. Like

Apollo with his chariot bringing out the sun, she turned the darkness to light. We reached the base of what I assumed was a cliff.

There was an opening in the wall, and she entered. Again, I followed her. The water began to recede as we made our way through this hallway carved from the rock. The walls were cold, wet, and still rough, as if the hallway were freshly cut. The air grew warmer, and the sand beneath my feet went from wet and firm to dry and hot quicksand. It was like walking out of the surf and across the cool wet sand packed hard from the crashing waves to struggling through the hot sunbaked sand back to your blanket. Except we weren't at the beach, we were under it, and this shouldn't be happening. She pressed on with me following right behind her.

The hallway opened up into an enormous cavern. There was a whole world beneath the sea. It was an incredible paradise that shouldn't be here. Bright sun, azure sky, flowing grass, and blooming trees? How could this be possible? How could this place even exist?

With her back still turned to me, she said, "Welcome to Elysium, land of the Gods."

Her voice was deep and sultry, yet vaguely familiar. She slowly turned to face me, the similarity of her features from hair to height caught me off guard. Watching her move, I decided I should probably spend more time in the gym. Her muscles were perfectly toned. When she turned completely around, facing me, my jaw dropped. I know it's rude to stand there staring at someone with your mouth hanging open, but I just couldn't help it. It was like looking in the mirror. Well, looking in the mirror after I spent some much needed time toning up in the gym. My chest didn't hurt back when I thought I was going to drown, but it sure as hell hurt now. Was this what a heart attack felt like? I clutched my chest unconsciously.

"You're not having a heart attack, Maurin. Get a hold of yourself. We don't have much time. I have too many things to tell you and nowhere near enough time to explain it all. We don't have time for this foolishness."

She kept walking over a small sand dune and through the tall, dry grasses that grew on the beach to a spot where the grass had grown green, soft, and lush. The span of this place was unbelievable. A river ran through a huge valley and down to the beach, feeding back out into the ocean depths we had just left. The valley seemed to go on for miles before disappearing in the shadows of the tall, dark-green hills that formed a natural barrier. This kept everything in the valley safe from whatever was on the other side.

She sat there in the grass, waiting for me. The grass felt like plush carpeting beneath my feet and brought back sweet memories of my childhood. Damn it, where were my Docs now? Those were my favorite pair. They were originals, imported from London. Not the cheap crap made in China.

"You will find yourself back in order when we're done. You are here with me now in Elysium. You really have no need for material things here. Elysium is anything and everything we want it to be. It can be found high upon the hill, deep within the earth, or far below the sea, but only if we choose to bring you. Alas, I didn't bring you here to simply show you the splendor of our lands. Come and sit with me, Maurin, let my words and wisdom guide you through the battle that is about to come," she offered.

She sat down, legs crossed, forcing her rich purple gown up over her knees. Motioning for me to sit across from her, she pushed her mysteriously dried hair out of her face.

Speechless for the first time in my life, I did as she asked. A warm summer wind, sweet with the smell of honeysuckle, swept over me and danced along my skin. My hair and clothes, all of me was dried by the warm aromatic breeze.

"Let's start at the beginning, Maurin. I am you, and you are me. We are one," she stated.

"That doesn't really seem like the beginning. It feels kind of like you left something out. We are one? Do you mean in that 'we are all brothers and sisters' kind of way? Because I still feel like me, the same person I was when I woke up this morning." Well sort of, but I kept that to myself. "And you, well I don't even know who you are, but you're you. We can't be one because I am me, and you are you, and we are separate bodies in the same time and place."

"Maurin, I do consider myself a patient being. I have waited centuries to come alive again, and that obviously takes great patience. I have already used up almost all of my patience, and you are really testing the little bit that I have left. Do not squander the last of my grace with your childish behavior. Of course you are still you. But you have never only been you. I have always been a part of you, lying dormant, waiting to be reborn. And so I have been. The time is finally at hand."

"I'm not quite sure I am following you here. Actually, I know I'm not following you. What are you talking about?" I asked.

Up and pacing, my bare feet sank into the soft, cool grass. Startled as it came suddenly to life beneath my feet, winding its way around my ankles and over my pants legs until I couldn't pace any more, I put my arms out to keep my balance.

She smiled at me slyly and motioned for me to sit. Except for the confidence she exuded, which I most definitely lacked but made up for in stubbornness, I doubt anyone would be able to tell us apart.

I watched as her hair, brown like mine with the same burgundy highlights I got last month, caught in the breeze. Her eyes were the same as mine but with specks of gold in them, and they were fixed on me.

She motioned for me to sit again and since I wasn't given much of a choice, considering the grass was still wrapped around my feet like ropes, I did.

I plopped down, a little harder than I intended, and the grass unwove itself from around my ankles.

The look on her face said she was done playing.

"Had you not isolated yourself from your people this way, I could have happened years ago. You do not know enough of your history to fully understand what is happening here. Unfortunately, now there simply isn't time. Rather than spending years learning your full powers and mastering your skills, you wasted precious time working with the humans. You'll be weaker because of your ignorance," she said brusquely.

"I didn't isolate myself, and I don't have people." I felt the need to defend myself. "It's not like I chose to ignore my heritage. There was no one there to teach it to me. Certainly not my parents. They hated every-thing about me. I was a loner, even as a kid. Especially when I was a kid. I never really fit in with anyone, Norms or Others." I said defensively.

"Your parents may not have realized exactly what you were, but they knew you were gifted," she said.

Right. Like my parents were magically educated people. Like they knew about me. The weird glances they used to give each other when I did or said something not normal wasn't because I was a freak, but because I was what? More powerful than they expected? I realized that I didn't want to think about my parents. "So what are we talking about here, some kind of reincarnation?" I asked.

"Yes and no. It is similar, but the knowledge of the previous life remains, any skills one possessed before death they will have when they are reborn. Many lifetimes ago, a war raged between the gods, and it spilled over onto man. We were gods. We could not be killed, but the faith in us could. When a new belief system swept over our lands, many of the old gods began to fade. Some, who were more powerful and held favor with darkness, began to prey on the lesser gods, absorbing their powers in order to maintain their own strength. Others, myself included, gave them-selves and some of their powers to the humans so that we could be reborn. The darkest of us all, the Morrigna, led the hunt against the weak and won. Morrigan herself has been waiting, meddling in the affairs of humans for centuries. She has been waiting for just the right time to unleash her full powers, and of course her sisters, on the world. But I have also been waiting, reborn through the years as many different women, each strong and powerful in their own right, but none of them quite like you. I have lived through all of them, patiently waiting for the most gifted and most powerful. The Chosen, and so here you are," she said.

"Okay. Believe it or not, I have heard stranger things in the last twenty-four hours, but who exactly are you then?" I asked.

If I hadn't heard the world was going to end at the hand of the *disii* and the old Pagan Gods and sat in front of Carnage and her Battle Lord with the rest of the Council today, I might have been freaking out right now. But this, after all, was a vision. It didn't have to be true. I could wake up back on the floor of Baylen's living room, and none of this would mean anything. It's all just some insane vision brought on by the stone. Right. I am not going to freak out.

That sweet breeze came back, thick and warm. I closed my eyes and leaned into it, letting it wrap around me like a blanket. She cupped my chin in her hand, turning my face back to hers. The warmth in her hand surprised me. I'd half expected it to feel like the icy hand of death. There was power in that breeze now, a static charge that had the hairs on my arms standing on end.

"I am the Goddess Scota." She spoke her name as if that explained everything.

"A goddess? Please. If I am a goddess reborn, then why do I have self-esteem issues? Shouldn't I be some super diva or something?" I tried for sarcasm, my favorite defense mechanism, but it apparently wasn't working because she laughed at me.

The look she gave me told me she knew I wasn't really

buying into all this goddess stuff. I'm not really sure when it happened, but at some point today I lost my poker face. I had a really good one too. Now everyone could read me like a book, a *Fun with Dick and Jane* book, no less.

"Maurin, you only need to hear my words now. When you return from the vision, there will be proof enough. You have already sensed changes. Your power has grown through your connection with me. My powers will be yours. It will be a struggle to contain your new strength at first. I would have preferred you had some sort of training prior to this challenge, but that simply isn't possible now. You will simply have to learn as you go," Scota said.

"Would I have had any abilities if it weren't for you? I don't understand what is so special about me! Why am I the Chosen One?"

"You have always been gifted and even if you were not the Chosen, you would still be strong. Your ability to see inside someone's memories is your own unique gift, and you really are more powerful than you know. You have barely begun to scratch the surface of your own ability. But you will come to see why you are the Chosen in time. It was written long before you were born," she told me.

A beautifully crafted pewter goblet appeared in her hand. The stem was thick, and it looked heavy. Beginning at the rim and running all the way down to the base of the cup was an intricately carved grape vine. She held the goblet out to me, and I could see a thick, golden liquid inside it. It was the color of honey but smelled like peaches.

"Goibniu's Ale, nectar of the Gods. Drink," she commanded.

I looked at the cup of Meade and brought it to my lips. I

hesitated as I smelled the drink. I had never been a big fan of any honey wine. She reached out and tipped the cup until the thick warm liquid was running down my throat. It was sweet, almost too sweet, which is why I've never liked honey wine. I hadn't had much to eat today and mostly coffee to drink, so something this sweet would definitely upset my stomach. I could feel the wine (or ale as she called it) slowly burning its way down to my stomach. That slow burn started to spread out through my body, coursing through my veins to the tips of my fingers. It felt like electricity was running through my body, and instead of feeling sick I felt ravenous.

Her hands, outstretched once more, were over-flowing with fragrant berries, crimson nuts, and catkin apples.

My stomach growled.

"Take in the harvest of Elysium. Food for the gods," she said.

I grabbed the first apple, tart and crisp, finishing it quickly—down to the core in just a few bites. I'd never seen crimson nuts before, but they were the size and color of pomegranate seeds, and they tasted like cashews. She poured the nuts and berries in my hand, and I ate them almost as quickly as they had appeared. I was still so hungry. How did vegetarians get full eating like this?

I felt invigorated, alive, like I had been sleepwalking through life all these years. Everything seemed more vibrant. Every blade of grass was visible. I could count them if I wanted. My body was zinging with power, like I could kick ass and take names.

She smiled, obviously amused with me. I was glad she found me so entertaining.

The pewter goblet was back in my hands and full of the ale.

"Drink more," she said.

And I did.

More food appeared in her hands as well. "Keep eating," she said.

I ate and drank until I could not eat another bite or drink another drop. Now I was the one smiling as I thought once again of *Alice in Wonderland*. Eat me, drink me. What wondrous things would happen to me when I woke? Would I find myself falling down some rabbit hole too?

I lay down on the cool grass, and it felt good against my skin, still flushed from the ale. My eyes were so heavy; I could barely hear Scota telling me about Elysium or my powers. Was it something important? Probably. I tried rubbing my eyes to stay awake, but it wasn't working. Her voice got farther and farther away as I fell into a deep sleep.

XI
ELEVEN

When I woke up, the plush green grass had turned back into the hardwood floor of Baylen's living room. The vision was over.

"Maurin? Maurin, can you hear me?" It was Baylen. He was snapping his fingers in my face.

I blinked. My eyelids were still so heavy. When I finally managed to open my eyes all the way, I could barely see him at first.

He knelt over me with a look of shock on his face.

"Maurin. Maurin." His voice sounded weird. He spoke firmly, but seemed nervous somehow.

I stared at him lazily, and then he gave me a hard slap on my right cheek.

"Have you completely lost your fucking mind?" I asked, as I yawned and stretched out my whole body, forcing him to back up.

Arching my back, I reached my hands out and pointed my toes down. It felt good. That first big stretch when you get up from a long nap always felt great. A chill ran down my spine, shivering, I started to stand.

Baylen reached out to help me up, and I pulled away. He kept staring at me like I had six heads, as if he were unsure if it was really me or not.

"What is your problem? Man, I feel like Rip Van Winkle, like I slept for years. How long was I out?" I asked, stretching more to crack my back.

Baylen was about to answer my questions, but Agrona didn't give him the chance.

"Fifteen minutes," she said.

"Really? That's it? It seemed longer than that." I couldn't believe it had only been minutes. It had felt like hours.

"You fell as soon as you touched the stone. We waited for you, for something to happen. When it appeared you stopped breathing, Baylen came to your aid. He was barely by your side before you gasped for air and started breathing again." Agrona wasn't the least bit concerned about my not breathing. She was irritated I hadn't put on more of a show.

I ignored her for the moment and looked down at the floor. By my feet was the stone. I reached down and picked it up.

Baylen backed up further, like he didn't want to be anywhere near me while I was holding the stone. He kept giving me weird looks. "There is something different. Your eyes…they were not that color before."

I just stared at him. I hadn't seen my reflection yet, but I had an idea of what he meant. Scota's eyes were rimmed in gold with small specks of gold inside the black and now mine must be too. Great. Just what I needed. One more thing to make me different from everybody else.

I was still holding the King Maker in my hand. I looked around the room, and everyone's eyes were on me. Seamus's and Amalie's eyes held concern, unsure what had happened to me. The weres were sure I had changed. They could smell it with their heightened senses. They just didn't know what exactly I had changed into. I kept scanning the room. I felt like there was something in the room that I needed to find. Or maybe someone. I stopped when my eyes met Oberon's.

I knew those eyes. I suddenly felt like I knew him. Walking past Baylen, I crossed the room until I stood in front of Oberon. Taking his hand in mine, I pressed the stone into his palm and let go.

Oberon held the Stone of Fal, and it flared to life. He closed his fingers around the stone and bright light seeped through the cracks between his fingers.

Satisfied, I brushed the tips of my fingers across his brow, down his temple, and tucked a stray hair behind his ear. He looked at me with longing and familiarity. The same look Rory had in my vision. My hands itched to touch him.

After managing to pull my hand away, I started walking to the small bathroom near the kitchen. I wanted to see these new eyes of mine. It was hard to walk away from him, and I turned to get another look over my shoulder. Part of me could have stayed there looking at him for all eternity, and the other part of me wanted to know *why* I wanted to stare at him for all eternity since I didn't really know Oberon any more than I knew Rory. Scota said that I would still be me, but I was starting to think she was going to have one hell of an influence. Pulling my gaze away from

Oberon, I told myself the need to be near him was just left over from the vision. Once I got to the bathroom and there was a little more space (and a door) between us, my head would clear up.

I was curious and nervous to see my new and improved reflection, to see if Scota had changed more than just the color of my eyes. Toned triceps would be nice. I barely made it to the foyer when Agrona called to me, her voice iced over with anger. Apparently I had ignored her for a little too long.

"How dare you walk out on the Council!" Of course, when she said Council, what she really meant was her. No one else seemed to care. "No one here has dismissed you. We expect an explanation for what has occurred here in this room!" The harsh cold of her voice was quickly replaced with the heat of her power rushing out to me. She was going to try to force me to stand there.

I wasn't a member of the Council, or any group represented here for that matter. Until today, the Others were just fine to leave me hanging in limbo, straddling both worlds but never accepted by either, I most certainly didn't need her permission to leave the room. Tired of her constant need to display her dominance over me, I turned to face her and walked back to the living room.

Before Scota, I would have crumpled to the floor under the weight of Agrona's power, but not anymore. Let the battle of wills begin. As my anger and resentment grew, so did the power inside me. With my newfound strength running through my body my heart beat harder, working overtime to push not only my blood, but the power through my veins. I lowered my shields. It was too much.

Scota was right. Without practice, I wasn't going to be able to control this. I had to let it out. I did the only thing I could think of and pushed the building energy out of my body. Right back at Agrona.

I felt her power give and then withdraw as it crashed back into her body.

She stumbled. Her eyes turned ice blue and then black. Not good.

She practically flew across the room. I knew she wasn't actually flying, but she moved so damned fast it would have been hard for a Norm to tell the difference. She was so quick I didn't have time to brace before impact.

She had me by the shoulders and we continued to propel across the room together. We skidded through the foyer and slammed into the coat closet door. The door was solid wood which splintered apart, sending us crashing into a bunch of coats. That would have been fine actually, except for the empty wire hangers shoved in between them. The back wall of the closet, plus my limp arms and legs creating drag on the floor, finally stopped us.

Her fangs were drawn as she screamed at me. "You insolent bitch! I will teach you some manners!"

"Agrona, darling, I don't think it's wise to kill the psychic right now," Kedehern said.

Thank God.

He was by her side, pulling her out of the closet. She let him, becoming almost docile in his arms. They both left me there covered in coats. And something wet.

XII
TWELVE

I didn't even bother to get up. The warmth I felt running down my back told me that it wouldn't be a good idea. My arms weren't really cooperating right now, so I couldn't reach behind me to feel for sure, but I was betting the warmth was actually blood. If I could feel it running down my back, then odds were, I was hurt pretty good. Yup, if I was a betting kind of girl, I'd say the odds were even better I was going to have a hell of a lot of bruises and need a few stitches as well.

I could hear Roul and Olwyn arguing with the self-proclaimed vampire queen.

"She is not familiar with the ways of the Council. Perhaps we could have one meeting where Olwyn doesn't have to heal someone," Roul said angrily.

I don't think Agrona really gave a shit what they thought.

"She wasn't trying to escape. She's gone through some kind of metamorphosis since she touched that stone. I think she could have been allowed a moment to look at herself." Roul was all but growling now. His voice was rough, like he had been gargling with razor blades. I wondered if it was always like that or if in all the excitement his wolf side got a little too close to the surface.

"If we continue with all of this bickering and fighting, then nothing will get accomplished. Let me tend to Maurin's wounds. Then you can ask her civilly what happened. Agreed?" Olwyn was moving toward me as she spoke.

I assumed everyone agreed, since no actually voiced an objection. Olwyn took me by my forearms and began to lift me up and out of the closet.

My back screamed with pain, and I could feel the blood moving faster down my back. I let out a small cry, and Olwyn carefully moved me out into the foyer.

She went to lay me down on the floor, her hand sliding up my back until she hit the cause of all my pain. A large splinter of wood was lodged deep into my back. She turned me over gently and laid me down on my stomach. Then she ripped my shirt in two and unhooked my bra.

I could feel the wood and muscle shift as the tension from my bra strap was released.

Her fingers probed the wound. "Roul, I could use a little help here, please. Baylen and Seamus? Would you go get me a bowl of warm water and some towels?"

I heard footsteps. Some were moving away to the kitchen, and one heavy set moved toward me. Suddenly, even heavier hands were poking around my back. The fact that one hand was below my shoulder blade and the other was past the middle of my back said a lot. Just how much of the damned door got stuck in my back? It wasn't so much a splinter as it was a stake. Too bad it didn't get stuck in Agrona's cold heart instead.

"Roul, I need you to hold her down. She's stronger than before, and it seems she's gained some healing abilities. Not that she knows how to use them yet, but her body is obviously trying regardless. The skin is beginning to heal around the wood. I think I tore some of the scar tissue that was forming when I moved her. At the rate that she's healing, if we don't pull it out right now we'll have to cut it out. I'm not going to lie to you, Maurin. This is going to hurt like a son of a bitch," Olwyn said.

Oh, how I wished she had lied. Her honesty certainly didn't help any. Roul was holding my hands, left over right, against my back. The skin pulled around the wood, and it hurt like hell. With one hand still pinning my wrists, he moved the other hand to hold down my legs. A less experienced wolf could have done more damage, but the seasoned Roul was in complete control.

"On three, Roul. One, two..." Olwyn's hand was pressed against my back. "Three!"

With perfect timing, Roul pushed me against the floor as Olwyn pulled the wood out of my back.

I screamed as every inch was ripped out. The blood was pouring out now.

"There's skin and muscle attached to the wood, Olwyn. She's regenerating at a rapid rate already." Roul released me from his grip as he spoke to Olwyn as if I weren't lying there.

Baylen and Seamus were back with the water and towels, setting them in front of Olwyn. She dipped a towel in the warm water and started to clean my back. The water felt good. She was careful not to rub too hard on the gaping hole in my back.

"That really fucking hurt, you know," I whispered, as she cleaned away more of the blood.

"I do believe I mentioned that it would." I could hear the smirk in her voice.

"Olwyn, she's healed it completely. I've never seen a Norm heal so quickly." I was willing to bet Roul's jaw was hanging open.

"Um, hello, lying right here. You can stop talking *about* me and start talking *to* me anytime now."

"Neither have I," Olwyn said, as she wiped the last of the blood off my back. "I'm beginning to think she is far less human than we thought. We'll have to wait and see if you'll have a scar, Maurin. Healing, that's quite an impressive gift you've gained. Can you stand?"

Unsure, I pushed up slowly. With a lot less effort than I would have imagined, I was able to get up off the floor and keep a hold of what was left of my shirt. No need to give more of a show than I already had. I may have healed the wounds on the outside of my body, but I was still hurting pretty badly inside. Never a fan of showing weakness, I tried not to let anybody see my pain.

Olwyn stood up behind me, still marveling at my new ability to heal.

Her fingers slid up and down the new skin. No scab. Rolling my shoulders, I tried not to wince from the sharp pain in my muscles. The skin felt tight on my back. I was definitely going to have a scar. A big ugly scar at that.

Unsure of how much energy the healing had cost me, I stood there, watching everyone watching me.

Oberon moved to close the distance between us. I pulled away from Olwyn to meet him. He opened his arms, and I nestled in against the warmth of his body. Using his body to hold up my shirt, I wrapped my arms around his waist as he closed his around me and nuzzled my face into his chest like a cat might rub against your leg. Someone's throat cleared.

I looked up from the large expanse that was Oberon's chest to see Baylen's cold, hard gaze fixed upon me and Oberon. I wasn't sure what I did to deserve that look. He looked as if I had just slapped him in the face.

"Agrona, if we could move things along now. I would very much like to hear Maurin's explanation." He was trying hard to hide the anger in his voice and failing miserably.

What was his problem, anyway?

"Yes, yes. Let your new pet regale us all with her tale. I must admit that this little skirmish has peaked my interest in what she has to say. But you will do well to remember your place, Blue Man of the Minch. Fallen as you are, and tainted as your blood may be, I will not hesitate to drain every last drop from your body," the vampire queen threatened.

Apparently she thought the venom in his voice was directed at her. Luckily for Baylen, it's still considered tacky to drain your host.

"I would not have thought anything to the contrary, Carnage. Maurin, if you could pull yourself away from Oberon long enough to tell us what happened…" Baylen prompted.

And then the light bulb went off. He was jealous! If I

wasn't so pissed off, I'd be a little flattered. As it was, I couldn't figure out where the hell he got off. I hadn't known him long enough for him to have an opinion about my choice of shoes, let alone whom I cuddled up next to. Not that I could really explain why I was cuddling up to Oberon. I wasn't even sure these feelings were entirely my own.

I went back to glaring at Baylen and thought about standing there wrapped up in Oberon while I told them everything, just for spite. A smile crept across my face, but as quickly as it came it was gone. We didn't need any more pissing contests tonight. So, for the sake of actually getting something accomplished, I moved away from Oberon. Slipping my arms back into what was left of my shirt, I began to tell my motley audience what had happened in my vision.

XIII
THIRTEEN

I started with Rory and the water. How I thought that my lungs were going to be crushed and then about Scota. Eyes widened at the mention of her name. When no one offered an explanation, I moved on to Elysium and, if at all possible, their eyes got even bigger. Without stopping for questions, I kept explaining the rebirth and joining of powers. I left out the confusing 'I am me, we are one' conversation and for some reason, I omitted the food and drink I had consumed while I was with her. No one spoke, well at least not directly to me. There was murmuring and speculation mixed in with whispers that I couldn't quite hear.

"I feel like there is something you left out, Maurin."

My body tensed. I didn't go into detail about my despair at being parted with Rory in the vision. Could they have sensed that? When I realized it was Mahalia who had asked the question, some of the tension left my body.

"Did she not mention the Morrigna at all? That is, after all, why the Council has gathered and why you were ripped from your everyday life and dragged into this mess in the first place. Some of us would not have disrupted your life otherwise. Surely she would have given you some direction," Mahalia said.

"Afraid not." I felt a little guilty for not thinking of this while I was with Scota in the vision. "No big reveal on how to kill the *disii*. Just how the Triad gained more power. But I figured you already knew that," I told her.

Mahalia thought about that for a minute. "Tell us anyway. Perhaps if we know the motivation, then we will see the ends and be better able to stop it from occurring."

That seemed like wishful thinking on her part, but I humored her. I was exhausted by the time I finished telling them how the Triad wanted to be worshiped above all others.

"Then it is as I feared. Agrona, I have served as advisor to the Council for a long time, and I pray the Goddess gives me the wisdom to do so tonight. We cannot wait for Morrigan to attack first. It will be bad enough if the Triad is fully formed, but I fear impossible if they are given time to form an army. She doesn't know about Maurin yet, at least I hope she doesn't, and we must use that to our advantage," Mahalia said.

Agrona seemed to agree with her. They were deciding who should go where, who'd gather what, and who'd give orders. My mind took a break for a minute. If I missed something really important, I could get Amalie to fill me in over a cup, or three, of the old coffee in the kitchen because I was headed there as soon as this was over. I felt myself zone out, and then Mahalia was suddenly moving.

Mahalia moved over to Amalie. "We haven't discussed

this yet, but I have decided your path. You are a healer, like Arcana. Your apprenticeship with her begins tonight. You will go with her and Phallon to gather supplies. Juno and Oberon will stay here to keep the shields in place. Cicero and I will gather up the rest of the coven. We will meet you at the Witch's Closet and then return here."

Phallon looked like she was about to protest the separation from her sister Juno, and then seemed to change her mind. She gave her sister a quick squeeze and moved to stand with Amalie and Arcana.

I watched as the ethereal breeze gathered around them, whipping into a tiny tornado at their feet until it encompassed them and they simply faded away inside it. Thunder cracked, and then Mahalia and Cicero were gone too.

Well, so much for Amalie filling me in on anything. That'll teach me. I sort of missed her already. She was really the only person here I would have considered a friend, an ally. It felt kind of lonely without her here.

The party was officially over. Roul and Olwyn nodded to Agrona and Kedehern, about as close to a bow as the vamps would get. The alpha motioned to his pack, and they gathered by the door, looking as if they were in a football huddle. I couldn't make out every word, but it sounded like he was planning out a strategy for securing the perimeter. Olwyn was going to round up the rest of the pack and bring them back here. I had a moment to think about how strange it was that I could hear them at all. After all, I wasn't really all that close to them, and Roul was keeping his voice below a whisper. Making a quick mental note of my increased sense of hearing, I decided I'd have to figure that out later too.

There wasn't any creature better suited for security detail than a were. Well, maybe a vamp, but they only seemed to protect their own, not do security for hire. Weres, on the other hand, were typically ex-military or police force so they didn't mind so much. And with their superior senses, they were a hell of a lot better than a security camera. Not that I thought they could stop the Triad. We might have enough time for a head start, however, if we were lucky. I should have felt better about our situation, with my newfound powers. But even after the knowledge of Scota's rebirth, the supernaturals were all on edge. So naturally I was freaked out too. Like some urban legend, I hadn't even seen the Morrigna yet. But I knew they were a fearsome thing to behold, even if I had never laid eyes on them myself. The suspense of meeting them might actually kill me before they had a chance.

XIV
FOURTEEN

If I weren't so exhausted, and if I actually had the energy, this might be the part of my tale where I completely freak out. After all, a lot had happened to me so far. It was a hell of a lot to absorb in one day. Honestly, I did not know if I should be screaming or crying or what a reasonable reaction was at all. I numbly watched the vampires leave.

Agrona told Baylen they would be back after sunset. She basically commanded him to speak with Roul about bringing in neighboring packs. We needed the extra muscle, she said. While I can't argue with her on that point, she was so damned bossy. Agrona took the queen of the vamps thing a little too seriously in my opinion. She didn't care if you were a vamp or not, she was the queen and, as such, her word was final. 'God save the queen' and all that crap. Or maybe it was 'God damn the queen' when the Queen in question was a vamp? I tried not to laugh. That should be 100 bonus points for me for containing my crazy-person outburst in this insane situation.

Baylen walked the vamps out.

I was left alone for the moment with Seamus, so I decided to head to the kitchen for the dredges of that java. He said something about joining me. Maybe he'd tell me what exactly 'Blue Man of the Minch' is. That was definitely a title and not a term of endearment.

We walked past the powder room, and I caught a glimpse of myself in the mirror. I put the brakes on.

Seamus almost slammed into my sore back.

Shock was definitely setting in. My eyes! Holy hell, what was up with my eyes? They were luminescent now, in that cat eye sort of way. *Shit. Shit, shit, shit.* I reached into the doorway and fumbled along the wall until I found the light switch. In the process, I noticed my hair was a little different now too. As I watched myself in the mirror reaching for my hair, I expected it to feel different too. The mahogany lowlights I paid for last month were deeper, like a fine cabernet, making them a little harder to see now against my dark brown hair.

It was more than that, though. My physical condition had changed as well. I was basically the same size. I was the same shape, but a little firmer and more toned. Ok, well there's at least one plus. You know, I distinctly remember having a conversation with this goddess, and she said I would still be myself. Um, yeah, that was looking pretty unlikely at this point. While the toned arms and firm ass were serious perks, the abrupt change in my physical appearance was freaking me out. The numbness was wearing off again.

The crazy, shining eyes had stopped since the lights were on. People do not have eyes like this! My irises were smaller and edged with that same gold Scota had. They didn't have the same flakes of gold as hers. Instead, the dark brown of my natural eyes seemed to bleed into the gold ring. Well, the upside is that my job would be a whole lot easier. Hell, I probably wouldn't even need to use my psychic talents anymore. One look at these eyes, and they'd probably shit their pants and tell me everything. The Norms may not know what I was, but they would know I definitely wasn't human.

I didn't want to think about the ramifications of that or how I would explain this at work. It's not like I could say they were just contacts. They'd ask me to take them out. I could *not* afford to get all stressed out about it now. I'd have to deal with the captain when the time came and add this change to the list of things to deal with later. There were bigger and badder things to worry about.

My hair was a tangled mess from my trip through the coat closet with Agrona. Little pieces of drywall and splinters of wood were stuck in it. Seamus reached out to help me, and I damned near jumped out of my skin. I had forgotten he was there for a minute. Yup. Scary, badass medium for a goddess, that's me.

"It's just like when you first discovered you were different as a child. It will be awkward for a while, but you'll figure it out. You don't really have any other choice." He picked out the few pieces of debris in the back of my locks I couldn't reach.

Why was he always right? It just sucked. It's never fun to realize you're a bit of a freak and don't really fit anywhere. Nobody can do the things you can do, and there's no one around to explain why. Maybe this time would be different,

I'd be awkward for a while, learning curve and all, but then be the better for it in the end. I wasn't going to hold my breath, though. Life's a bitch. I've learned that much over the years.

As much as I wanted a shower, I didn't go upstairs. I turned off the light and headed into the kitchen. Baylen would probably be back in a couple of minutes, and I wanted to know what or who the hell he was.

XV
FIFTEEN

The smell of burnt coffee permeated the room, but I didn't care. I'd drink it anyway. A bit of a coffee aficionado, I'd still drink even the worst brew if I needed caffeinating badly enough. I've had my share of thick cups at the station. I grabbed my coffee cup from earlier off the table and went to the sink to rinse it out.

We were kind of pressed for time, so I skipped past the delicate and went straight for blunt. "So, Seamus, what's a Blue Man of the Minch anyway?"

He sighed audibly. "I knew it. The minute she called him that, I just knew you were going to hit me up for an answer. It's not really my place to say anything. I think it would be better if you wait to ask Baylen himself."

"Oh come on, Seamus. He won't mind. She'd find out sooner or later anyway." Medea seemed to materialize out of thin air.

You know, it might be good if these fucking cat eyes of mine were in the back of my head, because I was getting tired of all of these people sneaking up on me.

"I knew it. I knew there was something different about him. I knew that he wasn't entirely human. So what? Tell me." I tried to keep my smugness to a minimum, which was hard.

Still reluctant, Seamus knew he had no way out of telling me. Medea had kind of ruined that for him.

"If you're through gloating over your superior intuition, perhaps I can actually answer the question." Yup, he was mad at Medea for forcing his hand. "The Blue Men are men of the sea. They harness the wind, storms, and the water. All of it—they control it. Friend or foe to fishermen, on a whim."

As much as I was enjoying the fact Baylen wasn't just the extravagant and powerful human businessman he portrayed on the news, I couldn't figure out the reason for his secrecy. He was kind of like Storm from the X-Men. That was pretty cool actually. We, the Others, had integrated so well into mainstream society, I can't see him being cast out. In fact, weathermen everywhere might try to bribe him. And then, Seamus laid the rest of it out.

"Some legends say they are actually fallen Angels. Baylen is the last one. Or at least he says he is. Not the fallen Angel part, just the last of his kind. He hasn't talked about it in a really long time. He doesn't age like we do, but he doesn't seem to be ageless like Medea either."

"How old is he?" It didn't really matter, but I was curious.

They both shrugged their shoulders. Seems like even the people Baylen kept closest didn't really know all that much about him. If I lived through this, I was going to be doing a lot of googling later.

The front door opened, and we quickly changed the topic. Well, sort of.

"Baylen has a real knack for finding Others, most even before they know what they are." Seamus glanced at me. "Present company excluded."

"Well, I would have had to be the village idiot to not know what I had become. But I told you, Maurin, Baylen has wanted to contact you for some time. I think he had suspicions about what you were," Medea said.

I looked at Medea. She was trying not to be her normal bitchy self. "Yeah, it would have been nice to figure this out before now."

Baylen walked into the kitchen and by the look on his face, it was obvious he knew we were talking about him. *Oops.*

"Now that Seamus and Medea have no doubt told you everything about me, perhaps we could get back to work," Baylen said.

Seamus was glaring at Medea. Okay, the silence that followed was awkward. Baylen decided to ignore us and change the subject. That was fine with me.

"Roul has agreed to speak to the other pack leaders as soon as Agrona and Kedehern return," he said as he sat down at the kitchen table.

"Why wait? The sooner they get here, the better, right?" Judging from the quizzical looks I was receiving, that was obviously a dumb question.

"We can't risk splitting up any more than we already have. The Morrigna has ways of acquiring information. He will have to wait until dusk. If we're lucky, the Triad doesn't know that the Council has met," Baylen said.

"Um, Baylen, not to state the obvious here, but couldn't he just call them? I mean it's not like the Revolutionary War. He doesn't have to ride village to village on horseback, sounding the alarm. Maybe I'm a simpleton, but I'm pretty sure the other pack leaders have cell phones," I said.

"Horses are afraid of wolves. I doubt he'd get very far," Medea retorted.

"Shut up!" I snapped. Bitch.

"Ladies, please. There is protocol to follow. Roul's job cannot be done with a simple phone call. Packs are a balance of dominance and submission. There is no national pack leader. There is no, one wolf with authority over all of the other pack leaders. So Roul must meet with them individually." Baylen said all this like it would make sense to me.

"Screw protocol!" All of this political bullshit was lost on me. The world was about to end, right? So who really cares who's in charge if we're all dead, anyway? "If we're moving, then they're moving, and I'm pretty sure she's not following the proper protocol!"

◆ ◆ ◆

The Triad was moving. While I was starting to wonder about the incompetence of the Council—I mean they really should have had some kind of doomsday plan already— Amalie, Arcana, and Phallon were busy packing up half of the retail at the Witch's Closet.

They were busy all right—just not packing. I don't think any of us expected the Triad to hit the witches first. Or, at least, I didn't. I would have gone after the weres first, or maybe the vamps. Take out the natural killing machines, with their predictable six to eight-hour window of weakness. They seemed the most logical targets to me, but I guess the Triad didn't possess my kind of logic.

XVI
SIXTEEN

Amalie looked around, a little on edge. *I can't imagine why.* The streets in town were uncommonly quiet, especially this close to Halloween. Salem was always bustling this time of year. People flocked from all over the world to meet real witches who ironically lived in the town famous for torturing their kind. Of course, that was a long time ago, but they still came to read the quotes etched into the stones of the cemetery walls, get their picture taken with the *Bewitched* statue (any witch worth her salt fought putting that statue in town) and see the 'Witch Crossing' signs on every corner. They met at the Salem Witch Museum and headed out at sundown for the ghost tours before ending up at one of the local pubs.

The three witches walked past Toil and Trouble, the newest addition to the pubs on Arcana's street. It was doing really well, probably more for the cutesy names of the stuff they served, like 'Witches Brew', and not due to the reference to Macbeth. But tonight it was quiet. In fact, it was a little too quiet for Amalie's taste. They couldn't get inside the Witch's Closet fast enough.

Arcana fumbled with her keys and finally opened the door. "Just let me turn the alarm off," she said quietly. She went behind the counter, punched a few keys on the keypad, and the alarm was off. Of course the store was protected by spells, but to a witch thief that would be expected. Maybe they'd overlook something as mundane as ADT.

"Phallon, stay up front and keep watch while Amalie and I get what we need from the back," Arcana instructed. She gave Amalie a weak smile as she led her to the back, handing her a satchel as they went. Amalie couldn't shake the feeling something bad was about to happen. This place is where it had all started for her. Her normal day had spun totally out of control. Amalie tried to focus on the task at hand, but it was difficult. She winced as she heard Arcana's *Tsk* nearby.

"I told Seamus that he was free to take what he needed, but by the disarray of my stock, I'm guessing that you were the one filling a bag earlier today. I don't suppose you still have the things that you took?" Arcana asked.

Amalie knew Arcana wasn't really angry. She'd help put the store back the way it was, if she wasn't dead at the end of all this, that is. "Everything's at Baylen's," Amalie replied.

"Good, it looks like you already took a lot of what we need. Clever little witch. Someone was paying attention in their healing classes." Arcana said, smiling slightly.

Amalie perked up a little bit at the compliment. Twenty-four was about a quarter of the life span of a human, but she was still considered a baby as a witch. The fact that

Arcana had so much faith in her was actually a big deal. Moving through the cabinets and drawers, she loaded up her satchel with jars of this and bags of that until she hit the motherload. In the last cabinet on the right Amalie found Arcana's rarities stash. Normally she wouldn't be able to open it, but Arcana mumbled a spell, and the cabinet doors swung open.

"Holy shit! Ground Allicorn?" Amalie couldn't believe Arcana actually had it. She reached for the small jar that contained the rare powder. It was impossible to get because it had been banned. It was banned because only one unicorn ever walked the earth at one time in history. Taking and grinding down its horn was expressly forbidden. Not that Amalie had actually ever seen a unicorn. "Do I want to know how you even got this?" she asked Arcana.

"Probably not. Just be glad that I do. Nothing I have is better for healing than that powder. Mixed to a paste and applied directly on the wound, it can pull out the deadliest toxins and speed up healing." Arcana moved to take the jar from Amalie and put it in her own satchel.

"Arcana! You better come up here!" Phallon shouted from the front of the store.

"Don't you drop that!" Arcana shouted as she ran to check on Phallon.

Amalie put the jar in her bag and ran to see what was happening.

"What is it, Phallon, what's—?" Amalie started to ask. Amalie didn't need to finish the question. As she moved to the middle of the store, half hidden by a rack of velvet dresses, she saw six blood-red, glowing eyes glaring at them from across the street. There were three calf-sized, pitch-black dogs standing on the sidewalk opposite the store. If it weren't for the soft glow of the streetlight, they never would have seen them at all. Amalie jumped when she heard the first growl of the ferocious beasts.

"Arcana, what are they? What the hell are they?" Amalie asked.

"Black Dogs! Get back! Amalie, I said get back! Phallon, we can't wait for the others! We have to move! Now!" Arcana ordered.

There wasn't enough time. Glass shattered everywhere as the dogs leapt for them. The beasts were inside the store in the blink of an eye. Phallon tried to throw up a blockade. "Damn it, I wish Juno was here!" she screamed.

Amalie could see the reinforced steel barrier forming in front of them, but the spell wasn't complete. The dogs hurtled toward them, crashing through the unfinished metal wall. Now along with the glass shards, chunks of jagged metal came flying toward them.

Arcana tried to slow the shrapnel by commanding, "*Ceasi Seta!*" The pieces of Phallon's wall and the broken windows hung suspended in air, and still the dogs came for them. They had to get out of there. There was no way they could fight the beasts alone.

Amalie moved closer to Arcana. "Call the winds, Arcana! Get us back to Baylen's!"

Howls and snarls surpassed all other sounds. Arcana couldn't hear a word she said, even with Amalie right beside her. One dog stood in front as point with one on either side of it as the hounds moved into a makeshift triangle. The dog closest to them stood with his huge front paws on top of what was left of Phallon's wall. With his lips curled and teeth bared, he was terrifying. Two dogs behind him barked and snapped their jaws, thick saliva dripping from their canine teeth. The dog in front positioned himself to jump.

Arcana swung her arm outward, knocking Amalie aside. She used the precious seconds she had to get Amalie out of the way, and now the beast was on top of her.

The other two dogs moved to follow their leader.

Phallon began chanting a spell of protection. It was the same one they had performed back at the house.

Amalie joined in, unsure if her magic was strong enough for this spell. They needed three, didn't they? With more conviction than she had ever put into a spell, she repeated everything Phallon said.

The air in front of them began to ripple. Amalie could actually see the air bend and move.

Phallon kept chanting and moved backward away from the dogs and the edge of the protective shield they were forming.

The two dogs on either side began testing its strength. The shield wavered slightly and they padded around, trying to find the weakest spot in it.

Arcana screamed in pain. The lead dog still had her in his jaws. With its teeth clamped down firmly, the dog's mouth engulfed her right shoulder up to the collarbone. There was the distinct sound of bones snapping and Arcana let out another shriek. Blood was running down her arm and into the dog's mouth. Amalie fumbled in the chant, and the shield began to give.

The lead dog started dragging Arcana slowly toward the

dissipating shield.

Phallon quickly reached down and grabbed Arcana's hand.

"*Ignattia!*" Phallon screamed, barely audible over Arcana's cries of pain. She started to pull Arcana toward her, but the dog refused to relax the grip he had on her with his teeth.

Arcana screamed again as the flesh was torn from her crushed bones under the razor sharp teeth of the Black Dog.

"*Ignattia!*" Phallon screamed again.

Amalie stood there for a moment, unsure what to do. Phallon was teetering on the edge of dark magic. The fledgling witch never believed there was any gray area when it came to her magic. Never do anything that breaks the creed. This spell wasn't crafted for lighting the hearth fire. Phallon was invoking a spell with the intention to do harm. But the Black Dogs were here to kill them, right? And it wasn't like they were natural creatures, so did it matter? Faced with impending death Amalie decided it didn't. How could using a spell, even if it was dark, to save them from the dogs of death be bad? What if the only way to fight dark magic was with dark magic? There wasn't time to answer those questions. Amalie could only hope the cost to Phallon's aura wasn't more than she could bear.

A huge ball of fire formed in the air in front of Phallon's right hand, and she forced it toward the dog, careful not to hit Arcana.

The fire ball hit him in the side. He yelped and finally let go of Arcana.

Phallon pulled her close.

Arcana lay there broken and bleeding in a crump-led mass at Phallon's feet.

The smell of burnt flesh and fur stung Amalie's nose, and bile rose up from her stomach and burned the back of her throat.

The other two dogs continued to test the shield like a yard dog testing an electric fence. And then they were in. A large black paw with long, filthy claws pushed its way through the shield.

Phallon was calling fire to her again, but Amalie knew they couldn't stand here and fight, not if they wanted to live. She had only just begun learning offensive magic, and the incantations escaped her. Unable to remember the words, she reached out with her power alone and tried to call the winds.

She visualized the small winds, felt the wind in her hair. Air rushed in from the street, filling the room. Heat blew back in Amalie's face from the fireball forming in Phallon's hands. The surge of oxygen from her winds had turned Phallon's small fireball into a steady stream.

Phallon had become a human blowtorch. The heat was almost unbearable.

Arcana's groans were almost inaudible under the roar of the fire.

"Control it, Amalie. You called the winds, so you have to control them. Otherwise, you'll blow up the whole damned building, with us in it!" Phallon shouted.

Phallon pointed the flames down to the floor, creating a wall of fire behind the broken shield.

The dogs hesitated only for a moment before jumping across. The three dogs tried to form the triangle again with the wounded dog in the back this time. Slowly they pressed forward, closing the tiny gap between them and the witches.

Phallon slid Arcana's undamaged arm between her legs with her left heel and locked her feet around Arcana's forearm.

"Grab hold of my hand. We have to get the hell out of here. Goddess, I hope this works. Amalie, I need you to concentrate. If your magic isn't strong enough, if you waver in your concentration at all, we'll get stuck in the between. On my mark," Phallon said.

Amalie took a deep breath. She knew about this spell, knew about a witch who had gotten stuck in the between, who was still stuck in the between, she guessed. *Goddess, please. Give me the strength.*

XVII
SEVENTEEN

There was a thunderous crack, followed by a huge crash. Wolves howled. Medea and Baylen jumped up and ran to the front porch with Seamus and I right behind them. I couldn't believe what I was seeing. Phallon and Amalie were bent over something, something that was making disgusting gurgling noises. And then I realized what it was, or who it was. It was Arcana.

Roul and Grayson were running up to the house, almost trampling everyone when they got to the porch.

I could hardly see through the crowd that was forming. Moving forward, I gently shoved my way through to get to Amalie. My foot landed in something slippery, and I lost my balance. I pushed up off the porch with my hands in what felt like warm syrup. Shivering, I looked at my hands. *Holy shit.* It was blood. Arcana was going to bleed to death if someone didn't do something immediately.

Roul was shouting for the weres to return to their posts. The perimeter could not be compromised. This could be a trap.

Baylen and Seamus were shouting for Phallon and Amalie to tell them what had happened.

Juno came to kneel beside her sister. Through all the commotion, I could barely hear her tell Amalie she needed to heal Arcana.

"I can't heal this. I haven't learned regeneration. We need Olwyn. Roul, please, you have to get Olwyn," Amalie pleaded.

Roul repeated at least six times that Olwyn was already on her way back with the rest of the pack, but she wouldn't be here in time.

I called out to Amalie. "Heal what you can. Even if you can't fix all of her, heal some of her so she can hang on until Olwyn or Mahalia gets back. You're her only chance, Amalie!"

Oberon moved in behind me and slipped his arms around my waist. I didn't question his desire to comfort me instead of his fellow coven members, just welcomed his touch because I knew this was only the beginning of the horrors that lay ahead for all of us. Maybe he did too.

Juno held Amalie's hand in one hand and her sister's in the other. "We'll help you, Amalie. We'll lend you our strength. Invoke the spell."

I could see Phallon nodding her head in agreement with her sister. Power hummed through Oberon and across my skin where he touched me. I guess he didn't need to hold hands with anyone to share power. Amalie's voice cracked as she struggled with the words. What finally came out wasn't exactly what I'd call a spell.

"Argh, I am an idiot! Where's my bag, I was still carrying it when we left," Amalie cried out, panic-stricken.

None of us knew what the hell she was talking about, but I saw Seamus slide a dark-brown canvas bag over to Amalie. I watched in confusion as she pulled a small jar out of her bag. Juno and Phallon gasped in unison.

"How did you get that?" Phallon asked.

"Arcana let me take it. She said we'd need it. I guess she was right." Amalie's hands were shaking as she fumbled with the cork stopper. "I can't make the proper paste. I-I don't know what will happen if I put the powder directly on the wound."

"I've never seen it done either, but what else can we do? It will take too long for anything else to work. Just be careful, don't use too much," Juno warned her.

Amalie reached into the jar, her fingertips came out covered with a metallic dust finer than glitter, but just as bright. I'd never seen anything like it.

Oberon leaned into my ear and said in a hushed voice, so he didn't distract Amalie, "Allicorn powder." He didn't elaborate, so I guess he thought I knew what that was. He was wrong.

I watched Amalie sprinkle the powder over Arcana's wounds. I winced when Arcana began thrashing and screaming from the pain. It smelled like the Allicorn was cauterizing the wounds. The smell of burning flesh was barely noticeable, but I was breathing through my mouth anyway.

"That should stop the bleeding," Juno said, her voice quavering.

We were all watching Arcana so intently for any change that none of us noticed Mahalia arrive. That was completely stupid and careless of us. What if it wasn't

Mahalia who showed up?

She pushed her way through the crowd on the porch.

Amalie looked up at Mahalia with tears streaming down her face. My heart broke for her. Arcana was like her family, but I knew this was the first of many injuries or losses that were to come.

Mahalia tried to comfort Amalie. "You did all you could, all that any of us could have done in the same situation. The Goddess blessed us that the Allicorn powder made it back with you." She laid a hand on Amalie's shoulder. "Now that the bleeding has stopped, we should get her inside. I want to clean the wound. The Allicorn will fight any poisons from what I assume is a bite wound, but it won't do anything to mend the bones. Seamus, if you could bring her upstairs please. Amalie, come with me. You can tell me what happened."

Seamus carefully picked Arcana up off the porch and cradled her like an infant against his chest as he carried her upstairs. The coven followed him to a spare bedroom. Oberon slipped his arms from around my waist as he went to join the coven upstairs.

Instantly aware of the absence of his touch in more than a physical sense, I was irritated with myself for this sudden need I had for him. I tried to shake my thoughts of Oberon.

The coven members discussed what Mahalia was going to do. She'd clean and examine the wounds first, of course. If the bone and tissue damage were too severe, they wouldn't use a full regeneration spell. Instead, Mahalia would use charms to ease the pain and invoke a slower growth spell to insure proper healing and full use of limbs. I stood at the bottom of the steps and listened to them talk for a few minutes before heading into the kitchen for more muddy coffee. Coffee had to be the cure for whatever ailed me today.

XVIII
EIGHTEEN

I busied myself with making fresh coffee and fixing something for everyone to eat. Isn't that what you're supposed to do? Or is that just for a funeral? I set about my task, grabbing fruit from the basket on the counter and was rinsing grapes in the sink when Oberon walked in. Once again I found his presence calming. And frustrating. It was upsetting that he could make me feel better by simply walking into room. It was official, I was a mess.

Oberon padded across the kitchen to me. I'd have mistaken him for a were if I didn't know he was a witch, because he was stalking me like a cat. I couldn't take my eyes off of him. He was gorgeous. His hair, a little too long, was tucked neatly behind his ear. Tribal tattoos peaked out from beneath the long sleeves of his shirt. My knees went a little weak. Damn, I sure had a thing for tattoos.

Concentrating solely on rinsing the grapes, I had the skin nearly washed off of them when he came over. He took my face in his hands and kissed me on the lips. Before I could react, his lips were gone from mine as if nothing had happened. The loss of his touch momentarily eclipsed everything else.

I grabbed a paper towel and dried the grapes. If he wasn't going to say anything about the kiss, then neither was I. He grabbed a cutting board and a knife. I rinsed some apples and set them next to the cutting board. We were alone in the kitchen cutting fruit, and I found myself fantasizing about what it would be like to do this with him every day. To wake up with him, spend the day with him and do all the things that normal couples do. The only problem with that pretty little picture was that we were so far from normal.

We had set up a pretty nice spread by the time we finished. Grabbing some of the fruit, cheese, and bread, I headed over to the table and slid onto a bench. It was an old wooden table set in the corner of the kitchen with benches along the walls and chairs on the other side. Oberon slid in beside me.

In a voice that seemed to resonate through my entire body like a bow across violin strings, he said, "Maurin, I can't explain it. I know I just met you, but I feel like I have known you all my life. It's like I know things about you. It's like I know you in a way that is just not possible. I can't seem to help myself. You...you feel it too, right?" he asked.

I cleared my throat. "Yeah, I do." Reduced to rudimentary sentences, I couldn't come up with anything more eloquent.

He took my hands in his. Almost instantly, power rushed through me like a jolt of electricity.

Oberon's eyes flew open wide, and I shared his memories of Rory. He was the same man I saw in the vision. It was like the same thing with Scota, except I don't think Rory was a god. He was just a mortal in line for the throne. I saw all the things he saw and felt all the things he felt while he held my hands in his.

I fell back into the corner of the bench, and he struggled to catch his breath when it was over. He slid back a few inches from me, and I can't say I blame him. Neither of us could explain what had just happened, never mind how or why. I wouldn't be dying to touch someone after that either. So we just sat there in silence. We'd spoken only a few sentences in this lifetime, but somehow shared a lifetime of memories between us.

Baylen walked in, his gaze darkening as he looked at us. He grabbed some food off the counter.

Phallon came in behind him.

"Medea has gone to warn Agrona and Kedehern. She fears they will attack the vampires next, since dawn is approaching," Baylen said, as he made his way back to the table.

Phallon sat down at the table.

I pushed my napkin of fruit and cheese toward her. "I highly doubt the vampires would be caught off guard. They have security, right? They must have people who watch out for them during the day?"

Phallon looked at me. "They sent Black Dogs, Maurin. I don't know if you fully comprehend what they are, but they're probably one of the scariest things you can send after someone. You can't prepare for the Black Dogs. I mean, with only three witches, and two of them healers at that, there was no way. Maybe if I'd had Juno with me..." she paused, shaking her head. "Mahalia is taking the coven into town to clear the scene. We can't leave it like it is. She could wipe it down herself with no problem, but we haven't heard from the others, and she's not splitting up the coven anymore. They were supposed to meet us there, but we had to run before they showed up. I pray the goddess spared them and the Black Dogs were long gone if they ever did make it to the store. I managed to hurt one of those canine bastards, but not before it damn near killed Arcana." She slammed her fist on the table in frustration. "Oberon, let's go." With her head hanging down, she sighed deeply as she made her way out of the kitchen.

I felt Oberon tense beside me before he slid off of the bench and followed Phallon out. He glanced back only once before the kitchen door swung shut behind him.

I almost felt relieved that Oberon was going away for a little while. I'd probably be worried sick about all of them in five minutes, but at least I could think straight without him sitting next to me. Being near him muddled my thoughts obviously, since a few minutes ago I was fantasizing about playing house with him in the middle of a crisis of apocalyptic proportions.

Baylen was leaning back in his chair. I almost felt bad for how I had misjudged him. Almost. He obviously wasn't the selfish bastard I'd thought he was, or he wouldn't be doing this. But I still had a ton of questions about him. Seamus knew him better than anyone here, and I doubt even he could answer my questions. What did he do to become a fallen angel? For some reason, I was still having a hard time with the fallen angel thing. This was yet another manifestation of my stupidity. We're fighting an army of demons that are led by a Triad of pagan goddesses, and I am having a hard time with the fact that Baylen might actually be a fallen angel. We all have our limits, and my brain had reached mine.

Baylen broke the awkward silence that was beginning to fill the room. "Roul has assured me the perimeter is secure. More of his wolves have arrived, and the wolves on loan from neighboring packs will be here within a few hours."

"I thought you said he wasn't going to be able to ask for help until tomorrow."

"He had planned to ask in person, but after what happened to the Coven he made a call," Baylen replied. He was being short and not so sweet.

"So the Council does know how to use a cell phone. So what's the plan?" I was trying not to give him a hard time, really.

"So far we are gathering as many Others as we can. The fey will not get involved, so that leaves us with vamps, witches, and weres. And of course, us."

I thought about what he was saying for a minute. "It's not enough. There are sixteen wolves max outside, not including Olwyn and Roul. We won't have the vamps back until what time? 4:30 at the earliest? We can't stay here," I said.

"Well, well, well. It would seem you've been putting some thought into this. So, go on, what's your plan?" Baylen was a little irritated with me. For what? Stating the obvious?

I hadn't put any thought into it up until now. I was just going along with whatever the Council said. In fact, I kind of felt like I was operating on auto-pilot. "I think we should consider calling in the SPTF. They should know what's happening. They should be given a chance to evacuate the Norms or something."

Baylen snorted. "You're crazy. It's better if we don't. They'll just screw it all up. They're not equipped to handle this, mentally or physically. The Coven has ways of keeping them out. If we fail, evacuation won't matter. There's no where they could run that would be far enough, anyway."

"Okay, Mr. Doom and Gloom. We can't stay here. We need to go somewhere safe so that we can regroup and figure out where the Morrigna is hiding. Well, not hiding exactly. Hiding would imply that we had them on the run, and unfortunately it's just the opposite. Anyway, you know what I mean," I said.

"The Coven just left. We have to at least wait for them to get back. Roul is doing everything to insure our security. We have to stay here for now."

Is this like a test or something. "Look, you have maybe an acre of ground out there? Spread Roul's pack across it, and there are still some big holes in the fence. We're too vulnerable here. You can call the Coven back, you know. What is it with you and your aversion to cell phones?" I asked.

I watched him think it over. I watched all the different emotions run across his face. "Something will have to be done with Arcana. We can't take her with us. And we'll need a building. We can't squeeze our immediate party of eighteen wolves, a dozen vamps, two-dozen witches, Seamus, and the two of us in a bomb shelter. So where do we go?" he asked.

"I'm a psychic, not a four-star general! I don't know. I

kind of thought you guys would have a real plan!" I snapped.

"I was merely thinking aloud, Maurin." He didn't seem mad at my little outburst.

"So uh, the Black Dogs, are they like the Hounds of Hell or something?" Maybe if I changed the subject he wouldn't notice I didn't apologize for being an ass.

"Not like the hounds of Hell, they are the Hounds of Hell," he said.

"This just gets better and better. Can you at least try to lie to me when I ask questions?" I dropped my head onto the table.

"Maurin, focus. Where do we go?" He was being a smartass. Like he already knew the answer and was waiting for me to figure it out.

I barely raised my head to look at him. "Why is everyone so damned difficult all the time? Let me explain how this brainstorming thing works. I make a suggestion that we should leave, and then you make a suggestion about where we should go. God, Baylen, if this is any indication of the strategizing skills of the Council, then it's miraculous that you all have survived the hordes with pitchforks and torches for so long," I said.

And then, as if the words from my lips had reached the ears of an evil goddess, the wolves started howling. The head of the Triad was coming. You could call Morrigan a lot of things, but stupid wasn't one of them. She was a war goddess, after all.

Even if reinforcements arrived before Morrigan and her sisters completely obliterated us, they would just be joining us in our demise. Damn it. This is insanity. We are sitting at the kitchen table trying to come up with an escape plan while Armageddon is knocking at the front door.

Well I wasn't going to just sit here in the kitchen, waiting to be slaughtered. It was about time Morrigan and I were introduced.

XIX
NINETEEN

I got up and ran to the front windows. In spite of the incessant howling, I could hear the distinct sound of wings flapping. In the distance, the first signs of daybreak outlined the figures in the sky, and unfortunately prevented the vampires from coming back. Coincidence? I think not. The biggest flock of crows I have ever seen swooped down toward the house. They broke up the new light on the horizon with their violently flapping wings. Through my terror, I suddenly understood why a flock of crows is actually called a murder.

Baylen was right behind me. "She came alone. It's just Morrigan, not the Triad. She's the strongest of the three. She can take the few of us left here without her sisters," he said.

"Well I, for one, am offended," I said sarcastically.

I heard yelping and knew some of the wolves were already injured. Six red eyes were staring at me from the tree line. The Black Dogs were here. Morrigan didn't come alone after all. Were any of the wolves from Roul's pack alive? Could they survive the Black Dogs? The howling had stopped. Everything but the crows seemed to cease.

I watched with utter dread as the crows swarmed madly in front of the house and began to take shape in the driveway. Their wings flapped wildly, with beaks and talons occasionally visible through the chaos, and Morrigan's outline slowly appeared. The birds were fading, or melting, into her shape.

In seconds the birds were almost completely gone, apart from a few wings jutting out of her body. She ran her hands down her rib cage, smoothing out the wings and feathers until they seemed to disappear under her bodice.

She looked like a gothic nightmare. Her hair appeared black as pitch against alabaster skin. Baylen said she was a shifter, and I wondered if this was her true form or just the version of herself she wanted us to see. The dress, in true war-goddess fashion, had a black leather bodice over a black shift with billowing sleeves running down her arms. The long sleeves disappeared beneath the thick black leather of the bracers fitted around her forearms. There were markings burnt into the leather on her bodice and bracers, but I couldn't see them clearly. Ancient runes, maybe? Her skirt was long, almost dragging along the ground, and it was made of a stiff, flat-black material. Her skin seemed to soak up every last drop of the rapidly fading moonlight, making her look a little opalescent. She was the most beautiful nightmare I had ever had. What do you call it when your nightmare is staring you right in the face, but you're wide-awake?

Her voice wasn't the smooth and sultry sound I expected. Instead, it sounded like a chorus of crows. "Gone and left you all alone, have they, Maurin? The big bad vampires aren't so scary when the sun is rising, are they? How unfortunate for you and your furry little friends that my pets are so poorly trained. They never have played well with other dogs. And where is the rest of the Council? Did they think I wouldn't hear of their little discovery? Fools. Did they think I would not find you, Maurin? As if they thought that I would be content to survive on the bread-crumbs and milk left out for me by mortals. And when that stopped, when the fragile little beings forgot us and began to fear new gods, did they think that I would just fade away, just as the mortals' memories had?"

She didn't wait for an answer. She just crooked her evil finger at me, which had me frozen in place. "There is power lying just beneath the surface with you, Maurin. Is it all you, or are you truly a vessel? Pity that you've no idea how to wield it. It would be so much fun to test you," Morrigan said.

She came closer. One second she was in the driveway, and the next she was at the bottom of the porch steps. There was the sound of wood cracking and snapping. I could see drywall dust in the air. Morrigan tore through the walls with her bare hands. She was coming for me.

Power pricked along my skin. Was it hers or mine? I couldn't tell. She was right. It didn't matter that Scota had given me her power because I had no idea what to do with it. With all the effort it took to peel a banana she stripped the wall away and reached for me with those powerful bone-white hands. I tried to back up, but stumbled on some debris. There was nowhere left to go.

She had me by the hair and started to drag me out of

the house through the gaping hole she had made upon entering. Baylen grabbed my heels desperately, trying to keep me within the remainder of his walls. I heard him screaming for Amalie, whom I just noticed was practically frozen on the stairs.

"Holy shit, Baylen, don't let go of her!" Amalie screamed, as she found the courage to keep coming downstairs.

"I haven't been looked upon as holy for centuries, witch. Something I mean to rectify." Morrigan's laugh was a terrifying, screeching, cawing sound.

"*Ceasi, Seta!*" Amalie shouted from the stairs.

Morrigan freed a hand from my hair and raised it toward Amalie. I watched as a lime-green flame shot out from her hand and burst against Amalie's chest. Morrigan caught Amalie's spell and shot it back to her. Unable to stop it in time, Amalie was frozen mid step. I heard more shrieking crows. Morrigan apparently found Amalie's attempt to stop her from dragging me through the wall hilarious.

The chalk-like insides of the broken drywall scratched my skin as she pulled me through the hole. Broken nails and wood dug into my flesh, leaving little bits of me behind. The pain helped me to focus. The power vibrated through my core. I let it build and build until it felt like there was an ocean of magic pooled in my stomach. I drew the power up from my center and down into my hands. Heat radiated out from my palms as if flames would eventually burst through my skin.

Maybe I drew too much? I didn't know, and I didn't care. Clamping down onto her sides, I felt her body jolt and her back arch as if I had hit her with jumper cables, but that was all. I didn't even loosen her grip on me or knock her backward. The only thing I had managed to do was to piss her off.

Morrigan's fingernails dug into my scalp, and I realized she had barely been putting any effort into holding on to me before. Searing pain shot through my scalp. A warm rush of blood came down my temples, puddling in my left ear. She was ripping the hair from my scalp or worse, ripping my scalp from my skull. The more Baylen put his weight into keeping me inside, the more hair she ripped out. My thick hair could use some thinning, but this was fucking ridiculous.

Blackness crept into my peripheral vision, and unconsciousness was threatening to take me under. I quickly decided being dragged out through the crumbling wall was better than having my head ripped off. Kicking my legs wasn't working since Baylen had his arms wrapped around both of them, but I managed to dig a heel into his chest and push one leg free. My feet connected with his face until Baylen finally let go. The tension on my scalp eased as I snapped out onto the porch with her like a rubber band. She grabbed me by the neck with her free hand and held me in mid-air in front of her. Throbbing pain in my head increased with the blood flow from my scalp. The puddle of blood in my ear was now running down my neck, and the blackness was getting worse, creeping in like a veil over my eyes.

XX
TWENTY

Through the murkiness, I looked over Morrigan's shoulder and fixated on an object that seemed to be running up the driveway. *Wolf or witch?* They were moving at a good clip and rapidly closing the distance between us. I heard a low growl and saw a quick flash of canines. Wolf. At first I thought the blackness rushing in was unconsciousness finally taking me, but with the sound of viciously snapping jaws I realized that it was actually the Black Dogs. They had moved in and were having their way with my foiled rescuer. What I saw was so horrible I found myself praying for the blackness to take me completely. I tried to push Scota's power away so I could slip into the darkness and not see what was happening in front of me.

The yelps and barking of fighting dogs had been replaced with the screams of a man. My eyes shot open and I was now, much to my horror, wide-awake. His inability to stay in his wolf form meant he was hovering on the brink of death. I couldn't see his face, however. *Oh fuck, please, please don't let it be one of Roul's pack. Please say the other packs had arrived.* I didn't want anyone to die that way, but at least I hadn't met any of the neighboring pack members yet.

The screaming had stopped. There was more whimpering. Not the cries of a dog, but those of a man. It was as unbearable to hear him make those sounds as it was to see the Black Dogs eat him alive. They tore the flesh from what bones they had not broken. Their heads were thrown back, and they were snapping their jaws, working the meat down their gullets. The fur on their muzzles was matted in dark crimson. I prayed then that God or Goddess, or whomever he prayed to, that someone would take this man away from this horrible death and wrap him in an embrace that would end his suffering. By his sudden silence, I knew my prayers had been answered. All that remained were the sounds of the Black Dogs finishing their meal.

A familiar burn began making its way up from my stomach, scorching the back of my throat. Despite my effort to force the partially digested fruit and cheese back down, the nasty sting of vomit hit the back of my tongue and nose. I fought it hard, not because I gave a shit if anyone here saw me throw up but because I hated throwing up. I managed not to toss my midnight snack all over Baylen's porch. Gold star for me.

Morrigan laughed again, and the Black Dogs joined in. Their howls and barks mixed with Morrigan's crow-like cackling. It was a god-awful sound. If the devil had a choir and they crawled up from the bowels of Hell to stand here on this porch and sing, then that is what it would sound like.

There was a buildup of pressure and a sharp pop inside my ear, followed by excruciating pain and the warmth of a fresh flow of blood. I just barely got my wits about me enough to realize they had just blown out my eardrum. My eardrum, for fuck's sake! God, that hurt! Would the damage be permanent? Could I even heal that? I mean I could close a wound easily enough, but regenerate an eardrum? That would do wonders for my career, if I ever got to go back to it. I'm sorry, could you confess into my other ear, tad bit deaf on the right side. I wanted her to stop. I needed her to stop, before I lost my hearing completely.

The bracers she wore were made from a thick, stiff, high-quality leather. Great for armor, but it made it damned near impossible for me to get a good grip. Squeezing hard on her forearms until the tips of my fingers were white, I tried to steady my body so I could draw my leg back and kick her square between the legs. Not entirely as debilitating for a woman as it is for a man, but it still hurt like hell. If you were human, anyway. I seriously doubted I had actually hurt her but still managed to catch her by surprise. Having hurt me as badly as she had, I don't think she expected any fight in me at all. She dropped me. The evil chorus faded away, leaving her fury to hang heavily in the air.

I tried to scramble back to Baylen. There was no way I was going to stand toe to toe with her and live to talk about it. We needed to get the hell out of here and fast. All we needed was the escape plan. The one witch we had left was frozen on the damned staircase, and I was slowly bleeding to death and didn't see any more wolves coming to our aid. Baylen wasn't human, he was a Blue Man, for whatever that was worth. I had no idea what sort of powers a fallen angel had, but now would be a perfect time for Baylen to show some of them off.

And Seamus, where was he? Guilt washed over me as I realized I had completely forgotten about him. Was he even still alive? Did he go out with the wolves earlier, only to meet his death? He could have fired a warning off inside my head, but maybe there just wasn't enough time.

Baylen caught my wrist and pulled with all his might, dragging me back over the rubble and halfway into the house.

Morrigan clucked her tongue and pressed her black boot onto my leg, pinning me in place.

Morrigan seemed larger than she was a minute ago when she had been holding me by the throat. Now, as I was pressed under her boot and straining to look back at her, she seemed taller and broader. Was she growing? We couldn't handle her as it was, forget bigger and badder. It would be a cruel joke that someone with her powers and her strength could make themselves physically bigger too. I kept telling myself it was just because I was looking up at her from the ground. She couldn't actually be bigger, could she?

She drew back the foot that was not pressing me into the porch and kicked Baylen straight in the cheek. His face split, and blood spattered across the drywall, spotting my hand that was reaching out to him. Ruined. His beautiful face would be ruined after a blow like that. With Mahalia laid up, Amalie frozen in place, and Olwyn gone, there was no one to heal him. He raised his head, and I watched the blood stream from the huge gash she had opened on his cheek. I watched as the drywall rapidly sucked it up until a dark red stain began to form on the white and gray chunks of wall beneath him. He fell face first into the blood soaked debris, sending a small cloud of dust up into the air.

I was a dead woman. There was no other end to this, no escape but through death. Surely she would just kill me now.

XXI
TWENTY-ONE

Something deep within me stirred at the thought of my imminent death. My power struggled to rise up to the surface. It vibrated life through my body like someone tugging on a harp's strings, but after the beating I took, I just didn't have the strength to use it. The power was life. It was all that was keeping me alive right now. I had already lost a lot of blood, and the damage to my ear and scalp wasn't healing fast enough. My pounding heart just seemed to be forcing the blood up and out of the wounds even faster. If I let that power go, would I be forcing the life out of my body with it? Well, I was going to die one way or another. Better to die fighting, right?

Before I had a chance to use myself as a weapon of mass destruction, Morrigan yanked me up to face her, holding me in front of her with one arm held around my waist and her hand pressed into my spine. She leaned in for what seemed like a kiss and blew out a breath onto my face.

Instinctively, I closed my eyes.

She blew harder, and I kept them shut. Cold air rushed in

around me as her breath on my face turned to a bitter gust around my body. The ground pulled away from the soles of my feet, and I knew we were in the air.

My stomach churned with the ascent. I had never been afraid of heights until that moment. Of course, until now I had always been safely fastened inside an airplane at this height. There was moisture in the air. A storm was coming and the water stung my body like little pieces of glass slicing past my skin.

The sky was completely void of life, other than the creatures she called to her. That familiar swarm of crows swooped and swirled around us. The wind stung my sensitive scalp, and my damaged inner ear screamed from the change in altitude. There was no way to know how much ground we covered or where she was taking me. I hadn't dared open my eyes for the first few minutes of our flight. When I mustered up the courage to I look down no landmarks were visible.

Surely by now we had left Salem behind. She held me tight against her chest like precious cargo, and that made no sense to me at all. I had fully expected her to release me and send me plummeting to my death, but instead she held me firmly in her arms, pressing me tightly against her chest.

A horrible thought raced through my mind. What if she actually had a use for me? What would be worse? Freeing myself from her death grip and falling to my death, or waiting to see what creative, and no doubt painful, ways she had to get me to cooperate?

The immature part of my brain began talking to me and started to rationalize, quite convincingly I might add, that this was all Baylen's fault. If he hadn't put that damned book in my hands, then Ouzel wouldn't have seen me, and I wouldn't be held firmly in the clutches of Morrigan at this moment.

Just when I thought I would never stop shivering from the wind battering my body, we flew into a thick dark cloud. The moisture hanging inside the cloud was warm and heavy, and it clung to my skin. I could feel the two weather fronts begin to mix, and knew if we didn't change course soon we'd be flying right into a wicked storm. The sky lit up in the distance with the flash of lightning, and thunder roared through my body.

Morrigan turned a sharp right and rolled onto her back. She let her head fall back and threw us into a terrifying spiral descent. Unable to withstand the G forces she was creating as we rapidly fell, I blacked out. I could feel it coming. So, with the third bob of my head, I once again let the blackness take me. We were good friends, unconsciousness and I, so why not spend a few minutes in peace? After all the horrors I had seen so far tonight, and the horrors sure to come when I woke, I needed a few minutes of no thoughts whatsoever.

XXII
TWENTY-TWO

My eyes opened slowly, only to be met with blackness again. I started to rub my eyes as if it that would rub away the concussion I was pretty sure I had, but I still couldn't see even two inches in front of my face. I could, however, hear Morrigan's breathing. At least we had stopped flying and were firmly planted back on the ground—where those of us without feathers belong.

The air around me was cool and damp and smelled like turned earth. Were we in a basement? I tried to scoot myself backward to find a wall or something to lean against. What I felt under my hands was both unexpected and slightly disturbing. The hard smooth dirt, not concrete, beneath me gave me a little clue as to where we were and maybe a reason to be concerned. An old cold cellar? There were still a ton of them on properties around New England. It was too soon to freak out. I needed to keep my head. I moved back some more and farther away from the sound of her calm breathing. If she was closing the distance I was putting between us, I couldn't see or hear her doing it. Logic said she could see me. After all, she had picked this place for our destination.

When I finally hit a wall, the gravity of my situation started to hit home. More dirt, not block and mortar, formed the walls of this prison. Or was it a grave? Had she planned to bury me alive, leaving me here in this tomb to rot? There was no light coming from above, so it wasn't an open grave. At least I wouldn't be forced to watch her as she covered me with the dirt that would eventually crush my body under its weight, slowly killing me. That's if I didn't suffocate first.

Either death seemed excruciating and not how I pictured my death to be. Not that I've spent a lot of time thinking about how I would die, mind you, but being crushed or suffocating to death from being buried alive were definitely not on the top of the list. Nope, they were somewhere near the bottom, along with being burned alive.

Had it been a mere human who had brought me here, I would have risked feeling around for an exit. Since Morrigan had brought me, however, I didn't bother. If her magic was anything like Scota's, and I can only assume it was, given how we got here in the first place, she didn't drag me down any tunnel. My eyes were finally starting to adjust to the darkness, and I was able to see the faintest glow emanating from her skin.

"So what now? You're just going to leave me here, I guess?" I asked.

I didn't really want to know what she had planned since I had no real way to stop it, but the silence in my tomb was unnerving. And crazy as it sounds, part of me just wanted to get her talking and keep her talking because I didn't want her to go. When she did leave, I would be left alone in the painfully quiet darkness waiting for death to release me from this cell and lead me to whatever lay beyond. If I died here, would it be only Scota who was reborn, or would she take a piece of me with her as she searched for the next woman to carry her?

"I suppose this is the part where I, playing the villain, should foil all my plans by telling the heroine everything? Mmm, I think not. You see, despite what I have been told, I do not believe you are the reincarnate. Therefore, what happens to you is of no consequence to me. So, to answer your question, yes. I am going to leave you here, but not without some-thing to play with. Of course, if you are who they say you are, you'll find a way back to stop me like in those wretched movies you mortals love to watch so much. Just don't take too long, dear, or it'll be too late," she said.

A blast of icy air slapped me in the face, and she was gone. I was really starting to miss being around people who just walked to wherever the fuck they were going. All this flying shit was for the birds. Literally, in her case.

I got to my knees and started to crawl around, feeling for an exit. She'd said that she had left me something to play with, and I wanted out before I found out what that something was. My tomb was larger than I thought. It felt round in shape. When I tried to stand up my back bumped against the rounded ceiling. If it was domed, then the crypt must form a mound of some kind outside. Images from some-where beyond my own memories flashed through my mind, of a large mound covered in dark-green grass and encircled at the base with large rocks worn smooth by the ocean. A long path led from the burial mound to a circle of larger stones brought from farther away. Out further still was a trench dug around the site, surrounded again with more stones that were taller and wider than the others.

As fascinating as these memories were, I couldn't help wondering why I didn't see something a little more useful. For example, I'd like to know how the hell to get out of here. Now that would be a memory of hers I wouldn't mind occupying a little space in my brain.

The pain in my head came back with a vengeance, forcing me to sit back down. It was probably from concentrating on the useless, at least in my opinion, memory flashes I was receiving from Scota. All I could do was close my eyes and wait for the pain to subside.

I was still sitting there in the dark, trying to get the pain under control, when I realized I wasn't alone. The thick, low growl vibrated through my stomach and across my skin. A huge, filthy paw, matted with blood, hit the ground in front of me. Oh goodie, my playmate's here. And it sounded hungry.

The enormous dog's fur was so black it was practically invisible in the tomb. Only the luminescent eyes and sharp white teeth stood out in the pitch-black darkness. The massive jaws began to separate, and I watched the toxic saliva drip down from its top canines. I had no weapons. I had nothing to stop those bacteria-covered teeth from sinking into me.

If I waited for it to strike first, I was a goner. I did the only thing I could think of and kicked the dog hard across its muzzle. It was a risky move since the mouth of the dog was still open and its deadly teeth were still exposed, but I managed not to scrape or puncture myself on those razor-sharp teeth. Pushing forward, I scrambled across the dirt floor like a crab, kicking out as I went. The last kick was a disaster.

With a jerk of its head it suddenly had me, just grazing my leg. It still had a hold on my jeans and started thrashing its head around violently, shaking my whole body. It began to pound me into the ground repeatedly. My head hit the ground with an audible thump and, for a surreal moment, I saw stars underground.

It must have known I was temporarily stunned. It let go of my jeans and pounced on my chest. Air rushed out of my lungs. Thick, warm drops of the dog's saliva splattered against my cheek. Its crushing jaws and deadly teeth were just inches from my face. The weight of the dog on my chest was making it difficult to breathe. I could feel small puncture wounds on my chest from its nails. And yet, I couldn't help thinking it wasn't putting its entire weight on me or my chest would have been crushed already. It still wanted to play.

The small scratch on my leg was already inflamed with infection, and my chest and side would follow suit in just a few minutes. Apparently, the bite wasn't the only poisonous type of injury from the Black Dogs. If fever set in, then weakness and fatigue would follow soon after. I wouldn't stand a chance when that happened. As I dug my heels into the dirt, I also dug deep down inside for every ounce of strength I had left.

Grabbing onto its ears, I jerked hard to my left. The dog struggled a little against my pull. The weight on my chest was easing, and the demon dog was backing up. Scrambling out from under it as fast as I could, I barely managed to swing myself onto its back before it had bitten me again. The beast began to claw its way forward, thrashing its head left to right, but I held on with both arms wrapped around its neck. With my hands under its bottom jaw, I pulled back until my heels found purchase in the dirt again. I threw all my weight into the move and prayed for the awful sound of snapping bone.

Someone was listening. The huge beast fell limp, taking me with it and trapping my left leg underneath it. Exhausted, I stayed on my back for a moment, before pushing the enormous creature off me with my right leg. Talk about dead weight. My whole body screamed as I crawled a few feet away and collapsed on the ground.

I was tired, and the fever was finally settling in. Sweating and cold, I laid there shivering in the dirt, staring at the motionless black mound in front of me until I couldn't keep my eyes open any longer.

XXIII
TWENTY-THREE

Much to my disappointment, I woke up on my back, still in the dark, damp tomb. As I slipped into a restless, fever-induced sleep, I had almost convinced myself all of this was a horrible dream. The chills had eased a little, but the fever still burned, and I was incredibly thirsty. I tried to get some spit together to swallow, but my mouth was so dry there just wasn't enough. An infection was raging inside my body. Raising a weak hand to my eyes, I tried desperately to rub the blurriness away.

I rolled onto my stomach and let my head rest on my folded arms. In the distance I could see a horizontal beam of light. Either the fever or the concussion was playing tricks on me. I rubbed my eyes again. There was more light casting a soft glow in the room. The room must have been big if the Black Dog fit in it. Hell, we fought in it, but I didn't realize how much room there actually was. I blinked, sure this was a fever-induced mirage. Still there. I closed my eyes, kept them closed, and counted, certain I'd find nothing but darkness when I opened them. One

Mississippi, two Mississippi, three Mississippi. Nope, the light was still there.

The light was increasing in size from a little sliver to a rectangle the width of about two kneeling men. Staring at the light was starting to hurt my eyes, which had only recently adjusted to the darkness, but I couldn't look away. I felt my eyes well up with tears from staring so hard at the light. Like the sun cresting over the horizon, the light began to rise and fill a long tunnel before me.

If I'd had a light bulb, I would have held it over my head at that point. It *was* the sun rising! The tunnel would fill with light as the sun made its way up into the sky and lit up my escape route.

The sun hadn't completely risen yet, so the tunnel wasn't fully lit. I wasn't sure how high the passage actually was. Still exhausted from fighting the infection and from my body trying to heal the wounds while I slept, I forced myself up on all fours. Slowly I started to crawl for the tunnel.

The tunnel was a lot longer than it had looked from where I had been lying on the floor. Not a few feet into the tunnel and something already blocked part of the light. Was someone closing up the tunnel? I tried to scream at them to stop, that I was in here, but all that came out was a strangled rasp. My throat was too dry to make any audible noise.

I was in blackness again. Closing my eyes again, I tried to readjust to the darkness. I didn't care if they did block up the tunnel with a huge rock. The way out was up ahead, and I was getting the hell out of here, no matter what the obstacle was.

I kept crawling forward, pushing through the fatigue in order to escape. Having my eyes closed amplified my other senses. I could smell something like moss mixed with sea salt. It was a sharp contrast to the damp dirt smell in the tomb so I was definitely closer to the surface. The sharp smell of salt and the rush of adrenaline helped to clear the fever from my mind.

Something stirred in the tunnel ahead of me. Shit, I wasn't alone anymore. I should have known it wouldn't be as easy as just crawling out of here. Straining to hear the sound of footsteps with my good ear, I barely managed to pinpoint the sound. A soft padding on the dirt floor, different from the sound of the massive paws of a Black Dog, thank God, but still I didn't know what it was.

I opened my eyes, hoping they had adjusted enough to at least see the silhouette of who, or what was headed my way. They were getting closer. Light started to creep back in. The way out was still clear. All I had to do was get past whatever it was, and I was out of here. My heart was racing. For a second I forgot how sick I was. As more light flickered in, the outline of two very large people came into focus. *Damn!* I could handle one in my condition, but not two! My hopes were quickly fading.

It would be impossible not to see me once the light filled the tunnel completely. As much as every fiber of my being wanted to do exactly the opposite, I started backing up into the tomb. At least in there I had enough room to put up a fight. What little was left of me might not make a great opponent, however. I backed up through the entrance to the tomb with barely enough time to press myself up against the left side of the opening.

The first, of what I assumed was two men, was about to step through, and I let my hand fly, hoping to catch him off guard with a solid backhanded fist to the face. It took all of the energy I had left, but I wouldn't get a better opportunity once he was in the room.

He caught me by the wrist and pulled me out in front of him without saying a word, just held me there until the second man came to join him.

The sun had completely risen, and now that the two men were out of the tunnel and in the tomb with me, light poured in. Still held in the grip of the huge hand belonging to the first man and still too weak to fight, I chanced a glance around the room.

It was completely different from what I had imagined. I obviously had not been around the whole room. On a curved wall opposite me was a large rectangular pit large enough to hold a mattress—a straw one, I guessed. A little farther down on the same side was a built-in cupboard. It was like a house underground and yet, it was definitely a place for the dead.

The second man, with his bald head and reddish-brown mustache and goatee, spoke with a thick Scottish accent. "Well, she certainly picked a wee bit of a lass, eh Mac?"

"Aye, that she did, Angus, but I'd wager there's some fight still left in this one. If I let you down, will you promise not to make trouble?" Mac's voice was similar to Angus's, not as deep, but it had the same thick accent. His face was smooth-shaven, and he had salt-and-pepper hair.

I wasn't going to admit to being too weak to fight right now so I simply nodded, and he let me go. Mac stepped back and leaned against the wall.

"So, Maurin—"

"How do you know my name?" I cut Mac off. I loved a Scottish accent as much as the next girl, and if it were any other day I'd gladly sit there and listen to him talk over a few pints. Right now, I just wanted to know how the hell they got here and how he knew my name. "Who the hell are you guys, anyway?" I was trying not to slur my words, but it wasn't easy. I was still fighting the infection. My voice was scratchy and harsh from my dry throat.

Angus smiled, but made no attempt to explain. He was apparently leaving all the talking to Mac.

Mac looked at Angus and chuckled. "You'd think she never communed with the dead before."

The two men laughed, and it echoed in the empty chamber.

I was really tired of being the entertainment. It seemed like today I was either the butt of the joke or kissing it entirely. I guess the frustration showed, even through the bruises on my face.

"It's alright, Maurin," Mac said, as he tried to regain his composure.

"So you're dead? Is this some kind of side effect from Scota or something? Because really, it's just been a blast up until now! So why not throw some fucking ghosts in the mix, right? I mean everyone has just been piling the shit on today, so why not. There's an evil goddess running loose who wants to rule the world, not to mention raise an army of disii. I have become some sort of vessel for a whole different goddess. I got my ass kicked by a vampire, a couple people I truly liked are probably dead, and a wolf I hope I don't know is definitely dead. I've been bitten by a

Black Dog, and I am barely holding off the infection. So sure, why not two ghosts to round out my day? Fan-fucking-tastic!" I ranted.

I was managing a slow pace, back and forth, wearing a path in the dirt floor. What I wanted to do was run screaming, arms flailing from the room, but I was too exhausted so I just slowly hobbled back and forth in front of the two Scottish apparitions as I ranted and raved.

XXIV
TWENTY-FOUR

The two giant men stayed put, leaning against the wall as if the tomb would crash down around us if they weren't there. Mac sighed heavily, as if he was the one who was exhausted, and he hadn't even explained anything to me yet.

"Side effect? No, I doubt very seriously if you weren't unconscious that you would even see us at all. More of an out-of-body experience, I'd say. You've stepped outside yourself and in doing so, you're able to see us," Mac said.

Mac motioned to the floor, and there I was, lying lifeless in the dirt. I reached to touch myself and instantly thought better of it. What if I wasn't out of my body, but actually dead? The idea of touching my own dead body was almost as upsetting as the patronizing smiles from the two ghostly men.

Now, I was just pissed off at everything and everyone. I was so sick of all of this. Was it too much to ask for my old life back? The one where I didn't see ghosts or goddesses? My hands were balled into fists down at my sides, and I started pacing again. Pacing in front of my motionless body was obviously not going to calm me down, but I couldn't help it.

Being angry was about all I had right now so I clung to it, but I figured I should at least hear them out.

"So, I'm in a coma or something? This isn't even happening right now, it's a dream right?" Denial was fast becoming my answer for everything lately.

"Oh, you are still physically here in this tomb," Mac answered. "As for conversations with a goddess and a couple of ghosts? I'm not a doctor or anything, but that's not the sanest thing I've ever heard."

"Ha. Ha. You're a real funny guy-ghost-whatever. So, I *am* imagining you then. Probably because of the fever."

"Oh, all right," he protested. "The grand stories of a white light and people calling to you...well, they're a bit of an exaggeration. Now, when someone is like you are now...well it leaves an opening in your consciousness that is otherwise closed off. Humans, though your energy feels different from that of most humans, tend to close themselves off from the spirit world. Oh they all want answers to the afterlife, but none of them really want to have a conversation with a ghost to obtain them. When we try to communicate, they cry, 'Poltergeist!' and try to have a séance to cast us out. It's ridiculous!" Mac was suddenly on a roll.

"Um, any other time I'm lying on the ground in a tomb, probably unconscious and bleeding to death, I would so want to hear the whole life-after-death speech. But right now, I would much rather hear about how I can get back home. So do you think maybe, just maybe, you could actually help me with that?" Okay, I probably could have said that a little less bitchy.

Mac seemed to agree. "Hmph! You know, it's not every day a ghost offers to give you the secrets to the afterlife, and now all you want to hear about is getting out of this tomb..." he trailed off, waving his hand to imply that getting out of here was far less interesting than what he was going to say.

Mac folded his arms across his broad chest. He was finished. If I didn't want to hear what he had to say, then tough. He wouldn't tell me anything.

Angus gave him a swift jolt in the ribs with an elbow the size of a sledgehammer. Angus, it seemed, had finally decided to join the conversation. "He knows. He just likes to hear himself talk is all. As full of hot air in death as he was in life, that one is," he said, jutting his thumb out toward Mac. "Still not going to tell her, eh? Fine. I can't promise this will work but being from a line of Druid Priests, we know a little about magic. I can give you the invocation but beaten as you are, it may not be wise to use it. It will take a lot of physical strength, and I don't know how much is left in that body lying there right now."

"I was going to tell her. No one ever comes here anymore. I just wanted to have a bit of fun before we helped her. She must give us something in return, Angus. You can tell her yourself, but I want a token in return for your ruining my fun."

"A token? Sorry, boys, I left my purse back in Salem. I don't have any money." Something told me it wasn't really money that he wanted.

"Nay, not your money. A promise. Make me a promise. If

we tell you the invocation, then we can talk with you again," Mac said.

Well, that seemed harmless enough. I had no intention of coming back here, so there was no real danger in the promise. He couldn't talk to me if I wasn't here and practically dead. I was going to avoid those two things as much as possible. So?

"Ok, sure. I'll talk to you again. Now what's the invocation?" I asked.

Mac smiled at me, and something in that smile told me I was wrong to assume they could only talk to me here. Damn it, one day I'd learn. Nothing for nothing, right? I sighed. Once again, I had walked right into a trap.

Angus had a few more questions. "How do you plan to make the journey in your condition? You'll have to do something about it before you use the spell. Do you have enough energy to heal? There is a cost for that as well. Too weak and you could do more harm to yourself than good."

"Yo-you know what I am?" I guess I shouldn't have been surprised they could tell.

"Aye," they both replied in unison.

"Well I'm still not sure. When I got up and went to work this morning, I was just Maurin, psychically-gifted. But somewhere between lunch and dinnertime, I became a holding facility for a goddess. Even I'm not really sure what that makes me. It hasn't even been twenty-four hours since this all started. For all I know, I could just have a brain tumor that is causing serious delusions," I said.

The tumor wasn't sounding so bad actually. Normally, I would never wish sickness on myself, but even a disease was starting to sound better than all the weird stuff happening to me today.

"A reincarnate. That's what you are. But you are at odds with the transformation," Angus said gravely.

"No shit, Angus. Honestly, when you were alive, would you have just moved half your soul over to make room for someone else, regardless if she was a goddess or not? It's a bit much to process and seems even worse when you combine it with everything else that's happened. Not to mention that I'm not really a big fan of change in the first place." *So there.* You couldn't blame me for that. It was a lot to deal with in such a short period of time.

Mac never moved. He just stood there, satisfied with his bargain. He was going to get to talk to me again, the freak magnet that I am, and that made him real happy. It made me really uncomfortable. If I managed to get back, I was going to have to ask Mahalia what exactly I had gotten myself in to.

"Perhaps I would also be reluctant to accept it, but you must come to terms with it and quickly. If the things you said in your little tirade are accurate, then you need to be a little more embracing of your fate. You'll never defeat an evil force, War Goddess or otherwise, if you are divided inside. So I will leave you this invocation, but caution you to heal yourself before you use it. Invoking the powers of nature and the powers of this land can be dangerous. I recommend wind by the way, with no boat or small craft, faring the sea would not be a wise choice for a novice. Focus on the words. Repeat them three times. Then focus on the land of Erin and the force of nature that you wish to wield." Angus was already fading.

Mac winked at me. The wall behind him was becoming

visible through his suddenly transparent body. Instead of walking back out of the tunnel as they had come in, their bodies were almost evaporated.

"Wait, wait, I'm not a witch. Are you sure this will work? Hey, wait, you didn't give me the spell!" I called out.

They were gone. My physical body stirred on the ground, calling to me. My body sucked my consciousness back inside, pulling me down until my soul settled back into the deepest recesses of my core. Power hummed, and I welcomed it, welcomed her. They were right, my two ghosts, as much as I hated to admit it. If I didn't accept my fate, then I might as well stay here and quit. Was I an instant super-hero? No. But I was given this power, and I wasn't going to waste it. Not if I could help save the people I had left behind. People like Amalie and Oberon. Aw hell, even Baylen.

Now that I was back inside my body, I pushed that thrumming power through my blood, letting it plug up the holes in my flesh. How was I going to fix my ear? I thought about the pictures I'd seen on the wall at the doctor's office when I was a kid and tried to focus on that image. There was a rush of heat, and the pain subsided. If I was lucky, I had healed it enough to prevent any major hearing loss.

Weakened from lack of nourishment, not to mention the beatings I had taken, I stayed on the ground. My mouth was thick with the feeling of dry cotton. There was nothing I could do right now about my need for food and water, but maybe I could ease the muscle fatigue. Power coursed through my sore muscles like tiny jolts of electricity. It started pushing through my heart, gradually increasing my pulse. I might still look like shit on the outside, but I was actually starting to feel a little better on the inside. With a lot less effort than expected, I pushed myself off the floor, got to my knees, and tried to clear my thoughts.

XXV
TWENTY-FIVE

What had he said? That he gave me the invocation? But he hadn't, had he? Dammit, the words escaped me. *Think, Maurin, think.* What did he say? It was still dark in the tomb, the light having gone when my apparitions did. After the salty air dispersed only the stale air of the tomb remained. The exit was sealed, and the invocation was my only hope. I pounded a fist into the floor in frustration and felt something scrawled in the dirt. Tracing my finger through the shapes in the floor, the letters flared to life when I reached the end of the last shape. There on the floor of my tomb, glowing in a faint orange light, was the invocation. Well here goes nothing. I might not be a witch, but with every bit of my new and old powers I spoke the words etched in the floor.

> "I invoke thee, Erin Brilliant Sea
> Fertile Hill Bitter Winds
> I invoke the spirits of the East

From my land to this one I have come Grant me
the power, so my journey is done."

Taking a cue from the Salem coven, I repeated it three times. My powers mixed with the words as I imagined the same winds I had seen the witches call forth at Baylen's house. Thoughts of how they harnessed them for travel and how I wished to do the same, filled my mind. Awestruck, I watched the dirt begin to swirl around my feet. Holy shit, I had actually done it!

The wind grew in intensity, sucking the air from the tomb. I slowly spun myself into the wind, wrapping it around my body like a blanket, until a small cyclone formed around me. The dirt inside the spiraling wind started to cling to my skin and clothes. Eyes closed to keep the debris out, I focused on the wind and Baylen's house.

I pictured his house in my mind, the driveway, the porch, even the shower. God knows I needed the shower. With zero experience lassoing a tornado, all I could do was hope the need to get back to Baylen's would be powerful enough to make it happen. My feet left the ground again, but this time instead of riding Morrigan's power, I rode my own. My skin felt hot, like it was on fire, but not from fever. The magic and the dirt quickly filled the room. It was hard to breathe now.

I opened my hands, palms down, and made a thrusting motion toward the floor. I flew into the ceiling, knocking the air out of my lungs. Gasping, with the wind still swirling rapidly around my body, I stayed there pressed against the ceiling.

Unsure of what to do or exactly how to get out, I thrust my hands downward again. This time I sucked in air and forced it out of my lungs in a scream. I felt the hard, dirt-packed ceiling give way above my back. With the wind and my power, I broke through the mounded earth, sending rock and dirt flying everywhere. I hung there, above the demolished tomb that had been my prison as the winds I had called began to pull in the air around me.

As the tornado grew, so did the core, and I felt safe inside it. I had invoked this spell, called this wind. Nothing would hurt me while I was inside it. Again I thought about my destination and who would be there waiting for me. Oberon.

The magic—my magic—flared inside me with the thought of him. My power was swirling in sync with the wind outside my body. I could feel it moving. It turned inside me and forced my body to spin slowly inside the core of the winds. And then, with an excruciatingly painful snap, something happened. Scota. Our powers were truly becoming one. There were no longer two separate beings inside my body. We had a connection. Our souls were permanently fused together. Her magic mixed with mine. Our power was one, and I didn't fear it anymore. I welcomed it. I welcomed her and the new person I had become.

With this union came the knowledge of how to wield this power that was so new but felt so old. I pushed the lightning running through my body out. Arms outstretched, I threw the magic into the circling winds. I watched as the circle of ground beneath me widened until nothing remained outside the core of the tornado. Like a stretched rubber band, I let go of the power and instead of breaking, the sides came crashing back together, propelling me into motion. To Oberon.

All I could see were flashes of light that told me where I was. Not that I needed them. I knew right where I was going to land. As quickly as my flight had begun, it was ending. Still safe within the tornado, I could feel the descent. My ears popped with the change in altitude, and a jolt of pain shot through my inner ear, most likely because I hadn't put it back together correctly.

When the driveway leading up to Baylen's house came into view, I knew I was coming down too fast. My transportation hadn't come with an owner's manual so I didn't have a clue where the brakes were, but I needed to come up with something quick. I didn't even want to try healing two broken legs, and God knows what else, if I crashed at that speed into the driveway. I'd be picking gravel out of my ass for a month.

I tried to concentrate on nothing but slowing down, but it wasn't working. Maybe it was because of all the tree branches smacking into my legs and breaking my concentration. The ground rose up to meet me. There was no way I could slow down enough to land on my feet. If I couldn't slow down at all, then maybe I could just stop. *Stop. Stop!* I slowed, but nowhere near in time. With a great thump and a couple of bounces, I crashed into the driveway. Damn, that hurt a lot! Rolling from my side onto my back, I sucked in huge gulps of air to catch my breath. It was all I could manage.

XXVI
TWENTY-SIX

A wolf howled to signal the pack. There was no way for him, or her for that matter, to know I was the trouble they'd smelled on the perimeter so they sounded the alarm. The first wolf was joined by at least three more. Branches snapped and leaves crunched beneath their paws. They would be on top of me in a second. I tried to stand but barely made it to all fours before the unfamiliar wolves had me surrounded. Since I was already in the position, I kept my head bowed down, showing my intent to submit and that I wasn't going to fight them.

There were four of them snarling at me with their lips curled. Were they just waiting for me to make a move so they could pounce and tear me to shreds? From behind them, I could hear the soft padding steps of another large wolf. With my head still down I listened carefully, trying to make out the barks and growls. What were they saying? The two wolves in front of me moved to the side, leaving an opening for the fifth wolf to walk through. Two large, black paws stepped into my view, and for just a second I got nervous, thinking I had mistaken the Black Dogs for wolves.

As soon as he lowered his muzzle I knew who it was. He stuck his cold, wet nose under my chin and raised my head so I could see his eyes. Roul had very distinct blue eyes. Even as a wolf, there was no mistaking them. His coat was as black as his hair, but the wave was gone. It was beautiful, thick, and softer than I had expected.

Flooded with relief to see someone I recognized, I flung an arm around his neck and stroked his coat. Burying my face in his fur, I whispered my thanks for his timely arrival.

Roul pawed at my knee, and I let him go. He barked off what I assumed were some orders, and the other wolves left us to go back to their watch posts.

I looked into his eyes and knew that even though I couldn't understand him right now he could most certainly understand me. "Roul, we can't stay here. We have to go back to the house and get everyone who's left out of there. She'll know I got out of the tomb, and she'll be looking for me soon, if she isn't already," I said.

He cocked his head sideways at the mention of a tomb, probably wondering why the hell I was in a tomb.

A shrug was the only answer I had for that one. I still hadn't figured out why she had placed me in a tomb instead of just killing me.

He nudged me in the ribs, which I took as my cue to get moving.

Sore from falling out of the sky and onto the driveway, I didn't move as fast as he'd have liked. Every muscle in my body was telling me not to stand up, almost demanding I lie back down where I was before the wolves had found me. I didn't see any blood on the ground anywhere, and Roul didn't seem too alarmed by my appearance, so obviously there were no huge cuts or bones jutting out of my skin anywhere.

Once I was on my feet, I tried to brush off some of the gravel that was still stuck to my skin. Tweezers would be required to remove the rest. The first few steps were awful. I had to stop, not twenty feet from where I landed, to catch my breath, which probably meant I had a couple of cracked ribs.

"I gotta catch my breath a minute," I said to Roul, who was walking gracefully beside me. "I think if I just stop a sec, I might be able to heal myself a little."

Dropping down on the gravel, I pulled my knees into my chest. It felt good to stretch my sore back and helped me to relax. My breathing slowly returned to normal, and with each passing minute I felt a little better. After about five minutes, I stood up, arching my back and twisting side to side. The beatings felt days old, not hours. I could walk without pain shooting through my whole body. Sure, I was still stiff, but it was a far cry from what I felt like when Roul first found me in the driveway.

Roul was looking at me impatiently. I think he wanted to get back to the house more than I did.

"Okay, okay. Let's go," I said.

Roul padded out in front. He picked up the pace.

I pushed my short, human legs to keep up with the speed of his wolf trot. As the bottom of the porch steps came into view, Roul was nothing more than a cloud of dust in the driveway.

XXVII
TWENTY-SEVEN

Joy. It was the only way to describe being out of that tomb and back with the people who'd become strangely important to me. Making friends came easily enough when I was a kid, but it didn't take long before they figured out I was different and found someone else to be friends with. You learn not to get attached to things, places, or even people under those circumstances. It was unusual for me to be so deeply affected by so many people because I didn't let that happen. Ever. Normally my philosophy stated that if you didn't get close, you wouldn't get hurt or disappointed, but right now I would prefer to be hurt by these people than to not have them at all. For a second I thought I might cry. It must have been the dirt in my eye, and not some rash wave of emotion taking over. Still, I waited a minute before opening the front door to Baylen's house.

I walked through the doorway suddenly feeling like I'd been rolling in a pig pen as I looked around the room at all the clean faces and clean clothes. Dirt was stuck to my skin, hair, and clothes from the wind, and now I had sticks, leaves, and gravel to go with it. The small amount of bare skin visible was an interesting shade of gray and orange clay.

Baylen stood there staring at me. The exhaustion and worry on his face a distraction from the fading bruises marring his complexion.

Roul had shifted back to human form and had slipped on a pair of shorts. He was leaning against the wall Morrigan had torn down. The rubble I'd left Baylen lying in had been fixed. The drywall looked untouched and the paint fresh. It was as if she had never come, never torn down the wall and ripped me away to my underground prison.

Well, there's a nifty, little trick.

Roul's gaze was fixed in my direction. He was waiting for something, and I didn't think it was an explanation. There was something I was missing, something I hadn't seen yet.

And then I saw it—or him. I noticed the person Roul was waiting for me to see. He was sitting on the couch between Phallon and Juno, who both looked a little uncomfortable with him sandwiched between them. Blue hair, cut short and tapered around his ears was an unwanted distraction from his light-blue eyes. His frame was long and lean, and he was by far the least attractive man there. Cold blue eyes raked up and down my body, and I couldn't help feeling a little violated by his gaze.

"Amalie is upstairs with Arcana. She's taken a turn for the worse. Olwyn, Mahalia, and Oberon are with her too. Seamus is with the vampires, but he'll come back with Medea as soon as the sun sets. Go, get cleaned up." Roul's voice sounded tired.

I felt my shoulders drop in relief. It was calming to know where everyone was. I took it for granted that Roul's wolves were okay. He would have told me if the wolf I'd seen eaten alive was his, wouldn't he? I wanted to know. I wanted to grieve for the nameless wolf, but I wanted more to feel cool tiles beneath my feet and hot water beading up on my skin. Roul was right. I needed to get cleaned up. I needed to get the dirt out of my hair and check my body for any remaining cuts that might need to be cleaned and healed.

The stranger smashed between the two sisters rose from the couch. "We haven't been introduced yet, Maurin. I'm Cash." He held out a hand.

I did not reciprocate. "Just Cash?" I replied, unable to hide my disdain for his having delayed my shower.

"Yeah, just Cash.

"Well, just Cash, now we've been introduced. So, if you'll excuse me, I'm going to go grab that shower now." I didn't wait for him to say anything else, just turned and went up the stairs to my shower. Voices carried from down the hall before my foot hit the top step. It was mostly Olwyn cursing, and it was coming from the guest room Arcana was in.

"Damn it, Mahalia, this bite has more bacteria than one from a Komodo dragon. Even the Allicorn powder is having a hard time fighting off the poisons." The concern was so clear in her voice it made me pause.

I walked up to the half-open door and peeked into the room.

Oberon sat beside Arcana on the bed, helping her to drink something. Amalie looked up from holding her mentor's hand to give me a weak smile before she returned her attention to whispering healing prayers over her while Mahalia and Olwyn discussed which remedies to try next.

I smiled back. There would be time to talk to Amalie later. Right now she needed to be there with Arcana, and I needed to be in the shower.

The door to the bathroom closed with a soft click, and I let out the deep sigh I'd been holding in since I landed on my ass in the driveway. I turned on the hot water and stared at the mess of a woman looking back at me from the mirror as steam filled the room. My hair was matted and filthy. The dirt and mud caked on my skin cracked and flaked off as I stripped out of my ragged clothes. A last glimpse of my naked reflection before the steam completely fogged up the mirror revealed already fading bruises on nearly every inch my body in varying shades of yellow and green.

Scratches and cuts from the nails and framework of the broken wall were almost gone. Bright-pink skin replaced the scabs that had been there only an hour or so ago. In just a few more hours, there would be no evidence left of the beating I had received. Remnants of Morrigan's boot print lingered on my chest, but the tread marks would soon be gone, leaving only a lingering ache in my muscles and bones. I looked at myself one more time before getting into the shower. It was a damned good thing I had recently gained the ability to heal, otherwise, I'd be dead for sure. No human could take as much ass-kicking as I had today and live to talk about it. At least none I'd ever met.

I drew back the curtain and stepped inside the shower. The hot water rolled down my skin, and I watched the brown rivulets run down my arms and legs before swirling around the drain. With my head back, I rubbed the water out of my eyes and face and tried to run my fingers through the tangled mess that was my hair. I knew as soon as I hit the first big knot there'd be a lot of lather, rinse, and repeat involved in cleaning my hair.

As I reached for the soap in the little dish on the shower wall, a hand wrapped around the edge of the curtain and slowly pulled it back. I hadn't heard the door open, and no one had called out to announce his or her presence. But with him this close to me, I knew who it was. The aroma of magic and fresh mint permeated the steamy bathroom. My heart was beating fast as he stepped into the shower with me. He was everything I had imagined he would be underneath his clothes, and more.

Every inch of his skin was smooth and flawless. His muscular body was decorated with black tribal tattoos, mainly on his arms and shoulders. They wrapped down to his chest. The tattoos were more than just tribal. They were a Celtic design. When I could finally tear my eyes away from him long enough to string a coherent sentence together, I would have to ask him what they meant.

Reaching for me, he pulled me close to him and wrapped me in his arms as the water beat upon our skin. He took the soap from my hand and lathering it up, he started with my arms, running the bar of soap and his hands along my skin as he washed away what remained of the caked on dirt. Turning me around so my back was to him, he washed and massaged my back, sliding his hands around to the front until he cupped my breasts.

I let out a ragged breath in anticipation of what he would do next.

He kissed my neck just below my ear, and despite the hot water I could feel the warmth of his breath against my skin. His kisses moved down my neck until he came to rest his mouth just at the edge of my collarbone.

I tried to turn around so I could return his kisses, but he held me there with my back to him and continued to wash the dirt and grime from my body. After he had familiarized himself with every inch of my skin, he nudged me forward under the hot water and used his hands to help the water rinse the soap away. He gently pulled my head back, massaging the shampoo into my hair and scalp.

He slowly spun me around until I faced him, wrapped an arm around my back, and pressed me to him as he walked us both back under the water. I closed my eyes and lowered my head back to rinse the conditioner away. Oberon held me there, kissing my chin, working his way down to the hollow of my neck and lingered there only for a moment before he started working his mouth back up my jawline.

I held his face in my hands, raised my head to meet his lips with mine and kissed him. We stayed there, our lips locked together, until the water turned cold.

He finally let me out of his embrace to turn off the shower and reach for a towel. My strong, masculine witch tenderly ran the towel along my body, scrutinizing every fading bruise as he dried the beaded water from my skin. Oberon wrapped the towel around me and tucked it in front to stay in place.

I sat down on the edge of the tub.

After drying himself and wrapping a towel around his waist, he turned my upper body back toward the shower wall, grabbed a brush off the counter, and slowly brushed the knots from my hair. When he'd finished, I turned around to face him with the intention of kissing him again only to have him kneel down in front of me and rest his head in my lap.

I pushed him back and slid off the tub and into his lap. Somewhere in that moment, with him holding me in his lap, I fell a little bit in love with him. While part of me wanted more, wanted him to finish what he had started in the shower, the rest of me loved him for knowing just what I needed right now. I felt so comfortable, so safe there in his arms. If I could just close my eyes for a few minutes, I would feel even better. Nuzzling my head on his shoulder, I rested my forehead against his neck, and slipped into sleep while I had the chance.

XXVIII
TWENTY-EIGHT

Darkness devoured everything except the flicker of candles from atop the altar draped in a dark burgundy fabric where Morrigna stood. Two wrought-iron candelabras with three candles each on either end of the altar, shot up from the table like two giant pitch-forks. Between the candelabras, a man was stretched out with his hands and feet bound and his mouth gagged. There was a blade held high above him in Morrigan's hands, ready to strike.

"My warriors, on the eve of battle I give these gifts to you!" Morrigan shouted to the throng.

She screamed over the war cries from her soldiers and thrust the knife down into the man's chest. Unable to turn away, I watched as she carved up the man on the altar. Blood ran down the altar, leaving dark matted lines in the fabric beneath him. The unidentified man's back was arched, and his body convulsed as she twisted and turned the blade inside him. His cheeks, puffed and red, were the only sign of the screams muted by the gag in his mouth. His head rolled to face me, and I watched him watch me until all the life had left him and his eyes had closed for the last time. Using her hands like rib spreaders, she ripped open his chest and pulled out his dying heart.

"I give to you the heart of Indech! Eat of his heart, and you shall have his strength in battle!" Morrigan proclaimed.

I watched in disgust, still unseen and wanting very much to stay that way, as her soldiers came to the altar one by one to eat from the heart of Indech. With long, bony fingers, they each took the heart in their hands and brought it up to their black lips. They took a bite out of the still warm heart.

The blood dripped from their mouths. It was barely visible against their charcoal-colored flesh. She wasted no time drawing her blade again. Morrigan flipped Indech onto his side and buried the blade, hilt deep. Once again, she tore through his body, stealing his organs to feed her masses. Organs fell onto a large silver platter with a gooey thud as she shouted out to her soldiers again. "Even you wretched evil things can have valor, and I give it to you now, here in the kidneys of Indech! Fill your vile mouths with these pieces of Indech, and you shall have heart in battle! You will give cowardice to your enemies! They will run from the battlefield at the sight of you!"

Cries of war ripped through my ears again, and I just wanted to weep. I had never seen him before tonight, and I would never have missed him if I hadn't witnessed his death and the desecration of his body, but this was horrible and should never happen to anyone.

The chanting of the soldiers slowly turned into mur-

murs, and a path was forming in the crowd as the sea of monsters parted. Feet stomping in time, could be heard from the back, and I saw two lines of soldiers six deep marching up the middle. Dressed in full armor, they stood out from the rest, and I could hear the lesser soldiers whispering to make way for the *An ChaipBhais*.

The *An ChaipBhais* marched up to the altar as she stood there waiting with a platter in each hand held out for them. With razor-like teeth, they tore into what was left of the man's heart and kidneys. Their captain licked the platters clean before handing them back to Morrigan.

Her two sisters took the platters as she walked around the altar to meet her elite warriors.

The Captain took her hand and led her down the steps to stand next to the *An ChaipBhais*.

The soldiers began howling like hyenas. Someone fired a gun, and others joined in. A small cloud of dust erupted as pieces of the stone ceiling fell around them. Swords banged on shields, and the howling grew louder. *Bang, bang, bang!* Morrigan turned, raised a hand to point at me, and the banging grew louder. *Bang, bang, bang, bang!*

"Maurin!"

A scream tore from my lips as I woke safe on the floor with Oberon still holding me.

"Maurin? Maurin?" he called, and I could hear the fear in his voice.

I tried to speak, but couldn't seem to form any words. There was a bang again, and I practically jumped out of my skin. This time the bang was followed by Phallon busting through the bathroom door.

"Oberon, what's wrong with her? What happened? Why

is she screaming like that?" Phallon demanded.

He looked to me for an answer.

No matter how hard I tried to find them, the words to describe what I saw escaped me. I could only turn to Oberon, bury my head in his neck, and quietly sob for what they had done to Indech.

Phallon was all out of patience. "Fine, don't bother to explain, then! You got the whole damned house in an uproar with you in here freaking out, but you don't have to tell me what the hell is going on! There are clothes for you in the guest room." She was still spewing off as she storm-ed out of the bathroom. Her swearing was growing fainter as she made her way back down the stairs.

Oberon pulled me away from the comfort of his chest and raised my head to look at him.

"Maurin, what happened? What did you see in your dream? It's okay. You're okay now. You can tell me what happened," he said.

I didn't want to think about, or see, it all again as I explained my nightmare to him, but I didn't have a choice. I tried to keep my voice from shaking, but I was failing miserably as I recounted my vision.

"A sacrifice. I saw her sacrifice a man, and she called him Indech. I don't know who he was, but she cut him up and fed him to her army. Her army," I said, grabbing him by the shoulders. "She has an army. She's ready, and she's coming. She said 'on the eve of battle'. I think what I saw has already happened!" I flew to my feet, almost losing my towel, and headed down the hallway for the stairs.

Oberon called to me, "Hey, you might want to get dressed first!"

I looked down, having almost forgotten my lack of clothes. "Probably not a bad idea," I said, as I turned and made my way past the bathroom where Oberon was leaning in the doorway and to the bedroom where my clothes were waiting.

Neatly folded on the bed were a pair of black pants, a long-sleeve, black shirt, and black eight-hole Doc's. There was even one of my black bra and panty sets. Obviously Medea had grabbed a few extra things when she got my clothes yesterday, because a guy probably wouldn't think to pick out a matching set. I was thankful she at least had had the courtesy to pick out one of my nicer ones because I would have died if Oberon saw me in my laundry-day granny panties.

I started to get dressed, fully aware of Oberon watching me as I slipped on the panties. The bra was on, but unhooked, when he came up behind me to hook it, pulling my hair out of the way so it didn't catch. The long-sleeve shirt was a tighter fit than I would have picked out for myself, but I didn't have much of a choice since this was the only thing in here for me to wear. The pants were the weight and material of camo, but without any pattern on them. I pulled the drawstring tight on my waist and then reached for my socks and boots. When I had finished getting dressed, I looked at myself in the long, standing mirror.

"Well, all that's missing is some black paint to put under my eyes. I look like a burglar who shops at Sunny's Surplus. Well, at least the blood stains won't show," I joked.

Oberon laughed, and I turned away from the cat burglar in the mirror to see if he had the same outfit. He did.

Enjoying the show as he dressed, I watched his muscles and beautiful tattoos disappear under the clothes. If it was this much fun to watch him get dressed, then watching him get undressed would be even better.

He must have known what I was thinking. With a wicked smile he walked over, very aware of his body, grabbed my hand, and dragged me out the door.

I found myself digging in my heels just a little after the way he had stalked over to me. This man could definitely be trouble. With a capital *T*. He gave my arm a gentle tug and with a little trip, I was right beside him.

XXIX
TWENTY-NINE

We had barely exited the steps when Oberon address-ed everyone in the room and started explaining what had happened upstairs. Not everything that happened upstairs obviously, just the dream part. The new were, Cash, was the first to stand.

"Well then, you're pretty lucky to have me at your disposal, I'd say," Cash said arrogantly.

He had to be on our side—otherwise Roul would have torn him to shreds—but something was definitely off.

Roul and Olwyn were both visibly irritated by his presence.

I was about to ask what I was missing when Olwyn caught my gaze. She shook her head as if to say not now.

Cash continued, oblivious to their intense and obvious dislike for him. Or maybe he just didn't give a shit. "Cash brought the heavy artillery. I've got something for everyone," he said, sticking his thumb toward his chest.

Oh, God, he talked about himself in the third person. I cannot stand it when someone talks about himself that way. Only boxers and professional wrestlers can justify talking about themselves in the third person, in my opinion, and even then it gets on my nerves.

Cash grabbed two long, black cases from beside the couch and set them down on the coffee table before dragging out a third. Closer to the size of a chest, this one was too big to set on top of anything. He flipped the silver latch on the chest and started laying weapons out all over Baylen's living room floor. Fortunately for Cash, it was a big room.

"This one here is a thing of real beauty," he said, as he pulled out a huge fully-automatic weapon. "HK416, 5.56X45mm enhanced carbine, 700-900 rounds per minute, equipped with the AG416 40mm grenade launcher. Pure genius at Heckler & Koch. This baby never jams. Ammo's modified, of course. Holy water rounds with a holy water grenade. Hold the trigger on this baby and you can cut a demon in half without ever getting close to him. You only get one shot with the grenade, though, so you'll have to reload if you miss your target. In other words, don't miss." Cash held the gun like he wanted to make love to it later.

Oberon leaned in, whispering in my ear, "Ex-military, he's a merc for hire now."

Well, that explained it. Military boys and their toys. 6666Man, did they love their guns! Cash reached into the case again and pulled out something I was a little more familiar with.

"Is that...is that a paint-ball gun?" I asked, unsure of why he would bring a paint-ball gun. It seemed a little like bringing a knife to a gunfight.

He looked at me with amusement. "Don't under estimate the Eco, honey. It's got a modified motherboard and can shoot a minimum of 18 rounds per minute. That's as fast as you can pull the trigger. It'll hold plenty of ammo in the hopper, and that isn't paint. They're filled with holy water. Perfect for you non-military types. But, if you still have your doubts when this is all over, you and I can play our own little war game. I'll be the Big Bad Wolf and you can be Little Red Riding Hood. I'll show you just what my gun can do." His hands were trailing down to places on his body my eyes did not want to follow.

What an asshole. If he didn't have all the good weapons, I would have told him so.

Roul stepped forward, lips curled. He had moved well beyond irritated and was just plain pissed now. I would have liked to think it was on my behalf, but I knew better. Cash's poor attempt at a sexual innuendo may have been the straw that broke the camel's back, but Roul was mad about something bigger than Cash being a pervert.

"You were warned before coming here, Cash. Your pack leader may tolerate disobedience and rogue behavior, but I will not!" Roul warned.

"Oh, I'll behave, for now. When this is over, we can settle up our differences according to pack law," Cash replied smugly.

"If that is a direct challenge, then we most certainly will settle up!" Roul's face grew dark.

"Before these witnesses, I challenge you. When we have finished this business, then we'll see who's truly the Alpha here!" Cash said confidently.

Oh, he wasn't just an asshole. He was a fucking huge,

gigantic asshole—guns or no guns. Thankfully, Baylen stepped in before the fur started to fly.

"Cash, if you would, the weapons? We have very little time to outfit everyone here," Baylen prodded.

A very neutral and tactful approach. Better than I would have done. I think I probably would have started with my finger in his chest telling him where he could stick his guns. The tension seemed to leave Cash's body as he went back to his beloved weapons. An image of him, getting off to the H&K catalog instead of *Playboy* or *Penthouse* like normal men, made my stomach turn, and I quickly pushed the thought away.

He moved to the smaller cases on the coffee table and continued with what seemed like the gunrunner 101 sales pitch.

"Okay, well, here we have some smaller hand guns— Springfield XD Subcompact 40S&W, the H&K USP Compact 9mm and the Benelli M4 Super 90 shotgun. All excellent weapons with modified ammo made from melted down crosses, but these are not long-range weapons. The XD and USP will leave a hell of an exit wound, and the M4 will make a huge hole on the way in and out, but they are last resort. If you have to fire one of these, you're too close and probably will be dead before the second round. And over here, I have a few IEDs. I only have a few of these. We had to make them special, and that can take some time, so again, don't miss the target. Make sure you get the hell out of Dodge before this sucker detonates. When it goes off, it will blast shrapnel from blessed steel crosses covering about a whole city block," Cash warned.

I stuck my hand up, ready to start asking questions. It

seemed to me there was something Cash had forgotten. Or maybe he didn't. Vampires and weres may live side by side, but they don't particularly care for one another. Sure there are exceptions but as a general rule, vamps stick with vamps and weres stick with weres. The relationship between vamps and weres was founded solidly on the principle of the enemy you know. Despite their mutual distrust, they'd still rather deal with each other than deal with humans. They managed to hold it all together on the basis of that. Better to work together and police themselves than leave it up to the humans. But still, Cash didn't seem like the kind of guy who would mind a few vamp casualties, even if we were all on the same team for now.

"Um, I don't want to sound ungrateful or anything, but won't these weapons and ammo pose a problem for the vamps? I mean, holy water and bullets made from melted down crosses? In the thick of it we might end up with serious casualties on our own side, even from friendly fire," I said.

Everyone turned to look at me, as if I had sprouted five heads. Maybe they had already thought about all this, but I wanted to know how we could expect the vamps to go out there while we were shooting bullets that could burn, maim, or kill them too.

"If you've got any better ideas, offer 'em up. Roul asked our pack for help, so here it is," Cash responded.

Why is it that I get nothing but attitude every time I ask a question around these fuckers? What I wouldn't give to be back at work posing questions to simple, everyday criminals. At least with them I could get the straight answers I was looking for. But seeing as how he was a killer for hire, and he could probably drop me before anyone in the room could stop him, I would play nice.

"I'm not questioning your weapons expertise, obviously. I just want to know our game plan? How are we going to keep the vamps out of the line of fire?" I asked.

Cash perked up at my feeble attempt at a compliment. "We're not. They were briefed on the risks and are willing to take them. We're treating the demons in a very similar fashion as we would vamps. A vamp is the undead. A demon is close to the living dead, right? Practically related in my book. The best information we have is holy items, like holy water, crosses, and the occasional exorcism are the best weapons against a demon. So that's where we are. We've got an attack plan for the vamps, so if you only shoot the demons we won't have any problems, now will we?"

"Nope, no problems at all," I managed through gritted teeth. I wanted to say. *How about a silver bullet so I can shoot you, you prick?* But I didn't. Another gold star for me today!

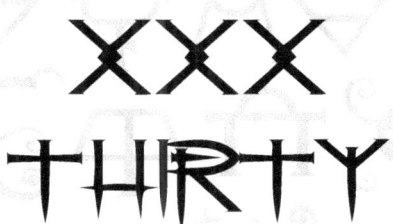

XXX
THIRTY

Cash was already handing out guns and clips to everyone.

Roul and Grayson had theirs. With the HK416s slung over their shoulders, they loaded up on clips and headed out the door.

The wolves came in pairs to get their weapons and ammo until all of them were armed and dangerous—even more so than usual for them. As they came and went, I started to notice a difference in the two packs here today.

Roul's wolves, while equally strong and deadly, had a more casual way about them. They came in quietly and politely, got their guns and gear and left. They all looked and dressed like bodyguards, but each had their own personal touch, like a piercing, a tattoo, or green hair.

Cash's pack mates, however, must have all been military at some point. Their identical haircuts and stance were a dead giveaway. High and tights came in pairs, stopping in front of Cash. Their legs were slightly spread, and their hands were behind their backs in the at ease position.

After they received their weapons, they made a sharp quarter turn and made their way back to their posts until they were ordered to leave.

The witches each took a USP Compact 9mm, but left the Eco and HK416s. They had their own weapons, and they weren't holy water or crosses.

Cash made his way over to me and handed me an XD Subcompact, an Eco, and one other gun that he didn't hand out to the rest of the group.

"I'd give you an HK416, but I hear you don't spend a lot of time at the range, so you get the Eco. And the XD has a short barrel. At 3" it'll have some kick, so if you do have to use it, just try to keep a tight hold on it." He handed me two clips for the XD. "You won't even use that much ammo for the XD, and you'd be dead before you unloaded the first clip, but take it anyways, just in case."

"Aw, gee, thanks. Now, could you stop saying shit like that? I mean, really, we all get it, okay. You don't have to keep telling us how dead we'll be and just how fast it will happen, okay?" I said.

I dropped the clips I wouldn't need into one of the large pockets on the side of my pant leg and waited for him to let me have it. He didn't. Instead, he handed me a very modern-looking shotgun. It was not at all similar to what I had seen at the station. Ours still had wooden stocks, the old-fashioned, double-barrel kind. Of course, we sawed ours down. Hey we're the cops, who's gonna turn us in? Besides, when you're faced with an angry vamp at close range, you usually want a big fucking hole in your enemy.

"Benelli M4 Super 90. You won't get too many shots with that so don't rely on it too much. The Eco is your primary weapon," Cash instructed.

That was all he said before he went back to his cases and started filling up his pockets with clips, grenades, and the IEDs.

Mahalia stepped forward. She held a small, teal satin pouch with gold cording and dark-blue velvet lining. She reached into it and held out a stone pendant dangling on a black-leather cord. The stone was a dark shade of green with bright red spots. Bloodstone, she called it.

"I have one for each of us," she said quietly. Looking to Olwyn, she said, "We took great care not to use silver clasps or fittings. Your wolves will have no trouble wearing these. These amulets will absorb your pain and injury. Like a sponge absorbs water, it will draw the pain away from your body. But take care. You may not realize how badly you are hurt while wearing it. It should speed the rate at which a vamp or were will heal and, for those of us not blessed by the Goddess with the natural ability to heal ourselves, it will keep us on the battle field a little longer."

She handed a pouch identical to her own to Olwyn who, after putting an amulet around her neck, went out to give them to the wolves. Mahalia handed the pouch to me and instructed me to take one stone and pass the pouch along. I slipped the amulet over my head, and Oberon pulled my hair through the cording. His hands brushed my neck and sent a thrill racing down my spine.

I handed the pouch to Baylen and noticed he wasn't carrying any guns. What would he do, I wondered? I still didn't know what his abilities were, but I was starting to get comfortable with the idea of having an angel, even a fallen one, on our side. Angels help cast out the devil and his followers, right? He ought to come in handy. Surely over the years he's crossed paths with a *disii* or two?

After we all had our amulets, Mahalia reached into the velvet pouch and called for Amalie. She pulled out the last Bloodstone and held it out to Amalie as she came down the stairs.

Amalie took the amulet, put it on, and turned to go back upstairs.

Mahalia laid a hand on her shoulder. "We have discussed this, Amalie. Arcana will heal. We cannot afford to leave you behind," Mahalia told her.

Amalie dropped her head. "Can't I just stay with her until my uncle comes to get her?" she asked.

"It's best if you don't. We will be leaving momentarily. Why don't you go outside with the others? I'll join you in a moment, and we will begin the prayer of protection," Mahalia said.

Amalie did as she was told, and the rest of the witches and wizards followed her, including my Oberon. There were more outside. I could feel them. Their power lingered in the air. It felt like the prelude of a summer storm, when the air is heaviest before the rain.

It was so quiet in the house now, with only Mahalia, Baylen, Cash, and I left.

Cash leaned against the mantle, feeling me up with his eyes, making me want to physically squirm as they raked up and down my body.

I suddenly felt like prey.

He looked at me like I was a rabbit in front of a greyhound, and he wanted to see if I could run. Cash raised an eyebrow and licked his lips.

That tingling feeling in my cheeks and excessive watering started in my mouth—two sure signs I was about to hurl. I can honestly say this was the first time a man made me want to literally throw up.

He had said we were lucky to have him but with the bad vibes he put out, I couldn't help thinking he was the lucky one—lucky he was on our side because otherwise he would certainly be getting an ass-whooping.

Baylen caught the last of Cash's tongue sliding across his lips, and it darkened his expression. Cash was just pissing everybody off. He really needed to work on his people skills.

"I believe your place is with the wolves," Baylen said to Cash.

"Fuck off! I don't answer to you. And I don't answer to that sorry excuse for a pack leader out there, either!" snapped Cash.

Baylen drew his hands into tight fists. The last thing I saw before the everything went dark was him shaking with rage. Black storm clouds rolled over the house, and thunder smashed above us. Lightning crashed down outside. The lightning was so close and so bright, it was like a flash grenade had detonated inside the house.

My eyes started tearing from the light, and when I blinked everything had that greenish blotch like from a camera flash, just a hundred times worse.

The lightning fell again, and this time I caught Cash's face in the flash of light. While he was trying to hide it, and not doing a bad job of it, I could still see the fear creeping into his eyes. He had completely misjudged Baylen.

Even though he might not be afraid of Roul, again a

misjudgment, he did fear Baylen. And while I found it interesting that Cash really thought Roul was his equal and not his superior, it was Baylen most of all that had me curious. Baylen was apparently a storm-bringer.

Cash backed down and backed up until he got to the front door without ever turning his back on Baylen.

Once the door clicked shut behind Cash, the dark clouds parted, letting the midday sun peak through. The air instantly felt lighter, making it easier to breathe, and the sun brought welcomed warmth back to the room.

"Well, Baylen, that was certainly one way to get him to leave," Mahalia said with amusement in her voice.

"It was better than what I had originally intended. I have no patience where that wolf is concerned," he stiffly replied.

She chuckled. "Oh, I'm not complaining. Though I fear Roul will have his hands full with that one."

"Yes, but that is Roul's problem for another day," Baylen said.

"Well, maybe the Black Dogs will eat him next and save us all the trouble," I said to them, almost cheerfully.

Baylen turned, giving me half a smile. "Perhaps."

He walked over to stand in front of the framed Michael Park's painting, *Gargoyles*, which was hanging above the couch. His wasn't a print like the one hanging above my bed. A soft click came from behind the frame, which I realized was on a hinge and swung out from the wall to reveal a safe. You always see those in movies. Who knew people really had them?

"It seemed a fitting choice, *Gargoyles*. They were meant to protect the castle or building upon which they were placed, so placing them over a safe seems fitting," Baylen didn't need to rationalize it to me. It would be a fitting piece to hang on any wall—safe behind it or not.

He opened the safe and pulled out something swaddled in dark-blue cloth. The cloth was old and worn around the edges. I had a pretty good idea of what was wrapped up in it. I guessed it to be about four inches across and maybe 37 inches in length.

When he finished peeling away the layers, my suspicions were confirmed. He held out a short sword, and it really was a beautiful piece of Celtic craftsmanship. Still holding the sword, Baylen let the weight of it turn his wrist. The sword lowered and gained momentum, humming as it sliced through the air.

Mahalia came to stand beside him.

"The Sword of Manannan, the Retaliator. It is yours now, and I believe you will find it more useful tonight than the guns Cash has provided." With one hand under the tip and another under the hilt, Baylen offered up the sword to me.

I reached out and took the simple and beautiful bone grip in my hands, half expecting to drop it. Having no prior experience with a sword, I thought it would be too heavy for me, but it wasn't. In fact, it felt like it was just the right weight and length for me. Aside from the bone grip, the sword was very traditional in design. You'd never guess there was anything spectacular about it.

As if reading my mind, Baylen began to tell me about the importance of this sword and the part it would play in our battle. "In the face of this sword, all strengths turn to weakness. No one can survive a wound from its blade. And it is with this sword that you will cut off Morrigan's head," he said, matter of factly.

In between laughs, I managed to get out "I'm sorry...I just thought you said...I had to cut off Morrigan's head. So, really, what did you say?"

I was wiping the tears of laughter from my eyes when he repeated verbatim what he had just said. He really expected me to cut her damned head off. There were a couple of major problems with this plan. A swordsman I most definitely wasn't and even if I were, I would still have to get close enough to her to strike the blow. And even if I could get close enough, I'd need an opportunity. Somehow I didn't think she would just stand there and let me cut off her head. I'm betting a goddess is just as attached to her head as the rest of us, especially if getting it chopped off would end her reign of terror.

"Why me? Why not you, or Mahalia, or anyone of the vamps? I'm willing to bet that anyone of the vamps is old enough to have actually used a sword in actual battle. Hell, Agrona could probably just rip her head off," I said.

Mahalia stepped closer to me. "I understand your apprehension, my dear, but it must be you, the goddess vessel. You are the only one who can strike the killing blow, the only one who can wield the sword of Manannan. For no other amongst us will the sword's magic work. Any of us could use the sword, but it would only be cold steel in our hands. It would not be The Retaliator. Baylen has been watching you for some time, we all have. He was certain it would be you. Admittedly, Agrona and I had our doubts, but that is of no consequence now. The point I am trying to make here, Maurin, is that this is your path. This is your destiny. You are the rebirth, and this task is meant for you. It must be completed by you."

My shoulders were immediately heavy with the weight of her words. It was impossible for me to believe my life had spiraled this far out of my control in just about twenty-four hours.

"Yesterday morning started out like every other morning. I didn't feel any different. And now, now I am a demi-goddess? How did this happen? Why did this have to happen to me? There is nothing spectacular about me. I don't have exceptional strength or beauty or anything to really set me apart. Shouldn't it have been a more extraordinary person in life before the rebirth?" I asked.

Mahalia looked at me with sage eyes. "So you say, Maurin, but there are others who would disagree. It is a heavy burden and a great deal that we ask of you now. I do not begrudge you that, but we ask it nonetheless. Take heart, Maurin, in the fact that she chose you. She is a wise and powerful goddess, and she chose you. So we all must trust in that, have faith in that." She looked at Baylen. "I want to check on Arcana once more before we leave. Mason should be here any minute to take her."

She reached out, laid her hand over mine that still held the sword, and whispered something unintelligible in Gaelic. With a gentle pat on my hand, she finished her prayer and went upstairs to check on her disciple.

XXXI
THIRTY-ONE

Baylen's confidence in me was unnerving. I was just starting to come to grips with everything, right up until he told me I was the one who had to chop off the head of a goddess—a war goddess, no less. My normal insecurities and fears took over.

"I don't really know what I am doing with this. I mean, I have no idea how to use it," I told him.

"Instinct and adrenaline, not to mention the likelihood that your power will take over. I had a back scabbard made for you. None of us expect you to go hacking your way through a sea of *disii* and *An ChaipBhais* to get to Morrigan. The rest of us will clear the way for you. But you must strike the final blow. That being said, please know that you are not alone in this battle, Maurin. You will not be alone," Baylen repeated.

I knew he was trying to comfort me and settle my nerves, but it wasn't helping. Nothing he said would make me feel better right now. I just needed a few minutes, well, maybe a few years, to absorb it all. Sending out a little prayer to anyone who was listening, I hoped he was right, that when the time came my powers would simply take over and without thought or fear I would be able to slay the "dragon".

Baylen went back to the safe and pulled out the black leather scabbard he had had made for me. He held it out.

With my right arm raised, I stepped into the scabbard. It slung over my shoulder and across my chest and back. I lifted the Retaliator and fumbled to slide the sword into the sheath. If I wasn't careful, I might cut my own head off. Adjusting my stance, I found my footing under the new weight on my back and ran my fingers along the smooth, hard leather now strapped across my chest. With any luck I didn't look as awkward as I felt.

Baylen started to speak, but I just held up my hand, giving him the universal sign for not right now. I walked away with the tip of the scabbard lightly tapping me on the back of my left thigh as I opened the front door and stepped out onto the porch. The witches and wizards were all gathered in the front yard waiting for Mahalia. Closing the door behind me, I leaned up against it, needing something to hold me up right now. Not from the physical weight of the sword, but the mental weight of it and the task that came with it.

Amalie and Oberon both stopped talking with the others and looked at me with very similar expressions of concern. They may not know why I had a sword strapped to my back, but it didn't take a genius to know that it probably wasn't a good thing.

The midday sun began its retreat from the sky and I did my best not to look at Oberon or Amalie. I didn't want to talk about chopping someone's head off, even if the head belonged to a goddess hell bent on killing me and everyone else here. Talking about it would make it real, and I much preferred to wait until there was nothing else to do but cut her head off to accept the reality of it.

Amalie looked like she was about to come over when the door opened and saved me from a conversation I didn't really want to have. Comforting words were useless, there was no way to make me feel better about what I had to do. Beheading someone was a violent and personal act. A verbal pat on the shoulder telling me it would be okay wasn't going to help me do it.

Mahalia breezed past me without a word, as if she knew what I was feeling, because she probably did. Without a word, her coven gathered around her, and awaited direction. Juno, Oberon, and Cicero stepped closer at the priestess's command. Phallon and Amalie fell back from the others as the circle tightened. Mahalia drew a short sword, or athame, from her waist. It had been hidden in the flowing fabric of the rich, chocolate-brown dress she now wore. She drew a wide circle around them with the tip of the small sword and then returned the athame to its place on her hip.

Without a compass to guide her, she turned to face true north. Cicero followed, turning to face east, then Juno to the south and Oberon to the west.

I inched closer, standing on the top porch step and watched their every movement.

Amalie and Phallon had moved closer to the porch and were within earshot. Amalie tried to explain what was about to happen.

"Each of the directions on a compass is directly related to an elemental power—north for earth, east for air, south for fire, and west for water. Facing the four directions to draw on the elements will add increased strength to a prayer or spell. They're about to begin a prayer of protection."

Mahalia began the prayer.

> *"The earth on axis turns, Air and wind will blow,*
> *The fire so brightly burns, Water will freely flow,*
> *Set about us your protective spirits, From all directions stand your guards.*
> *From all dangers, no matter what quarter, Whether from above or below keep us safe."*

"Around us, the God and Goddess are watching, may we do what is right, that they may protect us," the coven chorused.

Mahalia carved a circle into the earth. Ethereal fire burned in the trench made with her blade, golden flames licking and lapping at their feet, until with one great burst it rose up and out, passing over and through everything within sight.

I felt the power of the flame rush through me. It warmed me from the inside out, and then moved past me into the house. A golden hue lingered for only a moment in the wake of the flame, and then it was gone. The spell was cast.

Mahalia broke the circle, readying herself and her coven

for travel. They would teleport to Agrona's while I rode along with Baylen and the wolves. Mahalia called to the east, to the ancient ones and the winds came to her. The air moved around us, encircling the coven, followed by a thundering crack. Then they were gone.

XXXII
THIRTY-TWO

They would wait for us at the road that led to the long driveway of Agrona and Kedehern's castle. Cliché or not, they really live in a castle. Baylen came out as six black Denalis pulled up in front of the house. The trucks moved in a line, passing the porch until all of the SUVs were facing down the driveway to the road. The back doors of each truck opened and a wolf stepped out of each one, twelve in all, waiting for us to make our way to the vehicles. Baylen threw a small pack over his shoulder, took me by the arm, and led me down to the third SUV.

A beautiful wolf was standing by the rear passenger door. She had stark-white hair that was cut short in the back with long angled pieces in the front. The style complimented the angular features of her face. She looked too young to have such white hair, and I wondered if it was natural. Her white coat as a wolf must be beautiful.

"Mr. Knightley, you'll be riding in the second car. Maurin will be riding with us," the white wolf told him.

She motioned for him to go to the second SUV, but he

didn't budge. I watched as the muscles in her arms, fully sleeved with tattoos of wolves, flexed.

Baylen didn't back down. "That will not be happening. If there is not enough room for all of us to ride in this one, then I suggest you go up to the second truck. I will stay with Maurin."

There must have been something in the look he was giving her that said there would be no discussion because she went to the second truck after an intense stare-down between the two. She didn't seem too happy about it either, probably because she was now unable to stick to the dictated plan for our trip to Agrona's.

I grabbed ahold of the inside of the door and hoisted myself into the back seat. I slid in next to a wolf who had arms the size of my thighs and hair so black it almost looked blue.

He shot a quick glance in my direction and then went back to watching intently. It was almost as if he expected something to happen outside the truck.

Baylen closed the door, and we rolled forward.

We crawled about halfway down the driveway and then stopped. Out of the trees and surrounding woods lining Baylen's driveway came nine more wolves of varying shapes and sizes. They filled the last three trucks and we were on our way.

We turned left out of the driveway back out onto the main roads heading into town. I watched the street signs pass and tried not to dwell on the whole severed-head concern. We were making good time, already passing Salem Hospital. We'd reach Gallows Hill Park in no time.

Agrona and Kedehern had lived, or rather had been

undead, long enough to amass more money than the Massachusetts Lottery, and had bought Gallows Hill with their accumulated wealth. Nobody seemed to care if the park were privately owned, so long as it didn't turn into a parking lot. They'd had a large castle built on the edge of the park that towered above most of the surrounding buildings. It was weird to have a castle in Gallows Hill, but it was still better than some of the other plans that had been presented at the town hall meeting before construction began. I just don't appreciate abstract art sculptures. I don't think I ever will. So for me, a castle was a hell of a lot better than the modern-art garden some people wanted there.

We drove around the park to the vampire keep, and I took in the massive building. Made of large gray stones and mortar, the castle filled up the darkening afternoon sky. My eyes moved past the huge metal door. I can't blame them for not having a wooden one. No sense in having stakes made out of your own broken door just because you weren't a stickler for detail.

Two watchtowers topped the fortress. There were no windows to be found, just small arched slits in the stone that were originally designed for archers to shoot arrows through. It must have suited the vampires nicely, since it was well fortified and probably dark inside, extending the hours they could walk the halls of this place they called home. The only thing missing was a moat.

The caravan came to a stop and as soon as the doors opened, we were crushed by the sounds of weeping and groaning. As doors flew open on each SUV, the wolves stumbled out with hands clasped on their ears trying to soften the deafening cries. I did the same, but it didn't really do anything to help my freshly healed ear drum. I was glad hearing aides had come such a long way. I'd probably need one by the time this was all over. The pack spread out, searching for a woman I knew they would never see. With memories that were both mine and someone else's, I knew what she was.

"A *Caointeach*. Something's wrong. Something's very wrong in there," I whispered.

With the clarity of Scota's thoughts, I knew exactly what a *Caointeach* was. It was a spectral woman who weeps before death or heralds disaster. You never see her, only hear her presence in the most painful way. I feared she was here for both death and disaster today.

The closer we got to the castle, the stronger the sweet, metallic smell of blood was. The silence after I mentally reached out to Seamus sent my heart racing. Had the Morrigna gotten here before us? Where were Mahalia and her coven? My heart went from racing to a dead stop. Where was Oberon? They should have arrived before us. I called out for him, but couldn't even hear the sound of my own voice over the wails of the *Caointeach*. The wolves moved to the front, sides, and back of Baylen and me. We moved like a battalion, with two scouts in the front creeping forward through the lawn to secure the position. With sharp, short motions and hand signals, they moved us closer and finally we came up to the massive front door that was cracked open. There was no sign of forced entry, so someone must have come to answer the door. But who would that be if it were not Seamus? The vamps would have been dead to the daytime world. I doubted they would rise to answer the front door, even if it was almost dusk. Some of the older vamps could rise before full dark, but Agrona and Kedehern were too territorial for any of the really old vampires to live here. So if the two of them were not awake, then it had to have been Seamus who opened the door. And he didn't seem to be anywhere around.

We walked into a large, open room too big to be called a foyer. A pair of grand stone staircases, one on either side of the back wall, led upstairs, meeting at the top to create a landing overlooking the expansive room in which we were standing. There was an arched doorway on the left and right side of the room, leading to separate wings of the castle and there was a staircase leading into the bowels of the vampire lair. The thick walls of the castle deadened the sound of the *Caointeach*, and we could finally converse at a normal level again.

Roul stepped forward and began to break off the group. We would need to separate and search the castle to find everyone. Cash took four wolves from his own pack and headed upstairs. Always the alpha, Roul took charge, instructing two more groups of four to take a wing and search it top to bottom. The two groups, one going right and the other left, were each made up of two of Roul's wolves and two of Cash's. Roul shot down Cash's suggestion to break off into groups by pack.

I didn't care if Roul and Olwyn kept an eye on Cash, so long as they had one to spare for everything else.

Roul led the remaining wolves, plus Baylen and I, down the steps to where I assumed the vampires slept. We moved cautiously down the narrow, stone stairs. It was dark down here, but not as dark as the tomb I had been in, so no one in our group would have trouble seeing. None of us were human. I had been when I went to work yesterday—albeit a psychic, but I had still been mostly human. Those days were long gone now.

Roul stayed with Baylen and me as the rest of wolves moved up and down the hallway, trying all the doors. All of them were locked. There was no sign of a struggle down here, no strewn furniture or busted down doors. So where was everyone? How does a whole castle full of vampires just disappear?

XXXIII
THIRTY-THREE

A loud whistle came from upstairs, and we moved quickly and quietly back up the steps. Cash and Olwyn were waiting for us at the top of the stairs. The four groups searching the top level of the castle were clustered around the entrance to the left wing. We moved over to where they were standing. Roul pushed his way through the crowd. If it was bad enough to shake up the wolves, to make them break rank and forget to move out of the way of their pack leader, I wasn't sure I wanted to see what they'd found, but I couldn't shake the feeling that I had to.

Baylen and I were struggling to stay on Roul's heels when we broke through the crowd and almost stumbled into the first room. The smell of blood and meat hit us hard. I couldn't hold back the cough. The smell wasn't sweet and metallic now. It was more like the smell of decaying meat. If you've never smelled decaying flesh before, the closest thing I can compare it to is rotten ground beef covered in simple syrup. I held my arm over my nose and mouth, burying my face in my elbow in effort to prevent my mouth and throat from getting coated with the sickly sweet taste of death on the inhale.

The room was decorated with medieval style furnishings, four heavy, wooden benches, two lining each of opposite walls. Empty of any furniture, a long narrow rug divided the middle of the room from back to front. A few tapestries hung on the walls, but most of the space was still bare stone. The design on the tapestries and the runner was intricate and while the room was sparsely furnished, it still managed to look elegant. There were two high-backed chairs at the end of the room, and I realized that this was Agrona and Kedehern's throne room. I always thought of King and Queen as more of a title, but after seeing the throne room I decided I still had a lot to learn about vamp politics.

A door on the side of the throne was broken down off its hinges and blocked the doorway. Roul pushed the door out of the way, and we moved into another dimly torch-lit corridor with more rooms branching off of it. The floor of the corridor was covered in tacky, semi-dried blood. We followed a trail of blood to a room about halfway down on the right. I battled with myself about how much I did and didn't want to know whose blood it was as we stopped just outside the doorway.

Did I really want to go inside? Now that I was here I wasn't so sure, but it was too late to turn back. Still, I wasn't going to chicken out in front of all these people. I didn't ever see this kind of thing at work. Of course, I had seen my share of death inside someone's head and in crime scene photos, but never in person. I never had to experience the smell, the sight, and the taste all at one time.

My stomach was already roiling, and I hadn't even made it inside the room yet.

It was an interior room with no windows, and it was dark except for the sparse light creeping in from the hallway. We didn't need or want any more light in the room because what little existed was already too much. Medea hissed as she saw us. If it were any brighter in here, she would have gone insane. I could see what was in front of me just fine, but processing it mentally was a whole different thing. I blinked hard a couple of times, and every time I opened my eyes the same horrible sight was in front of me. Medea was staked to the wall, but not through her heart obviously, since she was still not dead. Though she hasn't been alive for a couple hundred years, 'not dead' was still the best way to describe her right then.

Rage and hunger filled her eyes and face. If we let her down off that wall, she would have ripped us to shreds. There wasn't a wolf that could stop her this far into her blood lust. More than hungry, she was injured and would need to feed in order to heal it. Her hiss turned to a low growl as she smelled us walk into the room, and I jumped. Medea smelled fresh meat and not the rot that filled the air before we walked in. She started thrashing her body against the wall, doing even more damage to herself in the process. Baylen pushed up his sleeve and walked closer to Medea.

I grabbed ahold of his arm and tried to pull him back. "What the hell are you doing? She'll tear your damn arm off if she doesn't bleed you dry first!"

"We need something to slack her hunger so we can get her down off the wall. I cannot, and will not, leave her hanging there!" Baylen shouted.

"I'm not saying we should leave her hanging there, but there has got to be a better way than this. What if she takes too much, what then? You're no good to anybody dead," I reminded him.

"She won't. There is still some control left in her. She will not take any more than she needs to keep that control. She'll heal a little before finding better prey. And I am certain that Olwyn can heal any wound that Medea might accidentally inflict on me," Baylen said.

There was no stopping him now. He moved forward and then took two big steps to his left in order to avoid something on the floor. I focused on the object he had sidestepped and realized it wasn't something—it was someone. And judging by the size of him, I knew exactly who it was.

It was Seamus, left crumpled on the floor, his body broken and twisted. Roul moved closer to where Seamus lay and, using his foot, pushed Seamus onto his side. There was a loud sticky sound as Seamus's bloody body broke suction with the cold stones. His throat was ripped out, and his body was slashed and mutilated. They had consumed some of his flesh after they had killed him. The image of what had happened here still hung in the air, and I could pick up on all of it. I fought back the stomach acid making its way up and succeeded only because it had been a while since I had eaten.

Hate flowed through me. And, as if someone had flicked a switch inside me, I suddenly could not wait to chop off that bitch's head. Being angry was good. Being angry would keep me from being sad. Right now, I couldn't be sad or think about the fact that maybe I could have been nicer to

Seamus in the short time I had known him. Anger would keep me from feeling regret. It would prevent me from wishing he had never shown up in the interrogation room yesterday morning.

I welcomed the anger because we were old friends. Anger and I went way back. It's an emotion I am pretty comfortable with, since I spent most of my time as a young adult being angry for being different and for the disappointments of my childhood—for being lonely and let down. I tried hard to let it all go, to be the bigger person, and on most days I succeed. However, when I do get hurt or really pissed off, I am haunted by all of those old feelings again. Slipping back into my anger was like putting on those favorite old pajamas. They're worn and torn, and you wouldn't let anyone see you in them, but damn they were comfortable and easy to be in.

Slipping into that anger like a comfortable winter coat, my body came alive with adrenaline and power, practically humming with energy. I was also beginning to realize a new use for my favorite emotion. It can be blinding to the senses. When I let the rage take me, it deafened me to the sounds of Medea licking and slurping at Baylen. It seemed wrong to let my senses be deadened, though. Wrong because I know in his last moments of consciousness, Seamus was probably hearing those same sounds. Except it was his flesh that was being eaten, and his own blood that was being drained. I tried to push that thought from my mind and focused on Baylen instead.

"Enough!" he cried.

She was going to drain him. I knew it. Staked to a wall, the vampire suffered numerous injuries, and was forced to watch as the *disii* killed and fed upon Seamus. Taunted and tormented by his blood being spilled, Medea's need was too great, and she was too far gone to stop herself. It didn't matter she would never have wanted to hurt Baylen. All she cared about now was the blood that would save her, and she would take as much as she could.

"Medea, enough!" Baylen shouted.

Baylen was not going to get through to her. I don't care how many times he told her to stop or called her name, it wouldn't matter to her.

Roul rushed forward, grabbed hold of the stake sticking out of her chest, and pulled.

Medea hissed in pain and as she did, released her grip on Baylen's arm.

He fell to the floor and with what little strength he had, he managed to push himself away from her.

I reached out and dragged him back to me as Roul struggled with Medea on the floor.

Medea managed to get her head raised high enough and with her mouth open and fangs out like a snake, she struck, barely missing Roul's forearm.

"We're going to need another donor in here, Maurin! Even after drinking Baylen almost dry she still thirsts, but we can't turn her loose to hunt. What if she stumbled upon an innocent first? More blood on our hands? No, it must be someone here," Roul said.

"Don't look at me! She's not sinking those fangs into any part of my body. How about Cash?" I asked innocently enough.

Roul laughed. "As much as I would like to throw him in her clutches, I don't think we can afford to have him on the disabled list."

He called for a wolf named Piet. Piet knew what had to be done, and he silently walked over to Roul and Medea. He sat down and gave her his arm. A small wince was his only show of discomfort as he tried to give me a reassuring glance.

"I've done this before, don't worry about it," he said to me.

"I wouldn't have pegged you for food," I replied, genuinely surprised that any wolf would let a vamp feed from him.

Most weres didn't like vamps all that much. Oh they tolerated each other and managed to share territories, but feeding? That was a whole different thing, and you'd be hard-pressed to find any wolf that would admit to serving as vamp food. Wolves were too high on the food chain themselves for anything to feed off of them normally.

"I'm not cattle. Just because this is *your* first time kicking the shit out of some demons, that doesn't mean the rest of us are novices. This isn't our first go round at protecting our way of life. Besides, a witch could never feed a vamp like this. Not if she wanted to live to tell about it. A wolf, or any shifter for that matter, can heal fast enough to keep from passing out or dying. But let's just get some things straight right now. I wouldn't let this scavenger feed off me at any other time. I am not a caged wolf. Got it?" Piet said.

"Got it," I said. I guess he had told me.

Olwyn came in just then, and I had never been so glad to see her. She was the healer for her pack. There was a huge difference between wolves and vamps, so she'd be of no use to Medea, but maybe she could help Baylen. He was so confident she could but after getting a good look at his arm, I wasn't so sure. She got to work, bandaging his torn skin.

I am sure Medea would have left two very discreet vampire bites had she not been so taken by her bloodlust, but in her current state she had ravaged his arm. Vampires have a coagulant in their saliva to quickly stop the bleeding once they pull back from a bite. This wasn't a simple bite, though. This was a jagged gaping wound. It had slowed the bleeding but hadn't stopped it, and the coagulant wouldn't piece Baylen's arm back together.

Olwyn pulled more bandages out of her small pack and continued to wrap his arm. The white cotton gauze quickly turned red. It looked like Baylen would bleed to death right there on the floor. A normal person would have blacked out by now from all of the blood loss, but Baylen wasn't a normal person. He was a Blue Man of the Minch, and this wound shouldn't kill him. The bandages Olwyn wound around his arm would hold him together until the bleeding completely stopped and the tissue started to regenerate. It would heal, but would his arm ever be the same? Would he have a scar or a deformity from the muscles being torn? Would he heal like a vamp or a were? Maybe neither. I didn't know enough about what Baylen was to even guess. None of that was really important. The only thing that mattered was that he would survive.

XXXIV
THIRTY-FOUR

There was a scratching sound near my feet like fingernails on a chalk board. I fought the urge to jump, and won. The scratching continued and was now chorused with the sound of a foot shuffling, pushing on the stone floor. Without looking down, I knew what was making that sound.

"Roul! He's not dead! Seamus isn't dead!" I shouted.

Seamus's movement was jerky and stiff as if his bones were fused together at the joints. There was a horrible cracking and as I watched him try to stand, it reminded me of one of those black and white mummy movies.

"That is not Seamus rising up off that floor, Maurin," Roul said.

"Yes, it is, Roul. I am watching him get up off the floor. It's him!" I moved toward him. What the hell did he mean it wasn't Seamus? He was looking right at him, and so was I for that matter.

Roul yelled for me to stop, and the fierceness in the Alpha's voice held me in place. I was glad I listened, because as soon as Seamus's head rotated around and I got a good look at those white filmy eyes, I knew what he meant.

"Oh, for fuck's sake, Roul! Why couldn't he turn into something normal like a vamp or a were? A demon, a fucking *demon*?" I shouted.

Baylen drew back from Olwyn, who had just finished the bandages on his arm. Blood was already seeping through the top layer of the white gauzy bandage again, but he got up and stood by me anyway. Guess he didn't heal as fast as the vamps or weres, or even me. He looked at me with pain vivid in his eyes.

"Draw your sword," he said.

I didn't move.

"Even if we could leave him like this, would you really want to? Would you curse him to be nothing more than a walking corpse? He was a good friend and a good man," Baylen said.

Of course he was right. Goose bumps ran up and down my arm as I slid the sword out of its scabbard. If I thought beheading Morrigan was bad, I was wrong. This was so much worse. I liked Seamus. Granted, it was only yesterday that I had been slightly bitter at him for dragging me into this shit storm, but I still liked him. He was nice to me and stupid as it sounds, I usually liked people until they weren't nice to me.

I lifted the sword above my head and couldn't bring myself to lower it down onto the back of his neck. The creature had managed to get up on all fours and that would have been as good a position to cut someone's head off as I could ask for, but I just couldn't do item mind couldn't separate the physical Seamus from the spiritual one. Baylen tried his best to encourage me to do what had to be done.

"It's not him in there, Maurin. I wouldn't, not for one second, ask you to do this if I thought even a piece of him was in there. Not if there was even the slightest chance that we could save him. But we can't. He's gone. He was gone before we even got here." The urgency and volume of his voice was increasing. "Do it, Maurin, do it now!" Baylen yelled.

"If you are going to fucking yell at me, then you can do it yourself!" I shouted back at him as I thrust the Retaliator deep into Seamus's back. Blood, thick and cold, splattered my neck and face.

The thing that had taken over his body thrashed on the floor as I pulled the blade out of his back. His body rose up off the floor with the blade. Once more I raised the sword. This time I shoved the blade hard and deep into the flesh until the tip of the sword sparked against the stone floor and the hilt smacked against Seamus's back. As fast as I drove the sword in, I pulled it back out, stumbling backward and gasping for breath. The flesh began to smoke and ooze, leaking a putrid smell. Sweat and tears mixed with the splattered coagulated blood, thinning it enough so that it began to run down my face.

"Forgive me," I whispered.

That was it. That was the moment it all hit me. From psychic to psychopath, what a slippery slope. Looking around the room at the broken antique furniture, at the blood and gore that covered the stone walls and floor and nearly everyone in the room, I wondered how I had gone from psychic investigator to the slayer of evil things and how I could go back to my regular life. Part of me wanted desperately to go back to the drab rooms and bad coffee the police department offered up to me every day. But part of me, from the moment the blade broke through the first layer of skin knew this is who I truly was.

I *was* different, and no matter how much I dressed like them, worked with them, and acted like them, I would never be the same as they were, never really be normal. This was the world I belonged to, as strange and unusual as it was. I fit here better than the little niche I had carved out for myself in everyday life. It should have upset me more to finally realize this, but it didn't. The emptiness I expected to feel after realizing the life I had worked so hard to make for myself was gone and never should have been mine in the first place didn't come. Standing there in the dark room with an ancient godly sword in my hand, and splattered in the blood of a demon that stole the body of my friend, I finally felt complete.

XXXV
THIRTY-FIVE

Medea was finished with Piet, who lay slumped against the wall next to her. He wasn't dead, but he wouldn't be any good to us for a while. Medea stood and wiped the blood from her mouth with the back of her hand. Her eyes were glassy, and her movements were sluggish. She looked drugged, if you could drug a vampire, which you can't. I think she was just high on Piet.

"Agrona wants you to release her," Medea said. Her words were slurred. We could barely understand what she said. She stumbled, and Roul was there to catch her.

"There's no one else here, we looked, and we only found you and Seamus," Roul told her. His voice dropped as he said Seamus's name.

Seamus had meant a lot to everyone here in this room, that was obvious enough. I was glad they couldn't see the things I had seen, like the way he died and exactly how they had turned him into the gruesome creature I had just killed.

Since I had never been to a crime scene in person before—there was never a need since I read people and not things, and people don't usually hang around the scene of the crime—I wondered if I could have always seen things so easily. Could I have seen without having to touch someone or something, or was it an enhancement to the skills I already had? I guess it doesn't really matter now, I would have preferred not knowing I could do it at all.

"She's calling for you. Can't you hear her?" Medea giggled. "Oh, right, you can't. She's in the catacombs. Come on, you'll never find it by yourself."

She was definitely high on Piet. Disgusting. The inebriated vampire pressed forward with Roul on her arm. We went back out into the hallway, through the throne room, and out into the large foyer. We passed the large group of wolves that had gathered there, Cash included.

We followed her single-file down the stairway. When we reached the bottom, she walked to the wall in front of her and pushed on a spot half-way down the wall. With a click it slid open. Medea slipped her fingers in the large crack and pushed the wall, that was actually a door, the rest of the way open. She was right—we would never have found this on our own.

Another set of steps. This set was narrower than the last, and the stones were old and worn. We made our way down to a small, dark room. It was cold, with no furniture —just a doorway. Medea walked through it, calling out for Baylen.

"None of the wolves will be able to get them out. You'll have to do it," she said.

Baylen brushed by me. I could barely see him pull the gun out of the shoulder holster he wore. He held his gun in one hand and a small Maglite in the other. The silver crosses strapped around the coffins gleamed, casting light out into the pitch darkness of the room. I couldn't help thinking that if he was just going to use a gun, then the wolves could've easily done that. They couldn't touch the silver obviously, but shoot it? Yeah, well, anyone of us could have done that.

Four flashes and pops of the gun later Agrona burst through her coffin. They had chained her, Kedehern, and the rest of her sleeping vampires in their coffins with silver chains and crosses. They had used silver so the wolves would not be able to remove the chains and crosses so the vampires would be unable to free themselves.

Clever. The city had built an enormous prison, paid dearly in tax revenue for the dwarves to build it, made deals with the witches to enchant it, and now we discover that all they needed were some silver chains and crosses on a coffin to hold the few vampires we had caught. Typical. The vampires were so very good at not getting caught that the vamp cell was almost always empty. I knew of only two vamp prisoners in the entire three years I had worked in the precinct.

Rage burned across Agrona's face as she looked at all of us. Baylen and Roul both seemed puzzled. Shouldn't she have been relieved we had finally freed them? I shot a quick glance at Olwyn. The knowing look she returned told me she had come to the same conclusion. Agrona was a proud vampire. The fact that she had to be rescued at all was enough to infuriate her. She turned at lightning speed and ripped the chains from Kedehern's coffin, her skin burning as some of the crosses touched her. The chains had barely slipped from her grasp before he broke through the coffin.

Maybe now they would finally give up sleeping in those damned things. It seemed so cliché to me anyway. Why not just sleep in a bed?

She moved around the room shouting curses as she broke the chains from the remaining coffins. The silver-toned flesh on her palms was black and charred. She would heal the burns quickly enough, but her beautiful skin would be forever scarred from the crosses. Shiny, new scar tissue had already formed under the blackened, broken skin on her palms. I knew if Agrona had her way, the Triad would pay dearly for this little souvenir. So far the vampires were the only ones calling Morrigan and her sisters the Triad. Everyone else referred to them as the Morrigna.

Kedehern ordered the vampires to go feed. They would need their strength. He glided over to his Queen, wrapping his arm around her shoulder, and she seemed to ease into him. She instantly calmed, and I was starting to wonder if it wasn't some sort of power he had. Was he the calm before her storm? With Agrona temporarily sedated in his arms, he looked to Baylen for answers.

"It would seem that the Triad has been busy. By the looks of you, Agrona and I have missed the battle entirely. Where is Mahalia? Why isn't she here with you?" Kedehern asked.

Oh shit, where were they? Somewhere between the *Caointeach*, finding Medea staked to a wall, seeing Seamus dead on the floor, and then having to kill the demon that had stolen his body, I had completely forgotten the coven had never made it. After remembering they weren't here waiting for us like they should have been, panic set in. Oberon was with them, and if the coven had befallen a similar fate as Seamus and Medea, then that meant Oberon had as well.

Kedehern was still asking questions about everything that had happened since he left us at Baylen's, but most of his questions had to do with why we were all covered with so much blood. Well, Baylen would just have to answer them. I didn't have time to stand here and play twenty questions. I had a whole coven to find.

With the sword still covered in Seamus's blood, I ran out of the room, back up the steps, out of the catacombs, and onto the next flight of steps leading back to the foyer where I smashed in to Cash. He was on his way down to see the vampire Queen and her King.

I was sure everyone down there would be thrilled to see him. I know I was. If we were lucky, Agrona would feed from him.

"Whoa, slow down. You're like a fucking barbarian, charging up the steps with that sword! You damn near chopped my arm off!" Cash said.

"Aw, too bad I missed. Move!" I said.

He did and mumbled something about me being a stupid bitch under his breath. At any other time, I would have shot back something witty and insulting, but I didn't have time to waste talking to that prick so I kept on moving. I was going to check every inch of this God forsaken place! I didn't care that both packs had already searched and given a very official "all clear". They weren't really looking for a witch or wizard, now were they? It was possible they had missed something, anything that would give us a clue as to where Oberon was. And the rest of the

coven, of course. If they had missed something, then I
would find it.

XXXVI
THIRTY-SIX

Barreling through the foyer and up the last set of stairs to the second floor, I searched each room. All eight bedrooms, an office, a parlor, and a small library. I pulled pillows and sheets off the beds and looked underneath each one, ripped cushions off chairs and looked in the closets and drawers. There was nothing up here. Not a single charm, scrap of clothing, or strand of hair. Nothing. But there wasn't any sign of blood or a struggle either, and that had to be a good sign. Of course, now that I was done ransacking the place, it looked like there had been a robbery.

Out of breath from running around like a lunatic, I stopped at the bottom of the stairs and tried to get my thoughts together. Deep down, I knew I wouldn't find anything. If they had been here when the demons came, then there would have been a bloody mess like we'd found downstairs. Someone would have seen something because I highly doubt the demons would have been able to take the entire coven without a trace. There would have been bodies or something. I told myself since there were none of these, since there was no trace of them at all, everything would be fine. They hadn't made it here on time for some other reason, and they were fine, all of them.

Tired of holding the Retaliator, I went to put the sword back in the scabbard and remembered it was covered with dried blood. I tried to wipe it off on my pants with no luck. The blood wasn't coming off without some water and scrubbing. *Hell with it.* Slipping the sword back into the scabbard, I walked outside for some fresh air and sat on the steps in front of the huge metal door.

It was a cool night and felt like rain. I closed my eyes and took in a deep breath of the clean fall air, picturing Oberon beside me, my head on his shoulder instead of on my fists. I wanted to hear him tell me everything would be okay, that I would be able to sleep at night without reliving stabbing Seamus to death, because I feared what I might see in my dreams. My guilt wouldn't let it be just a demon. No, it would be Seamus every time I fell asleep and my dreams took me back to the bloody room.

I opened my eyes and tried to focus on something, a tree, the moon growing brighter as darkness swept the sky, anything to stop thinking about Oberon. My gaze rolled over the grass and down the hill to a line of trees in the distance. I stared so hard and so long that the trees began to move. I closed my eyes, hoping they would refocus once I opened them, but the trees were still moving. Something was actually moving down there!

I shot to my feet like a rocket. What the hell was that? My eyes never left the tree line that was slowly closing the distance between us. I focused a little more intently. Maybe

I was simply overtired and seeing things that weren't really there. There was a light breeze. Perhaps it had caught the leaves on the trees and made them look as if they were moving. Still, the dark line kept moving out of the trees and onto the grassy field that lay between us. As they loomed closer, shapes began to appear like fuzzy figures in the dark. They weren't moving at a supernatural speed, just a normal walking pace. I turned to run and get someone, but stopped short as a thought came to me.

Stumbling as I spun around, almost forgetting I was on the front steps, I watched the figures that continued to walk toward me. Watched as their six shapes took form. Six, it was six people coming. Six? It had to be them. Oberon had to be with them! My feet were moving, closing ground as someone yelled for me to stop. It was Cash, whom I'd assumed had been told to take his big nose back upstairs.

"You don't know it's them, Maurin. It could be a trap, you dumb broad. Stop!" Cash shouted.

The vampires were awake, and there were enough wolves here that I would have plenty of time to turn and hightail it back to the castle so I didn't stop. There was more cursing, most of it involving my name and Cash shouting for Roul. I knew it pissed him off to call the Alpha for help. That was just an added bonus. My pace slowed a little as the ground began to slope down. There was no sense in ruining the moment by falling down the damned hill.

When I was close enough to see his beautiful face, I stopped just to watch him walk toward me. Relief washed over him, and his body visibly relaxed when he saw me.

Until he was close enough to see the blood, that is. He stopped only a few feet away from me, and his relief was quickly replaced with worry. I must admit I went a little weak at the knees knowing he was worried about me. Nothing compares to knowing your feelings are reciprocated this early in a relationship. Mahalia, Phallon, Juno, Amalie, and Cicero came to stand beside us.

Cicero spoke for the first time since I'd met him outside of his casting a spell. "Warding spell! We couldn't land after we teleported. We were stuck in between Baylen's and here, so we were forced to change our destination. We had to land back at the hospital." Cicero's voice was a little scratchy, and I thought maybe it was because he hardly ever used it.

"Yeah, and then we had to walk all the way here!" Juno piped in.

Amalie cut her off. "It was a strong one, too, because we couldn't break it. A warding spell is used to keep things away. They are used to ward something off—namely us! Mahalia thinks it was cast here. The *An ChaipBhais* had to have been…" She trailed off, distracted by my appearance. "Hey! What happened to you? For goddess' sake, Maurin, you've got blood all over your face and neck!"

"It's not mine." I said flatly. "Baylen or Roul can fill you in. Or maybe Medea. I haven't even heard what happened before we got here. Some of it we've figured out, some of it I could see when we walked into the room and stepped in the blood, and some of it I did, but Medea can tell you how it started. So ask her first. She'll know how the demons got in."

Amalie seemed excited. "The demons were here? So

Mahalia was right, the spell was—"

I cut her off this time. "Amalie, really, I can't. Please, they'll explain everything to you. I just, I just need a few minutes."

She looked hurt as they all started to walk up to the vampires' dwelling. She walked past me, and I grabbed her arm lightly.

"I am glad that you're here and that you're okay. I was worried sick, really," I reassured her.

I left out the part about the slight delay in realizing they weren't here yet. I didn't really see the point in bringing that up now.

She smiled, gave me a quick hug, and sped up to catch the rest of the group.

All but Oberon. He stayed with me at the bottom of the hill. He held my cheek with one hand and tenderly brushed the hair out of my face with the other.

I leaned my head against his hand, and he leaned in for a kiss. He had to bend down, so I stepped up on my tiptoes to meet him. Oberon's mouth crashed into mine, and I kissed him back with equal fervor. His lips were soft, and his breath was sweet and warm on my face. We stood there kissing at the bottom of the hill, and every bad thing that had occurred up to that moment washed away. The tears of relief I had been holding back since I first realized it was him slipped out, running down my cheeks, hitting his thumb and running down the palm of his hand. Pulling away from the kiss, he looked at me, knowing all too well the worry and panic I'd experienced during his absence because he felt the same way. He pulled me into his arms and held me tight. My arms encircled his waist, holding on for dear life, afraid he'd disappear.

It felt good to be held physically, but even better to have someone who wants to comfort you emotionally. I had forgotten how much intimacy I was missing, being alone the last couple of years. The long, miserable dry spell that was my love life seemed to be coming to an end. It's funny how independent you can become. After a while you tell yourself you don't need anybody at all. You're fine on your own. Thing is, if that was true and I didn't need anybody, then would I feel this relieved to have found someone and this excited at the prospect of a new relationship? This worried when I didn't know where he was? I had all but convinced myself I didn't need anyone before Oberon entered my life.

I was surprised at how well we fit given the height difference, but his arms seemed like they were made to hold me. His chin rested gently on the top of my head, and my cheek nuzzled into his chest. We held each other and for those few moments, everything seemed right with the world, like nothing could touch us. He kissed the top of my head and pulled back from our embrace. I knew it was time to go back, that we had lingered here together too long, but I didn't care. No one up at the top of that hill would make me feel bad for wanting to stay here with him instead of rushing back up to the Spanish inquisition that waited for me. Maybe Medea and Baylen had told them enough and they would leave me alone. Doubtful. Oberon must have known that, given the choice, I would much rather stay here with him. However, he took my hand and led the way back up the hill to the gruesome scene of Seamus's murder.

He still didn't know what had happened. So, even if

everyone else already had their answers, I would still have to tell him about Seamus and Medea, not to mention what I had been forced to do. I didn't really see the point in waiting until we got up there, so I told him everything as we walked back up the hill to the courtyard. Without interruption, Oberon let me deliver my awful monologue, taking in every detail, thinking it over and holding his questions until the end.

He only had one. "How did the *disii* manage to take the vampires by surprise? Medea and Seamus came here to warn Agrona and Kedehern. Shouldn't they have been waiting for an attack?"

I looked at him without an answer for the only question now gnawing at both of us and said the only thing I could. "The only person left who can answer that is Medea. The *disii* were gone before we found them."

"Well, then, let's go ask her. I'd be willing to bet it's one of two things though," Oberon said.

"And they are?" I asked.

"Either Medea and Seamus interrupted the *disii* in their attempt to sack the castle, or the error was just plain arrogance on Agrona's part," he said.

"Well, I doubt very much it was the first. It wasn't even close to dawn when Seamus and Medea left. I don't think the *disii* would be dumb enough to come here before the vamps were dead for the day, even if the *An ChaipBhais* was with them," I told him.

"I hope it's not arrogance on her part that cost Seamus his life but, knowing Agrona, she would think they were all safe inside the castle walls. She wouldn't have expected the *An ChaipBhais*. A few *disii*, the black dogs maybe, but not a small army of them. Anything less than what it seems the Morrigna sent, and they probably could have held them off until we got here. It would have taken several *disii* to ward the grounds and hold it for that long. And then several more to trap that many vampires, never mind staking Medea and killing Seamus," he said.

"But I thought Agrona and Kedehern were this fierce, terrible force together. I mean, Carnage and the Battle Lord? With names like those, names that they earned from humans, it seems as if she's got a little bit of a right to be arrogant," I chuckled.

"Speed, strength, and an insatiable appetite for the blood of your enemy do not make you a military mastermind. This is a war goddess we're talking about, not a bunch of medieval villagers with torches and pitchforks. They should have been expecting more. Maybe Seamus would still be alive if they had," Oberon said grimly.

I wondered how long it would take to stop seeing the sword rip through Seamus's back and down through his chest every time someone said his name. I was hoping it would be soon, but betting on it being never.

XXXVII
THIRTY-SEVEN

By the time we reached the top of the hill, Mahalia was already beginning a cleansing spell. She was going to try and lift the ward. The smell of salt and sage, mixed with other herbs I couldn't quite name, hung in the air.

Oberon pulled me to a stop. I was about to cross and break the circle that went completely around the castle. She must have used a massive amount of salt and herbs to outline the circle she now stood in. As I stood outside her circle, I found myself more than a little curious about how they carried around all this stuff. It's not like you ever saw them with a suitcase or anything.

Standing right next to the edge of the circle, I could almost make out the rest of the ingredients. I recognized flax and caraway seeds, but there was something else there too. If I remembered to do so later, I'd have to ask what that other one was. Mahalia's voice bellowed around us.

> *"About this house, establish your place of warding. Remove those placed before your own.*

Stand watchfully at the corners.
Be a shield between this house and all that have worked evil against this place.
Guard this land and all that claim its protection.
Here, on the border, I ask you stand watch.
Offering not only words, but gifts placed before your marker.
Watcher on the border, the steward of this land offers this grain to you.
Undo the evil set about this house.
For you are the watcher and only your ward shall stand."

The ground hummed gently at first, but then it grew stronger and somehow larger. From beneath Mahalia, the spell rippled out through the ground like liquid beneath my feet. The ground moved, not like hard packed earth, but like disturbed water after someone throws a stone in a pond, with ripples moving out in rings from where the stone broke the surface. It kept spreading out from under her. There was a deep gonging sound, both low and rich, that resonated through my body. The humming had grown to a strong vibration, and was now almost a violent shaking. As far as I knew, there wasn't a fault line anywhere near here, so this earthquake-like shuddering was all Mahalia's doing.

It lasted only a minute, and I was pretty sure it didn't extend beyond the park grounds and into town. If it was anything other than Mahalia, power lines would be down and the town should look dark from up here by now, but it didn't. As far as everyone else knew, all was right with the world. The lights still twinkled throughout the town, undisturbed, unaware. It would be nothing short of a miracle if we could keep it that way.

Even though I couldn't see anything, I knew Mahalia was finished and the watchtowers were raised. The watcher had taken up residence. Through him, Mahalia had lifted one ward and replaced it with her own. This ground, and all who stood on it, were safe from harm. That is, until they left it. She had called to a watcher and, if properly honored, they would protect your land from border to border. They would protect you as long as you were on that land, but they couldn't keep you safe once you crossed the border of the protected grounds. The circle of salt and herbs was all but gone, absorbed into the ground. Only a few glimmers remained, which meant the watcher had accepted the offering.

She turned to me. "Now that that's out of the way, why don't we continue with the timeline? We've been working our way backward through the day's events. We seem to be caught up to when you arrived with Baylen and the packs. We didn't want Medea to begin without the two of you."

She looked at Oberon inquisitively, asking with her eyes if he knew everything that had happened while they had been forced to abandon their magic for a more human mode of travel.

He nodded, telling her he knew everything without ever saying a word.

"Well then, Medea, if you would?" she asked, and everyone waited to hear the rest of Medea's story.

Medea stepped forward to answer Mahalia. The

vampire moved slower than she had before, and I wasn't sure if she was actually nervous or still wounded. Either way, she began to tell us what happened to the one person among us that couldn't heal himself—the only one of us left who was truly mortal. Medea looked to Agrona and Kedehern, and there was hesitation in her eyes. She was nervous, afraid to say the wrong thing because if she did they would make her pay for it. When this was all over, and we had long forgotten it, the vampires would remember even the smallest betrayal.

I shivered a little at the thought of what kind of torture they would make her endure. No one seemed to notice me trying to physically shake those thoughts from my head. Enough bad thoughts lingered in the corners of my mind from the shit that had actually happened. I didn't need these newcomers running around inside my head too.

Oberon moved a little closer, wrapping himself around me from behind. Maybe he thought my little shake was from the October chill setting in.

I didn't bother to tell him otherwise. Medea was about to tell us what happened to Seamus, and I wanted to hear every word.

"We did tell them." She motioned to Agrona and Kedehern.

She would definitely be paying for this later. I knew she didn't mean to throw them under the bus, but the two of them wouldn't see it quite that way.

"We told them what had happened to the coven in town, but none of us thought they would really come here, at least not that many of them. Had there been fewer, then I think we could have held them. Seamus could have held them, even without me, if that had been the case. Did you know that, Maurin? That not only could he read minds, but that he could control them? I knew him for years and never knew that he could do that. He told me that even a dark, twisted demon's mind could be controlled. It was how the Triad was keeping them in their service for so long. At least, that's what he thought. I think they had other reasons for helping the Triad," Medea said.

Yeah, like the prospect of turning the town that was named after peace into a hell on earth. The irony never quits. Oh, and I can't forget the all you can eat buffet of human flesh. The Morrigna may be able to control the lesser *disii* with mind control, if that was even what they were doing, but the *An ChaipBhais* required payment in blood, and there were plenty of innocents here for them to be paid in pints. I didn't actually say any of this out loud, since I didn't want her to stop talking, not yet anyway. She would reach the part about my stabbing Seamus soon enough.

"The *An ChaipBhais* came, and none of us expected to see them here. Would you have thought that they would have left the side of the Triad, Mahalia? Foolishly, neither did we. So, with only assumptions to go on, everyone here began to prepare to "die" for the day. I felt safe with Seamus in the inner room. There was no sunlight in there, and I could spend the day with him. I knew that it would cost me to stay awake. I'd lose some strength, sure, but only for a little while. They never broke through the castle walls or the door. One minute it was just Seamus and I in the room, and the next the *An ChaipBhais* were there. I have lived a long time and heard many stories of the *An*

ChaipBhais, but not once did I hear that they were not only elite demon warriors, but they were sorcerers as well.

Seconds after appearing in the room, they had Seamus pinned to the floor, and I was staked to the stone wall. He fought, and they literally broke him, snapping the bones in his arms and legs. They left me pinned to the wall to watch as they ripped and gnawed at his flesh with their razor-like teeth. They took their time waiting for my wound to drain my strength along with my blood, knowing it would send me into the throes of a blood lust while remaining unable to quench it. They left me unable to heal myself and also unable to die from my wound.

"He was stronger than I am. He never screamed or begged for them to stop. He wouldn't allow them to feed on his emotions as they fed on his flesh. When they had finally killed him, when the blood had gone thick and cold and no longer flowed from his wounds, only then did they finally leave. And then you found us. I don't know if they meant to turn him into a *disii* or not. Maybe they had hoped that he would survive long enough to do some damage from within. Baylen and a delicious wolf named Piet let me feed, and Maurin killed the *disii* that was previously Seamus," Medea finished.

A lump had formed in the back of my throat from trying not to cry for Seamus. The feeling of having people who are important to you was still foreign to me. And it kind of sucked actually. It came with worry when they were apart from you and sadness when they left. This was way more emotional baggage than I was used to carrying around, and my heart was heavy from the weight of it all. Seamus had grown on me quickly, like poison ivy. The lack of him would leave me feeling a lot like a bad case of poison ivy too, absolutely miserable.

XXXVIII
THIRTY-EIGHT

A familiar click came from behind Medea and I looked up to see Cash's gun raised. Those of us not facing the park turned to see what the hell he was aiming at. Something was moving quickly across the park. In flashes of movement, they moved so fast it was hard to determine just who or what it was.

Kedehern knew. He reached out at lightning speed and grabbed the barrel of the gun, crushing the metal in his massive hand. "They're with me."

Cash's brow creased, and his eyes drew tight on Kedehern as he examined the crumpled metal that was left in his hand. "That was an H&K USP 9mm you just crushed like a beer can, not some shitty street piece. You will replace that."

"Don't test my patience, wolf. I would just as soon split your skull, letting your blood spill to feed my flock," Kedehern warned.

Now there was a thought that could bring the warm fuzzies back. Almost as quickly as I had grown to like

Seamus, I had decided that I did not like Cash. Maybe I was being too judgmental.

"Fortunately for you, you are here with Roul, and we have agreed to extend to you the same courtesies that we do to his pack. So, be careful when you challenge me, wolf. I am not bound to pack law and can show you why I am called Battle Lord without any of the wolf formalities to stop me." Kedehern sneered.

Cash growled but before the sound could fully escape his mouth, Kedehern had him by the throat. Kedehern raised him at least four feet into the air. He was about to crush Cash's windpipe when Agrona, of all people, stopped him.

She wrapped those long, silvery-white fingers around his shoulder, squeezing gently. "My darling, there will be plenty of time to feast upon this wolf afterwards. You know how unsatisfied you are when you rush. You will hunger again shortly after."

Hmm, sounds like me with Chinese food. I thought about how weird it was that I was relating Kedehern feeding on someone to me eating take out. It probably would have bothered me yesterday to hear the vampires talk so openly about feasting for pleasure on someone. But now? Maybe my morals were slipping or, maybe after everything that had happened so far, it just didn't seem that big a deal. Or maybe I just disliked Cash that much.

Kedehern let him go and bruising was already visible on Cash's neck. Some of the swelling from his ego-inflated head seemed to have moved down to his neck. I didn't feel the least bit sorry for him, either. I wouldn't shed any tears when Cash was gone. Nope, I'd be all too happy to see him go back to his own pack and get the hell out of Salem. He'd only make trouble if he stayed, or he'd get himself killed. More than likely he'd end up dead, which would just start a war between the neighboring packs. If the rest of us made it out of this alive, we'll have had our fill of war for a while.

Roul and Olwyn looked all too pleased at the prospect of Kedehern feasting on Cash, sure would be an easy fix to the problem of Cash's challenge. I doubted very much that Roul feared Cash, and doubted even more that Roul would lose a fight to him. But what if he did? A challenge from any wolf was a potential problem, never mind one who wasn't from within your own pack. Roul knew the men in his pack. He knew how they would move and fight. And I bet that all of his wolves would fight fairly. Now Cash, on the other hand? He had dirty fighter written all over him. Only an extremely arrogant wolf, a complete moron, or both would rock this boat the way he'd been doing. As I looked around our little group, I didn't see any friendly faces rooting for Cash. No one seemed to want him there at the moment, but he stayed anyway. Rather than wait for Cash to piss someone else off, I suggested we get ourselves together and go.

"The way I see it, it's the Morrigna one, us zip. All this infighting isn't going to accomplish anything. I'm tired of the bitching and bullshit. Let's just go," I said.

It was already fully dark. At this rate, it would be midnight before all of us were ready to go hunting for the war goddess.

A vampire I didn't know, not that I really knew any until this weekend, said in a voice that held the same eternal youth that her face did, "Got an itch for battle, this one does."

She was turned young and probably back in England, since she still had a thick accent. The vamp, with her ratty Sex Pistols t-shirt, red-and-black plaid schoolgirl skirt with black leggings and worn black combat boots, just stared at me. She was the epitome of punk rock, and I'm pretty sure if I dug back far enough in my own closet I would find a similar outfit from my high school days.

"Yeah, that's what it is. Nothing I'd rather do than go kill some demons and lose some friends. Now, that's what I call a good fucking time!" I shot back.

Wasn't it just me who said something about being tired of all the bitching? Oh, well. She had struck a nerve, though. I was itchy. Not necessarily for a fight, but just to have this whole thing finished.

"Okay, love, you don't have to bite me head off. It was just an observation. Besides, bitin' is best left to a vamp, eh?" She shot me a toothy grin, and I couldn't help but crack a smile myself.

She left it at that, and everyone slowly began to walk away. I stood there alone as I watched the different groups gather together. The wolves, vamps, and witches were all in their own little circles, ironing out their plans. But there was no circle for a psychic goddess vessel. I mean, how many of us were there? There was just me, as far as I knew. Baylen moved in, closing the distance between us. I had hardly noticed he was even here.

"We've decided it's best to travel together this time," he said, trying to fill the awkward silence between us.

"Seems like a good idea, since the whole splitting up thing hasn't worked out too well so far," I responded.

"That's a mistake that we won't be making again," he agreed.

There was no point wasting my breath reminding him they'd already done it twice. First, by letting some members of the coven go into town, which ended with Arcana unable to heal herself, or anyone else for that matter. And now this, which was far worse, ending in Seamus's death. I couldn't help but wonder why it was always Mahalia's people who were sent off on their own, separated from the rest of the group. The vamps I understood, they should have been safer here during the day, but why the witches? The coven could heal, but they are nowhere near as fast as a were or a vampire. Salves, potions, and charms all took time to work. The witches couldn't take a beating and just get right back up. There wasn't a whole lot of logic behind it. Then again, maybe I wasn't giving Mahalia enough credit. She didn't seem like a foolish woman, and she knew perfectly well what she and her coven were capable of.

"We'll all have to squeeze into the trucks. There isn't enough time to arrange for additional transportation," Baylen said, interrupting my thoughts.

"What?" I asked.

Wrapped up in my thoughts about the coven, which always seemed to come full circle to Oberon, because it was ultimately him I was worried about, I stopped listening to the conversation. I didn't want him to be separated from the group. More precisely, I didn't want him to be separated from me.

"Forget it, just go over there. It is painfully obvious that you would rather be talking with him," Baylen said.

There it was again. That hint of jealousy in his voice,

and I still didn't know what I had done to give him something to be jealous over. We weren't an item, not now, not even before, so I couldn't see what the problem was, but I didn't have the room in my brain to worry about it now.

I didn't go over to Oberon, though. At that moment I only had eyes for Roul, who had his hand to his ear and appeared to be talking to himself like a madman. I knew better, though. In true James Bond fashion, the alpha was busy giving someone orders, something to do with our departure, no doubt.

I wasn't sure where we were going or how any of them had figured out where to go, for that matter. The time to ask passed me by as tires crushed their way up the gravel drive. I didn't look to Baylen for instruction, and he didn't attempt to give any. We just moved in unison to the trucks that pulled up in front of the stone keep.

The last of the witches were back from scouting out the area. One even gave a report on Arcana. By the look of relief on Mahalia's face, I could tell that there was some improvement. Finally, we had some good news. We were all accounted for at last and ready to go. Roul gave a whistle, but that didn't seem to get everyone's attention, so he opted for shouting over the crowd instead.

"We're going to break up the groups. I want to have a few from each party in each truck. In this way, no group will lack any particular strength. This is it, people. Let's mount up." Roul said.

It's funny how loosely everyone uses the term "people" or "person" now. When the vamps and weres first came out, most "people" referred to them as "it" and dropped any reference to gender. It wasn't until the census came out and the humans realized just how many "its" there actually were, that they stopped ostracizing the Others. Still, it took a while for human families to realize that their ideal of the American dream had changed and to figure out a way to accept that. Personally, I never understood how having Others was any less American. We were, after all, a melting pot society. What did it matter if the pot was actually a cauldron, or some of your friends got furry on occasion? Not everyone held the same ideals, though. It was a couple of years before they really began to reconcile, before friends and neighbors found ways to live together again and words became just words again. So it was 'mount up people' and no one thought anything of it. No one looked around to see if there were any actual humans here, ready to pile into the caravan of SUVs. At any rate, who wants to say 'Mount up weres, vampires, witches and wizards, and of course the Blue Man of the Minch and the goddess vessel'? It loses some of its impact in the translation, doesn't it?

XXXIX
THIRTY-NINE

The time had come. My heart pounded again, and I tried to slow it down with no success. I took a deep breath and rubbed my sweaty palms on my pants. Grabbing the strap of leather from the scabbard that ran across my chest, I doubled-timed it over to Roul.

"Where do you want me?" I asked, not wanting to just hop into any old truck. Roul seemed to have a plan, and now that we finally had a plan I wasn't going to throw a wrench into the works.

"Uh, I'm not sure yet, actually. Let me get everyone else loaded up, and then I'll figure out where to put you. It'll be easier to find a spot for you once I assign everyone else to a truck."

The pack leader went back to counting off the groups. Like Noah, he loaded the trucks by twos, making sure each SUV was loaded up equally. Any of us left over would just squeeze in somewhere, I suppose. He did a good job of it, actually, putting one offensive and one defensive-skilled witch or wizard, two wolves, and two vampires into each truck. The vampires gave Roul the most trouble with placement, since the real differences in Agrona and Kedehern's family were their auras. They were all evenly matched in strength and age. The King and Queen were careful not to allow any vampires older than themselves into the family, but their auras were still varied.

Medea, for example, was sex on legs. She oozed sex appeal from her pores, which made it easier to trap her prey. I'm pretty sure Kedehern's involved a sedative of some sort. Ironic, I know, that a vampire, the only creature besides a polar bear documented to hunt humans, would have that aura as his gift, but he could squelch Agrona's hot temper with little effort. I felt it myself. There was something in his voice when he spoke. Maybe he used it to his advantage when he hunted, making his prey feel relaxed and unafraid of the fangs he was about to sink into their jugulars.

The rest I wasn't so sure about, since they didn't go around advertising these particular perks of their already enviable eternal lives. Especially since they were the most feared group of Others after the shift. Weres, and shape shifters in general, got off easy, since it is a virus that spreads their "condition". The Fey had it the best, since humans always thought of fairies and pixies as cute, kind of like Tinker Bell. They never did catch on to the dangers of the Fey who had strong powers. Some of them possessed very old magic and were closer to the old gods than any other group. Vampires, on the other hand, unless made by a cruel and bitter master vampire, consciously decided to become a member of the undead. That really seemed to freak out a lot of humans. So the vampires were all too familiar with mobs armed with stakes and torches. A community decision was made to keep a few secrets, and individual auras were one of them.

Agrona offered to help Roul assign her vampires their places in the trucks. She knew better than anyone what her "children" could do. They may not advertise all their powers to us, but she would be a fool to bring another vamp into her family without complete and absolute knowledge of their strengths and weaknesses. Not doing your research when a vampire asks to serve you could get you killed. Permanently. Any old and powerful vampire could slip through unnoticed, slowly taking control of the younger and lesser vampires until the newbie was in charge and the former leader was dead. Not just undead, but *dead* dead. You don't get to be the queen by being careless, so she knew everything about her vampires from the time when they were living humans up until the present.

She was down to the last two vampires, except Kedehern and herself, when I heard the sad song of the *Caointeach* again. She wasn't crippling us with ear-piercing screams anymore. It was more of a serenade, soft and sorrowful. Her weeping was only heard in between verses. The lyrics were barely audible, but I didn't recognize the song. Her voice sounded like Tori Amos, but the song was more like one by Enya. I would have preferred *Tomorrow Wendy* by Concrete Blonde as my death melody, but the Caointeach didn't take requests. I tried to remind myself this wasn't spectral karaoke, but a serious warning. The song of the *Caointeach*, which I know should have sent me reeling into a panic, was actually keeping me calm as I watched the small army we'd gathered finish throwing their gear into the trucks before climbing inside.

Music has always been an escape for me and while I have zero musical talent, it's an important part of who I am. A smile crept across my face as I remembered how my mom would yell at me for having my stereo on full blast while I did my homework. And how I loved the record store I worked in while I was in high school. It's weird what you think about while a spectral woman warns you of your impending death. I wondered if everyone thought about the beginning before the end? Her lyrical words washed over me, swaying to her serenade as I fought off regret and awaited my orders. Regrets like I could have been a nicer person and not so stubborn. I could have liked myself and let others like me a little more. I've heard people talk about how your life flashes before your eyes before you die and if this was it, it sucked. It was altogether possible I wouldn't die. After all, I had gained the ability to heal myself along with some other nifty side effects since becoming the new living quarters for an old pagan goddess, but the *Caointeach* had me convinced otherwise.

Had she always been a specter or did some horrible fate befall her too? Was she trapped here with the rest of us, seeing terrible things but never actually being seen herself? Was this her purpose or a curse? Similar questions weighed heavily on my mind about my new life. It was a hard pill to swallow, but I didn't feel like I was choking on it anymore and accepted my fate. I stopped fighting against the new powers taking over my body, mind, and spirit, but only time would tell if it was the blessing everyone around me seemed to think it was. Right now it seemed to be more of the same shitty luck I had been born with.

Roul walked over to me and threw his arm around my shoulder. He could practically use me as an arm-rest, since I was so much shorter than he was. I was glad for the interruption of my thoughts. "Come on, you're riding with me, Mahalia, and Kedehern,"

I walked with him to the truck, curious to see who else was going to be riding with us. The rear passenger door opened, and Roul motioned for me to climb in first. There was just no ladylike way for someone my height to haul her ass up into this truck, but I managed to get myself up and in, sliding across the back seat until I bumped hips with Kedehern. The vampire king smirked as I scooched over, mistaking my need for a little more personal space for fear. I wasn't afraid of him—not anymore. Sure he could snap me in half without giving it a second thought and drain me dry before a cry for help could escape my lips, but I'd had my ass kicked by Agrona and a goddess all in the same day, and I was still around to talk about it. That had changed my perspective a bit.

Settling into the seat, I gathered all the confidence I could muster. 'I am not intimidated by anyone here, anymore,' I repeated to myself. Kedehern seemed to notice my effort and smiled some more. Growing tired of the vampire beside me, I looked around to see who else was in the truck and saw Mahalia in the driver's seat. Seeing her sitting there behind the wheel gave me a little cause for concern. How much driving did she actually do? Teleporting seemed to be her favorite means of travel. The pretty wolf with all the tattoos that came to pick us up from Baylen's was in the front seat as well. We were short a vampire and a witch—the only truck not loaded up two by two. Though if you just measured power, Mahalia and Kedehern would probably each count as two. I wasn't surprised Oberon and I were in separate trucks, but I was surprised Baylen wasn't riding with me. He's been glued to my ass since I returned from Elysium.

No one was talking. It was too quiet, and that was suddenly making me very nervous, draining the energy I'd had building inside me. And I had been pretty pumped, ready to go a few moments ago, but all that heavy tension quickly brought me down. Maybe the silence was some sort of pre-fight meditation. They had certainly all seen more battles than me, so I couldn't accuse them of being scared. I tried to do a little meditating of my own, but it wasn't working. Instead of finding a Zen state of mind, I just found the tune of *Cadence to Arms* by Dropkick Murphys, which I began to hum out loud without even realizing it. It wasn't until the wolf, which I had yet to be formally introduced to, started humming with me that I knew I was even doing it.

Kicked back in the front passenger seat with her legs crossed and the heels of her black motorcycle style boot resting on the dash, she belted out the tune. Her head was cupped in her hands, which were folded between the back of her head and the headrest. I couldn't see her face, just some of her white hair and her tattoo-covered arms sticking out from the headrest like chicken wings. The wolf dropped the visor and flicked open the small mirror in a swift but cool motion, positioning it to see me in the back seat

She had switched from *Cadence to Arms* to *Shipping Up to Boston* and was no longer humming, but was instead singing the words. The desire to join in when she got to the chorus was irresistible. We both laughed a little, enjoying the noise we made. I can't even pretend it was music. The wolf wasn't that bad, but I could drown out even the best voices with my atrocious singing. There were a few eye rolls from Mahalia. Kedehern drove his fingers into his ears in an attempt to drown out the racket and she even got a "Mairead, for the love of the hunt, would you please shut up!" out of Roul, which only encouraged us further. Our voices rose, practically shouting the words now, like two kids trying their best to drive their parents crazy on a road trip. "...Sailor Peg, and I lost my leg! I'm climbing up the topsails 'cause I lost my leg! I'm shipping up to Boston! Whoa oh oh! I'm shipping up to..." We didn't get to finish the chorus.

XL
FORTY

A bright flash of green fire smashed into the truck in front of us. The explosion rocked our truck, blowing out the windows. Instinctively, we ducked down to avoid the flying shards of glass. When we got up off of the floor of the truck, there were flames and smoke coming from a twisted hunk of metal in the driveway.

Nothing resembling an SUV remained. Thick, black smoke rose up from what used to be the lead car in our caravan. A round, burning object, I think was a tire, rolled away from the flames and down the hill. The doors had been blown open, but I didn't see anyone trying to get out. Shouting and commotion came from every direction except the fire in front of us. I was frozen for a moment by the thought of those who were in there, trapped and burning. What if they were unconscious and burning to death?

I started shoving Roul, who was already halfway out of the truck and headed for Kedehern, who was crouched behind the rear door. People ran up to help. They wouldn't get there in time. Before any of them could even get to our truck, Roul was shouting at me. "Get out, get out of the truck! Move, now!"

The flames were beginning to lick at the front of our truck, and the fire was forcing sweat to build on my forehead. The heat alone started to burn my skin, and I hoped everyone caught in the explosion had died on impact. Trapped in a fire and burning to death was one of my irrational fears. I already knew who attacked us. I just didn't know exactly *where* she was, but I looked up just in time to see the next fireball coming toward us.

Mairead was out of the truck and pushing me backward. "Go!" I was moving, but she kept her hand in the middle of my back, forcing me to move faster.

We were almost behind the third truck in line when the molten ball of death slammed into the one we had just escaped from. The force of the blast had us airborne, throwing us up and back. I slammed down on the hood of the fourth truck, smashing the windshield with the back of my head.

Mairead landed hard in the grass next to us with a heavy thud and a loud exhale of breath. The air had literally been knocked out of her. It would take a minute for her to get up from that one, even if she was a were. I wasn't actually getting up myself. It was more of a slide to my feet off the hood and into a roll along the side of the truck and around to the back.

Roul had moved out from behind the truck and was trying to drag Mairead back behind the truck to some sort of cover.

We couldn't stay there much longer. Morrigan wasn't

going to give us a chance to catch our breath. Another fireball would rain down on us any second. All of the trucks were empty. Everyone had poured out of them. They were all running back to the castle toward the only shelter on the grounds where we could figure out whom we'd lost and regroup. The real battle hadn't begun, and the casualties were already mounting up. We couldn't keep sustaining losses like this and walk away the victor.

Shouts for everyone to pull back could be heard over the roar of the fire in front of us. Black, thick, and toxic smoke hung in the air from the burning tires, blocking the stars and leaving no light to guide us. My throat was starting to burn, and I couldn't stop coughing. If the wind shifted direction, we would be lost in the poisonous cloud, unable to make our way back to the vampire haven or to each other's aid. We would be easy fodder for her and her demon army if that happened.

The wind shifted south suddenly, blowing the smoke down the hill and away from us, thanks to Mahalia. It was going to leave us vulnerable. We would be out in plain sight for a minute until it rose high enough to meet Morrigan, where it would block her view of us for a few precious seconds. If we wanted to see, then the Triad was going to see us too. There was a hum of power, followed by a hard push. A huge wave of energy came rolling over us and the earth. Someone was trying to block her attack.

The third firestorm came. This time she hit us with a volley of fireballs that burned with even more intensity. They lit the sky like fireworks and burned a brighter, hotter green than they had before. The fire crashed into the wave of power and ricocheted back out to the one who had cast it. Like a tsunami after an earthquake, the power rolled back, crashing into us and knocking some of our fighters off of their feet. I felt it rush out from under my feet, like the ocean receding back off the beach. The power rippled and wavered in front of me before it finally snapped back into place.

I looked around. No one in the coven had cast a spell to put up this shield. Not one of them was in the ethereal breeze that came when they called their magic. Then I remembered the Watcher. Mahalia had called to a Watcher to protect this land. He had accepted her offering and would do what was within his power to fulfill her request of him. So were we too far outside the circle the Watcher had raised, or had Morrigan done something to weaken the Watcher? The way the power rolled down, clearing the area and then resurging, it felt like he had to set the circle all over again. That couldn't be good. What good was having a Watcher if she could get past him?

The smoke cloud in front of me was beginning to swirl around. Morrigan had called winds of her own. It hit the circle and bounced back. I felt the circle almost give.

Roul was shouting for me to fall back.

Mairead was on her feet next to him, waving me in.

Someone had managed to get a large metal door open on the side of the castle, and they were holding it open for us. I didn't think holing up inside the vampires' home was going to do any good for any real length of time, but I seemed to be outvoted.

Large stones that made up the walls of the castle could hold against any barrage of magic, but they could just as easily become our prison. Once Morrigan and the *disii*

surrounded the castle, there would be no escape. We would
be trapped, and she would simply wait us out. There was
no doubt in my mind she could wait longer than we could.
Sure the vampires were all well fed now, but just give them
a few days. The bloodlust would take them, and we'd be
slaughtered like cattle. They'd finish us all off for her.
Without any bright ideas of my own, I started to haul ass
toward the door, in spite of my reservations.

XLI
FORTY-ONE

I was healing the ribs that had broken when I smashed into the hood of the SUV, but the muscles were still sore as I ran. My injuries seemed to be well within range of what I could heal, I just hadn't mastered the new skill yet. The energy I had expelled in trying to heal the bone had left me unable to heal the muscles. At least if I got inside, I wouldn't be running and might have a little more energy to use toward healing myself. There was no way I'd last the night, fighting injured.

I made it inside. This must be where the vamps normally entered the castle. Benches lined one wall with hooks fastened above them. Coats in various styles and sizes hung from the hooks, giving small clues as to the age or era of the vampires residing within the castle walls.

Several pairs of shoes were neatly lined up under the benches. I thought we had searched the whole place, but we had only been in the rooms the vampires wanted us to see, leaving far more of their home undiscovered. More rooms and hidden hallways like the one that had masked the sleeping quarters branched off from this side of the estate. The front rooms we'd explored must have been for show. Vampires have a taste for all things dramatic. When company came, you wouldn't find Agrona and Kedehern sitting in matching Lazy Boy recliners. They would be sitting in their matching thrones. But this, this was the gateway to their personal space. A place no one outside of their family was ever allowed to see. Until tonight.

We were going to have to fight them now. I looked through the sea of faces crammed into the dark hallway with arched ceilings. My eyes finally came to rest on Roul, deep in thought. He was the man who previously had the plan. I was hoping he had another one now.

"Hey, Roul, we better get into some kind of position before she has time to dig in. Otherwise we'll be trapped inside. So? What now, what are you thinking?" I asked.

Everyone looked at me like I was the village idiot who had finally said something smart.

Tucking a flyaway piece of hair behind my ear, I stared back with my eyebrows raised, managing to show both my curiosity and my agitation. "What?" I said, trying to holding back my irritation.

No one said anything, instead they turned their amused little faces to Roul, who didn't like having all eyes directed at him either. The Alpha tried to put something together, and all I had accomplished was to draw everyone's attention to the fact he didn't have a plan B. Roul just stared down the hall at me, without uttering a word, his face dark and drawn, piercing eyes boring a hole in my forehead.

I wiped a hand across my forehead, half expecting there

to be smoke coming off my skin.

Never one to let silence hang in the air, I kept going. "Okay. Well, what if the witches took up places at the arrow slits? They're the only ones who can fight effectively from a distance and might be able to distract the *disii* long enough for us to get our shit together."

Heads whipped back to me, yet again. Obviously everyone here was not used to the village idiot stringing sentences together to form coherent thought, because this time no one bothered to snap their jaws shut.

"What the hell is wrong with you people? What did you think the Police Department did? Put an ad in for a really stupid part-time psychic? I'll have you know I went to the academy like everybody else, and I even studied for the detective exam." My pointer finger was waving around at everybody, and my voice was rising. "You'd think I came to all of you begging to be let into your little club, but I sure as hell did not. Oh no, you all came looking for me!" My finger switched from a random wag at the crowd to poking myself firmly in the chest. "I'm still not a hundred percent sure why, but you did. So stop treating me like the dumb mortal. Which I'm not anymore, by the way. Mortal, I mean. I was never dumb." I added.

Baylen and Oberon were the only ones laughing. They were mirror images of each other, leaning against opposite walls of the narrow hallway, arms crossed over their chests and both thoroughly amused with my little tantrum.

I let out a long sigh. "Fucking hopeless. You're all fucking hopeless," I muttered under my breath.

Cash spoke up finally, ordering the witches to man the arrow slits along the castle exterior walls like it was his frigging idea. What an ass. But even more disturbing was the fact that people were moving. What the hell? I watched them go and threw my hands up. Sure I thought, the girl with the badge makes a suggestion and no one goes anywhere. They all just stand around and stare like I have seven heads. But the crazy gun-for-hire prick says something, and suddenly everyone is moving. I watched the witches go, all but Mahalia and Oberon, who both gave me a little wink. Normally I would have found the mild flirting cute, but right now I was seething over the fact the coven was listening to Cash. Of all the damned people here to listen to. Sure, he was ex-military, but he was still just a pompous ass.

The sensation of wolf and testosterone shot out through the hallway, practically bouncing off the stone walls and slamming into anyone who was inside the room That snapped me back from my pity party real quick.

From what I'd picked up about wolf behavior so far, and based on that little display, I'd say Roul didn't much care for Cash chiming in either. He may not have had an alternative to offer, but he was still running the pack here. If he wanted the advice of another wolf, he'd ask for it, and if he wanted someone else to be in charge of something, he'd delegate it. He didn't, however, and he would see that as a challenge to his authority, especially if it was coming unsolicited from a wolf outside of his pack.

The air was charged in the hallway, and goosebumps ran along my skin. We'd have to move if they were going to fight it out, and it looked like they were about to because Cash wasn't backing down this time.

Kedehern stepped forward and sent his liquid-cool aura

out to calm everyone down. The air was so charged with electricity that my hair felt like it was standing on end. Someone should have reminded Kedehern that water and electricity don't mix because the more he poured that aura into the hallway, the more jacked up Roul got. The air crackled like a downed powerline with the power Roul was pumping out.

"Don't use your aura on me, Kedehern!" Roul growled. "This wolf's been looking for a fight ever since he got here, and I'm finally going to give him exactly what he wants!"

Roul tore down the hallway, pinning anyone he passed against the wall with his broad shoulders and stride.

Cash was standing in the middle of the hallway waiting for him, feet planted firmly in a fighting stance. He readied himself for Roul's charge, and the rest of us scrambled to get out of the way.

Roul didn't charge. He simply lunged, knocking Cash backward onto the floor.

Someone's elbow smashed my cheek as they made their way down. Pain seared across my face where my cheek had split open. I reached up and wiped away some of the blood running out of the gash.

Okay, now I was really pissed! Not only was this piss-poor timing, but I got bashed in the face too? Anger and irritation flashed hot across my skin. Reaching down deep into the power that was pooled up in my stomach, I pulled it up until a fire raged in my chest. The flames increased, ready to burst from my body and leave nothing but ash in the hallway. I pushed the heat and power outward, rocking everyone off their feet and slamming them into the walls.

Roul and Cash took the brunt of the blast.

I sent them crashing into the two little steps in front of the door that led out of the hallway and back into the castle. I could tell that Roul still wanted to fight, but he didn't move. Cash, on the other hand, made a terrible mistake. It was one I wouldn't have expected him to make because he was so arrogant, and he allegedly had so much combat experience. You'd think they'd teach you this kind of shit in the military. Maybe he'd just been given too much leash. He'd become a little too cocky, and he had forgotten there were people tougher than he was in the world.

He let a little fear slip across his eyes, and I pounced.

I wasn't sure if I could use my power in the way I was about to, but I tried anyway. If I let him get up now, knowing I saw the fear there but had held myself back, he'd take it as a sign of weakness, and I had no intention of letting him think he was dominant to me. I focused in on him, directing my power at him like a crushing weight. He tried to move out from under my gaze, but the more he moved the harder I pushed. Unable to resist the increasing pressure, he finally gave in, sulking down on the floor like a dog with his tail between his legs.

I had aligned myself with Roul, and the rest of the Council, that first night at Baylen's, so any victory here in this hallway would belong to his pack.

Roul stood up and started brushing himself off. He ran one of his massive hands through his thick, wavy black hair, smoothing it back and out of his face.

The pack leader watched me with dark, intense eyes. I think he liked me, and maybe he'd eventually consider me a friend to the pack, but right now he wasn't sure what to make of me. It was written all over his face. He hadn't expected me to have so much power and seemed to take note of the lack of energy I'd exerted taking Cash down. Pushing him and then pinning him down beneath the weight of my power seemed effortless.

Roul shot a look at Cash, just with his eyes, and my gaze followed his down to the floor where Cash still lay pinned. Shit, I didn't even realize I was still holding him there. I didn't pull my power back in a rush because I didn't want to draw attention to the fact I was using so much power with so very little concentration. Instead, I just let it slowly slide back in place under my skin, pooling back up in my stomach. It felt good—like when you drink something hot on an empty stomach and you can feel the warmth move down inside you.

Roul drew his gaze away from Cash and back to me, confirming I had been discreet. No one seemed to notice the shift in power levels in the room. Maybe it was the mix of wolf, vamp, and whatever the hell my power was called that helped hide the full amount of magic I had used. I still wasn't sure if it even was some kind of magic, since no one had really explained that part.

Agrona and Baylen were looking at me as if I were a prize to be won—as if I were a trophy to keep high up on a shelf. I guess some people had noticed the change in me after all, and apparently I was stronger than they'd thought too. None of them expected me to gain so much strength so fast. And now that they knew, what would they do with me? They were starting to creep me out, staring at me like that. The chase was on. They would hunt me down until one of them had succeeded in mounting me above their fireplace.

Agrona ran her long fingernails through her tightly

coiffed bun, checking to see if any strands of her auburn hair were out of place. She was still staring at me, and I thought I caught a little tongue flash across her canines. She was definitely sizing me up again. She had already tested me once, but she obviously thought she had misjudged me. She kept those hazel eyes fixed on me and amusement, both evil and painful, swam in her eyes.

I wouldn't be kept by anyone, but right now if I had to pick someone to stick me in a display case, it would definitely be Baylen. At least he wasn't staring at me like he wanted to eat me. Poke me and prod me in a lab somewhere, maybe, but I was pretty sure I wouldn't have to worry about Baylen making a meal out of me. I wasn't the only one who had noticed the change in their demeanor. The wolves could smell it too. The thick, choking mix of adrenaline, aura, and my power had thinned out, leaving behind Baylen and Agrona's crippling desire. Desire for me.

Roul cleared his throat, his voice still a half growl. "Grayson, Tybalt, go check in with Phallon. Cash has wasted enough of our time, and now we have surely lost the outer grounds to the *disii*."

The two wolves did as they were told, leaving quickly to find Phallon and the others.

Roul was right. We had wasted enough time. Time that was far too precious to just throw away on testosterone and pack bullshit. I knew outside of this situation, pack law was extremely important. Without it, the wolves would have no order, and they wouldn't be able to survive in the world. Even in a world totally aware they existed. The thing that made it so easy for society to accept the wolves in the first place was pack law. Without it, they were no better than the vampires, so their rules, and the order they maintained, were important. It kept them and everyone around them safe. But, in that moment, it didn't seem to matter. It could not compare with what was outside. The sound of heavy footsteps running toward us solidified that for me.

XLII
FORTY-TWO

"We've got a problem!" It was Grayson. "Phallon says–"

Mahalia interrupted. "The Watcher's going to break. He can't hold her back much longer. If we lose the Watcher, we lose the protective circle around the grounds. It's the only thing keeping back the full force of her attack."

"I know you're a witch, but it still really freaks me out when you do that shit. Phallon said you better do something quick because they won't be able to hold them back alone," Grayson said.

Mahalia gave him the comforting smile I thought was reserved for only me and told him to go back to Phallon and wait for further instructions.

The situation looked pretty grim to me. Similar sentiments were mumbled around the room. We had wasted valuable time that had gone from precious to priceless in seconds. Without the Watcher to help keep Morrigan and her army of demons back, we were vastly outnumbered. The ground wavered beneath my feet, like a large rock hitting a still pond, as the circle fell. Morrigan made easy work of the Watcher, and that had me more than a little worried.

The ancient goddess enjoyed toying with us. She could take us anytime she wanted. There was no holding the castle. We would have to go out and meet her, face her out there on the grounds and do it quickly, before the last of the remnants of the circle's magic disappeared.

I didn't wait for anyone to say anything. They'd just argue over what to do or who to listen to, and by the time they settled on a plan, we'd all be good and dead. Every single one of us. Permanently. So I headed for the heavy metal door that would open to an army of demons and Morrigan.

"Whoa, whoa, what the hell, Maurin? Where are you going?" Oberon was hot on my heels.

He was trying to pull me back down the hallway and into what everyone seemed to think was the safety of the castle. I saw it more as prolonging the inevitable. Morrigan was going to get us, whether it was out there or in here, it didn't much matter to her. She could break that circle and the Watcher any time she wanted to. Personally, I wanted go out and meet her with a little bit of my dignity intact, rather than wait for the inevitable slaughter.

Yanking my arm out of his grasp, I trudged back up the hallway. My hand encircled the doorknob, I was poised to step outside, to finally stand toe to toe with the goddess and her army when I stopped. Oberon wasn't the source of my anger, and if something happened to one of us, I didn't want it to end with me storming out on him. My shoulders dropped as I let out a sigh. When I turned to look at Oberon he was standing right where I'd left him.

"I don't know about you, but I'd rather go out there now, while there is still a circle, and see what I can do than wait until it breaks and the flood of *disii* comes pouring in. You can stay here with the rest of them," I said, waving a hand around, "Or you can walk out there beside me. It's up to you. And that goes for the rest of you too."

The sound of footsteps came from behind as I turned to go. Without turning around, I knew it was Oberon. A weight lifted in my heart at the same time a knot untied itself from inside my stomach. He was so close, his breath hot on my neck before I could even get the door open.

"If you're going, then we'll go together," he whispered.

I would have turned to plant a kiss right on those beautiful lips of his if it wouldn't have ruined the moment of me being the tough girl, walking out of here to go kick some war goddess ass.

"Wait," Baylen called after us. "You need a plan. You can't just go out there. Not without some kind of a plan."

"Why not? You don't have one. Nobody here has one and if they do, I am betting it's not one Morrigan hasn't already planned for herself. I mean, hello, war goddess? Besides, going out there without a plan is—in its own twisted way—a plan. It's simple. Go out there and meet them. Don't let me hold any of you back, though. If someone's got something to say, then let's hear it." I scanned the tight corridor, searching for someone to throw out an idea. "Anybody else got anything? *Anybody*? Fine. See ya."

They were going to do exactly what I had thought they would, stand around and talk shit out until it was too late to act. Well I didn't feel like just waiting around to die. I took hold of Oberon's arm, and we both reached for the door at the same time.

Baylen called out again, this time clearly agitated. "I said you can't just go out there."

What is wrong with him? What part of me going is he not understanding?

"What the hell is wrong with you? Okay, Baylen, I'll bite. Why can't I go out there?" I asked.

"Because you're the bait, dear," Agrona answered for him, looking at me more like I was an appetizer than bait. "You don't just throw the bait out before the trap is set."

With my hands on my hips, I looked around the cramped quarters we had made in the hallway. My blood had reached its boiling point. I wouldn't have been the least bit surprised if there was steam coming out of my head. Baylen and Agrona I would have expected this from, but Roul and Olwyn?

Oberon's grip on my shoulder told me enough about his involvement, which was nil, apparently. He didn't know anything about it. Something about Mahalia, some kind of vibe I had received from her earlier, made me think she couldn't have known anything about this either. I could feel my eyes draw tight, narrowing down on the two wolves. If looks could kill, then I would have dropped them right there.

Olwyn looked shocked, almost offended, that I would think they would stoop to this level.

Roul just raised his hands up in a very casual motion and stepped back, distancing himself from Baylen and the vampires.

"What, Baylen, surely you told her? Here you fitted her

with this lovely sword and all this wonderful equipment, but you never bothered to tell her she was nothing but cheese for the mouse trap?" Agrona taunted.

"Really? I was supposed to be cheese for the mouse? Well, the mouse out there could certainly kick your ass, and when exactly were you going to set the trap? The only trapping that *I've* seen, has been done by the *disii*. Or did you lock yourselves in the basement?" I shot back.

Baylen was moving toward me in an attempt to plead his case. But I wasn't having any of it. I didn't want him anywhere near me.

"You need to stay right the fuck where you are. Don't come near me. You know, I knew you were an asshole even before I met you. But stupid me gave you a chance, and what do you do? Take an extra-long time at proving me right. You almost had me, though. I'll give you that," I said through gritted teeth.

"Really, Maurin, it's not as bad as that. It's not as bad as she makes it sound. Sure, at first we wanted to use your natural gifts, but as for you becoming a vessel? Well, I had hoped, but that wasn't certain. As for everything else? Your increase in strength was unforeseen. You're more than bait now." Baylen looked almost sheepish for once.

"Oh, well, in that case, no problem, glad to help! Of course, you need me now. Now that I have the power of a goddess coursing through my veins, right? Prior to that I was simply disposable. You're not helping yourself here, do you realize that? The more you talk, the worse you are making it for yourself."

"Uh, this is coming out wrong." Baylen fumbled for the right words.

"You think?"

"Please," he pleaded. "Yes, you were initially bait, but...what I mean to say is...I'm sorry. I should have been honest with you from the start. I knew after you saw Ouzel that you would be more, and I should have been honest with you from the start."

"Aw, isn't that nice. I'm all warm and gooey inside after that apology, really. Tell you what. If you feel that bad about it, then why don't you come with us? You can go out there first and make sure we've got a clear path. If something comes at us, you can block it with your face." I'd have been all too happy to use him as a shield.

"There is simply no reasoning with you, you know that? She'll kill you if you go out there alone. Can't you see that? We have to come up with something that will work!" Baylen's frustration with me reached an all-time high.

"The Triad will kill us anyway if we stay in here, and she's not going alone." Oberon opened the door and pushed me through. "The cheese and I are going out there together. If you've got a plan or something rolling around in that cruel, calculating mind of yours, Agrona, now would be a good time to share." He slammed the door behind him and took my hand in his.

From outside the thick metal door, we could hear muffled voices, which we knew came from the others shouting inside. We started to walk around front, his hand gripping mine more tightly with each step. When we were about to turn the corner toward the front yard, he stopped. Backing me up against the wall, his body pressed against mine, he leaned in to kiss me.

I started to protest, to tell him that this wasn't the time, kissing could wait until later, but then I remembered that there might not be a later.

Oberon's lips were soft and gentle. His mouth was a perfect fit for mine, as if his lips were made for nothing but kissing me. I wrapped my arms around him, loving the way he felt next to me.

His hands inched slowly up my sides, sending a shiver through my body, which had been aching for more ever since he had joined me in the shower. They stopped when they reached my cheeks. With my face in his hands, he continued to kiss my lips, and then my nose and my forehead. Oberon stopped kissing me, but left his lips pressed against my forehead, just breathing me in.

I moved my head out of his hands and leaned into his chest. It felt so right that I fell into the rhythm of his heartbeat. For just a moment, the world seemed to stop spinning. It was just the two of us. No army of demons. No Morrigan. And no pain in the ass Council. It was just the two of us, here in the dark, holding each other, and it was a perfect moment.

He gave me a final squeeze, followed by that telltale rub on the back that lets you know the embrace is over, and I looked up at him. His lips found mine one last time, and then he stepped back.

"I just wanted to, you know, just in case something..." he stammered.

I put my hand up to his mouth to stop him. "I know."

He held out his hand, and I took it. We walked around the corner and out into the front yard, hand in hand. My heart was pounding, not just from my desire for more than kisses, but also from the anticipation of what lay around the corner. When we finally stepped out into the courtyard, it was much worse than I had feared.

XLIII
FORTY-THREE

The sea of *disii* swept over the dark-green grass and all the way down the hill to the field in the park. The rustle of the changing leaves died down, leaving a bone-chilling silence in the air. There were no stars speckling the black night sky, and there was no moon to light our way. We walked through the darkness to the edge of the circle, our footsteps matching the beat of the *disii* drumming their swords against their shields.

The hum of the Watcher's magic was barely audible over the clang of metal against metal. It was a primal beat that drowned out any sound of the creatures that normally roam the night. With a call like cackling hyenas, the *An ChaipBhais* sounded their war cry. In the distance, I could see a black cloud moving quickly toward us through the otherwise still night air. I heard a familiar flapping of wings and watched in awe once more as she took shape in front of us.

The goddess made one hell of an entrance. I had to give her that. The crows beat their wings and thrashed about, crashing into one another until they formed Morrigan. She hovered in front of us just outside the Watcher's circle before finally landing with such force she shook the very ground beneath our feet.

"Are you so confident in your rebirth that you would dare to face me alone, Maurin?" Morrigan asked.

I started to speak, both my mind and my mouth ready to form some witty comeback, but Oberon answered her before I had the chance. "She's not alone. I stand before you with her."

"Do you mean to frighten me, witch? You'll have to do better than that. You will find that I am not easily intimidated. Certainly not by a useless vessel and one pathetic witch! You two are hardly worth dragging out the *An ChaipBhais*. Tell me, Maurin, why is it that in your hour of need everyone has abandoned you?"

"If you are trying to psych me out, it won't work. I've had abandonment issues my whole life. I'm used to it. Looks like you're the one who's afraid, seeing how you dragged every demon out of the bowels of hell to come here and kill me. I would have thought the mighty Morrigan would have been able to kill little ol' me all by herself," I stupidly egged her on.

"You are an amusing specimen. Perhaps I should cage you rather than kill you so you can entertain me for all eternity. Don't flatter yourself, child. There is much to be done after I am through with you. Once the *disii* have picked their teeth with your bones, we still have the rest of the world to conquer. Before the sun rises, the sniveling little humans will kneel before me, begging for mercy!"

A chorus of howling and cackling rose up behind her in

praise of her speech.

"Do you think this meager circle will keep you safe? Foolish girl!" Morrigan raised her hands above her head. With arms crossed, she swooped them back down, creating a small but strong gust of wind that almost knocked us off our feet.

Fighting to keep my balance, I caught a glimpse of what looked like two comets igniting the pitch-black sky. They looked a bit like the fire bolts she had rained down on the trucks little more than an hour ago. I hoped the Watcher's circle would keep us safe from the fiery orbs she had created.

She was certainly stronger than the Watcher. Her magic was much older than his. Our safety in his circle was questionable at best.

I'd thought from the invocation Mahalia had used earlier that the whole vampire grounds would be covered with the protection of the Watcher, but that didn't seem to be the case. Either it wasn't a literal spell, or Morrigan had already reduced the bounds of the protection from the property lines down to the actual circle Mahalia had drawn around the castle itself. Either way, I was pretty sure she was just toying with us and could break the circle anytime she wanted to. Then why hadn't she done it yet? What was she waiting for?

The balls of fire barreling toward us burned so brightly against the blackness of the sky it was hard to keep my eyes open, and my pupils were straining to adjust.

Oberon threw an arm out across my chest and knocked me to the ground. He was on top of me, shielding me from the blast as the two fireballs crashed into the ground in front of the circle. The ground erupted into a wall of flame, licking at the rapidly weakening circle that barely separated us from the crazed war goddess.

Two women rose out of the flames like the phoenix had risen from the ashes. As they emerged from the flames and charred earth, I had an answer. I was just asking the wrong question. Not what, but *who* had she been waiting for?

The women slowly stood up. Their skin was flawless, despite the fire raging around them.

I knew immediately who they were, and for the first time, the Triad formed itself before us.

Badb rose up out of the flames in a motion more suited to a 1950's pin up girl than a demi-goddess. Pale, opalescent skin reflected the multitude of colors that made up the flames. Different shades of orange and blue shone through her skin, revealing the temperature of the fire. A mix of red and orange hair, almost camouflaged by the fire kissing her skin, topped her head in a tangled mass. Eyes red with the fury and rage that always burned inside her, searched us out.

Nemain was quite the opposite. Of the two of them, she most resembled Morrigan. Her skin was the telltale difference between her and her older sister. Not having the same silvery sheen of Morrigan, Nemain's skin was a light gray, dull and lifeless. Her eyes were blacker than the *disii's*, her face was drawn tight, not with rage like Badb, but with hate. Filled with a hatred so strong and so deep it oozed out of every pore of her sickly skin. Everything else about her was a smaller version of Morrigan. Same hair, same features. Of the three of them, Nemain was the only one I could come almost eye-to-eye with.

The onyx eyes, too numerous to count in the army of demons before us, slowly began to burn with Badb's rage. Their eyes glowed a shade of red so bright it rivaled the flames of the fire scorching the ground in front of us.

The flames might not be able to breach the protective circle, but the heat they gave off was still killing the grass inside it. I looked at the grass, shriveling and curling back down to the ground. The heat was penetrating the cool, moist fall dirt, killing even the roots normally protected beneath the surface. The lush carpet of grass would never recover. A circle would be burned into the earth, forever a reminder of what was about to happen here.

In timing perfected through centuries of battle, Nemain's hatred fell like a thick fog over the battalions. Her battle craze would sweep down through the troops of *disii* and mix with Badb's rage to create an insatiable bloodlust. As if a demon needed any help in that area. Weren't they born and bred for mayhem and madness, anyway? Recruited from the worst of what humanity had to offer? Now the Triad would unleash an already deadly army, equipped with weapons far better suited for this battle than those made of steel.

The Triad was older than the concept of hell itself. Born of a religion much older than anything we recognized today, the sisters had been waging wars far longer than demons had filled the depths of the underworld. When their offerings and sacrifices were gone and new religions swept across their lands, they waited. They had all of eternity, after all. Plenty of time to strike their bargains with the gatekeeper of a newly-created hell. There was plenty of time to wait and see which side was winning the favor of mankind. Evil sleeps in the heart of every person. With each generation, the evil flared more frequently. For a species that claims to be so inherently good, humans just can't stop themselves from doing increasingly horrible things to each other.

The Triad would seize this opportunity, since this was certainly proving to be the darkest time in the history of man. When the age of enlightenment arrived, the proverbial light came on, providing new and exciting ways for man to maim and kill not only each other, but the very planet that gives them life. This was true of the Me generation, the X generation, and the most recent generation as well. They would serve as the rapture so many mortals prayed for, the salvation that never seemed to come. The Triad would take back the altars and places of worship, casting any denouncers down to the torturous depths of hell. Their army—what was once the worst of mankind, banished into damnation after a lifetime of wretchedness—would sweep across humanity, snuffing out the last of the innocence. I had seen it all before in Ouzel's mind, but I hadn't fully understood it until now. Not until the Triad had explained it to me. Not with actual words, but with pictures in my head. Morrigan and her sisters showed me all of the terrible things that would happen once they were done.

If only Seamus were still alive. He'd pull these pictures from my mind, I could tell someone without the Triad knowing what I was doing. And then it hit me. That was precisely why Seamus had been singled out. Because they did know he could talk to me without ever making a sound. The images faded, and the world around me was coming back into focus. I felt someone or something, besides the Triad, staring at me. The weight of the gaze now fixed upon me felt so familiar.

When my vision finally cleared, I met the two black, beady eyes, like a rat's, but larger. I had seen this creature in a different form. It was with human eyes that he had pried into my mind and spoke my name. He stood before me now as his true self.

The demon kept a basic human shape, but the skin that was once fair and flawless was now a dark, rotted green, covered in scars and pockmarks. Nothing human remained in his goat-slitted eyes. Brittle and broken straw-like hair hung past his ears. He fit in well with the army standing behind him. I may not have recognized him at all, except for the pull of his gaze. Ouzel smiled wickedly at me as he stood in front of the *An ChaipBhais*, smashing his sword into a large and elaborate shield. The shield was almost as tall as I was, and it was rectangular in shape, with symbols carved into it. However, they were too small and too far away for me to decipher. His sword clashed into his shield again. *Clang, clang, clang.* Pause. *Clang, clang, clang.*

The *An ChaipBhais*, followed by the rest of the *disii*, joined in. Their swords banged against their shields again and again in the same primitive beat. *Clang, clang, clang.* Pause. *Clang, clang, clang.* Another battle cry tore through the night with terrifying ferocity.

I stepped back with Oberon shadowing my movements. The flames began to die down now, taking away any warmth they had brought, and leaving nothing but bitter cold and darkness behind. As I stood there fighting off the shivers from the cold autumn night air, I began to have serious second thoughts about venturing out here to meet her.

The three goddesses drew swords from the folds of their long skirts. In unison, they wielded them high above their heads and drove them down into the damp, soft ground of the circle's edge. Blood spurted up from the ground, soaking the grass.

My eyes hadn't fully adjusted to the darkness. The blood looked more like thick crude oil. It shot up from the ground like a geyser. Before long, the circle that was once made of salt and herbs had turned completely black. The volumes of thick blood had made it so. A familiar metallic smell rose up from the ground and filled the air. It filled my nose and mouth, and left a taste on my tongue as if I had been chewing on tin foil. The blood no longer gushed from the cuts from the Triad's steel alone, but was now seeping up all around us. We stood inside the tainted circle with the warm blood from the soil creeping toward us.

The Watcher was dead, and the circle of protection was completely broken. They hadn't just driven their swords through the thick grass and damp earth, but also through the flesh of the guardian. He was the earth, the sky, and the stone and mortar. His very essence was tied to the circle and the land it protected. To destroy the circle was the same as destroying the Watcher. Had it been a lesser being attacking him, I believe the Watcher would have been able to hold this place. And that was why she had waited. She had needed the power of three, of the Triad, to break the magic that was so different from hers. It wasn't any more powerful. It was just different, conjured for one purpose, and channeled in such a way she could not break it alone.

Blood hadn't penetrated my boots yet, but I could feel it all around me. The ground was so saturated it could not absorb another drop. It squished beneath my feet as I backpedaled away from the three of them. Dry and cracked from the fire, the ground soaked up as much blood as it could. It oozed up from the cracks in the earth.

I felt naked standing in front of them without a circle to protect me. There had never been a need for me to be inside one before tonight. Tucked safely within the walls of my interrogation room and protected by the cavalry hiding behind the two-way mirror, I had no need for magic other than my own psychic abilities. The big bad ugly may have been sitting right across from me, but he or she couldn't actually touch me. Oh, I'd had a few come across the table but by the time they did, I was always out of reach. Being inside someone's head does have its advantages. Once I was in, I could see everything. Every thought, whether it was tied to a memory I was reading or not was audible once I slipped inside a mind. The brain has to tell the body to move and as soon as the thought was created, as soon as the synapses fired, I could see it. Then I got the hell out of the way. Right now, I very much wanted, no needed, a circle between me and the Triad. A circle, a continent, a lifetime, anything between me and the three of them would suffice.

Oberon stepped closer to me and placed a hand low on my back, pressing the cold sweat beading up on my back between my shirt and my skin. The soaked fabric clung to my skin, and I shivered from the cold.

Nemain smiled with satisfaction. She thought they literally had me shaking in my boots. They did, but I'd be damned if I gave them the satisfaction of knowing it.

Plucking up what felt like the last of my courage, I drew the Retaliator out of its sheath and readied myself for battle. Channeling Scota's power, I fell into a fighting stance with my sword raised high, ready to drive it into the flesh of my enemies. I'd already driven it deep into the body of someone I had considered a friend, so piercing the meat and bone of an evil goddess or *disii* would certainly be easy in comparison.

Morrigan's eyes narrowed in on me, but I stood firm under the weight of her gaze. She raised her sword, still coated with the blood of the Watcher, ready to engage. Silence fell with the motion of her blade. As she got into her stance and each battalion of demons saw her sword, a hush fell over them. The rhythmic beat of their swords and shields stopped.

She attacked and I blocked the first of many blows to come. The sound of steel on steel cracked the still night air. Tiny sparks shot out as our swords collided. Morrigan's powerful blows rocked through my body. Gripping the handle tighter to keep from dropping the sword, my arms vibrated from the impact.

She raised an eyebrow, smiling at me, as if impressed by the fact I had not simply crumpled like paper under the force of her strike.

The muscles in my arms screamed as I brought the sword up and around for another blow.

Morrigan came at me again, and this time I dodged out of the way to the ground. Lunging forward, she sliced through the air as I rolled away. Her sword pierced the ground, narrowly missing my shoulder. My sleeve was pinned between the blade and the ground.

I yanked my arm, tearing the black cotton shirt. The fight would be over before it began at this rate. I needed something to separate the three of them. If the Triad was broken, we might actually have a chance. What I needed was a distraction.

And, as if reading my mind, Oberon jumped into action. The hairs on the back of my neck began to stand on end as the air became charged with electricity. Oberon had called lightning to him. There was a sudden, fierce crack of electricity. I couldn't afford take my eyes off of Morrigan, but I saw Oberon gathering the storm in his hands out of my peripheral vision. He directed the blast at Nemain just before Morrigan charged again. The edge of my sword stopped the blow.

Every attempt to parry her blows was costing as much strength as if I were on the offensive, and maybe more. If I kept blocking her, I wouldn't have any strength left to make an offensive strike of my own.

With my sword high above my head and with as much strength as I could muster, I swung down hard, knocking her sword from her loose grip. Had she not underestimated me, I never would have been able to do it. A smug, satisfied look took over my face. It didn't matter to me if she wasn't really trying. I'd knocked her weapon out of her hands. That was a major accomplishment.

A bright flash shot back at Oberon. He was flung back into the massive stones that formed the outer wall of the castle. His feet dug in and made a trench in the grass in his wake. I heard the air rush out of his lungs with the impact and knew he had been knocked unconscious. At least, that was what I was hoping—that he was just knocked out.

Anger reared up inside me, and I charged with the Retaliator pointed straight out in front of me. I had to chop her head off, but I knew I'd have to get her to her knees to do it. Cutting her somewhere else, anywhere else, could help me get her there. She swatted my sword away with her bare hand. Just swatted me away like a pesky fly.

I stumbled, but managed to catch the tip of the Retaliator in the ground and keep myself on my feet.

Morrigan held out her hand, palm up, and flexed her fingers, calling her sword to her.

I watched in horror as the sword rocked back and forth and then flew up off the ground and into her hand.

She wrapped those long spindly fingers around the handle once more. I shouldn't have expected anything else. Neither Lady Luck nor her sister Fate had ever been on my side before, so why the hell should they start now?

No movement or sound was coming from Oberon, and there was no way I could get to him.

If I turned my back on Morrigan to go check on him. I'd be killing us both. Where the hell was everyone? Why hadn't they come out to help us? I know I said I was going with or without them, but that was before she had killed the Watcher. Not to mention the fact I didn't really believe they wouldn't be forced to come out eventually.

"Agrona!" I growled.

If she had a trap, now would be a good fucking time to spring it on the Morrigna! No answer came. Not that I really expected one from her. But Mahalia? Oberon was out here with me, and Mahalia had to know the Watcher was dead. She had to feel the magic returning to her after the

Triad had killed him. Why didn't she do something? Why weren't the witches firing down on the *disii* from safe behind the arrow slits in the thick stone walls? Even if they were only safe for the time being, it was much better than the position I was in! Why the fuck was I out here by myself? And when the hell did any of them start listening to me? Obviously, I was talking like a crazy person in the hallway a while ago. They could have done a little more to stop me from coming out here.

Nemain and Badb stalked over to Oberon like two large cats.

The sight of them closing in on him threw me into high gear. Adrenaline washed over my self-doubt and second thoughts. I was out here now, and nothing I did would turn back the clock. I'd rather be dead than submit to the three of them anyway.

Neiman and Badb kept their attention focused on Oberon, inching closer and closer to him. Their bodies moved like liquid death, and it seemed ironic that two warriors could move so delicately. I didn't know what they wanted with him, but they weren't going to take him. Not while there was still life in my body.

I backpedaled, positioning myself between the demi-goddesses and Oberon.

Morrigan stepped forward, fully aware I wouldn't be able to simultaneously hold off the sisters from the side and her from the front. They continued to close in. Morrigan lowered her sword to her side, no longer feeling any need for her weapon, she snatched me up by my neck. Again. My windpipe began to crush under her powerful grip.

A thought tried to form in my head. It was something about opportunity, but I couldn't put it together. The pain and lack of oxygen were fogging up my mind. They were making it difficult—no impossible—to think. Pressure was building in my ears and behind my eyes. My head felt like it was going to pop. Words were still fighting to get through, flashing through the pea soup that had become my mind. I think "now" flashed in my mind a dozen times before I finally got it.

The weight of the Retaliator in my hands pulled on my arm. Managing to get a foot up, I planted it firmly in her chest. Hanging there, suspended in her arms like a child, I struggled to push myself away from her. My arms were free thanks to the cradle hold she had formed around my body. My foot pushing on her chest as she tried to hold me close created enough tension to turn her into a harness. When there was finally enough room between us, I lifted the sword and managed to get the tip just under her chin. I pressed hard enough to draw blood, forcing her to drop me.

She ran the back of her hand under her chin to wipe away the blood. The rage boiling up in her eyes was quickly washed away by shock when she discovered I had actually managed to cut her.

My ass softened the blow of my landing, sending a shock up my spine. I scrambled to get to my feet before she had ahold of me again. Morrigan wouldn't be bothered with taking the time to enjoy the kill. She'd just kill me, denying herself any pleasure in it, just to have me out of the way for good.

There was still no noise coming from Oberon, but the

sisters were within my peripheral vision. I wanted to turn and look at him to make sure he was breathing, but I couldn't risk turning my back to Morrigan. Keeping the two sisters in my line of sight was going to have to suffice for now. If Nemain and Badb moved, then I'd have to chance it, but I didn't want to stand there staring Morrigan down either. She'd win that contest and see that she had already scared the shit out of me. That was something I sure as hell wasn't going to let her see willingly. Instead of looking her in the eye, I looked at her shoulder. That trick seemed to work. I managed to avoid direct eye contact, but still kept her in my sight.

Something stirred behind her in the back line of her troops. The battalions of *disii* soldiers broke, losing formation as something attacked them from behind.

XLIV
FORTY-FOUR

A flash went off briefly, casting a light above the army of demons. Painful screeching replaced the foggy feeling stuck inside my ears. Then there was another flash, followed by more awful screeching. And then I heard it, a low familiar growl. I don't know how they got behind the *disii*, but Roul's growl was unmistakable.

He was there with his pack, and they were fighting their way up to us. The *disii* was suddenly cut off from the Triad as the vampires moved out from the shadows.

Agrona had answered me.

Or maybe I had just served my purpose. Had she baited me into coming out here, played me for the impulsive hothead that I was, and pissed me off enough that I walked out here and created a diversion? Whether or not I was really bait on the hook before didn't matter. By telling me that's all I was, she had insured I would come out here and do something. And I did. I may not have looked pretty creating the diversion they needed and perhaps should have found another way, but it worked.

Roul and Cash were moving up through the *disii* fast, each with their pack behind them. Flashes of light exploded around them. It was from the grenades Cash had made! A thick, putrid smell rode through the air, and I gagged a little. Worse than old garbage festering in the hottest summer sun, it rose thick and steamy into the air. It was the smell of death and spilled demon blood. Despite the fact the awful reek had made me vomit a little in my mouth, it actually helped clear my head.

I reached for the Retaliator, which I had dropped when Morrigan dropped me. Sword in hand, I stood. By the time I was on my feet, the Triad was moving down the hill toward the vampires, who were pressing the demons back to the wolves. Guns and bombs cut through them with ease. Holy water bullets sliced through the demons like hot knives through butter. Demons made a nice shield for the vampires, keeping them safe for the time being from the holy water being fired by the wolves.

They would be finished with the *disii* in no time, and it was a good thing too. The guns, the explosions, and the screams of the dying were so loud that all of Massachusetts would hear.

Captains on both sides of the battle lines shouted orders barely audible over the earth-shaking booms of the IEDs. Pieces of wolf, vampire and demon were splattered all over the field.

We had to end this fast. There were plenty of humans who risked living so close to the vampires, never really believing vampires considered people a food source. Obviously they didn't have too much interaction with Agrona and Kedehern.

I'd bet a town meeting with them would change a few minds. Maybe the real estate was too good, or maybe some families had simply been there too long to be uprooted by a bunch of vampires. Whatever the reason, they were there on the outskirts of Gallows Hill. Close enough to feel, never mind hear, the explosions. Goddess help us if they started coming out of their homes in their jammies and slippers to see what was going on. They would rightfully demand the police check it out.

Our hands were already full. We didn't need to add human police into the mix. I liked most of the people I worked with, but I had worked with them long enough to know this was no place for them to be. This pushed too hard against the sanity of everyday life. I think people had accepted all of us fairly well since the shift, but this was more than any of us could ask them to understand. Demons running free from the chains of hell? Sure, you hear someone spewing off about demons from behind a pulpit, but to actually see them running around up top? Let's just say it would do more than fill a few pews.

Searching through the mass of bodies, some veiled in shadows, some covered with slick gray skin, and some furry, I tried to find Roul. I'd seen him as a wolf earlier. Hopefully I could pick him out if he'd shifted. I needed to get to him and figure out a way to get close enough to Morrigan to chop her damned head off before my human coworkers arrived.

The wolves were relentlessly firing holy water bullets into the demons, leaving gaping burning holes in their leathery gray flesh. Cash might be an ass, but the guns he had supplied worked with the efficiency and accuracy he'd promised. I couldn't fault him there. A few more blasts from the IEDs were followed by screams from both demon and vampire. As I had feared, there were vampire casualties. There was just no way to contain the shrapnel and holy water once the grenades went off. But so far they had lost fewer members than the wolves. The vamps tried to keep a wall of *disii* between them and the wolves, but the ones closest to the *disii* were taking pretty hard hits.

The burning in my eyes and nose from that horrid demon smell eased up, which unfortunately meant I'd gotten used to the smell, not that there were fewer demons. We were killing them. They were piled high, but also so great in number it didn't seem like we had gained any ground.

Wolves from the rear and vamps on the front lines blew holes in the *disii*. But when one fell, another was right there to take its place. I kept scanning until I finally found the wolf I was looking for, plus one I wasn't.

Roul and Cash were moving forward. They were about halfway up the field, but had to stop every few feet and hack their way through more demons. If I wanted to talk to Roul, I would have to go out and meet them.

First things first. With the Triad's attention drawn to the fight, I risked checking on Oberon. He was still unconscious, which was probably for the best. Who wanted to be awake if they were just going to be in that much pain? I'm no nurse, but his pulse seemed normal, and that was something to be thankful for.

I slid a hand down the collar of his shirt and pulled out the bloodstone amulet he was wearing. The stone had turned a shade of red so dark it was practically black. It had absorbed all of the damage and pain it could. I unfastened the cording of my amulet and tied it around his neck. He needed it more than I did.

If I were lucky, Mahalia would have another. *There I go again, counting on luck.* It had never done me any good before. And now that I had thought it, I had pretty much guaranteed Mahalia had already given her last one away. Damn Murphy's law. Not that it mattered. I would rather go without than know I could have given it to Oberon, sparing him pain and possibly permanent damage. After placing a kiss on his forehead, I gave in to the urge to kiss his supple lips for perhaps the last time. Mahalia could heal him, and I could heal myself, but neither of us could do it without time. And time was something we were a little short on right now. It was hard to get up and leave him lying there unconscious and alone, but I forced myself to walk away.

I hadn't walked five steps when I caught sight of someone running toward Oberon. Crouched protectively in front of him, sword raised and ready to strike, I realized it was Amalie. Almost a second too late.

"I almost killed you, you know! Do you realize that?"

"Um, yeah, the sword pointed at my head kind of clued me in."

"Seriously, Amalie! Why didn't you say something? You know, something like, 'Maurin, wait, it's me Amalie.' Or how about, 'Hey, Maurin, I'm taking Oberon to Mahalia?' You know, something along those lines? Something that wouldn't almost get your head lopped off!"

"I *was* yelling. I'm still yelling, actually. I think that your hearing is a little messed up from all of the explosions!" Amalie pointed to her ears.

I don't know why I was surprised. My hearing had been shitty ever since my eardrum was blown out earlier. Maybe I didn't heal it correctly. If I managed to walk away from this alive, I'd have to get that checked out. I told her I planned to find Roul and asked her to look after Oberon for me. "How are you going to get him inside? I mean you can't carry him by yourself. You're not going to just stay out here with him, are you? Because if that's what you were going to do, then I'll help you get him inside before I go find Roul."

She smiled at me, and I was glad to see something chase the worry for Arcana and Oberon from her face.

"Actually, I thought I might just use magic," Amalie chided.

I snapped my fingers. "Right. Witch." I turned to go, waving goodbye to her as I started walking away. *How are you going to get him inside?* What a stupid question. I chuckled, glad for the chance to laugh at myself or at anything, for that matter. It's always been my sense of humor, dry and sarcastic, that got me through all the really bad shit in my life. This was no exception. Monty Python's *Always Look on the Bright Side of Life* came to mind, and I hummed it out loud as I made my descent down the hill. I hummed that tune with all my heart until a *disii* knocked the wind right out of me.

I hadn't seen the blow coming, not that I was really looking for one. Not that I expected to make it all the way to Roul without a tussle, but I didn't expect a seven-foot, three-hundred-pound *disii* to come charging at me from the side either.

Thick, charcoal flesh half covered with an incomplete

set of armor slammed into my right shoulder hard enough to send me flying back onto my left side. My hip throbbed instantly on impact. Black eyes seemed to pierce my skull, as he followed me down. I bounced a little when he landed on top of me, and some more air rushed out of my lungs. He had me partially pinned from the right. My left side was grateful not to have taken the second blow plus his weight.

A helmet hadn't been part of his armor, so he definitely wasn't *An ChaipBhais*. He was too small to be A Cap of Death anyway. The breastplate and gauntlets he wore dug into my right arm and side under the weight of him.

I couldn't read the rune words etched into his armor. Mahalia could probably decipher them from the imprint left behind on my skin. As heavy as he was, it should leave a clear enough mark. Maybe it was it a spell or some kind of enchantment to aid them while they were roaming the Earth.

With the Retaliator hopelessly pinned beneath me, I reached for the XD. It was the only gun out of the three Cash had given me that I still had. The Eco and the Benelli were in the truck Morrigan had blown up. I hadn't given them a second thought until now. Baylen's little pep talk about chopping her head off kind of made me forget about the guns. The XD and the Retaliator were attached to me when I got out of the truck. Otherwise, they'd be melted in the crispy remains of the truck too. Fortunately for me, the two men who saw fit to arm me also thought about different ways for me to carry the weapons around. With my left hand wedged between my back and the ground, I fought to pull the XD out of the holster. Easier said than done. The holster was on my belt, and it was on my right side, so it didn't hit the scabbard for the Retaliator every time I took a step. I tried to roll and managed to get a little lift, just enough room to shove my hand another inch. Muscles and tendons screamed in my shoulder as I stretched beyond my limits of flexibility. My fingers reached the butt of the gun, but couldn't get enough of a grip to pull it loose from its holster.

The demon raised his upper body slightly, still holding me in place with the crushing weight of his enormous legs. He was almost sitting on me and drew back, ready to land a blow to my face.

I turned to the right and shut my eyes before the blow landed. If he hit me before I got my gun loose, I didn't want him breaking my nose. With some of his weight off my chest I was able to roll my upper body a little more, giving me just enough space to get the gun loose from the holster, but not in time to avoid the blow.

His massive hand smashed down on my left cheek, splitting it wide open. It felt like he had shattered a couple of bones too. Maybe it would have been better to just let him hit me straight on. A nose job was probably easier than an entire face realignment. I was seeing more than just stars. It was more like the whole damned Milky Way. He was pulling back for another blow by the time I could finally see again.

This time I whipped the gun around and stuck it right in his armpit. I'd never get through the breastplate, so that was the next best place I could think of. He might have seen it coming if I'd tried to blow his face off.

He was a demon, but that didn't make him dumb. Quite the contrary, in fact. Demons were devilishly clever, no pun intended, and frighteningly attuned to the movements of humans. I was still human enough not to take the risk of him seeing a gun moving toward his face.

I pulled the trigger three times, as fast as it would let me.

He reared back, howling in pain as the bullets tore through the skin, sending blessed water into his blood-stream. Veins faintly glowed under the skin as the holy water ran through them. Steam or smoke started seeping out of his pores as his body burned from the inside out. His face, contorted and hideous with the pain, helped keep his focus off of me long enough to fire three more rounds into his forehead. He dropped like a ton of bricks. Fortunately for me, his head was so big that when combined with the force of the impact, he toppled over onto his back and away from me. I would have had a hell of a time trying to roll him off of me.

I stayed where I was for a few seconds, trying to slow the bleeding from my cheek. Concentrating on my face and what it looked like before the *disii* crushed it under his massive fist, I imagined my reflection staring back at me in a mirror. The blood slowed and finally stopped, but there was still a burning sensation in my cheek.

I slid the gun with half of its twelve-round clip remaining back into its holster and reached across my face to feel the cut on my cheek. The gash wasn't as wide as I had feared and if I focused on it hard enough later, I might not get a scar. Even though nothing seemed broken, I was still going to have to learn how to heal bones properly. It proved to be a very worthwhile skill to have. If the rest of my life were anything like the last couple of days, then that new skill might be the only thing keeping me out of traction.

Back on my feet, I made my way to where Roul and Cash were, shockingly, fighting side by side. I guess the old adage 'the enemy of my enemy is my friend' is true. Things would go back to normal soon enough, though. When this was all over, if both of them were still standing, they would go right back to despising each other. Cash's challenge would be met, and pack law would rule once more.

Roul saw me coming and shouted something. I couldn't hear what he was saying at all, however. Either everything around me was too loud, or my hearing was getting even worse. Damn, I was really going to have to get my ears checked after this. He yelled again, and this time I caught the words "Behind you!"

In one swift movement, I pulled the XD back out of the holster and whipped around. One of the *An ChaipBhais* was headed straight for me. Those sons of bitches were bigger than your run of the mill demon. Weighing in at over four-hundred pounds and nine or ten feet tall, I would need more than a step ladder to see eye to eye with him. The ground shook violently as he charged toward me. I'd never get out of the way in time.

An ChaipBhais dressed in full armor, and he was no exception. The skullcaps they wore were reminiscent of medieval times, with the slightly domed top and a thin sliver of metal that ran down the nose. His suit was made up of several pieces of thick linked chainmail with a small-skirted breastplate over the top. He had thigh and shin guards, which were dented and dull from previous battles, and a pair of war boots to complete the set. It sounded like someone was shaking pots and pans filled with change as he ran toward me. There were fewer soft spots to hit on this one than the *disii* I'd just dropped, making it harder to put him down with just the XD.

I gripped the gun and aimed for his face. It was hard to keep it aimed on a moving target, but the XML mini-light attached to the underside of the barrel helped. Exhaling, I steadied myself. A tiny red light bounced off of his skin, and I fired. Four pulls on the trigger. *Pop, Pop, Pop, Pop!*

The gun was compact and fit nicely in my hands. It was comfortable and easy to hold. My fingers didn't feel stretched between the butt of the gun, which was slightly extended from the twelve-round clip, and the trigger like other guns I had trained with. It's almost like it was purposely made to fit a woman's smaller hand. Though I doubted that, once I really thought about it. I seriously doubted a guy would intentionally design a badass gun this compact that could blow a nice-sized hole in someone yet still fit into a dainty handbag. It didn't quite have the kick Cash had promised, but I could definitely feel it more without the end of the barrel pressed against the forehead of my target. The first shot panged off his helmet. I hit him at least once below his eye, blowing out his cheek and leaving his face a bloody mess. Another bullet hit him square in the eye, sending bits and pieces flying out of the socket. What was left dangled there liked a chewed up cherry tomato. Gross.

Ever the unlucky one—my luck might be bad, but at least it was consistent—the shots weren't enough to get him to his knees.

He picked up his pace and was only a couple of steps

away from me.

I didn't need the little laser on the end of my gun this time. With my stance squared, I raised the gun just a little higher, and pulled the trigger two more times. One bullet went through his already-mangled cheek, and the other blasted through the corner of his mouth. He still wasn't dead. For the love of all things holy, why wouldn't he just die already?

He lowered his upper body, almost hunched over to my level, and prepared to ram into me. What the hell is with these demons anyway?

I pulled the trigger again. *Click. Oh, fuck! Click.* Empty. Continuing to pull the trigger even after you know you're out of ammo is a little like tapping the face of your watch after the battery dies. It's completely pointless.

I must have miscounted somewhere. The clip held twelve, but I was already out of bullets. Maybe the *disii* I dropped first had cost me more ammo than I thought? *Shit!* He was too close to reload now. With him bent over, we were almost eye-to-eye. I held the XD in my left hand and shoved up and out with my right palm. What was left of his face, all the splintered bone and blasted flesh, slid back under the force of my blow. His helmet slid back off of his head, taking with it a disgusting mash of his flesh and bone. Only then, with his face completely caved in, did he finally go down. The smell of burning tires struck my nose. It had to be from the holy water. He was dead before he got to me, he just didn't know it. It was working its magic on the inside of the demon corpse lying at my feet.

Scanning around me, I tried to find a clear path to Roul and Cash. There wasn't one. Battles raged on all around me. Everywhere I turned, the way was blocked with fighting or piles of the dead and dying. Grabbing a clip from one of the pockets on the front of my pants, I reloaded my gun. Tossing the empty clip on the ground, I kept moving, firing at anything that got in my way.

Roul and Cash were back to back, turning like arms on a clock. They kept a circle clear around them with a steady stream of bullets, blasting through the demons that had closed in on them and leaving a heaping pile of sizzling, smoking dead all around them. By the time I got close enough to get hit in the crossfire, the shots had stopped. The *disii* were on the run, moving on to other prey. They'd find some prey that was less likely to leave them looking like melted Swiss cheese. I had to practically climb over the dead to get to Roul.

"I don't know how long Mahalia and the rest of them can hold the shields. If we can't finish this soon, it's going to spread," he said when I got close enough to hear him.

"What?" I asked. "I didn't even realize she was doing that. I was wondering why there weren't any blue lights flashing or sirens blaring yet."

"If you look up, you can almost see it, like a haze over the sky," Roul said.

He was right. There was something clouding the night sky. I had just assumed it was the Triad.

"Hey, you two might want to quit stargazing for a minute. Looks like they're about to do something up there!" Cash called out.

Roul and I turned to see the Triad standing in the middle of the battle, athames pointed toward the heavens. Morrigan reached for a small pouch on her belt and pulled out a large black stone. The three began to chant.

I couldn't understand all of the words, but I heard enough to know that it wasn't anything good.

> *"As spears, as swords, as arrows,*
> *Let the Sun send out his rays.*
> *Weapons from the hands of these mighty warriors to strike down all who cannot withstand the day!"*

The stone, now floating in the air just above her open palm, began to liquefy. It hung there suspended, like thick, black tar. Something stirred deep inside my mind and with great conviction, I knew it was Obsidian. It was used to change time or season, allowing things that were normally done during the day to be done at night, for example. Slowly the sky began to lighten. The black blanket drawn over us was slowly being pulled back, and sunlight began breaking through. They were changing time. They were actually making the damned sun rise!

"Oh for shit's sake!" I sighed, at a loss for anything else to say.

"I'll second that sentiment," Cash replied.

Roul never took his eyes off of the Triad. "Looks like they're through leaving it up to the *disii*. That's going to take out about half of our forces. If Baylen's right about what you have to do, we've got to get you up there and fast. If they can make the damned sun come up, then you've got to finish this soon, before there's nothing left of us."

Shadows began darting in and out of the rays of sun shooting up from the horizon.

Vampires were scattering to find shelter from the deadly sun.

Roul began to climb up and over the corpse wall. Blasting his way to the Triad, he left Cash and I scrambling to catch up.

After the two burly wolves made their way out of the neat wall they'd formed around them, it completely collapsed, leaving a seeping messy pile. I had a hell of a time, stumbling my way through the limbs, trying not to step on a torso. It seemed wrong, demon or not, to be walking on anything dead. Hopping over the last of the bodies, I picked up my pace to a light jog to catch up to Roul and Cash. If getting me to the Triad was the goal, they were doing a piss poor job of it, since I was still this far behind them.

My clothes were soaked with blood from climbing and crawling through the massacre that Roul and Cash had left behind them. Not that I'm complaining about the *disii* casualties. It's just that I doubted very much the matted hair on my head was from sweat alone. Between my tatter-ed, bloody clothes and my filthy hair, I must have been quite a scary sight. *Carrie* just wasn't a good look for me.

The two wolves in front of me were blowing a hole in anything that got in their way, making a clear path to the Triad. Night had almost been completely turned to day, and small bursts of light and smoke began erupting at every turn.

I soon realized what I thought were exploding IEDs were actually vampires. Helpless, suffering vampires who either couldn't find shelter before the sun washed away the darkness, or who were held there, forced to face the thing they had given up when they became undead. One of the few things that would make them truly dead—the sun.

Like small funeral pyres, the burning undead dotted the field, and I couldn't help but mourn them. I had heard once that even a burnt vampire could come back if his or her ashes weren't properly scattered. There wasn't much of a breeze, and I wasn't sure if that was a good thing or a bad thing. Would they be forever trapped in a pile of ruin in an undead state? Or would they slowly reform themselves and find little critters to feed upon until they regained enough of themselves to hunt the larger prey they loved so much? Would the feet stomping across the ashes be enough to scatter them? I couldn't think about it anymore. The horrible sight of it, the sadness of it all, would suck me in and pull me down into a bottomless pit of despair. Casualties are expected with this sort of thing. What you don't expect is to see an ally or a friend burst into flames before your eyes.

Much to my surprise, I hoped Medea wasn't one of them. The vampire had suffered enough, tortured not only with physical pain, but also the ruthless murder of Seamus right in front of her. She had been forced to watch them kill him and then turn him into a demon. For her to die now would be doubly cruel. Maybe she wasn't even out here, having recently been staked to a stone wall and left to drip dry. Sure, she'd fed and healed the gaping hole in her chest, but maybe it wasn't enough to fully regain her strength. She could be within the castle walls, safe for the time being, since they hadn't breached the outer wall yet. I wasn't willing to lose anybody else I knew, even the ones I didn't particularly care for.

XLV
FORTY-FIVE

Sparks and cinders floated on the air, and the smell of burnt flesh and bone had my stomach churning. The Triad had opened a floodgate of demons by bringing on the daylight. I may have had a hard time believing in them, but that didn't mean I didn't know anything about them. I'd had a pretty scary Sunday school teacher when I was a kid. She had told us terrifying things in order to make us behave. Who knew it would actually come in handy later? Thinking demons weren't out during the day was a common misconception. Demons could, and did, walk among us all the time, just waiting to seize an opportunity of human weakness. Without the vampires to help hold them back, the *disii* were easily over taking the wolves now.

The path to Morrigan was quickly blocked by six *A ChaipBhais*. Standing shoulder to shoulder, they formed a mountain range of metal and muscle.

Cash threw a grenade, sending bits of dirt and *disii* flying into the air. Similar small explosions came from both my right and my left. I didn't realize how much we were holding back in the way of explosives while the vampires were still out here. One after another, grenades were launched from HK-416s. Explosions rocked the ground after a few more IEDs were detonated.

The gap between me and Roul filled with demons, causing me to fall further behind. I couldn't even see the back of his head anymore. No one could hear me over the demon war cries and the wails of the dying. The *disii* closed in, pressing and shoving closer and closer. Being trapped in a demon mosh pit was definitely not on my to-do list. It was going to be impossible to haul ass out of here. If I moved right, they moved right. They were quickly closing in on me.

I wished now that I still had my bloodstone amulet. These things were about to bring on the pain, and having a bank to put it in would be kind of helpful. Now this was really going to hurt like hell. If I'd thought about it for even half a second before I left Oberon with Amalie, I would have taken it back. He didn't really need it with Amalie there to help him. Well, it is what it is. Pain or no pain, I was going to have to fight my way out of here.

Heavy footsteps and the distinct sound of armor clanging came up to my left. I'd be damned if one of those things was going to charge me again. Turning, I thrust my foot up and out in a hard front snap kick. It landed square in the demon's jaw, sending him tumbling ass over teakettle to the ground. He was flat on his back, and I pounced, dropping my foot onto his face. My knee was raised chest high, ready to drop another bomb on his face when a demon grabbed ahold of me by the shoulders and tried to pull me down. I let the force building in my leg go and dropped my foot on the face of the demon still on the ground. Something cracked and gave way in his face. If that had been one of the *An ChaipBhais*, I'd have been in real trouble. A foot to the face would hurt, but it wouldn't split skulls when they had helmets on. This was just a *disii*, so his head was more vulnerable.

The demon at my back let go of my shoulders and was now trying to rip off my scabbard and the Retaliator. *Oh, hell no!* I shoved an elbow into his stomach. A flash of pain and heat instantly flared in my elbow as it met with the armor plating covering his stomach. He laughed, and that was all the motivation I needed. I ate the pain in my arm like candy and thrust my fist up and back into his face. It connected with his mouth. Blood spurted from his busted lip and started running down my hand and arm. When it was still dark, I had thought the blackness of the demon blood was a trick of the eye. It wasn't. The sunlight was glistening on the black blood now running down my forearm. It slid down my arm slow and thick, like molasses. I tried to rub it off on my pants. Some of it came off, but the rest just smeared on my skin like engine grease.

The blood seeping out from his split lip ran slowly, but the blow to his face didn't slow him down at all. He hit me hard in the back with a closed fist, and with such force I couldn't even get my hands out in front of me to break the fall.

I went from standing to face first in the dirt in three seconds flat.

The demon had grabbed my ankle and started dragging me.

Scrambling to get free of his grip, I dug my fingers into

the ground, clawing and scratching in the grass as he pulled me behind him. He only had a hold on one ankle, so I kept kicking at his hand with my free foot. His grip only tightened. They say you eat a pound of dirt before you die. I think I ate about six pounds as my head bounced along the ground. The pain that started when he hit me was only getting stronger, no thanks to the unnatural bend in my back from having my foot raised so high and my upper body pressed into the ground as he dragged me along. With my fingers still tearing through the dirt and grass in a desperate attempt to slow us down, I winced as I felt two of my fingernails rip right off. I looked back at the trail of my claw marks and finally conceded it wasn't working. The blood rushing to my head was also making me feel a little dizzy.

From the angle we were on and the length of the grooves I had made in the grass, I'd say he had me about halfway up the hill. Halfway back to where the Triad was. *Shit!* I was trying to get to them, but not alone. Morrigan was problem enough. There was no way I could take on all three of them by myself. My head skipped over a rock, and I could feel the cut it made on my temple. Blood wasn't pouring out of it, so I figured it was superficial. No sense wasting energy on something so small. I'd need every ounce of it when this dumb hulk dropped me off for the Triad.

The war cries of the *An ChaipBhais* had nearly drowned out the wolves. Things had taken a turn for the worse. Without any vampires, we were grossly outnumbered. Even with the coven sending volley after volley of magic down on the *disii* from the tower tops and behind the arrow slits in the castle walls, there were still too many standing. No one would come to help me. It was hard enough for them to stay alive, never mind hack their way up to save me.

My hands and fingers ached from being raked through the dirt. Barely able to make a fist, I reached behind me and tried to pull out the Retaliator. The sword slid almost completely out of the scabbard, but without the room to swing my arm around, the tip was stuck in its sheath. If we reached Morrigan before I freed the Retaliator, I was in big trouble. Not that I wasn't in trouble already. I could scarcely deny that being dragged off to three ancient sister goddesses wasn't trouble. Unfortunately, it was exactly the kind of trouble I was looking for. However, getting there without some kind of weapon in my hand was not.

I took my hand off the grip of the sword and let more than half the blade hang out of the scabbard over my shoulder. Grabbing hold of the blade and squeezing tightly so that it didn't slip out of my hand, but not so tightly that I cut myself, I pulled the sword free. Letting go of the tip of the scabbard with my left hand, I swung my arm out in front of me. Still holding the sword by the blade, I carefully swung it over my head. Steadying the sword with my left hand, I repositioned my right hand back onto the bone grip. Having the Retaliator back in my hand gave me renewed confidence, but as much as I wanted to get myself turned around and hack this demon to pieces, I didn't. My attempts to fight him off before hadn't worked. I was going to have to try something else. What that something else was, I had no idea. If I was going to do something, I had to come up with it fast.

We were almost to the top of the hill. I tightened my grip on the handle of the Retaliator and did the only thing I could think of. I played dead. We reached the top, and he tossed me like a broken plaything at the feet of the Triad. Air rushed out of my lungs but I managed to force back the yelp that almost crossed my lips. Dead people don't cry, and Morrigan needed to believe I was dead.

The Retaliator was stuck underneath me. That was good and bad. Good that the blade was not on its side so I didn't slice a chunk of my torso off when I hit the ground. Bad because a dead person doesn't roll over and pull out their sword. That was a major kink in my plan. Because I was forming a plan, even if it was a simple one. No fancy explosions or sword fights to save the world from total domination, just a plain and simple little idea. And it all hinged on the Triad falling for one of the oldest tricks in the book.

Unsure if the gift that had been dropped at her feet was really and truly dead, Morrigan kicked me hard in the ribs. I felt and heard something in my chest crack. So I could add a couple of broken ribs to my growing list of injuries.

I fought the natural instinct to stiffen against the blow. Instead I stayed limp, letting my body go with the impact. The force of her kick rolled me onto my back. My arm draped across my chest, the Retaliator loosely held in my hand at my side. *Pretty convenient.* Almost like I had planned it that way. I tried to hold onto the sword. A tight grip would give me away, so I left my fingers loosely wrapped around the grip. The bone handle was smooth and cool against my fingers, a chilling reminder of how close to my death I actually was.

Even the smallest twitch would give me away under her watchful eye. I concentrated on being dead, which wasn't hard to do, since I felt like death warmed over anyway. My body hardly put up a fight playing dead. In fact, I'd say it was downright cooperative. Since I hadn't mastered healing myself, I needed time to stop and concentrate to do it. This was the first chance I'd had so far. Unfortunately, I couldn't think about healing right now. All I could think about was being still. Silently cursing myself once more for letting the bloodstone amulet go, I tried to slow my breathing. She would be watching to see if my chest fell back into a natural rhythm. When it did, she would make sure I was truly dead. Short and shallow breaths were all I'd allow myself. I was too afraid she'd see me if I took a deep breath.

It was a good thing I wasn't breathing deeply because, from what I could smell, anything more would have me heaving. The smell of boiling, spoiled meat, and trash permeated the air. Hot and thick, the smell wafted past, and my stomach roiled. I tried to ignore it and imagined I was breathing through a coffee stirrer. I fought desperately to keep the panic of suffocation in check. By sheer will, I slowed my heartbeat and lay there dead, as far as anyone could tell. At least, I hoped so.

Finally satisfied with my performance, she turned her attention to the *disii* who had brought me to her. She spoke in a tongue I've never heard. I couldn't understand the words, but it sounded like she was bestowing a blessing on him and then dismissing him. She sent him back out into the carnage that was once Gallows Hill Park.

He grunted some form of thanks and left. His heavy

footsteps grew softer and softer until the distance between him and us was too great to hear or feel his presence. The three sisters were overjoyed with their success so far. It was easier than they had expected. Morrigan's voice was enough to rocket my heart up into my throat as she spoke to her sisters.

"Is your cauldron complete, Badb? This will be finished soon, and I do not want any delays. Once the cauldron boils over and the land is barren, the people will look to us to make it right. They will worship us and lay a great sacrifice before us to return the dying land back to its greener glory," Morrigan said to her sister.

"It was I who presided over that cauldron for centuries before the mortals abandoned their pagan shrines, sister. I have fanned the flames beneath it, stirred the great cosmic brew of life and death for more than an eternity. Of course it is ready," Badb replied, with an acid tongue.

"Take care, sister, we have come too far and we are too close to the end for foolish errors. I am well aware that you preside over the cauldron, which is why I look to you to for assurance that all is prepared," Morrigan said.

Badb seemed irritated with Morrigan for even asking, but reassured her sister nonetheless. "All is prepared and as it should be, dear sister."

I waited, hoping at least one of the sisters would leave or, at the very least, become distracted. It looked like I'd be waiting a long time. I had a plan, albeit not very well thought out. Or even a complete one. Actually, my plan got about as far as playing dead. Mission accomplished. Now, all I had to do was come up with part two.

Morrigan called the captain of the *An ChaipBhais* to her.

I'd never be able to pronounce his name and decided it wasn't worth trying to file it away in the recesses of my mind.

My heart tried to pick up the pace as I lay there listening to her plans.

Having practically wiped the field of all resistors, it was time to turn their attention to the cowards within the castle walls. They had plenty of demons left—enough to divide their forces. Should there be excessive losses, then Ouzel could simply call more. Ouzel! I had almost forgotten about that rotten bastard.

Morrigan ordered her captain to assemble a large group of *disii* to tear the castle down. The demons would dig under one corner of the castle, forming a tunnel, and then set a fire. Weakened by the lack of support under just one corner, the castle would crumble, and the flames would spread. When the diggers were in place, he was to take the rest of the *An ChaipBhais* and storm the castle. Once inside, they could do whatever they wished with its inhabitants. All but the High Priestess, that is. The priestess would be brought directly to Ouzel, who would dispose of her in his own way. Morrigan sent the captain away to gather his forces and called for Ouzel.

He came quickly, walking with the same arrogance with which he spoke. The ground vibrated with each step he took. His stride seemed overly confident for a demon who had failed to accomplish a task as simple as kidnapping a psychic. There weren't any hostages on top of the hill, and so far they'd made no mention of one.

"Despite your many failed attempts to secure the psychic, here she lies. The vessel finally lies before my sister's feet, but she is not there by your hand. No, not by the demon that was charged with this task, but by a *disii* who can't even walk among the mortals. By a demon that is only free to roam the earth because we called him here. You, who are free to walk among them, the trickster, the demon caller, cannot even manage to discover the chosen human. How many precious hours did you waste, Ouzel, tracking and killing the wrong human?" Venom all but dripped from her lips as Nemain spoke to him.

Fuck. I was the psychic? Isn't that just great. Why didn't I just stick a fucking apple in my mouth while I was at it? Bet this wasn't part of Baylen and Agrona's master plan.

Badb jumped in, "But you must admit that his last attempt was most amusing. Turning the human and then leaving him for the little vessel to kill?"

"We did not bring him here for compliments, dear sister," Nemain snapped.

Ouzel was way too full of himself to stand there and listen to this. "I may not have found her, but it wasn't me who left the job undone in the burial mound," he replied, cool and confident as ever.

They should just kill him now. I definitely did not want to help the Triad in any way whatsoever, but he was so damned arrogant while speaking to a demi-goddess, albeit an evil one, that I wanted to kill him myself. Not that I didn't have my own reasons to slit his throat.

"You dare to question the Morrigna? Please, sisters, let us rid ourselves of this gobshite." Neiman practically begged her sisters for permission, and her power, her craze, pricked and pinched along my skin like needles.

Badb was actually keeping herself under control. "You

have been measured, demon, and have been found wanting. Morrigan offers you a chance to redeem yourself. Do not fail again. I assure you, you will not like our response!"

"I am at your disposal, Morrigan, as always." He addressed her directly, dismissing the other two demi-goddesses.

"You would do well to stay within my graces, demon. I would caution you not to dismiss my sisters so carelessly or I may make you their plaything. They do so like to play after they have labored through a long battle," Morrigan warned.

She must have heard it too. There was something in his voice that didn't just dismiss her sisters, but also said he would turn on her the second an opportunity presented itself. He was a power leech and the second a stronger being came along, he would latch on like the parasite he truly was.

"I am here only to serve you," he said to her.

"Of course you are." She laughed and it was a terrifyingly cold and cruel laugh. Yup, she had heard it. She apparently needed him for something else, however, because instead of killing him on the spot, she gave him new orders. "Well then, gobshite, let us see the depths of your devotion. My captain will bring you the priestess. I expect you to rid us of her. Heed this warning, Ouzel. Do not make the mistake of thinking there is additional value in your service to us. You continue to walk this plane simply because I allow it. Fail me again, and I will tenderize your flesh with my best whips and marinate you in your own blood before feeding you to the Black Dogs."

Morrigan said all of this casually as if she was ordering a

value meal, but I believed her completely.

"As my lady wishes, so it shall be," he said.

Oh, I could just vomit. What an ass. He had to know he was dead either way. She'd kill him if he couldn't kill Mahalia, or kill him even if he did, having served his purpose. The question I wanted answered was why did she want to kill Mahalia? Apart from the obvious reasons of knowledge, experience, and strong magic, that is. But none of those seemed to warrant bringing her out to Ouzel for execution. Why was she singled out and not Baylen? Surely the *An ChaipBhais* could handle her. Unless she was more powerful than I thought, or knew something I didn't, which wasn't that hard to believe.

Ouzel took his sweet time about leaving. I was pretty sure she had dismissed him with the whole 'feed you to my dogs' thing, but he lingered a few seconds more before finally turning to leave. It seemed like an eternity waiting for him to depart. Waiting for whatever was going to happen next.

Still immobile on the ground, I was completely at a loss as to what to do. There was no way to warn anyone or tell them what I'd heard. If Seamus were here, then I could talk to him without ever speaking a word. No one else here could do that, at least not that I knew of. It would have been a good idea to find that out before. God forbid something like this should ever happen again, but if it did, we were going to have some sort of checklist. Psychic gifts? Check. Ability to regenerate or heal thyself? Check. Good things to have on a list before you go out to fight the bad guys, right in between guns and flashlights. Right now, I didn't have a clue as to who could really do what. When this was all over, if I was still alive and had all my working parts, I just knew someone was going to say, 'Well why didn't you just say so? If you had only touched the mental link…', and I was going to bash them right in the eye when they did.

A tremor ran underground from the bottom of the hill. The little tremors grew and grew until they were a full-blown quake. Like thunder, the footsteps of the *An ChaipBhais* and their legion of demons rumbled past me. In droves, they stomped up the hill to the designated corner of the castle. Pulling up the rear was a slower moving group of *disii*. They moved together in a unified but labored pace. Their heavy breathing and grunting told me whatever it was they were carrying up the hill was extremely heavy. Was it something to help them take down the castle wall? The drumming of their footsteps got farther away from me and closer to the demise of everyone inside.

Roul and Cash hadn't even gotten close to where I was. It was time to face facts. They were either badly hurt or dead. From what I could see over the shoulder of the *disii* who had carried me up here, most of the wolves had been ripped to shreds. Pieces of them were scattered across the blood-soaked ground. An occasional whimper could be heard in the background.

Some had shifted in a last ditch effort to heal themselves. When a were shifts, their whole physical make-up changes, speeding up their healing process. It's part of what makes them so hard to kill. But they couldn't regenerate limbs, and no amount of shifting would stop the blood loss from having your arms or legs ripped off.

My heart ached for Olwyn. Her husband, like most of her

pack, was destroyed. Even if she walked away from this, I don't think she would survive losing her mate.

A loud boom of wood against metal snapped my attention back from remembering the horrible images of the battered and torn bodies of the dead and dying. There was another deep boom and then a crash. Demons must have broken through the massive metal doors that led into the castle. Warmth from the crackling bonfire slowly made its way over to me as the Triad's plan continued to unfold. The castle had been breached, its cornerstones compromised. Any second now, Ouzel would drag Mahalia out for her execution.

XLVI
FORTY-SIX

The clean smell of mint and herbs floated through the air. All my senses flared to life as the rot and musk of the demons was cleansed from my nose. My body felt instantly restored and my courage renewed. Without thought or fear, I took a deep breath. It wasn't just his scent that permeated the air, but his essence as well. I pulled him into me as the air filled my lungs. The smell was so thick I could taste it and feel it on my tongue. Oberon was here. With each breath of him, my strength and spirit grew. Breathing didn't just bring a rush of power, it brought the attention of the Triad. My eyes flew open, and my grip on the Retaliator tightened.

Mahalia's voice cut through the painful silence, and Morrigan turned with a hate like I have never seen before in her eyes.

Badb and Nemain kept their eyes on me.

Mahalia began an invocation and with each syllable, her confidence and power grew. The air was electrified, and the static charge had my hair standing on end.

"Arawn, Lord of Annwfn, I call to thee.
Master of the Cwn Annwfn I call to thee.
Let your hounds of justice free.
Let them hunt.
Let them track the scent of those who have
preyed upon the innocent."

Morrigan screamed and spun around, her burning eyes back on me. With a crushing weight, the power of the Triad smashed into me. The hate, the fury, the bloodlust, all of it pushing, trying to keep me down. I knew Morrigan would strike while they tried to hold me with the force of their combined powers. And she would move at lightning speed when she did. But as I lay there on my back looking up at her, she seemed to be moving in slow motion.

I watched her come for me and tightened my grip on the Retaliator. The muscles in my hand ached. My knuckles were white from the effort of holding onto the sword.

She was diving down with her spindly fingers out-stretched, ready to wrap them around my neck.

I raised the sword, tilting the blade slightly, and let the weight of her body do the work.

It sliced clean through the flesh on the side of her neck and grated against the bone. There was no hiding the shock on her face as her mouth hung open. Her eyes widened as her own weight pushed the blade deeper into the bone. Blood, still warm, splattered across my face. She wasn't dead. Morrigan's head wasn't cut off. And I wasn't sure how to get out from under her. Sliding down the blade past the hilt, the goddess fell onto my chest. The weight of the

Triad's power eased back until all that remained was the physical weight of her body pressing down on me.

Badb and Nemain were weakened by Morrigan's current state. Stunned, they stood there motionless, staring down at their wounded sister.

The power that had been building since I first sensed Oberon hummed through me, reminding me it was there. I focused my power, focused it on moving her. With one hand off the sword, I balled the power up and forced my hand in between us. With my palm flat against her shoulder, I pushed, lifting her off of me. One more good push and I rolled out from underneath her.

My hand was stained red with her blood. Even after I tried to wipe it off on my pants, it still filled the little lines in my skin.

She hit the ground with a thud and a gasp.

Badb and Nemain seemed unsure whom to attack first. Should they start with Mahalia, who had been joined by Oberon and Phallon in her call to Arawn? Or should they attack me, since I had just slit their sister's throat?

They made their decision relatively quickly, but before they took their first step, the thunderous pounding of hooves kept them frozen in place.

I never took my gaze off the sisters, who stood frozen in fear from the sight of the herd speeding across the field. Morrigan laid next to me, her hand clasped to her neck, clinging to life as power and blood poured from her wound.

The pounding of hooves got louder, the soft vibration increased to a pounding inside my chest as they got closer. My blood pumped in time with their stride as they came up behind me. It wasn't until they came up alongside me that I realized they weren't horses at all.

At least nine massive, ethereal white dogs padded up around the Triad and me. The dogs stood somewhere around four feet high at the shoulders—a little taller than a Shetland pony.

I got on my knees and still only came about chest high on the huge dogs.

If the dogs attacked me, I'd have a better chance if I were on my feet. Not wanting to alarm them, I slowly stood up. The dogs, who could pass for large Great Danes if not for their ethereal intensity, watched my every move with a patient curiosity. With only a slight tilt of their large rectangular heads, they were almost eye-to-eye with me.

I looked at them with their powerful, smooth-muscled bodies and regal stance. Short white coats highlighted their muscular physique. Their cropped and pointed ears didn't have the usual pinkish color inside. Instead, the flesh inside their noses and ears was blood red. There was a faint lining of red around the edge of their mouth as well. The red flesh against the pure white coats made them look albino. They looked like very scary albino ghost dogs to me.

Red eyes turned to the Triad, and I watched their curiosity turn dark and deadly. They focused in on their prey. With lips curled and teeth bared, they emitted a low growl from their throats. These ethereal creatures made the Black Dogs look like pups. Not only were they bigger, but there was something in their appearance that was even more unsettling. Maybe it was the pink stains on the white fur on their muzzles that was more noticeable once they curled their lips back.

A voice boomed out from somewhere in the distance. With the dogs watching the Triad, I risked looking back. I can't explain why I felt like the dogs were on our side, but I did. Maybe it was because they were staring and growling at the Triad instead of at me.

A tall man with reddish-brown hair and eyes like liquid gold, wearing a long sleeve, dark-gray velvet tunic and black pants tucked neatly into knee high boots, made his way up to the top of the hill. There was something regal about the intricate silver embroidery around the V-neck collar of his tunic, and he had a braided, black leather belt fastened around his waist. His voice was deep and rich, sounding just the way chocolate tastes. "My beautiful beasts can strike fear into even the darkest hearts." The stranger stepped forward until his feet were right beside Morrigan's head. "It has been many moons since I have seen the three of you. I see Morrigan has already been judged, though her execution is not complete. It is highly unusual for this to begin before I am called. Have the others been tried as well?"

Badb and Nemain stood still. The only visible motion was a quiver in their hands hanging by their sides.

"I will take all this silence to mean no. You there, has judgment been rendered here? A punishment decided?" the man in the tunic asked.

He was asking me? Okay. "No, no it hasn't. Not for any of them."

"Really? That is most interesting. So Morrigan was wounded in battle? My, my, my, you have gotten rusty, Morrigan." He pushed her over onto her back with his foot.

She lay there looking up at him. Her blood pumped out

between her fingers in a seemingly endless supply, despite the pressure she was applying to her neck.

Pulling my gaze from her and the powerful man who had appeared out of nowhere with his ghost dogs. I looked past Badb and Nemain to the familiar outlines standing in front of the main gate of the castle. A smile reached my heart when I saw Oberon standing with Mahalia

He started to walk toward me, but Mahalia threw an arm across his chest to stop him. That was puzzling, to say the least. Why wouldn't Mahalia let him come over here? I could obviously use the help, and he wanted to come. So why stop him? Maybe Amalie wasn't able to fix him? Maybe he wasn't up to it yet? I had just assumed that because he was here helping Mahalia with a calling that he was healed, but maybe he wasn't. Any relief I had felt when I first saw him was once again chased away by worry.

The man in the tunic with the delicious, deep voice brought my attention back to him. "I am not used to being ignored by those who call me. Usually I have their undivided attention," he said.

A hand gripped my shoulder and spun me around. "There, that's better," he said.

I could feel my face scrunching up in confusion. "What? You're talking to me? I didn't call you," I told him.

"Yes, actually, I *was* speaking to you. Perhaps if you were focusing on the three goddesses and the lord before you, you would have heard me," he said angrily.

Oops. What do you say when a lord is scolding you? "Uh, right, sorry. Undivided attention."

"I do hate these modern times. If you didn't call me, then could you focus long enough to point me in the direction of whomever did?" he said.

I started to point him toward Mahalia, but something in her face stopped me. Didn't she call him? If she didn't do it, then who the hell did? Why didn't she want him anywhere near her? I didn't understand what was happening, but I stupidly engaged him in conversation anyway. "Hey, I don't even know who you are. How could I know who called you?"

He sighed, clearly annoyed he had to tell me who he was. He obviously thought I should know.

"Honestly, I have no idea why the three of you, the mighty Triad, wanted to come here." The man shook his head at the three sisters, before turning back to me. "I am Arawn, Lord of *Annwfn*. These beautiful creatures, the *Cwn Annwfn*, are mine." He gestured to the white dogs. "Never mind about who called me. It really makes no difference. I know why I am here," Arawn said.

He was about to give me the brush off, but something made him take a second look. "Do I know you? There is something so familiar about you," Arawn said.

Morrigan tried to say something, but all that came out through the blood was a gurgling sound.

"No, I don't think you do. Anyway, I'm pretty sure I would remember meeting a lord such as you," I told him.

He perked up at that. His chest puffed out with the idea of being unforgettable. "Yes, I suppose you would at that."

He held his hand out, and one of the massive white dogs padded over in two long steps with its softball-sized paws. The rest of his pack moved, all of them eager for a piece of his attention. They waited around his feet for a quick pat or stroke, like dogs around a table waiting for scraps.

"Thankfully, no verdict has been handed down, and my trip is not a waste. Let the hunt begin. The *Cwn Annwfn* shall seek the offenders."

The leader of the Wild Hunt called out something to his dogs in Gaelic, and they jumped to attention at his instructions. Ears back, they stood ready to track their prey. With another command they split into two groups of nine. The number of dogs I had previously counted had somehow doubled since they'd arrived. Not that I was complaining. He could bring a hundred of those dogs if they were going on a search and destroy mission for all of the bad guys.

The first group of nine was further split into three more groups of three as they made their way down the hill toward the legions of demons. One group stayed straight, one went right and the other went left. Terrible screams came from the demons as the *Cwn Annwfn* tore them apart. The three groups methodically moved through the masses across the battlefield, leaving the wolves alone. They really could tell the difference between the enemy and us. *Cool.* The remaining nine at the top of the hill broke apart into two groups. Six remained here with Arawn, the Triad, and me. The other three walked over to the main gate where Mahalia, Phallon, and Oberon were standing.

Pieces of Ouzel and the *An ChaipBhais* littered the ground and more were being hurled out from inside the gate. The castle was weakened at the corner where the fire raged on, and the rest of our group poured through the gate.

All of the familiar faces from the Council were there. Most of the new faces weren't. They had fared better than I thought they would inside the castle walls, but there were still many of us among the dead.

Three dogs weaved in and out of the crowd forming outside the main gate. They were searching for demons that hadn't already been killed, stopping occasionally to check the remaining pieces, just to be sure. Or at least that's what I thought. They kept moving from one person to the next until they finally stopped in front of two people who remained just out of my view. Gasps broke out, and the crowd started backing up. Once everyone had backed far enough away, I could finally see who it was.

I couldn't believe it either and didn't bother to hide my shock. The dogs had stopped in front of Baylen and Medea. What the hell was going on?

Right on cue, Arawn said the guilty had been found, and the search was now over. I guess this would normally take a long time, but this case was pretty cut and dry.

Morrigan, her sisters, and their army of demons. Evil. It was that simple. There was just one loose end, Baylen and Medea. What did Arawn want with them? They weren't guilty of anything. Well, okay, they were probably guilty of a lot of things, but nothing to do with this. The *Cwn Annwfn* had made a mistake. This couldn't be right.

"Wait! They made a mistake!" I shouted, in an attempt to stop whatever was going to happen next.

Arawn gave me a look that had the hairs on the back of my neck standing on end. Maybe I should have just kept my big mouth shut. Baylen's a big boy. He could handle this himself. If there was ever a time I wanted to take back something I'd said, that was definitely it.

"You dare to question my judgment? This is what the

Cwn Annwfn do. They follow the scent and the soul of wrongdoers. They hunt their prey into the ground—hunt them until they can run no more. They do not make mistakes. This is but a taste of what they are truly like. If the Blue Man should run, then you will see. So what shall it be, Blue Man? Falsely declare your innocence and try to escape? Or come with us willingly? I do hope you try to escape. My dogs have long been absent from the hunt. They do miss it so," Arawn said.

Baylen and Medea didn't move. She whispered something to him, and he nodded, but they didn't try to run. It was a wise choice, given the desire to chase that burned in the eyes of the *Cwn Annwfn*. I just didn't get it. How could Baylen be guilty? How was he involved? He didn't proclaim his innocence, but he hadn't admitted guilt either.

I needed answers so I decided to press my luck. I know what they say about curiosity, but it was certainly getting the best of me. Besides, if Baylen was guilty, then that meant I was right about my first impression of him and wrong about everything else. That I let myself be tricked into trusting him meant it had all been a setup. I couldn't swallow that. Not without a hard slap in the face with some reality. It'd probably feel more like a punch in the gut if Baylen confessed.

"Okay, the dogs don't make mistakes. Maybe he's guilty of a lot of other things. I'm pretty sure he is, actually. Couldn't they just want him for some of the other stuff he's done?" I asked.

Arawn's eyes softened just a little. "You know, one of the things that I have always adored about your kind is your innocence. Perhaps that is what inspires me to do what I do. But you border on the naïve. And while I find it endearing, it is growing tiresome. Think back to the beginning, child. He hasn't been with you since the beginning, has he? No, no, he hasn't. The *Cwn Annwfn* have chosen. All his deeds have been laid before me. And he has been busy, hasn't he, ladies? Why don't you tell the child all that he has done?" Arawn prodded.

He bent down to meet Badb and Nemain at eye level. Their torsos were held firmly in the jaws of the ethereal dogs. The fur, once stained light pink around their mouths, was now a dark red from the blood of the sisters.

Nemain tried to speak, but all she managed was a fit of coughing, which ended with her spitting blood everywhere. Badb didn't even bother. Blood was already pouring out of her mouth and nose from the pressure of the massive jaws clamped down around her midsection.

He stood back up and looked inquisitively at Baylen.

"Perhaps you would shed light on the matter then, Baylen Knightley? Or you, Medea, what do you have to say for yourself?" Arawn asked.

This was surreal. I mean everything up until now has been insanity, but this was just un-fucking-believable. And Baylen still wasn't denying it. He just stood there like a fucking mute. Well, if he wasn't going to say anything...

"Okay, fine. You don't deny it, so I'm going to assume you did it. You wanted world domination? Okay, I'll buy that. Crazier things have happened in the course of history. Even in the course of a weekend. But what I don't get is how you can let your best friend get fucking eaten and turned by a bunch of demons!" I shouted at him.

There. He had to deny it now. An innocent man wouldn't keep silent after that accusation.

"He didn't mean for Seamus to die. That was an accident!" Medea screamed in his defense.

"You son of a bitch. I'm going to kill you! You are going to rue the fucking day you gave me this sword." I whirled the Retaliator and was ready to storm over to him when Arawn grabbed me by the collar and snatched me back.

"This is not how it is done. You wield the sword of Manannan. There is a different task laid before you. As for this one, the one with whom it all began, he is mine. You, executioner, must finish what you have started," Arawn said.

He let me go and started walking over to Baylen and Medea. The three remaining *Cwn Annwfn* closed in on them. They snapped their teeth, and their saliva dripped in anticipation of sinking their teeth into sinful flesh. But before Arawn could give the command, Medea made their escape. She wrapped the shadows around herself and Baylen. Cloaked with darkness, they disappeared. They literally vanished and were gone.

No one moved. That is, no one moved except Arawn. I think we were all in shock that they were actually stupid enough to believe they would get away. Shock, however, was not a word I would use to describe how Arawn was feeling.

He closed his eyes, threw his head back, took in a deep breath and exhaled.

"I think I will give him a head start. I want to enjoy this. If I leave now, it will be over too quickly. It has been far too long since anyone believed in, let alone invoked, my name. I shall take my time. I'm actually pleased with the choice Baylen and Medea made. To be perfectly honest, I wanted them to flee. The *Cwn Annwfn* need the chase. It's been far too long since they've had someone on the run. Let them relish the look of fear in Baylen's eyes every time he glances over his shoulder and sees the ethereal dogs behind him. As far as I'm concerned the Blue Man and his nightwalker made the right choice, the only choice. As for you, executioner, are you going to wait until she regenerates herself and her sisters? Or perhaps you would like to finish it now?" Arawn said.

"Regenerate? Shit, she can still do that?" I asked in shock.

I didn't wait for him to answer. I had no intention of waiting around to find out the hard way. I stood over Morrigan with the sword held high above my head. With one hard swing, I brought the blade down into her neck. The tip of the sword dug in, and I was surprised by how easy it was to drag it back through the ground and her neck. I swung that sword with enough force to cut through the bone. It sliced through the muscle and skin on the other side as I pulled the sword back to me. It was done. Morrigan was decapitated.

Her head followed the tip of the Retaliator as I pulled the sword away from her body. It wasn't the dramatic ending I had pictured—blood spurting everywhere, severed head falling at my feet. The little roll after I had completely cut through was almost anti-climactic. Now ask me if I cared. She was dead, and I was alive. I couldn't ask for a happier ending. Ding Dong, the witch is dead!

Badb and Nemain cried out as they watched the life and

magic leave their sister. They wailed in pain as her body began to rapidly decay before their eyes. Their cries were so raw, and sounded so similar to the weeping of the *Caointeach*, that I almost felt sorry for them. Almost.

Unsure of what to do, I looked to Arawn. Should the blade of the Retaliator meet the flesh of their necks as well? Would they meet the same end as Morrigan had, or did he have other plans for them? I waited for my directions. None came.

The *Cwn Annwfn* devoured what was left of the Triad with the same battle lust and fury they had unleashed on us. It was a gruesome sight to witness. Nothing you see on Animal Planet could prepare you for the sight of six massive dogs in a feeding frenzy, tearing through flesh and crushing bone. Badb's and Nemain's cries of heartache quickly turned to screams of physical pain. Without Morrigan, they knew they were vulnerable. They felt every rip and tear of their skin and muscle and every break in their bones until finally there was nothing left of them but unrecognizable bits and pieces. All that was left were some small chunks of muscle, a few shreds of skin, and tiny shards of bone. This was, without a doubt, the worst thing I had ever witnessed. I thought what had happened to Seamus was the worst, but I didn't actually see him consumed by the *disii*. Killing the demon that rode his body was horrible, but this...this was a Wes Craven horror show.

It didn't matter if they deserved to die or if death was a justifiable punishment for all of their crimes against humanity. What mattered is that I was not accustomed to watching people die, and I didn't want to be. I believe in capital punishment only because there are some crimes that are so heinous in nature it is warranted. More than one piece of evidence found its way to a police officer because of the work I did. Evidence to prove that someone who had committed a crime was deserving of it. But I never went to stand witness at an execution. I've just never had the stomach for it. Maybe it was because I knew it would affect me too deeply or change the way I viewed my job. Maybe it's just fucked up to watch someone die.

The answers to those questions would come the first time I closed my eyes to sleep. They would torment me in my dreams. Dreams that were sure to turn to nightmares about the person I was becoming. A person who could so easily drive the blade of a sword into someone they knew, possessed or not. Someone who could cut off the head of their enemy without hesitation.

Exhausted, I sat down in the grass with my knees tucked into my chest. Warm rays from the sun fought off the chills from the shock starting to set in. Oberon's clean scent rolled over me, and again I breathed it in deeply. Without looking up, I gave the ground beside me a little pat. He plopped down next to me, wrapping an arm around my shoulder and pulling me to his chest. It felt good to be held and damned good that it was finally all over.

Arawn picked up the shards of obsidian and crushed them. He opened his hand and let the breeze catch the black dust. The particles turned the blue sky black.

Part of me was relieved Morrigan's spell had been reversed. Day turned back to night, back to the way it was before she spoke the words and used the stones to kill the vampires. The rest of me wanted to stay in the warmth of the sun. Anything to keep away the darkness and the sleep that comes with it.

Mahalia came to stand beside Arawn, and together they put out the flames that still burned beneath Badb's cauldron. Lingering gray smoke and smoldering coals were all that remained of the fire. Arawn whispered something over the cauldron and spilled out its contents.

I realized why Mahalia was such a threat to the Triad. She knew to call Arawn, and she knew how to extinguish the flames of destiny. Mahalia was the only one here who knew how their magic worked and how to stop it. I just couldn't figure out why she didn't want Arawn to know she was the one who had called him.

He peered over the side of the cauldron at me as I sat on the ground curled up next to Oberon. "All that remains is for you to bury them. Bury Morrigan's head separate from her body. Then bury what remains of her sisters. You must bury the dead seven times 'ere the earth rejects them. I am ready to begin the hunt. I do believe that I have given Mr. Knightley and his companion a fair lead. More than generous," Arawn said.

He whistled, and the *Cwn Annwfn* came running, shaking the ground with their gigantic paws. He gave me a nod. "Executioner."

I nodded back. "Thanks." There was a look of puzzlement on his face, and I didn't know why.

"I am once again struck with the feeling of familiarity when I look at you. I—"

Mahalia cut him off. "Thank you, Lord Arawn of *Annwfn*. From you came the answer to my prayer. From me comes an offering of gratitude. This is what I give to you, a grateful offering with grateful words. Blessed be you, and blessed be us."

"The balance is kept. I do not only know how to take. I know how to give. Your offering of thanks has been accepted, and I offer you this blessing in return. May all that you do be done well. May what is done be done rightly. May all that you do be done according to justice. May truth prevail and falsehoods fail. May your words and deeds and thoughts be just." He walked back down the hill the way he came, with the *Cwn Annwfn* hard on his heels. Without a backward glance, he disappeared into a thick fog that rolled up to meet him.

The beautiful white coats of the ethereal dogs were almost invisible as they followed Arawn into the fog. Once the last of the *Cwn Annwfn* had stepped inside it, the blanket of clouds began pulling back off the field, taking the bodies of the *disii* with it. When it was completely gone and the moon hung bright in the sky again, only the wolves remained.

Roul and Cash led their packs through the bodies of our dead allies, which littered the ground. Worse for wear wasn't enough to describe how awful they looked as they dragged themselves along the blood-soaked ground. They looked like they had passed through a shredder and had been taped back together again.

Olwyn certainly had her work cut out for her. Roul winced in pain as she ran past us and into his arms. She wasn't just his pack mate, she was his soulmate, and looked haggard from worrying and waiting to see him again.

It was over, for now, at least. It wouldn't be truly over until Arawn caught up with that son of a bitch Baylen, but I wasn't too worried about that. Arawn might take his time, but he would find that traitorous son of a bitch

A genuine smile crept across my face at the thought of him catching up to Baylen and Medea. What I wouldn't give to be there when he did. I wanted to hear his explanation. I wanted to hear him beg for mercy and receive none.

On second thought, never mind. I've had my fill of the gods for now. The Triad was gone. All that was left to do was bury them. And then the reality of what Arawn had said finally hit me.

"Hey, uh, Mahalia? Was he for real? Bury them seven times?" I asked, as I unwrapped myself from Oberon and stood up.

A smile broke out on her face, and it didn't stop until it reached her eyes. They were alight with amusement. "Oh yes, he was for real."

"Ah, man." I hated to sound like the whiny kid, but seven times? How freaking deep was that, anyway? Too deep for me to be digging it.

"Maurin, I don't think there is a person among us who would argue that you haven't done your share tonight. In fact, you have done all that was asked of you and more. Isn't that right, Agrona?" Mahalia dared her to object.

I never even heard the vampire queen's approach. Not that I was supposed to. You only heard them if they wanted you to, and Agrona was one vampire who enjoyed the element of surprise.

"As much as I would like to argue, Mahalia, I cannot," Agrona said.

I'd pretty much had my fill of her too. Forgiveness her for using me as her pawn, not to mention her fight with me back at Baylen's. She could show a little gratitude, for crying out loud. I bit the inside of my cheek, trying not to say anything that would land me in a ditch with a shovel in my hand.

"Well, that's mighty big of you, Agrona. Thanks," I said.

There were a million other things I wanted to say, but I was too tired, and it just wasn't worth it. I ignored her glares and turned my attention back to Mahalia.

"So, does that mean that you've got it from here? I can finally go home?" I asked.

"Yes, my dear. We'll take care of the clean-up. We've been cleaning up this type of mess ourselves for centuries. Those of your kin who escaped the sun should be quite refreshed, Agrona. Perhaps they could join us?" Mahalia asked.

Mahalia may not be the head of the Council, but she was the High Priestess and the Council advisor. She said I could go home, and I was going. The aches and pains set in as soon as the adrenaline stopped. I planned to stay in the shower until the water ran cold and then slip under my comforter and sleep for a week.

XLVII
FORTY-SEVEN

I don't remember the trip home, the shower I must have taken, or how many days I slept through. The smell of coffee and not my alarm awakened me for the first time in I don't even know how long. Either I'd had the foresight to set the auto start on my coffee pot, or there was someone in my kitchen. Throwing back the comforter, I forced myself out of bed and staggered into my kitchen like a total drunkard. Eyes only half open, I misjudged the doorway and bumped into the wall.

The pain in my shoulder woke me up enough to realize someone had definitely been here. A few days ago I might have been freaked out at the thought of someone being in my apartment—your home is your sanctuary and that should not be violated—but not anymore. What lasting impression could a home invasion have when it is compared to a couple of pissed off goddesses and their army of demons? Exactly. Nothing. Besides, how many burglars would make you coffee and leave a plate of croissants on the table? It smelled like heaven in my kitchen. If it was a burglar, then they could have the stinking TV if they had made coffee and brought croissants. Right now, it seemed like a fair trade.

Grabbing my favorite, Cheshire Cat coffee mug out of the cabinet above the coffee pot, I filled it up, until there was the perfect amount of room for milk. Which meant when I opened the refrigerator...no milk. Shopping hadn't been high on my to do list. Black coffee it is. After stirring an extra teaspoon of sugar into my cup, I plopped myself down in front of the plate of buttery goodness. The front door opened, and I didn't even bother getting up. If it was someone who meant me harm...oh well. We all die eventually and if this was my time to go, then face down in a plate of flaky French pastry was as good a way to go as any.

"I see I'm just in time." The sound of Oberon's voice was music to my ears, and my heart did little flips in my chest as he walked into the kitchen with a little brown bag. "Want some milk for your coffee?" he asked.

"Yeah, that'd be great. The mugs are above the...well I guess you know where the mugs are if you found the coffee, noticed that I had no milk, and got out a plate for the croissants. Thank you for those, by the way."

"I can't take the credit for that one. Amalie dropped by this morning to check on you. She brought those with her."

"How long was I out?" I asked as I picked apart a croissant.

"Just since the night before last. Not too bad, considering everything that happened."

"Yeah, so that would make it what? Tuesday? Shit, I better call in. Matthison will have my ass if he hasn't fired me already." I started to get up to grab the phone off the counter when I remembered he sent me home with instructions to wait for his call. A call I was pretty sure never came. There was no point in checking my messages, so I sat back down and started picking at my breakfast again.

"I don't suppose that anybody called while I was crashed out?" I knew the answer, but I couldn't help myself. I picked at my breakfast, avoiding eye contact so Oberon couldn't see the disappointment.

SPTF didn't know Seamus was dead, or about anything else that had happened. How the hell was I going to explain this one?

"Don't worry about it. Roul and Mahalia have already been into the station," Oberon said, while he poured himself a cup of coffee.

"What? What did they say? What did they tell him?" I asked. I couldn't believe they had gone down there and talked to Matthison.

Oberon took the seat across from me, set his mug down, and leaned back in the chair, looking delicious all stretched out in my kitchen in his jeans and an old T-shirt. I think he was very aware of how good he looked and the effect he had on me. Grabbing a croissant for himself, he started to tell me everything that had happened with Matthison.

"You know that the Council lets the police know what's going on in town, right?" Oberon began.

I sighed. *No, because nobody friggin' tells me anything.* But I wasn't going to tell him that, at least not yet, anyway. "Yeah, so?" I said.

He just gave me a little wink and kept going.

Damn, he knew I didn't know. I was still too tired to put

on a good poker face.

"Well, they do. It's sort of a courtesy. We've been policing ourselves for centuries, so as long as we let whoever's in charge at SPTF know when something big is happening, we get to keep it that way. They know what a fine line we're all walking. There's lots of stuff that the humans don't need or want to know. If they did, we'd never be able to live together. Anyway, Matthison knows all about it," he explained.

"He does, huh? Why do I get the feeling that's a major overstatement?" I asked.

"Maybe a little. He knows that Seamus is dead, and now the file is officially closed on him. He knows some serious metaphysical shit happened over the weekend. He knows that we kept it under control, and he knows that it's over now. Does he know that it was centuries-old goddesses come to take over the world with an army of demons? No. We kind of left that part out," he confessed.

I sort of chuckled at that. "Yeah, I guess I would have left that part out too. Besides, who the hell would believe that, anyway? What about Knightley? Did they tell him what a rotten bastard he is? Did they tell him he was involved?" I asked.

"Mmm, no. That poses a problem. See, if they tell the captain about Baylen, then they have to tell him about Arawn, which then leads to a conversation about the Triad. So they decided to leave that part out too. Besides, I don't really think Arawn wants the Salem Police Department cramping his style, do you?" He let out a chuckle of his own.

"So how do they plan on explaining Baylen's absence?

Someone's going to notice he's missing," I said.

"His companies are big enough to function without him. We've got some time for Arawn to catch him. When he does catch him, I guess the Council will stage an accident or something." Oberon didn't seem to really care about what happened to Baylen's businesses and financial holdings.

"So has anybody figured out why he did it? I mean, what did he have to gain from setting us all up?" I wanted to know what the Council thought, because I sure as hell couldn't figure it out.

"Mahalia's theory is that he grew tired of waiting for absolution. If he couldn't be with his God, then he would align himself with a new one," Oberon explained.

"So being away from his god for too long drove him insane?" It hardly seemed a good enough reason to me but like he said, it was just a theory. We'd probably never know all of his reasons.

"Basically." He brushed crumbs from his croissant into a little pile on the table.

"But why the big ruse? Why did he give me the sword? Why did he help us at all?" My head started to throb just thinking about the treachery. I much preferred it when people just acted like themselves.

"He wasn't helping us. He was helping the Triad. He was probably feeding them information the whole time. As for you and the sword? Not giving it to you would have been suspicious, but they'd planned for you to be dead long before you had the chance to use it."

"How did you find that out?" I suspected as much, but it was still hard to hear.

"I just put two and two together. Looking back, it was pretty obvious. I don't know why we didn't see it before."

"Your deductive reasoning is mind-blowing, Holmes."

"Why thank you, Watson. There are memorial services tomorrow. Attendance is mandatory for everyone who works for the Council." Oberon winced as he said the last part.

"So I guess that means you're going. If you don't think anyone will object, I'd like to pay my respects too," I said.

"Oh, I can pretty much guarantee that no one will object," he murmured.

"What was that?" I asked, behind gritted teeth.

"Ah, there's probably something else that I should mention. I wasn't supposed to say anything, but maybe it's better if you hear it from me first," he said nervously.

"Spit it out. I can tell already that I'm not going to be happy about it." I didn't mean to sound so agitated. I'm pretty sure it wasn't his fault, but he was the one sitting here, so he was the one who got the attitude.

"They sort of told Matthison about you," he mumbled.

I practically flew up out of my chair. "What? They did what?"

I knew I was going to have to tell him something to explain why I looked a little different, but I most definitely wasn't going to tell him I was some sort of medium for a pagan goddess. He'd hand me my pink slip so fast it'd make my head spin, and probably call the men in the white coats while he was at it.

"Why would they do that without asking me? It's my life! Or did they forget that part? Who the hell do they think they are, anyway? I don't answer to any of them. They have no say in what happens to me." I shouted.

Fuming and beyond pissed off, I couldn't believe they made decisions for me while I was passed out. I was pacing like a tiger in a cage when he gently grabbed my wrist.

"Would you sit back down? Please. There's more," he said calmly.

"No. Just say whatever else you have to say." I pulled my wrist free and continued pacing back and forth between the counter and my table.

"Let's start with the good news. Nobody knows what you really are. Roul just told Matthison that your powers have grown, which they have. He just didn't say exactly how they have increased, or what they've changed into."

I was going to wear a path in the vinyl floor if I kept pacing like this, but I didn't know what else to do. "And the bad news?" That last question almost came out like a growl. I was going to feel bad later for being mean to him, but right now I needed to be angry with someone and again, he was the one who was sitting here.

"You sort of work for the Council now," he said.

I stopped pacing and leaned up against my counter, exhausted all over again. I should have known my life was going to be turned upside down. I should have known the Council wouldn't let me off so easily. Once they got their claws in, there was no escape.

"You're the new liaison. Well, the first official liaison to be exact. They sort of created the position for you," Oberon said, sounding excited about the idea.

"Is that supposed to make me feel better about the whole thing? Is having a job created especially for me supposed to make me feel all warm and fuzzy about people making decisions about my life for me? Because it doesn't!"

"Hey, don't shoot the messenger. I'm not even supposed to tell you. Roul wanted to do it himself, so you'd better act surprised when he does. And maybe faking a little gratitude wouldn't be a bad idea, either. He thinks it's a great idea."

"Are you serious? You want me to show a little gratitude?" I asked sarcastically.

"Look, Mahalia and Roul went to a lot of trouble to make this happen. Agrona would have been perfectly happy to just out you to Matthison and leave you to figure out how to fix it. Roul, on the other hand, thought that this was a good solution for everyone. This way, they can help keep what you are under wraps. Until we figure it all out anyway. And you get to keep your job, sort of. I know it's not the same, but at least you'll still be working with the department," Oberon explained.

"Yeah, that's comforting. I'm sure they'll all welcome me back with open arms too. Most of them don't get what I do as it is. They just think I'm some spooky freak." I pushed away from the counter and headed back to my room.

"That's all the more reason that this new job will be a good thing. Besides, they're not even going to know. You don't actually think Matthison is going to tell them that you're even more powerful now, do you?" he asked, confused by my anger.

"You just don't get it, do you? Nothing's a secret there. Everybody finds out everything. And most cops don't like strange and unusual. Since I was the strangest and most unusual thing working at SPTF, I already had enough problems. Ratchet up my strangeness, and it's going to be even worse," I told him.

He looked at me with those beautiful eyes and a little of the sadness that had been there when I'd first met him returned. My reaction had hurt him. Did he really think this was a good thing, now that I was losing my job on top of everything else?

I tried to see it from his perspective, and from Roul's and Mahalia's too. I just couldn't. I had been so focused on the present that I never stopped to think about what would happen when it was all over. It never occurred to me I wouldn't go right back to my old life. Or that Scota wouldn't go away after the Triad was dead. It would take time to process everything, and it was getting too hard to stay mad at sad eyes over there. Which was probably the point. None of this was his fault, so yelling at him solved nothing. My shoulders dropped on a heavy sigh.

"Look, I'm not mad at you or anything. I still don't feel good, and this is all a bit much, you know. I'm going back to bed. If you want to stay, stay. If not, I hope that you don't mind if I don't walk you out," I said.

I didn't glance back as I walked to my room, shutting the door behind me. With an ear pressed to the door I listened for a second before crawling back into bed. Silence. Not scooting of chairs, not the closing of the front door, nothing. Was he still sitting there in my kitchen? That probably wasn't the response he had expected from me. Then again, Amalie had been here earlier. If she knew what was going on, then she probably came to give him a fair warning.

Guilt for being so rude to him came more quickly than usual, but I should have known it would. If I was going to be pissed off at anybody, then it shouldn't be him. Roul and Mahalia? Maybe. Agrona? Most definitely. Something told me she was the motivating force behind all this. Oberon deserved an apology.

Cracking the door, I peeked out half expecting him to be gone. I know I would have left under the same circumstances.

He was standing outside the door in my hallway.

I looked up at him and gave him a little smile.

He smiled back. It reached his eyes, chasing away the sadness that seemed to make a home there.

"Was that our first fight?" he asked, amusement in his voice.

Laughter bubbled up as I grabbed his hand and dragged him into my room. Climbing back up on my bed, I slipped under the covers and gave the mattress a little pat.

"Will you sit with me until I fall asleep? I wasn't just trying to get you to leave when I said that I didn't feel good. I'm still so tired, like I could sleep for days," I said.

Oberon didn't say a word. He just stretched out on the bed next to me.

I slid over closer to him and laid my head on his chest.

He dropped one arm down around me and held me tight against him. God, he smelled good.

My eyes were getting heavy and as I lay there feeling safe in his arms, I thought about how strange it was that I didn't feel strange being this close to him. It didn't matter that I had only met him a few days ago and now he was lying here next to me in my bed. It was like I'd known him all my life, like he was the one person I was meant to be with. Of course, things could be different tomorrow. They usually were with me.

I fidgeted a little, trying to get more comfortable and push all of the problems swirling around out of my head. At that moment, I didn't care if it all changed tomorrow. This was just what I needed. He was just what I needed. I also needed to get some more sleep. Everything else could wait. The Council, my new job, all of it could wait.

Oberon gave me the softest kiss on my forehead and whispered, "Go to sleep."

My eyes grew heavy as the words reached my ears, as if he had mixed a little magic in with them. That's not entirely impossible, I suppose. I let the warmth of Oberon's breath, the strength of his arm wrapped around me, and the feel of his body pressed against mine comfort me as sleep took me.

In the morning I'd have to face the world and the new things I had learned about it. I'd have to try to accept the changes that had happened because of them. Tomorrow I would begin my new life. Whether I wanted to or not.

Dear Reader,

I hope you enjoyed my debut novel The Morrigna! I love reader feedback and can't wait to hear what you think. Please leave a review on the site where you purchased your book. Keep reading for a sample of Witch Hunt, book 2in the Maurin Kincaide Series.

Want to know more about new releases, events, contests and giveaways? Be sure to check out my Facebook page www.facebook.com/TheMaurinKin caideSeries. It's a great way to keep in touch and I try to interact as often as I can on the page.

Thank you so much for your continued support.

Rachel Rawlings

www.rachelrawlings.com

twitter: @rachelsbooks

www.facebook.com/TheMaurinKincaideSeries

www.tsu.com/rachelsbooks

www.hallowread.com

www.facebook.com/hallowread

CONTINUE READING FOR A
SNEAK PREVIEW OF

WITCH
HUNT

Nothing is as it seems.

ONE

My head was killing me and it wasn't going away, no matter how much I rubbed my temples. The migraine that was moving through my head like a freight train had started almost immediately after I'd walked into Captain Matthison's office. I worked for him up until a couple of months ago, when all hell broke loose in Salem.

I'm psychometric. The police once used my talents to interrogate the suspects that they brought in and I was pretty skilled at it. Then Seamus walked into my interrogation room. That's when my nice little life started to fall apart. I helped Seamus and the Council defeat the Morrigna—a centuries-old triad of pagan goddesses who had come back to reclaim their place at the altar of mankind. My reward for said good deed was my removal from the Salem Preternatural Task Force and a brand new assignment as the Council's liaison. This all took place while I was recovering from the ass-kicking that I had received while I was helping them. Of course, Seamus was dead, so I guess I had nothing to truly complain about. It could have been worse. If there's one thing that I've learned while working for the Council, it's that things can always get worse.

So far my new job entailed pretty mundane stuff, such as notifying my old department when we were going to have long-term visitors or keeping them informed of any trials and disciplinary actions within the Others. The Others consist of beings such as vamps, weres, witches and all things fey. The Council was the judge, jury and executioner of the Others. It was a rude awakening to find out just how much discipline they actually doled out. The only time the SPTF ever got their hands on an Other was when the crime spilled over to the humans; even then, the Council had to approve it. I could count on one hand the number of times I had interviewed an Other in an interrogation room.

I may not have been thrilled with my new position, but the Council certainly was. Agrona was thinking up new ways to use me to infiltrate other vampire communities by going through the "vamp tramps"—humans that whored themselves out to vampires just for the erotic buzz that donating gave them. Mahalia was definitely excited about finally shutting down the dark covens and their forbidden human familiars that had been growing in Salem. Roul, a were, was the only one who didn't seem to have an ulterior motive; then again, maybe that's what this visit with Matthison was about.

Today was far from mundane. On the surface it looked like a typical extended visitation pass, but Matthison was no idiot. He knew this particular werewolf's return to Salem was more than a vacation. This was like trying to pass off a cage match for the ballet, and he wasn't buying any of it.

The Wolves are very secretive about what happens in the packs. Humans only accepted the weres because of pack law. It's civilized on the surface; sure, it's archaic at times, but it is similar to the human justice system. If Norms really knew how pack law worked, or the necessary violence woven into their laws, then it might make cohabitation a little complicated.

After the Shift—when the Others came out to the world—humans basically fell in line when they realized that they were severely outnumbered by the Others. Weres make up the second smallest percentage of the Others— only slightly greater in number than the Fey. They just can't reproduce at the same rate as vamps or witches, for example. Most people don't survive a were's bite or the infection that follows, and the infant mortality rate of those born to weres is sky-high. The packs keep their secrets, because fear doesn't just motivate—it unites. Humans may not have pitchforks and torches anymore, but bullhorns and signs aren't much better. So if word got out that a lieutenant from a neighboring pack was here to challenge Salem's pack leader in a fight to the death for control of the pack—well, you get the idea.

"Maurin, who are you kidding? I've heard about this guy and I'm not just referring to his last visit. He's certifiable. You honestly expect me to believe that he's here taking in the sights?" Matthison's eyes were trying to bore a hole in my forehead from across his desk. It never worked when I was on his payroll, and it wasn't working now either.

Male weres are supposed to be issued a pass for any

stay over a week. I'm assuming that policy exists specifically for reasons like this. Weres are pretty territorial. If a
were wasn't petitioning to join a pack, then they were
usually coming to challenge that pack's leader. None of
that had anything to do with the humans, except that it
could get messy and the SPTF would prefer to know what
was going on before it showed up on the six o'clock news.

It was all formality, really. If Cash (or any other were)
came into Salem, the Norms would never really know the
difference. Matthison would notice more Wolves, but what
could he really do about it? Lucky for him—and the rest of
the Norms—the Council loves formality. There are
hundreds of different types of Others and they all have
their own laws. The Council upholds them all.

There are groups on both sides who want things back to
the way they were before the Shift, especially the religious
groups who believed that the world was ending. And there
are other groups within the Others who believe that they
are superior to humans. But the Shift was about cohabitation, not controlling the Norms. The Others just didn't
want to hide what they were anymore. It was a balancing
act, but complying with human rules is easy. They're
nowhere near as strict as the laws that the Others have
imposed on themselves. This was why I was confident that
I'd be getting that pass.

"Yeah, actually I do," I casually replied, leaning back a
little in my chair. I was about to put my feet up on his desk
then thought better of it. "That's what I've been saying for
the last hour. He'll be here in two days. So are you clearing
the extended pass or not?"

"When did you become so indifferent? You act like

everyday a were like Cash comes into town—like I should take him on a tour of the city!" He was shuffling papers around; the conversation was finally coming to an end.

"Mmm, I think I stopped giving a shit somewhere around the time you sided with the Council and took me off SPTF." That comment probably wasn't going to help me.

He let out a sigh. "Against my better judgment, yes, you've got your pass. But if I catch one paw out of line, then I'm hauling his ass in and sending him back to Boston." He was obviously irritated that he didn't have enough information to officially deny the request.

"No arguments from me. Let me know when the paperwork is ready and I'll come by and pick it up." What I wanted to say was, 'It's about friggin' time! You kept me in here an hour to say what we both knew you were going to say when I first got here?'

I walked out of his office, grabbed the new cell phone that the Council had given me and texted the word 'Done'. I'd fill them in on the Captain's suspicions later. It was too much to type on my phone anyway. Cash's pass was approved. That was the most important thing to convey to them right now.

I meant what I had said to Matthison. He wouldn't get any arguments from me if they hauled Cash's ass back to Boston. I'd worked with this Wolf before. We may have spilled some demon blood together and sent the Triad back to the Underworld, but that didn't make us friends. In fact, I couldn't stand him. He walked around half-cocked all the time, which may not have bothered me so much if I hadn't seen the arsenal at his disposal. Maybe they'd pick him up on a gun violation. My instructions were to get the pass. They did not include helping him stay once he had received it.

TWO

I'd barely gotten outside before my cell phone was ringing. It didn't ring with one of my favorite songs, though, so I glanced at the little screen to see who it was before I answered. SPTF's main line? I'd just left.

"Maurin Kincaide." That was my professional greeting.

"It's Matthison. You need to- " I cut him off.

"Too late. You already approved the pass. You don't get to change your mind now." He wasn't going back on the pass, not after I had already sent word that it had been approved.

"First, I only said yes to you. You don't have my signature on the form yet. And second, I absolutely could go back on it if I wanted to, and there isn't a damned thing that you could do about it. But that's-" He didn't get to finish.

"I could get someone to whip up a potion. I know people." I interrupted.

I was almost to the corner. I pulled my coat a little tighter. It wasn't officially winter yet, but the Solstice was only a week away. I could almost see the sign for the Daily Grind; coffee was almost within my reach.

"They wouldn't and you know it. I didn't call about the pass, Maurin. You need to come back in." The friendly banter was over.

"Come back in? You make it sound like I'm wanted for questioning. Am I a person of interest, Captain?" I asked.

Something was up—so much for a decent cup of coffee. Looks like I'd be slurping down more of the sludge they keep in the coffee pot in the break room.

"You are one of the most interesting people that I know. I need to talk to you about a case." I could hear him talking to someone, but his hand was over the receiver, muffling his voice.

"Wow! Sounds like you need to meet some more people. Don't you have any cops working for you anymore, or did you transfer all of them too? Why didn't you ask me about this when I was in your office?" Of course, I had already turned around. My curiosity was definitely peeked, but I didn't want him to know that.

"I'm looking at it now for the first time. Just get your ass in here." He hung up.

When I got back to Matthison's office, he was gone. It didn't take me that long to get there; I was right outside, for crying out loud. I scanned the desks outside his office and found him bent over a folder with my least favorite detective—Masarelli. The one good thing about not being on SPTF anymore was not seeing Masarelli's ugly mug every day.

I walked over to Masarelli's desk. "Captain." I didn't even bother acknowledging Masarelli, the prick. I did, however, try to look at the file on his desk.

Before I could get a good look at anything, Matthison scooped up the folder and waved me into his office. Masarelli turned his best thousand-yard stare on me – as if I was intimidated by him. I was a better interrogator than he was and he knew it. Of course, he would say it's because I have advantages that he doesn't. While it is true that I have what I would call "helpful abilities", it isn't my fault that I have them. Besides, I was convinced that I would be a better interrogator than Masarelli even without those abilities. I gave him a wink and a smile over my shoulder, and then followed the Captain into his office.

He dropped the file onto his desk. "I need you to make a call."

I shut the door behind me. "I'm sorry, what?" I hadn't expected him to ask me to make a phone call. Talk to a suspect for old time's sake maybe, but not a phone call.

"You're the liaison. I need you to call the Council. Mahalia, specifically." He started rubbing his forehead, which was always his tell that something was very wrong.

"Okay, and what is it that you'd like me to ask her?" I asked. It was never good when he reminded you what your job was. Something was definitely wrong.

He dropped down in his chair. "Tell her that I've got a dead witch on my hands and I need her to ID the body. She can meet us at the morgue. They've already finished processing the scene."

"How are you so sure it's a witch? If they only just finished at the scene, then there's no way you have lab confirmation. What makes you say witch?" I was really hoping that he was jumping the gun on this.

There were lots of Norms who liked to masquerade around as witches in Salem. You could find a body in front of a cauldron with a broom in one hand and a wand in the other, and it still wouldn't mean you had a real witch. True witches have a slightly different genetic make-up than Norms, but you'd never know it without the lab work.

He slid the folder across his desk, spilling its contents. "Besides the 'thou shalt not suffer a witch to live' carved into her abdomen, you mean?"

"Shit." I picked up a photo off his desk. "Are her, are her hands cut off too?" Despite all the gross stuff I'd seen recently, I was still swallowing hard.

"Yeah, and her tongue was cut out too. Why would someone do that?" He wasn't really asking me, which was good—because I didn't have an answer.

"I'll call Mahalia," I said quietly.

She was waiting for us in the hallway outside the entrance to the morgue, her deep burgundy dress in stark contrast to the white of the walls and floor. "Captain Matthison. Maurin." Mahalia nodded at each of us in greeting.

"Ms. Amarelle. I'm sorry to see you again under these circumstances." Matthison's cop face was back on.

"Yes, well, I certainly appreciate your attention to this horrible crime. Even if she turns out not to be a member of my coven, the message seems to be directed at us." Matthison gave her a questioning look. "Oh, I hope you don't mind, I saw the medical examiner and asked him a few questions." She slipped her arm through mine as we headed to the double doors.

"Normally, I would mind, but I'm hoping that you'll be

able to advise us as an expert in the study of witchcraft, regardless of the victim's identity. You'll need to know what we know. For the most part." Matthison stopped just outside the door. "Norman's not usually the chatty type. You didn't do anything to him to get him to talk, did you, Ms. Amarelle? I can't have him running his mouth to the press, you know," he asked suspiciously.

"Call me Mahalia, please. I wouldn't think of it, Captain. I think he just took pity on an old woman." She gave my arm a light squeeze as we walked into the medical examiner's room.

Old woman, my ass! I've seen exactly what Mahalia can do; whatever she had done to get the medical examiner to talk had better wear off quickly.

Mahalia walked right up to the table. The sheet wasn't pulled over the girl's face. She was young and pretty. What a waste. I was hoping Mahalia didn't know her, and that she wasn't a witch. Not knowing the name of the dead always makes it easier; it makes it less real.

"Her name is Laura Youngston. She recently moved to Salem. She wasn't a full-blooded witch, but she was making great progress in developing her latent gifts. Maurin, if you would? I'd like to know who did this." Mahalia motioned me over to her.

She was holding my hand, but not because she needed the support. Mahalia knew me pretty well and asking me to read a dead girl would have definitely caused the old Maurin to bolt. I've never read a dead person before, but Mahalia was so confident in me that I felt as if I had to at least give it a try. I moved closer to the body. It was better if I just referred to her that way, I decided.

Matthison was mumbling to himself. "She's never been able to do that before. Would've been helpful..."

"Oh, I think you'd be quite surprised what our Maurin is capable of, Captain. Go ahead, dear," Mahalia said as she nudged me. Her voice was calm and sweet, as if she were pointing me toward a plate of cookies and a glass of milk instead of a corpse.

It was suddenly hot in here, which was odd for a morgue, so I knew that it was brought on by my nerves. I unbuttoned my black wool peacoat and moved in a little closer. I tried to tamp down the butterflies in my stomach as I lifted the sheet to expose her hands—and then I remembered that they weren't attached anymore. This felt wrong, so very wrong. I felt like some sicko necrophiliac or psychopath. I felt as if I were invading the dead girl's space, or violating her privacy. I let the sheet fall and looked at Matthison.

"I need to see the hands," I said. My tongue suddenly felt thick and dry in my mouth, like a piece of dentist's cotton that no longer belonged there.

Matthison winced. "I'll get Norm."

A couple of minutes later he came back in with Dr. Norman Walters. They were complete opposites. Matthison is tall, fit and well dressed, while Dr. Walters looked like an overweight Columbo. I could see the looks Normal—I mean Norman—Walters was giving me. Guess I can't blame him, though. I'd think the same thing about someone asking to hold a dead girl's amputated hands if I were him. He put a metal bin on one of those implement stands and rolled it over. And then he left, but not before giving me one last look. Suspicion and fear flickered in his eyes briefly, and then disappeared. Walters closed the door gently behind him, as if the dead girl were simply napping on the cold, hard table.

"He didn't say that I could touch them. He didn't say anything, actually. Did you tell him what I needed to do? Of course you did. That's why he didn't say anything." I was stalling.

"Yes, that's why he was looking at you like you had six heads. Do you what you need to do, Maurin, so we can get out of here. Twenty years of practice does not make this place any more pleasant." He pushed the tray a little closer.

The delicate hands were palm up in the bin, thankfully. I didn't want to touch them anymore than I had to. I reached into the bin, my fingertips barely grazing hers. I was immediately overwhelmed with pain, excruciating, crippling pain. I couldn't see anything beyond it.

I bit back the scream building in my throat. If I let it out, then the pain would completely overtake me. Every muscle in my body was suddenly exhausted. My fingers, lacking the strength to hold the connection to the dismem-bered hands, slipped away. The pain pulled back a little, but I could feel my knees start to give out, with no way to stop them. I was about to hit the floor when Matthison reached out to hold me up. He helped me over to a stool against the wall. Thank god for the wall, or I would have been headed for the floor again. I could barely find the strength to hold my head up.

Matthison grabbed my face with both hands, forcing me to focus on him. "Maurin, what the hell just happened? What did you see?"

I didn't answer him. I had no idea what had just

happened. And I wasn't ready to tell him that I hadn't seen anything. "Mahalia, I think I did something wrong. It isn't supposed to hurt like that, is it?"

She looked at the body on the table, her fledgling coven member, then back to me. "Perhaps this was not the best candidate for your first time."

I was starting to get my second wind. "Perhaps we could have a little more instruction next time."

She let out a somber laugh. "Perhaps. Dare I ask if you saw anything?"

"Nothing. Except for some flashes of light, like the pain was coming through as color, but I saw nothing useful at all." I was frustrated. It didn't matter if this was my first time trying to read the dead and I wasn't a traditional medium. Everyone expected me to perform with my ever-growing powers and I couldn't. I felt like a hack.

"Let's try the old-fashioned method for a change. My guys are working the evidence as we speak. We'll be chasing down every lead. Just out of curiosity, is there a time limit on this new ability of hers, or can we come back to it if we need to?" Matthison thinks of everything, no wonder he's Captain.

"We have some time. Maurin, let's get you some-thing to eat. You need to regain your strength." Mahalia was already leaving.

"What I need is a real cup of coffee," I said, as I followed them out the door to the hallway.

THREE

The three of us sat in Matthison's office, each with a cup of sludge and a stale Danish. It was a far cry from my favorite chair and perfectly-brewed cup of coffee at the Daily Grind, but it would have to do. This wasn't a conversation we should be having anywhere besides his office.

Matthison was drumming his fingers on the mug his kids had made for him a couple of Christmases ago. It had 'Number One Dad' on one side, and a family photo on the other. The mug certainly didn't match the man sitting across from me right now.

"I feel confident in saying that this perpetrator targeted the Salem Coven. Unless something happens or some other evidence comes to light, we'll proceed as such. The other arms of the Council don't appear to be under threat, so that narrows down our list of suspects," he said.

"Captain, surely you know the history of the Salem Coven? The witch hunts? The pointless persecution? The list of suspects is longer than you might think. There are too many to name off the top of my head actually, though we do keep a thorough database on the extremists. I'll get a copy of our files for you immediately." Mahalia got her cell phone out of a small velvet bag that hung from the rope belt around her waist.

I sat there, still recuperating. I heard her give instructions to someone on the phone to copy everything that they had in their database and get it over here immediately. Matthison thanked her as she hung up the phone. He said something about how it would save them a lot of time; their time was better spent on evidence, rather than chasing witch hunters on the Internet.

I gulped the rest of my coffee and fought the shiver that made its way up my spine from the bitterness of it. I got up to get a refill. I asked if anyone else needed one and, when neither of them raised a mug, I made my way over to the coffee pot.

The room outside Matthison's office was pretty quiet, despite the brutal murder that had occurred. Salem didn't have a high murder rate and a case like this, involving any faction of the Council, didn't usually hit a detective's desk. I would have expected more of a commotion. Someone slammed a phone down. I looked around to see who it was. I saw Masarelli grab his coat off the back of his chair and sprint for the door. The only problem was that I was in his way. He could have gone to his right—around another desk—but chose instead to barrel straight into me. I tried to move out of his way, but he still managed to clip me with his shoulder. My hip hit the desk next to me and my mug crashed to the floor.

"You're an asshole!" I shouted to his back. He gave me the finger and was out the door. I looked down at the broken pieces of my coffee mug; half the witch on a broomstick that made up SPTF's badge stared back at me from the shards of ceramic. And then it clicked. Masarelli was going to another crime scene. I looked up to find Matthison standing in his doorway.

"You and Mahalia are coming with me." He pulled his keys out of his pocket and walked out.

Mahalia and I were right behind him. I was hoping that she was going to speak up and say that it wasn't necessary for us to go to the crime scene. They weren't really my thing. You'd think after the Triad and the whole demon army thing that a little crime scene wouldn't bother me, but it still did. In the heat of battle, everyone feels invincible; crime scenes have the opposite effect. It's like they remind you of your mortality, even for those of us who are supposed to be immortal. Nothing is truly immortal, there is always a way to kill it. Even the immortals. Ironic.

There were at least half a dozen police cars, all with their lights still flashing, by the time we pulled up to the Witch History Museum. I can't recall the last time we had a serial killer in Salem. Matthison parked behind Masarelli's unmarked Impala. Yellow police tape was everywhere. Barriers were already set up to keep the media and onlookers back. We got out and followed Matthison, since he was the only one of us with the credentials to get behind the tape.

The body was sprawled out across the front steps of the museum. Flashes from the crime scene photographer's camera lit up the darkening evening sky. I rubbed my eyes to get the flash burn out. As the body came back into focus, its delicate curves and small frame told me that the second victim was also a woman. Shit. A pattern was forming. My heart skipped a beat as I wondered if this time it would be a witch that I knew. 'Please don't let it be Amalie,' I thought.

Matthison was bent over the body. He looked up and waved me over. I held my breath, not because of the smell, it was too soon and too cold for that, but because I was afraid of whom it would be. As I got closer, I saw the hair and relief washed over me. Jet-black hair with red tips fanned out from the pale face. I examined her fine yet striking features, trying to figure out if I had ever met her before. I fought the urge to look away when I realized that her eyes had been sewn shut. Matthison drew my attention to her exposed chest and the carving across her stomach.

'Witches deserve the heaviest punishments above all criminals of the world'. The letters were small and neat, as if the killer had used a scalpel or something similar.

I was struggling with the killer's logic. Witches deserved the harshest punishment? Really? I could think of several people, the killer included, who were capable of worse things than any witch that I knew had done.

Whatever the logic, the point of these messages was crystal clear. The person who was doing this hated witches. The choice in victims so far meant that the killer was attacking the coven from the bottom up. We were dealing with a fanatic—an extremist—and that worried me more than having a murderer running loose in Salem. This was like a terrifying mix of suicide bomber and serial killer. You can't rationalize with a fanatic. You can never explain away their belief systems. Their hatred is ingrained in every fiber of their being.

Matthison brought my attention back to the dead girl on the steps. There'd be time to profile the killer after we evaluated the latest crime scene.

"Who is she, Mahalia?" he asked.

"Julienne Blanc." Mahalia's stoic façade was starting to crack. "Julienne was a pure blood. She was stronger than Laura, but not as strong as any of the witches you know, Maurin."

"Okay, so that pretty much confirms what I was thinking. Whoever is doing this is eliminating the weakest members first," Matthison said.

"Well, of course they are. That's what serial killers do, right? It's about power for them – it's about preying upon people. And predators go after the easiest prey. I can't recall a case in history where the murder victims were all your size, for example" I said.

If we weren't standing over a dead girl then that kind of logic might actually have earned a smile from Matthison. Right now, it just had him staring at me like I was nuts.

"What? You know it's true," I said, in my typical defensive mode.

He waved it off. "No, no. You said 'they'. Why did you say 'they'?"

"I didn't even realize that I had," I replied, suddenly confused.

He was pacing. "These two murders were too close together for just one person to have committed them."

"Um, I hate to break it to you, Captain, but Jack the Ripper was one person and two of his murders were very close together." At least I thought I read somewhere that they were.

"You're missing my point. It's not that there are two murders this close together, but it's the way that the murders were committed. If you consider the lack of blood around the body, then she obviously wasn't killed here. The words are meticulously carved into her abdomen. Her eyes were sewn shut and I'm willing to bet if we opened her mouth we'd find her tongue is missing just like the other victim. This wasn't rushed, but rather relished." He paused.

There was something different about Julienne. "Why weren't her hands cut off?" I asked.

Matthison turned Julienne's hand over with as much care as if she could still feel him touching her.

"Not cut off, but cut deep enough to be useless. See it all the time with attempted suicides."

"Why?" I wondered out loud.

"They don't mean to, they just cut too deep. So-"

"No. Why did they take their time with her and not with the other victim?"

"That's a question for Mahalia, but if I had to guess then I'd say that there's a difference for the killer between half-blooded and full-blooded witches. It's like they wanted it to last longer with her." He turned to Mahalia.

Mahalia went white as a ghost. Which isn't really an accurate comparison in real life; I've seen ghosts and they're a lot more lifelike than you'd think. Something had her scared and I've never seen her scared. I reached out and touched her arm. She jumped. It was small, but I felt it.

Matthison noticed too, except he mistook it for shock.

"My apologies, Mahalia. I don't mean to be inconsiderate. This must be disturbing for you—seeing two of your coven members like this in a matter of hours. I can have one of the officers take you home if you like."

"Don't let the grey hair and wrinkled body fool you, Captain. I am not that frail and I have seen far worse than this in all my years. Maurin simply caught me deep in thought," Mahalia replied tartly.

I started to say that it felt like more than deep thought to me, but decided not to interrupt her. What she said next made my jaw drop, however.

"There is no difference in half-blood or full-blood to them, Captain. Any trace of witch blood is too much. I know who did this," she said quietly.

"What?" Matthison and I asked in unison.

"I know who is attacking us," she said louder.

"Okay, would you like to share that bit of information with the rest of us?" Matthison asked.

I was getting the feeling that she had suspected someone before we even got here, and now I was starting to get pissed off that she hadn't said anything sooner.

"Inquisitors." She practically choked on the name.

"Inquisitors? I've never heard of them before," I said, still stunned that it had taken her this long to fill us in on her thoughts.

"Well, you wouldn't; you're not a witch!" she snapped.

I could feel myself shrink back from her. She'd never spoken to me like that before—like I was an outsider.

"I'm sorry, Maurin. I didn't mean to take my anger out on you." She sighed.

"Mahalia, how can you be so certain that it is this group,

these Inquisitors?" Matthison asked. "We're not even finished here, we need to compare all the evidence that we're collecting from both crime scenes. There could be more than what we see on the surface."

"Well, of course I can't be one-hundred percent certain, but we have been fighting groups like this—the Inquisitors specifically, for centuries. I'll know more after I complete a recollection," she said.

"A what?" Matthison asked the question that was on the tip of my tongue.

"Normally a recollection is a simple spell that is commonly used to draw out suppressed memories or to heal amnesiacs. This one will be more difficult, since I won't be using it on the living. Hopefully we will have the same results, though I may need to consult with a necromancer," Mahalia said.

"What?" I felt like I was saying that a lot tonight. "A necromancer, isn't that a little on the darker side of things?"

"Like all things mystical, necromancy has gotten a bad name. They don't raise legions of the dead. Well, some have tried, but most help the dead find their way to the other side. It's a lot more shamanic than demonic. I have a friend I can call if need be." She sounded tired.

"Why didn't you try this back at the morgue?" I asked, trying to hide the anger and confusion in my voice.

"I can understand why my decision would bother you, but the outcome would be the same. Julienne and Laura would still be dead. I am certain the Captain's forensics will tell him the same thing," she said.

"But why did you make me go through the whole failed

reading if you could have just done a casting?" I asked, irritated.

"I believe I mentioned that this was a much stronger version of the recollection. And by stronger, I mean harder to accomplish with a much larger power drain. I had hoped that your reading would be a success and I wouldn't have to drain the coven's power base only to find out that my suspicions were wrong."

"But they aren't wrong. We could be chasing these guys down already!" I was practically shouting.

I was pissed off and she knew why. There were people that mattered to me in her coven. If it had been Amalie on those steps, then I would have completely lost it. The only thing keeping me from total panic about Oberon was that the Inquisitors seemed to be going after women. This only seemed to prove my earlier theory about serial killers.

"I get it. Calculated risks. Why unnecessarily drain your power base? If it weren't the Inquisitors, than you'd be left weak and possibly unable to defend yourselves against a different enemy. At least this way, now that we're all on the same page, we can help protect you until you recharge," Matthison piped in.

"Are you fucking kidding me?" I almost laughed. "The Council still exists for a reason, Matthison. You can't protect them any more than you can protect yourself from them."

I didn't say anything else. I just walked back to the car. It was pretty obvious to me that we were done here.